CRIMSON BONES

CRIMSON BONES

An Anthology Edited by

Heather and S.D. Vassallo

Edited by Heather and S.D. Vassallo

Proofed and formatted by Stephanie Ellis
Cover illustration and design by Elizabeth Leggett.

www.archwayportico.com

First Edition: June 2023

ISBN (paperback): 9781957537566

ISBN (ebook): 9781957537559

Library of Congress Control Number: 2023931790

BRIGIDS GATE PRESS
Bucyrus, Kansas
www.brigidsgatepress.com

Printed in the United States of America

Dedicated to the grandmothers, who always made sure we had stories to read when we were young.

Content warnings are provided at the end of the book

CONTENTS

ACKNOWLEDGEMENTS

A big thank you to the ever-talented Elizabeth Leggett, whose art graces the cover of this anthology, and so many of our other books.

Thanks to Stephanie Ellis for her editing, proofreading, and formatting. She keeps us on our toes—no matter how perfect or done I think a manuscript is, she always has corrections for me to implement.

Thanks to all the wonderful and talented authors who submitted their stories to us. Their passion and talent shines brightly through the stories in this anthology.

A big thank you to Agatha Andrews, whose passion and love for all things gothic played a large role in the inspiration for this anthology.

Thanks to the gang—Max, Laurie, Steph, Kim, and Cindy—for your constant support and encouragement.

And thank you to all our readers. These stories are for you—may they keep you company on many a stormy night, as you sit in your favorite comfortable chair before the fireplace, with creaks and groans and the occasional strange noise sounding in the house.

S.D. Vassallo
from the wide windswept prairies

FOREWORD

BY HEATHER VASSALLO

Like most things with me, it started on a rainy day with a book discussion over morning coffee. It started because I'm a sucker for gothic romance. Frankly, gothic anything. And, like most things with me, it twisted and grew into something beyond my original intention. Something different—something more broadly gothic.

We had submissions that bent my idea of a 'Happily Ever After' or 'OK for now.' There were stories that made me stretch my boxes about romance, dark fiction, relationships, and/or the gothic genre. And though I fought the good fight to keep this anthology Gothic Romance alone, in the end I couldn't do it. At least not only Gothic Romance.

In the end, we chose the stories that haunted us, that we couldn't keep from discussing and rediscussing, that we couldn't let go of even though we claimed we wanted to. I like to have my lines moved. I love the stories that give me pause, that make me reconsider, that make me abandon leaving breadcrumbs on the forest floor. In some way, every story in this anthology did that to me—for me.

Heather Ventura Vassallo
from the stormy Kansas prairies

INTRODUCTION

BY AGATHA ANDREWS

The Gothic genre appeals to us sensually. We feel the fog on our skin as we wander through Yorkshire moors. Our feet grow cold as we wander, at midnight, through the dark hallways of a crumbling house. We taste the metallic warmth of blood as a vampire feasts. There is intense sensation at every turn, and *Crimson Bones* explores them in a range of stories, from traditionally gothic to gothic romance, with a few that feel like a new take on the genre.

Like the trope of a young bride arriving at her new, isolated manor, I had romantic expectations as I wandered into these stories, but found strange and unsettling rooms in this house of secrets instead.

I meandered through the dark hallways, unsure of what I would find, as the stories veered from the romance I anticipated, to ones of dread, where the atmosphere itself takes center stage, and surviving it was the point. Like that young bride, my journey through *Crimson Bones* revealed an important truth, that the journey through gothic will always keep you guessing.

This anthology began as a call for Gothic Romance, and I know some of you are expecting that as you read these stories. Though the selection of stories no longer centers on that theme, it is not devoid of those stories either.

Desiree M. Niccoli delivers a gothic romance wrapped in a delightful eco-horror package that pays homage to two beloved folktales. In her story, "The Feast of Dead Man's Hollow," you are treated to a bog, a woman in black riding a white horse, and a nod to beloved headless characters.

A. R. Frederiksen offers us a traditional gothic romance in "As Twilight Falls on Sandthorn Hall," with some of my favorite tropes, including a second-chance romance mixed with a twist on the scarred hero. I think of this story as I venture into my own garden, wondering about the power of my plants to heal or harm.

"Bleeding Art," by Ariana Ferrante," is a twist on vampiric gothic romance that is as fun as it is gruesome, all the while managing to be rather sweet.

Other stories you'll find here are gothic with no intention of a hopeful ending, instead designed to unnerve us like Poe's atmospheric and chilling tales. They speak to hidden desires or horrors that pique our curiosity while making us want to look away … but we can't. I will never be the same after reading "The Cottage," by Mire Marke, a dark erotic horror that remains consensual despite the brutality. Marke's use of a cottage also unbalances us by mixing our sense of safety in a quaint home with our fairy tale association of cannibalistic witches in the woods.

Whatever you wish to find from gothic, *Crimson Bones* offers a spectrum of stories rich with atmosphere and dread. Twenty-three stories, including one of my own, that will make you dream or make you scream. Either way, I hope you enjoy wandering through them, preferably at night with a candle to light your way.

STAR-CROSSED

BY VALO WING

Dying, of course, had always been our plan.

But now, with Ro sprawled in shadows on the other side of our candlelight-splashed tomb, brows devastatingly furrowed as they scribble the details of yet another failed attempt in a worn journal, I wonder—and, not for the first time—if we severely miscalculated.

Because we can't seem to stop.

One vertebra at a time, I peel off the icy stone floor. The fresh stab wound in my chest screams. Sinew and bone, muscle and skin, tangle its fingers together, going about the business of making me appear whole. I wriggle my toes within their prison of satin slippers. Bring bloodied fingers to tear the fabric of my dress from its low neckline to waist. Slip free. Exhale relief.

Ro glances from the journal to me, mischievous gaze traveling north to south, then north again. "Every time, Liet." They laugh. "Don't get me wrong, I enjoy the show—" A twitch at the corner of their mouth. "But you're so lovely in that gown."

"Yeah, well, it's not for your enjoyment," I snipe.

Ro's mouth parts, mock-wounded, pen dripping ink between long, pale fingers.

"Fine, maybe a little," I begrudge, hating myself. "I just … can't take it anymore. Each death returning me to this damn outfit, this cursed"—I rip at the long strands of burnished gold magically regrown and tumbling to my waist—"*hair*. For once, I'd love it if

7

dying and resurrecting didn't mean …" I can't finish the sentence. Wraiths welcome me home. The tomb is cold.

Silence stretches agonizingly between us.

Then, Ro, sotto voce and dry: "You always cut your hair and dress as you like when we're"—they gesture vaguely—"*out there.*"

Black lightning crackles in my veins. "And that's supposed to be enough? At least you knew who you were half a millennium ago. Had family support. I wasn't granted such freedom." Pain, nebula explosion; violent in my veins. "My apologies for being unable to accept a few stolen hours here and there, knowing no matter what I do, I always wind up looking as I did that damn night."

"Hey, now! That's our wedding night you're damning."

"Technically," I correct, stepping out of burgundy satin (sweet relief!), "the night after."

"Semantics."

"You're being an asshole."

Ro runs a hand through their short, curly hair. Grins. A dark strand falls over one eye. "Shall I make it up to you, then? Come *here*, darling. Please. I'm wretched and starving for you. My fingers tremble for your skin, my bones ache. Soothe my need, appease my thirst."

"A *dramatic* asshole," I amend.

The hole in my chest finishes suturing itself. I exhale and the pain becomes a ghost, joining the myriad other specters haunting this crypt. Shadowy fingers press bruises in my sides, leave reminders of each story, each end, we've sung. My body, nothing more than a canvas of memories, cells never regenerating, never shedding to become new.

Ro flips the pen between their fingers. Muses, "I do love it when we wake in New York. Thought our last performance went pretty well, too. The Met is my favorite stage to die on."

"It's dusty and the curtains smell of sweat," I complain.

"But, the chandeliers! When they rise to the ceiling it's like watching a meteoroid shower in reverse."

"Big disagree." Those chandeliers could never come close to the real thing.

Ro's mouth thins. "Okay, you're being terribly cross this resurrection."

"Yeah? Bite me."

They snort, expression wicked. "Come closer and I will."

Stubborn, I kick away the fabric puddle gathered about my feet. Walk to the nearest wall in nothing but my now anachronistic undergarments, encircling the length of our prison, dragging two fingers along cold stone. Candles gutter in my wake. Ghosts cling to my shoulder blades. I stop once I've circled the entire perimeter; stand above Ro like a desperate, invisible god.

They tip back their head, shut their eyes. "You have to admit the productions are infinitely better than they were a hundred-something years ago; that last one wasn't even trying to be subtle about my role not being a man—for the first time, it actually *felt* like us up there." They hum a snippet of Bellini's final duet.

I stare into the emptiness of our crypt, an icy dark bereft of stars. "Speak for yourself."

A sigh. "Come *here*, beautiful." They reach for me and I relent.

Sliding onto their lap, I plunge my nose into the warmth of their neck. Inhale poison and sweat and blood. Home. One of their hands comes about my waist. Despite it all, we still have each other. Solidarity in this strange hell. We've never been separated. And I love them, even now. Even though I am changed and so much more while they remain the same.

Pulling me close, they slide their second hand around me, tangling in strands of my long hair. A small growl escapes their lips. They love me like this. And although it brings me pain, I can suffer these small moments so long as they welcome the real me *out there*.

Which, I know they do.

The journal slips from their fingers and falls open on the dark floor. I move to push it away.

And stare in disbelief.

In the beginning, we used to huddle together, them recording every aspect of our latest venture, me watching over their shoulder, looking for any clue, any key to break us from this endless cycle of death and rebirth. But the years stretch on, and I've left them to it. For our fate has yet to alter, despite our location and circumstance and year. Always the same, every time. Where they go, I follow. Two meandering shadows glued to one another, fated never to part, tasting only a glimpse of life before—

Poison. And a knife.

And I can no longer stomach reliving our demise on paper knowing we'll reenact it in person all too soon. Ro assured me they could handle the task and has dutifully continued the records upon each return to the tomb.

Except.

I see no writing on the page. Instead, sketches cover every inch of white: the stages we've sung on, the food we've eaten, city skylines, those fleeting encounters with people who have no idea who we are and no idea we'll never cross paths again. And, also, images of me. Except … not. Sketches of Liet through their eyes; the Liet of their dreams. Liet of their youth. Liet of whispered wedding vows. Someone false. Someone not real.

Liet of the tomb.

"What is this?" I hiss, swiping the journal from the floor.

They scrabble uselessly at the backs of my hands, but I have the journal and I'm not letting go. I jump from their lap. Stumble to the far wall. Bile burns in my throat, the pressing dark too severe, no longer safe and welcome. Page after page, the same. I swallow lightning and broken glass. Another turn of the page. All alike. Clearly, they stopped analyzing our journeys, stopped looking for the crack into which we could wriggle free some time ago. Fine. That, I can accept. But this, these sketches of me always in that vile gown, my hair long and plaited and crowned in roses, this I cannot stand.

"Give it back, Liet." Their voice, quiet but unmoving.

"All these years." I will not break for them to watch; my body now more iron, more steel than flesh and blood. "All these years, and this is *still* how you see me? When you know it's not true, when you know how unhappy, how trapped I feel here in the tomb and on the stage? This is the spouse you want?"

They spread their hands, palms up. Say, simply: "You're beautiful."

"But only like this."

Ro bites their lower lip. Refuses to look at me.

"You don't want us to break free," I accuse. The journal escapes my fingers and thuds dully on the floor. "You love this purgatory we're in."

It was only supposed to be once; one dramatic performance, one extravagant lie, in exchange for a lifetime of freedom. Instead, we keep dying. Doomed to play our roles ad nauseam with no sign of relief.

Still, without meeting my gaze: "I thought you'd have realized that by now."

Oily shadows smooth vicious valleys in Ro's face beneath bladed cheekbones. I wonder—a touch daftly—if the next time we find ourselves on stage, I could simply pluck the bones from their face; stab myself with them instead of whatever knife I'm handed by the stage crew. Slide the diamond edge between my ribs, soft as a sigh.

Poison wafts from their skin, heavy in the velvet darkness, bruisingly saccharine, and I can't do this; I need stars, I need the darkness of real night.

I stagger. They're across the crypt in a comet-flash, one arm around my waist. "Don't," I plead. "Please." I can no longer stand the chivalry when they won't accept it in return, I can't—

"Hush, darling." Their lips a brush against my ear. "It's going to be alright."

"It's not." I blink rage-water from my eyes, take in the familiar crypt, effervescently dark, blistering black and velvet; home. "This is no life."

Their grip on me tightens, lips insistent against skin. "And who's to dictate what makes a life? It may not be conventional, but it's *ours*."

"Things are different now, Ro. I see them, in the audience, past the fourth wall, phantomlike and blurred, only there and real. People like us—lovers, who don't have to hide." My nails curl into their wrist, desperate. "We're finally in an age where being ourselves might be safe, if we could just find a way to break the cycle—"

"And? Spend a handful of years together, then die? What we have is a gift. What we have is forever."

Forever.

"You're wrong." My voice, brittle-sharp: "This is no gift."

Ro nips at my ear and withdraws, clearly exasperated. "Such a pessimist, lover."

Darkness swirls about their ankles as they walk to the other side of the tomb, swipe the journal from where I dropped it. They slide down the wall and flip through the pages. I battle nauseous jealousy at the easy set to their shoulders, the vest unbuttoned and collared shirt beneath, wrinkled yet true.

Ro—who faked their death as a child to live the life they wanted, whose family supported the decision and told the world they'd adopted a son to try and appease their grief over the loss of their daughter—never has to suffer as I do. When we fell in love and the secret came out, they told me we could do it again; feign death to achieve freedom. Blitzed by youthful infatuation, I agreed. Little did I know, each return to this tomb they'd remain themselves, while my noose tightened. I thought at least they understood my rage, my despair, my grief.

But the journal proves they see only the person they wish I was. And I don't know how to change that. Or if it's even possible for someone like them to like the real me. And yet ...

At the end of our most recent second act, two women(?) sat in the front row, hand in hand. They carried themselves similarly, both in trousers, both with short hair. A confident gleam in two sets of eyes. As Ro drank the poison, leaving me to fall upon them— inconsolable and tragic, blade in my ribs, blood spilling forth—I focused on the two faces in the front row until the curtain came down, dragging me home. On the way they looked at each other with blatant and unquenchable desire. The way they rose to their feet amidst the applause (our requiem) proud and sure. When the opera ended, they would walk back to their lives, untethered and free.

To have what they do with Ro …

It's possible. It has to be.

A glitter of gold in the shadows. Ozone in the air. The tomb tilts; a world jolted from its axis. Vertigo sings within my chest. Two beings unfolded. A blink, an exhale, and—

"New York?" Ro shoves up on their elbows in the middle of Central Park. Above; a sky of blue and wispy white tinged gray with smog. "But we were just here."

And so it begins again.

"Thought you loved New York," I grumble, avoiding the pointed stares from passing people who clearly think we're actors on break from some Shakespearean production. I'm not sure what returned us already to Manhattan; our resurrections normally randomized; wherever in the world, through whichever media form happens to be showcasing our tragedy at the time.

Warmed summer grass and asphalt collides in my nose. I sit, brushing freshly cut blades from my ancient undergarments. In my veins, the shimmer of anticipation, despite the bitter knowledge of how the charade plays out. At least I get a few precious hours first. And I treasure them. Possibly more than anything. Maybe even more than Ro. "Come on. I need new clothes. And a haircut."

They groan, pushing me to my back. The sky becomes their face; laughing and handsome and eternally young. "Can't you keep it long? Just this once? For me?" They brush a kiss on my forehead, my temple, the corner of my mouth. "You're so beautiful, my Liet, my love, my—"

I remember the journal; the sketches. The fact that no matter how many times we resurrect, how many times I chop my hair and buy new clothes, I always return the Liet I was when we met. My heart roars.

The years crash about me. The pain and the blood and the music and the lights and the applause. The betrayal and lies. The end. For that's all Ro and I will ever be: a constant end, on loop until the planet melts in flames. Until the universe as we know it is no longer recognizable, changed indeterminately for both the better and worse. And although we were granted a beginning, mine was false, while they had the chance to start over. So, for us, a beginning and an end. Never a middle. Always, an end.

I shove them off. Scowl. "No."

They groan in encore, over-dramatic, then stand and hold forth an ink-stained hand for me to grasp. "As you wish, wife. Let's find you a barber before it's time to die."

To die and die and die.

I move to shove my hands in my pockets, but these clothes don't have any. Of course they don't. Fury crashes in my ears. Ro walks ahead of me, tall and shoulders straight. Hands out of sight, an infuriating whistle leaves their lips.

I ignore them until after my hair has been shorn off, the weight gone, new clothes acquired thanks to the money that magically appeared in their pocket.

When we exit the Fifth Avenue department store, gleaming windows many stories high reflect the me I know in secret and love. Pulse a vivid *accelerando*, I want to weep, to scream, to grab Ro around the waist and swing them about in wild joy. This particular barber did an excellent job, my gilded strands artfully tousled yet erect, the back of my neck exposed to the wind and sky. I adjust the lapels of my new sapphire suit. Smile wide and turn my head to examine the severity of my profile, the jut of strong nose and square jaw. Golden hour surrounds us, limning Ro with intoxicating light. They're devilishly striking, like a god. The supposed love of my never-ending existence. I move to kiss them, to pull them close in this sacred time before we must don our costumes and act out our inevitable demise.

They quirk an eyebrow and dodge me, quick. "We're going to be late."

Right. Can't have that.

Dejected, I shoulder past and make for Lincoln Center while New York howls and hisses with vibrant life.

The Met glitters pearly white and diamond-bright, smearing sunset in watercolor pastels over swarming couples eager for this night's performance. I halt at the central fountain, inhale water droplets and beg a silent prayer for things to be different.

"Liet," snaps Ro.

I lick my lips, taste imminent death, and murmur: "Meet you in there."

They sigh and leave my side without so much as a loving touch, a kiss, or glance. It shouldn't matter. It *doesn't* matter. In the end, it's always the same. I'll blink and be on stage, dressed in another wretched gown, scratchy wig dug into my skull, a fresh knife in my hands.

"Please tell me this opera pisses you off, too."

Surprised, I turn, taking in the person standing at the fountain beside me: hands thrust in the pockets of their white suit, brown skin luminous, short, dark hair wavy and caught in the breeze. No one ever speaks to us when we're here. Not unless we initiate. Ro and I; eternal wraiths, shadow-beings who slither along the recesses of reality. "Excuse me?"

They snort lightly, glance at me askance. "I always find myself wondering what would happen if she drank the poison first, leaving the knife for him."

A storm, previously unseen and unrealized whispers through my veins, crescendos over the miracle of a stranger's unprompted voice directed at me. But … drink the poison first? Impossible. "You've seen this production a lot, then?"

"This *story*," they correct, mouth twisting. "In pretty much every form it exists. Opera, ballet, play, movie. I despise them all but can't seem to quit—call me a masochist, I just"—they grimace and something takes flight in my chest—"keep waiting for someone to come along and tell it differently. Oh well. Hanging onto hope." They laugh and hold out a hand, rings on every finger. "Ignore me. I've heard this show's two stars are phenomenal. I'm sure it'll be great. I'll sit and watch in agony, then drink myself into oblivion to forget I keep putting myself through this. Imara, by the way. They/ she."

Imara's hand is warm, the many rings cool against my skin.

"Liet," I offer. Then, swift as a thunderclap, and, without hesitation although never before verbalized to Ro or anyone else, "They/them."

"Nice to meet you, Liet." They smile, gaze lingering on my mouth, my nose, my hair, before coming to rest on my eyes. "Any chance I can sweep you off your feet for something a little more affirming? Care to ditch this bullshit?"

A breeze caresses my brow, loosening a strand of hair. I sweep it off my forehead. Clear my throat. "Ah, I'm uh, kind of expected in there."

"A date?" She smiles crooked, exposing the world's most perfect singular dimple.

"I suppose that's one word for it." The stage, the costumes, the conductor and lights. The knife. Ro and their plaintive wails before drinking the poison, leaving me to follow behind. Death. Then the tomb. Always, the tomb. My long hair returned, my bridal gown pristine, the fresh hole in my chest screaming shut. Ro and their journal, sketching the person they wished I was instead of the person I am.

Doubt crackles unsteady but electric sharp beneath my skin. A swirling storm of lightning and shadows glitter in my lungs. Hunger. Desperation. "Actually, you know what? Why not. I know a place, if you're interested."

Imara smiles glorious as dawn. "Awesome!"

We fall into step, side by side. I don't look back at the opera house, at Ro waiting impatient within. Any moment we'll be reunited, any moment the earth will tilt and I'll be on the stage, lungs full of lies, throat full of false words, tongue sharpened and ready for blood.

But maybe, just this once, I can procrastinate.

Together we cross the street, towards Hotel Empire. I saw the invite on Ro's magically materialized phone earlier this afternoon; a glamorous cast party post-performance that we'd never be able to attend. Well, fuck that. My suit is exquisite; the stage hasn't summoned me yet. And, too, this stranger at my side; ravishing beyond belief. When I rush to the door and hold it open for them, a small smile tugs at the corner of her mouth. The elevator ride skyward is a quiet affair, the both of us sneaking glances and pretending we're not, hands somehow incapable of leaving our pockets. I lean into the wall, crossing one ankle in front of the other, counting every beat of my heart, every inhale that's *mine* and mine alone. Before fate calls me home.

Shiny doors glide open, revealing a modern penthouse. Greenery, flower arches, entire trees, decorate the interior. The air's perfumed by lilac and peony. Votive candles flicker a warmer yellow than the anemic glow of those in our tomb. Laughter and the clink of crystal glasses pull us deeper, the event still being set up, empty save for us and hired staff.

"What is this?" Imara asks, eyes wide and glittering.

I bite my lower lip in attempt to hold back the grin blossoming. My throat, molten gold. The powdered glass in my veins somehow softer. "Maybe a place we can tell our own story instead of sitting through someone else's."

A stranger greets me with confused enthusiasm at our early arrival. Leads us through the forest until we enter a room lined with racks of clothes. They gesture, saying, "Pick out whatever you like, it's part of this," then leave us alone.

No. Granite squeezes my heart; diamonds broken and dull scrape their knuckles over my wounded soul. I look to Imara. Say, resolute, "I'm not wearing a costume." The very word a poison to my ears.

"That's fair, me neith—" She whistles low through her teeth. "Wait, holy shit, I need this."

Apprehensive, I come to their side, watch as she shoves dresses and suits aside to reveal a spectacular set of faux chainmail and pauldrons. My tongue salivates with inexplicable want.

She glances at me and chuckles. "There's more than one. We can both wear armor if you'd like, no rules against it."

Unable to speak, I nod, reaching for silver. Slip out of my suit jacket and pull metal over my head. Imara helps strap the pauldrons over my shoulders, her touch soft, yet sure. I help her in turn. My pulse has sped, and I know any moment now I'll blink, be on that stage, staring into Ro's familiar self-assured face. But I can't go back, I can't suffer it anymore, I need—

"Shall we?" I extend my hand. They twist their fingers into mine.

We enter the main room, resplendent. Floor-to-ceiling windows expose Central Park, the sun almost vanished, sky nothing more than a violet smudge of atmosphere. I pray for stars. For those celestial orbs denied to me since the night of my wedding hundreds of years ago. Of late, all I know is day, and the dark of the stage. The dark of the tomb. And, there are no stars in those places.

Imara guides me to the balcony. Outside, the air is cool, velvet-soft and full of promise. I hold my breath. Count the beats of my heart, every thrum closer to tearing me from this moment, this magic, this gift. We stand, side by side, hands gripping the silver railing. I catch her watching me, eyes sparkling, naked want trapped in the corners of her lips. Wings erupt from my veins, formed of glass shards previously designed to hurt, now magnificent and pearlescent.

"What?" I tease as their smile becomes something mischievous.

She shakes her head. Swipes a hand through short hair, faux armor gleaming quicksilver radiant. "I just"—they break off, eyeing me again—"can't believe I convinced someone *this* hot, a total stranger, too, to ditch their plans and be my date for the most absurd party of the year."

Brightness. Ringing in my heart. A roar to the wet fire of my blood. The catch of strange light on mirrored skyscrapers glimmering and dusted in shadows. Darkness blooms. I'm supposed to be on stage. I *should* be on the stage. Ro is most likely beside themself.

Courage, now.

I sink to one knee. Reach for her hand. They place it gentle and obliging in mine. I draw brown knuckles to my mouth. Press a lingering kiss to skin smelling of hope and stars and joy. Raise my eyes to theirs, slowly, oh so slow, for I fear when I look up she'll be gone and I'll be returned to the tomb. Always the tomb. Always Ro and death and a game of pretend. Our plot, our desperate ploy for freedom twisting us in mocking fingers. We planned to die. But maybe, just maybe, I finally want to live. For this night, this armor, this exhale.

For me.

Darkness smiles. I look to the sky, searching for stars and instead find a night luminous and laughing lit by the myriad jeweled lights of the city. For a moment, Imara's hand in mine becomes the knife. Poised and ready, so used to my grip, my resignation. For a moment, I forget to breathe, convinced blades will erupt from knuckles and spear me through. Across the avenue, Ro hesitates, their usual cue gone, unsure what to do without me there. Confused as to why I'm not. Wondering what changed this time when it never has before.

Ro: unable to sing without me, unable to play their part, unable to fathom any other way.

Well. How very sad for them.

Calm and certain, I rise.

Imara winds her fingers around the back of my neck, thumb grazing my jaw, irises a beautiful dark. "Goddamn," she murmurs. "Who the hell even are you?"

Catching their chin in my hands, I lean close. Inhale and smell freedom. "Someone who finally decided to drink the poison first."

REMNANT

BY ALLISON WALL

Of the circumstances which brought me to the shores of that cursed island it is not important to relate, save that I was sailing nearby it unaware in a small boat, fleeing a life to which I could not return—to which no woman should return—when I was beset by a capricious winter squall. The wind whipped my hair across my face, and the world was reduced to lashing rain and waves. My boat was driven upon unseen rocks, smashed. In the collision, I hit my head and was, for a time, insensate. Next I remember, I was upon a beach of sharp stones. My head ached. My vision blurred painfully and blood ran down my forehead. The rain continued, now lanced with ice. My feet, knees, and palms were cut and abrased, but numb from cold, so that I could not feel the extent of my injuries. I was, in short, in a weak and wretched state. I crawled blindly away from the punishing sea, hoping for shelter. If I had known what sort of shelter I would find, I may very well have turned back and thrown myself into the sea.

Even so I am glad I did not know, for if I had, and had made the rational choice to save myself, I would never have met Aurora. It was she who found me upon the beach; she who knelt beside me and sheltered me with her mantle; she whose face I saw—her eyes a deep blue-black, ringed by long lashes, her cheeks pink with the cold; she who looked upon me with so much gracious kindness. I looked up and saw her, and there was a halo of light round her, and I fell once more into darkness.

I was ill for some time. The blow to my head, the chill and wet, and the all-encompassing fear with which I had fled for my life and fought the ocean contributed to a prolonged malaise. As I drifted in and out of awareness, I slowly gained knowledge of my surroundings.

I reposed in a narrow bed. Opposite, there was a hearth in which a fire burned, and through a slat-like window high on the wall, gray winter light shone. The room was small, and it was built in an odd fashion: long flint shards stacked together, without mortar, each stone fitted perfectly in place. It was the same stone that had cut me upon the beach and, even here, no attempt had been made to file down any sharp edges. In all, the room gave a very cell-like impression, though whether penitentiary or monastic I could not tell.

The only person who attended me was Aurora. She was beautiful, with long, black hair, straight brows, and expressive eyes that inferred the great depths of her soul. I longed to know everything about her, but I was not at first strong enough to converse. My head ached often and she would not have me suffer, so we only spoke what was necessary. She told me her name, she assured me I was safe, and she asked after my needs. When she was in the room, she was all I saw, and when she was away, she was all I thought about. She wore black robes, somewhat like the clothes of cloistered nuns. She wore no head covering, and her hair was long. It lay like silk upon her shoulders. Did she live alone on this island, as a religious recluse, perhaps? Then again, she had never prayed with me nor mentioned anything about the Divine or saints, even in passing. She seemed, in short, utterly secular in her demeanor, yet to me, she was as a goddess.

This period of holy mystery came to an abrupt end one evening, when Aurora happened to leave the door open. As she tended the fire with her back to the door, someone passed by. They held a candle in the near-total dark. Like a shadowed specter they were, and I felt chills. So Aurora was not alone. Then, they looked into the room. The face—that face!

I gasped, barely keeping myself from shouting with fear.

It was an old face, an ancient one, over-wrinkled. Candle shadows caught in each fold of skin, disfiguring the visage horribly. Beneath the cliff of the brow, the eyes lit up orange-red in the flame. Worse and worse: seeing my fright, the face grinned, showing sharp and broken teeth.

I did call out then: "Aurora!"

She was at my side in an instant.

"Someone. Something terrible!" I pointed to the door, and the face was gone. The hall, empty.

Aurora closed the door. "It is your head injury playing tricks upon your vision."

"I have only ever seen bursts of light, or blurred images. Not … that. Nothing so awful."

Aurora put her hand upon my forehead. "Are you fevered?"

I leaned away from her. "I know what I saw. Do not try to dissuade me. We are not alone, are we? Who—what—is with us? Where are we? What is this place?"

"You should not be so excited. You will undo your progress. You need to rest."

"Do not leave me! I will not be able to rest, and I will refuse rest, until you tell me. My mind will spin tales, whispering that you are keeping secrets from me, and I will fall into paranoia and do myself even greater harm."

Aurora looked at me, no doubt determining whether to humor me. I waited, scarcely breathing.

Finally, she sighed. "No one beyond this island knows what I am about to tell you. You must swear to secrecy."

I assented readily.

She settled herself on the bed. She took my hand upon her lap and, as she spoke, she began to change my bandages.

Aurora told me we were upon an island, which had a name, although I will not record it here. Upon this isle was an ancient abbey, in which we were currently situated, which will remain equally nameless in this account. The abbey was populated by a secretive order of nuns.

Surely it had not been a nun's face I had seen in the hallway—such an evil visage!

I shivered.

"Are you all right? Do you need another blanket?"

"I'm fine. Please go on."

According to Aurora, the nuns were the last of their particular order. They hid from the world, devoted to holy lives in community with one another. They had not come to see me, and likely would not, as their order forbade them from interacting with outsiders, male or female. Had I been a man, they would not have permitted Aurora to take me in at all.

"I suppose I would have died, then. That does not seem a very charitable attitude."

Aurora shrugged. "It is their way."

Not for the first or last time, I thanked Fate I was a woman.

"The nuns are all quite old," Aurora said, removing the last of the bandage. "I haven't been around anyone near my own age in so long." She brushed her fingertips over my palm. Her touch awakened a fluttering, tickling sensation, which ran from my hand up my arm and settled in my stomach. "It's healing well," she said, so demure, so sweet. And she kissed—yes, kissed—my hand, before washing it in a bowl of warm water she had brought for that purpose. Her hands cradling mine—the sensations threatened to obliterate all thoughts from my head.

Rather breathlessly, I asked, "How did you come to be here?"

Aurora frowned. "I can't remember the circumstances of my arrival." She dried my hand gently. I struggled to maintain focus on the substance of her words, not on the way her lips moved as she formed them. "The passage of time does play with memory, does it not?" She smiled at me, showing the single dimple in her left cheek.

I smiled back. "I suppose."

"I was young, with nowhere to go. The sisters agreed to take me in, feed me, teach me, and join me to their order when I reach a certain age. It is the only home I've ever known. I owe them my life."

We were quiet for some minutes. Aurora wrapped my hand in a fresh bandage and began the process with my other hand.

"What is it like to live here?" I asked. "It seems very dark and solitary."

"I have the nuns to keep me company."

"And is that satisfying?"

Without looking up, Aurora asked, "Satisfying in what way, exactly?"

I touched her cheek. It was soft as down.

She let out a breath and closed her eyes.

"Satisfying in this way," I whispered. I pushed back her hair, which spilled like dark water down her neck, her back. And then I kissed her.

After, she looked at me with stars in her eyes.

I almost asked her to run away with me then. I refrained. I feared Aurora might be too attached to her abbey and her nuns, and that asking this of her so soon might sever the new bond between us. I wish I had asked. She might have said yes, and we might have been spared the anguish we were yet to endure.

Once I regained strength, and my headaches lessened and grew farther apart, we went on walks—arm in arm for support, and for the joy of feeling each other so near. We explored the abbey very little. Most places were off-limits to outsiders. I saw several hallways, the kitchens, and a large entrance. The building was vast, with ceilings that reached up into cobwebbed, black-flint darkness. Everywhere, doors, doors, doors—leading where? Hiding what arcane secrets? I could not hold back my curiosity, especially when I learned that Aurora herself was not fully initiated and did not know all of the abbey, despite living here for years; she was always vague on the exact amount of time.

Mostly, we strolled out of doors, despite the frigid weather. The sea wind invigorated my spirits and whipped blood into my cheeks. My head cleared. There was something oppressive about the air inside the abbey, a feeling of freedom upon leaving it. Aurora's voice grew louder and she laughed more, too, so I assume she experienced a similar sensation. At the time I attributed the phenomenon to the constant fires, to the windows shut against the winter cold, and to how many days I had spent in that little room. We did not speak of it.

Aurora pointed out where she had found me, and we saw the wreckage of my little boat washing up onto shore. At low tide, she told me, the island wasn't an island at all, but a peninsula, connected to the mainland by a rocky land bridge of several miles. Far in the distance, on clear days, one could just make out the mainland. It was dangerous to cross in winter, even at low tide, as the sea spray froze upon the rocks and made them slick.

One day, there was a long, black spine, exposed, extending across the waves.

"The land bridge," Aurora said. "It's a new moon tonight, and the tide is out."

We stood together, looking at it.

It was a path, a way out, a chain linking us back to the world. I had made no plans for myself once I was recovered; I did not think I would be allowed to stay. Now, seeing the bridge, passable though treacherous, I knew I *must* not stay.

A sense of urgency swept over me.

I took Aurora's hands. "Leave with me. Now. This very minute."

Aurora looked at me in confusion, sea spray clinging in pearls to the edge of her hood.

"Together, we could be happy, happier than we've ever been. I know this is your home, and—"

"I will go with you."

"Truly? You would forsake your life?"

"You are my life now."

And so we exchanged vows of love, and we made plans for our departure. Both of us spoke in hushed voices, despite the booming sea that surely covered all sound. We spoke as if we were planning something illicit, an escape. There were no locks on the doors, nor guards near them. A nun-in-waiting may choose to break her vows. However, the unspoken truth was that Aurora would not have been permitted to leave such a secret cloister, even without being initiated into the fullness of its mysteries.

We could not make the land bridge crossing empty-handed. It was several miles long, and the mainland on the other side was uninhabited, as the salt from the sea poisoned the ground for many miles more.

It was also too exposed in daylight to walk out across the bridge. Anyone watching from the abbey might see. We intended to meet in my cell at a certain hour. Aurora would bring what supplies she could secret away from the kitchen. Under cover of darkness, and with the low tide that would return at that time, we would cross and begin a new life together.

Aurora insisted that I nap after dinner to conserve strength. She would come and wake me when it was time. But she never came.

I woke with a start. It was the black of night. Silent as a tomb. Yet something had called me to consciousness.

"Aurora?" I whispered.

No reply.

Then I became aware of what had awoken me. There was a presence. Something was here, in the abbey, in the dark.

With trembling hands, I stirred up the coals in the hearth. The fire flared. The room was empty. My mind screamed that something was with me, yet I saw nothing, heard nothing.

It was the oppressive air of the abbey, intensified. No—it *was intensifying*. Something was gathering. Something was approaching.

Within the abbey, it crouched, a predator, waiting for the inhale before the strike.

It was past the designated hour, and Aurora had not come. She was determined to leave with me. She would not have missed our appointment. Something had kept her, against her will. She was in danger—as was anyone within the walls of this abbey on this night. I had to find her.

I dressed—I had been given a set of nun's robes, as the clothes I had arrived in were torn beyond repair. In spite of my dislike of the robes, I was grateful for them now, for their ability to conceal my identity. I dressed myself like a nun, pulling the deep hood over my face. I ventured out into the hall. I did not take so much as a candle; I dared not risk any light for fear of discovery, for I knew I would be venturing into forbidden places.

Save for Aurora, I would never have done so. I would have hidden in my room until the presence had passed. Thought of her was what kept me brave, kept me lucid, kept me moving, blind, through the dark abbey. I knew not where I went; I only knew I had to find her. I opened doors I had never seen. I crossed strange chambers and descended stairs. My search was unimpeded. All was deserted. I would have believed I was the only living thing there, if not for the ever-intensifying presence.

Did it draw me? Perhaps. Perhaps that is how I found my way through the labyrinthine abbey to the stairwell. It yawned suddenly before me: a vast round pit, walled in sharp flint stone, like a massive well, with stairs about the edges, coiling down, down, down. In a sconce, a black candle flickered. Wax ran down its gnarled sides and dripped to the floor like blood. More candles were lit at intervals along the descent. They shone like will-o'-the-wisps—ill omens hovering in the dark.

I descended, with no small amount of trepidation. Round and round I went. There was no railing separating me from the drop, and I clung as close to the flint wall as I dared. I grazed my knuckles, my cheek, my shoulder upon the stones.

The time was drawing near.

Time for what? I did not know, nor did I know from whence the thought entered my mind, yet I was gripped with terror and urgency. I hurried, faster, ever faster, now running down the stairs, long robes clutched in my hands. Round and round and round until I was giddy with the spiral I traced. And finally: gravel and sand. The bottom of the stairwell.

The presence here was so thick, I could feel it compressing my lungs. A dark, rounded hallway opened before me, like a mouth. This was a threshold—of what, I knew not, and it did not matter. I had no choice. I proceeded.

Inside, the passage was narrow and low-ceilinged. The curved walls were not stacked flint, but hewn directly into bedrock. Nothing upon the walls. Not so much as a chisel or hammer mark. They were smooth. Impossibly smooth. The floor, also, was perfectly even, without a single crack. With a loathsome chill, I found myself thinking, *not human made.*

A red light glowed at the far end of the passage. And from that direction emanated the first sounds I had heard during this torturous night: the sounds of human voices, raised in unison, speaking together in a rhythmic chant. The words—if there were any—echoed and distorted along the stone passage. I could not make them out.

This was where the nuns had gone. I was approaching some secret rite. I did not know what they would do to me, if I, an outsider, was discovered violating their ceremony. I pulled the hood more securely over my face. I moved silently through the remainder of the passage, to its end. Here I hesitated.

The nun's voices were loud, rising in volume. They were nearing some emotional climax.

I steeled myself—and there is no way I could have prepared myself thoroughly for the horrors upon which my eyes fell. Slowly, so slowly, I moved my head around the stone, and when one eye had view of the chamber beyond, I stood rigid, frozen by what I saw.

It was a massive space. From where I stood, the ground sloped down, as a bowl. Indeed, the space was completely spherical, perfectly so, of the same singularly smooth construction as the passage on an enormous scale. Though this was not what horrified me.

Within the stone sphere were gathered the nuns. There must have been at least one hundred. They held black candles, and they were completely naked. Not a one of them looked less than eighty years old. They chanted, and they waved their candles and writhed their bodies. Their faces, uplifted, were terrible to behold. Though this is not what horrified me.

At the far side of the sphere, across the sea of ancient women, were erect two stone pillars. Between these pillars, a woman had been restrained, suspended some twenty feet in the air, one wrist and ankle secured to each pillar. She too was naked, and I knew her. It was Aurora.

She did not scream or resist or flail. She dangled, limp and unaware of her hideous surroundings.

The chanting of the women shifted, increased in speed. It was a language I did not know, a language of the chest and throat, of snarling and gnashing. Spittle flashed in the air.

I stared at Aurora, willing myself to find a way to get to her, to cut her down, to escape, but the hundred nuns were between us. Even if I could have avoided them, their attention was bent upon her. They lifted clawed hands to her, exalting her, emphasizing her presence within the rhythm of their chant. There was nothing I could do.

As I watched in misery, something began to change. The stone behind Aurora, opaque at first, began to change color, to clear, to turn transparent. It *thinned*. Through this new opening were shapes, black shapes, not human, not animal, and the shapes coalesced into a singular being so awful it was beyond comprehension. I cannot describe its aspect with anything like precision. I can only compare it to an unholy amalgamation of many deep-sea creatures pressed together: tentacles, spines, webbing, teeth, fins, eyes, nothing in proportion, every part blasphemous and accursed.

The monstrosity crawled through the opening in the stone, and expanded, and unfurled, until it covered the curved ceiling entirely.

And with it came a crushing, near-physical blow. For this was the source of the presence. It was here, above me, breathing foul wind, slavering and grinning, with claws like the rib bones of a cow. There was no escape. I clung to the wall of the passage and despaired.

At the sight of the beast, the nuns grew frantic, with ecstasy or fear I knew not. They chanted and screamed, throwing their hands in the air, flinging them toward the pillars. Toward Aurora.

The beast took notice. It approached Aurora, rippling and undulating grotesquely across the ceiling. It hung over her, dangling limbs, tentacles, spines, wings. It paused, as if considering. Then, with one precise claw, it slashed her open. The beast opened her skin like the pages of a book, exposing the wet flesh of her muscles, the bone, the organs. A river of blood flowed down her legs. And it began to feed.

Aurora screamed.

Next I can recall, I was running, already halfway up the stairwell, suffocating: racing heart, gasping breath, echoing sobs. I could not fathom escape from such a creature, but where my mind failed, my body took charge. I knew only the animal instinct to survive.

I paused at the top of the stairwell only to retch uselessly. Acid burned my throat, my tongue. I kept running, my head pounding, flaming, burning. I found the doors, the doors to outside, to freedom —and they were locked.

I pushed, pulled, pounded. I felt for handles, locks, for hinges I might pry from the wood with my fingernails. The door was unassailable.

I tried other doors, all the doors I could find. All locked. All save one.

I let myself in with a sob of relief—only to realize it was my own cell. The window there was too high, too narrow. It was no good. I turned to find some other means of escape. The door had shut behind me, and it would not open.

I spent the dark hours before dawn beneath a crushing intensity of horror, watching the door. I was certain that at any moment the beast would come to kill me, that the nuns would enter and drag me back down to the hell beneath these very floors. And ever before my eyes was the image of my beloved, still alive, being consumed.

When the sun rose, I was alive and untouched. Could I now escape safely, in the light of day? Even as I began to gather the courage to try, the handle of my door rattled, and the door itself, opened.

I shrank back against the protruding sharpness of the wall, ready to scream, ready to fight, to claw out the eyes of whoever entered, to make them remember me, to make them pay a price for my life—but the person who entered was Aurora.

Whole, breathing, walking. Even cheerful. A flush to her cheeks and a sparkle in her eye. She smiled at me warmly. She *spoke*: "Good morning. How are you feeling?"

I gaped, unable to form any intelligible response.

"My manners. I haven't met an outsider in years. Apologies. My name is Aurora. The nuns told me about you, that you'd wrecked your boat on our island, and that you were unwell. I'm to care for you through your recovery."

"But we've met."

She laughed, that beautiful sound, incongruous, loathsome in this nightmare. "I do not think so."

I took both of her hands, rather roughly. "You don't remember me?"

Her brows furrowed. I had seen the expression upon her face before, when she had spoken of her inability to recall the circumstances of her arrival on this accursed island.

She withdrew her hands. "I am sure it is a trick of the mind," she said, again cheerful and blithe. "No more."

She began the morning routine, now so familiar to me, of tending the fire, of tidying.

"You do know me," I said. "And I know you. We have known each other these past weeks. You were the one who found me upon the shore. You were the one who has cared for me. You were the

32

one who showed me this island, the land bridge, and you were the one who agreed to go away with me."

As I spoke, Aurora's motions slowed. She stood, her arms hanging at her sides, her head bowed, her back to me.

I approached and, gently, put my arms around her. "You are the one I love. The one who loves me."

She shuddered. "I feel that you speak the truth. I know your touch." She grasped my hands. "But I don't remember."

I luxuriated in her touch—I thought I had lost it forever—but we could not linger.

I told her, "We are in danger here. We must go. Now."

"What? I don't—I don't understand."

"I saw you die last night." And the grief and horror of it all permeated my voice.

She turned and looked into my eyes. "I'm right here. Surely it was a dream. A nightmare."

I told her what I had seen.

She was shocked. "The nuns wouldn't do anything of the sort! They care for me. And the creature you speak of, such things don't exist. Surely that is proof it was a dream."

I admit that my confidence in my memory wavered. It would have been far easier if Aurora had been right. Yet here, upon my hands and arms were the abrasions from the stairwell. My body bore the proof of what I had witnessed.

Aurora said, "There's nothing to fear. We are safe here."

"There is no place on this earth less safe. We must away."

"This is my world. My life."

"You were willing to leave with me yesterday."

She quirked an eyebrow. "Well. That was before I died."

Anger flashed through me. I could not suffer her to make light of my torment. "Come. I will show you."

And I took her forcibly by the wrist and led her through the abbey. Aurora quailed beneath my intensity of purpose. I regret that I frightened her, but she would have been far more frightened than that, had she remembered what had happened to her.

I feared I might not be able to find my way, that any number of nuns might stop us, that any number of doors might now be locked. My memory did not fail me. Nor were we stopped. Perhaps the nuns were asleep, after their nighttime demonic ritual. Nuns: the word was wrong, clearly, for the women of the abbey. Did such creatures need sleep? Were they even human?

Ah—the stairwell yawned below us.

"Does this not look familiar?" I asked.

Aurora frowned. She did not answer.

We descended. No candles now lit the way; a window in the high ceiling let in the gray winter light. As we spiraled into the heart of evil, as we trod the impossible rounded passage, the light grew distant. At last, we stood in the center of the spherical cavern, at the point of deepest depression. The dark was nearly complete around us.

Aurora turned, slowly. When she faced the twin pillars to which she had been chained, the wall that had opened to admit the monster, she started backward. She shrieked. She covered her face with her hands and fell to the ground.

I was at her side instantly.

She could not speak for the violence of her sobs. She clutched at her chest, her stomach. She ripped away her robes. The skin beneath was smooth and unblemished.

I tried to take her hands. She evaded me.

"I remember!" she exclaimed, despair and agony coloring her voice.

"Last night?"

"Not just last night. All of it. Every new moon, they bring me here. Every new moon, they give me to that—to that—monster. I die. And when the sun rises, I'm alive again. I forget again. I let them bring me here. Over and over and over."

Her hands trembled. She felt her stomach, touched her chest, her throat, looked at her fingers as though for blood.

I watched the pillars, the place between them. There was no movement.

"Why?" I whispered. "Why do they do this?"

34

She looked at me, her eyes suddenly and violently wide. "The Great Beast rises from the earth, the last of its kind. From the depths it rises. In the perfect darkness it demands sacrifice. Without one, the Beast would devour the world."

"They worship it. They call it forth."

"They hold back horrors."

"By enacting horrors upon you." I took her by the hands and raised her to her feet. "You will not be sacrificed again. You have spent years in hell. No more."

"But the world—"

"Let the world be devoured. I would rather be devoured with you than know that I allowed you to be subject to torture and death."

Aurora flung her arms around me.

Then her body went rigid. Simultaneously, I became aware of a sound above. A rhythmic noise, as of drums, or knocking. Or footsteps. It had not begun in that moment; no, it had been steadily growing louder, louder, and had only then broken into the forefront of my awareness.

Aurora cast about wildly. "They know I remember, that I have broken the spell they laid upon me. They're coming."

I took her hand and we ran out of the spherical cavern, through the rounded passage—the only exit. At the bottom of the stairwell, where the gray patch of light shone, we looked, and saw: the nuns had already begun their spiraling descent. Drawing nearer, shuffling footsteps, hissing voices. There was no way past them. No other way out. We were caught in a stone trap.

Aurora wilted against the wall, built of that enigmatic flint. She gave up hope. I, however, grew angry. Before this island, I had saved myself from an evil fate. I would not succumb now. Nor would I allow Aurora to be taken by one even worse.

I had a desperate idea. I put my hand upon the wall, feeling in the semi-dark, and, once I found a suitable flint, I put pressure upon it. It snapped off in my hand. The flint was long as a butcher knife and just as sharp; it drew blood from my fingers at a touch.

The first nuns were only several revolutions from the bottom of the stairwell. They bared their teeth—sharpened to points—black circles beneath their eyes, which glittered red.

I gathered my nerve, my resolve.

To Aurora, I whispered, "Do you trust me?"

She looked at me with a dead expression, and she nodded.

I grasped Aurora about her shoulders, pulled her into the square of daylight, and I held the flint to her throat.

I shouted, "Look, you! Let us by, or I will kill her."

The nuns hissed louder, but they ceased their advance. They leered down at us. In one voice like grinding stone, like rusted iron, they spoke: *Kill her, and you will take her place.*

"I would sooner die." I mimed cutting first Aurora's throat, and then my own, in one smooth motion. "One way or another, we will be free." I gripped Aurora tighter and brandished the flint. "Go back! Let us pass! Or I will do it."

For one protracted and awful moment, the nuns seemed inclined to surge, to fall upon us from above, to overwhelm us. Then, there was movement at the top of the stairwell.

They began to retreat.

Aurora and I began to ascend, one harrowing step at a time. The nuns gave ground with excruciating slowness, all the time walking backward, their red eyes fixed upon us, upon the flint blade. Sweat dripped down my forehead. My hand cramped around the flint, and I feared for my grip. Once, Aurora slipped. The nuns growled and lunged *forward*. I shouted and they were again forced into their unwilling retreat, hissing curses upon us.

At last, we attained the summit. I kept our backs to the wall so the nuns could not surround us.

"The exit," I muttered into Aurora's ear. "I do not know the way."

She was nearly incoherent with fear, sensate enough to guide me, to step in the direction of freedom. Finally, I felt the wood of doors at my back. They opened. We were out, our feet upon sandy soil. The nuns gathered at the threshold, snapping their teeth together. they did not pass through.

"The daylight," Aurora panted. "They will not hazard it."

"Quick, then. Quick!"

We ran, sprinting, finding within ourselves new reserves of energy, and there, that black spine stretched across the water. Here and there, it disappeared, covered now and again by waves, or submerged. The tide was not low enough.

We could not afford to wait. We did not even pause to discuss it. I put Aurora ahead of me, and we ran as quick as we dared, now slipping upon ice, now upon shifting rock. Bitterly cold waves struck us, stiffened our clothes with salt, with ice, freezing in the constant wind.

Overhead, the weak winter sun began to fall in the sky. We were driven onward by the threat of night, of the darkness which would force us to slow, to crawl, to feel our way with our hands. The darkness which would unleash them. They would swarm along the rocky land bridge, seizing at our legs, dragging us down, dragging us back. In my exhaustion and terror, I imagined these rocks were the black vertebrae of the beast, which they would awaken. It would roll, flinging us into the sea, and it would impale us with tooth and claw.

We went forward, upon numb feet. The water rose around our ankles, around our shins. I did not know if Aurora could swim. I had no breath to ask. I only pressed my hand to her shoulder, hurrying her on.

At last, at last, we fell upon the sandy beach of the mainland. The sun was setting. We grasped each other's hands, picked ourselves up, and ran. We knew not what sort of life lay before us, but knew it would be—knew it *must* be—better than the horrors we fled.

BLEEDING ART

BY ARIANA FERRANTE

They told Mairead many things before she picked up a sword.

They told Mairead that vampires prowled the frozen wood, flitted like bats and were just as dark. They told Mairead they came down from their castles in the mountains each night to feast, to suck the cattle and the vagrants dry until their skin clung to their bones like wet hair to the scalp. They told Mairead until she mastered a blade, she could not even *entertain* the thought of venturing out after sunset.

So she mastered a blade. And then another. And another, and another, until she did not venture inside or out without at least three on her person. They told her the vampires preyed on women like her, with her wine-red hair done up in a bun and a heart-shaped face flanked by rosy, dangling coils. Told her they preyed on women with crimson-painted lips, women with eyes so dark brown they nearly rivaled the night itself.

They were right, she supposed. She *was* quite the catch. Cut down seventy-nine bloodsuckers over the course of her career. More than any other hunter in the region. When she wasn't stalking the woods for rogue vampires, she circled the town, blood-flushed skin pulsing, *glowing* with life. The sight of that much skin was enough to drive vampires wild, wild enough that they didn't notice the blessed silvered blade she slipped so swiftly out of her boots until she'd already lashed it across their throats, spilling their stinking, blackened blood over the earth.

And then *she* came for her—not on ink-black wings but in a cloak about as dark. And when Mairead saw her, she thought her heart had stopped—thought, for a moment, that she was as cold as the woman in front of her.

They never told her a vampire could be so beautiful. Never told her, never *warned* her, that a creature so stunning existed. But there she stood, clad in her fur-lined mantle, pale fingers covered in golden rings set with multicolored stones. Her vulpine face, pale and gray and bloodless, stood out against the wood behind her. And the vampire smiled at Mairead, eyes amber-colored like sap from a tree, beautiful and soft and ensnaring all that came close.

Mairead steeled herself, waiting to feel the tell-tale signs of a vampire's hypnotic gaze so that she could wrestle free, but nothing came. The beauty was her own doing, and Mairead's attraction hers.

The vampire did not bite. She did not hiss, did not lunge at Mairead, claws bared like so many others before her—a level of restraint she greatly appreciated. She merely smiled and tucked a lock of inky hair beneath a pointed ear. The vampire told her that her name was Isla, and that she lived on the opposite side of the mountain. And then she looked the huntress up and down and inquired which cordwainer made her boots.

A discussion of boots led to a discussion of dresses led to a discussion of everything. They spoke for hours on end, the moon lifting higher and higher overhead. Mairead hardly noticed the passage of time, save for twinges of growing exhaustion in her legs. Time wasn't the focus. Time wasn't necessary information.

"You haven't asked my occupation," Mairead said. "Every other subject you've asked about, but not that."

"I hardly have to," the vampire chuckled. "Word passes quickly when you can fly."

Mairead couldn't stop the smile that pulled at her lips. "You aren't attacking me, either."

"Not every vampire is foolish," Isla said, shrugging. "At least, not any vampires that want to last longer than a decade."

Mairead laughed. "You could say they get better with age, then?"

It was Isla's turn to chuckle. "Do they pay you well, the townspeople?" she asked, quickly digressing. "For your 'work'?" She drew her legs up and sat in the air, resting her chin in her hand. A pang of jealousy rippled through Mairead's aching legs at the sight of that, but she distracted herself with an answer.

"Not nearly," she said. "It's enough for a home, but a home isn't much here."

"It's nicer in my castle," Isla said, fangs showing in her smile. "I could show you, if you'd like!"

A laugh caught in the back of Mairead's throat. "What can you offer me?" she asked, admittedly intrigued. It wasn't every day she had the chance to speak with her *clientele*, and a part of her, some gigantic invisible part, begged the vampire to give her an excuse to follow her home.

Isla looked up as if trying to conjure an invisible thought, rubbing her chin with a dead-gray hand. "Well, when you are as old as I am, you amass quite the fortune. Plus, I have been looking for a model for one of my paintings."

"You paint?" Mairead asked, thin brow quirking.

"Oh, almost every day!" Isla exclaimed, amber eyes lighting up with excitement. She dropped her feet back to the ground to continue. "Well—every night, rather. However, since I cannot see anything during the daytime I cannot paint nearly as many things as I would like. As it turns out, castle walls became a boring subject after the first hundred years."

"Do you *pay* your models?" Mairead inquired, only half joking.

Isla's smile spread wider, pale-fingered hand spreading out over her unbeating heart. "On my unlife, I swear to make it worth your while."

The declaration was all she needed.

Mairead followed her through the frozen wood and up to the southern side of the mountain. Isla did indeed have a castle there, all dark stone and spires, the candlelight in the windows like dozens of watching eyes. The frigid snow outside clung to the buffeted stones like paint to a canvas, almost lace-like in its swirling, delicate patterns.

The doors to the castle opened, and so did Mairead's mouth. Hundreds, no, *thousands* of paintings clung to the walls like a second skin, hardly any hints of the stone from the outside visible beneath the multicolored layer.

Mairead wasn't sure that paint could come in so many shades. Every color under the sun decorated the walls: lights, darks, and in betweens. Some paintings were portraits of other vampires—she guessed as much by their dark attire and pale faces, stark against the dim backdrops Isla set them in front of. Other paintings were more abstract—a mess of splatters and blocks and circles and squiggles Mairead could not hope to keep track of. Others looked to be paintings of assorted items, but when she squinted, she noticed the hundreds and hundreds of individual dots making up the various objects.

"There's so *many*," Mairead exclaimed, unsure of what else to say. She had guessed that would be the case, certainly. An immortal creature like Isla needed to find *something* to occupy her time, after all. But the number in Mairead's mind was nothing compared to the presentation of it all, nothing against the vibrant, eclectic display of canvas upon canvas upon canvas.

"There's more in the dungeon," Isla noted offhandedly. "I cycle through them when I want to spice things up."

Mairead blinked, intrigued. "You have a *dungeon*?"

Isla's plump, dark lips parted, and she laughed. It was a warm and jubilant thing, her laugh, and it flowed through the air like the howl of the wind did outside. "No self-respecting vampire has a castle *without* a dungeon. It doesn't get much use, though. I primarily use it for storage."

"Your paintings are beautiful," Mairead said. Her gaze continued to wander the plastered walls, but each time she switched to the other side she became distracted, her attention drawn helplessly to the vampire. *You're beautiful too*, she wished to say, but the words refused to pass her lips. Given the way Isla looked back at her and winked, however, it seemed she hardly needed to.

"I'll take you to the guest rooms," Isla said, turning back around. She hurried to a set of stairs, leading her new companion to the second of many floors.

"Guest *rooms*?" Mairead echoed, mouth threatening to drop open again.

"Mhm. Haven't had anyone around in ages to actually *use* them, so I'm a little excited!" Isla said, giggling and clasping her dark-nailed hands together. She led Mairead down another painting-coated corridor, stopping at last at a wooden door. "I think this one should be fine. If you have any problems with the bed, there's six other rooms to choose from." She lifted a hand and gestured to the other doors lining the wall.

"Might try one for each day of the week," Mairead said, utterly serious.

"I like the way you think!" Isla laughed, clapping a hand on her shoulder before just as quickly releasing it. "Now, if there are any problems that can't be solved by a change of rooms, you come to me, okay?" Her face turned serious. "My room is ten doors down on the right."

Mairead nodded. "Ten doors down," she agreed, and Isla returned to joviality.

"See you tomorrow then, Mairead! I'll wake you when I'm ready to paint if you haven't already gotten up!"

Without another word Isla dashed down the hall, feet barely touching the ground as she whizzed to her own room, not stopping until she reached the entrance. Isla opened the door, turning and giving Mairead a final wave before shutting it behind her.

Mairead watched her go, not moving from her spot until long after the vampire's departure.

She already missed Isla's voice.

Mairead woke the next morning. At least she assumed it must be morning. Predictably, all of the windows in the guest room were closed, barring any access to the sunlight. She sat up in bed, wiping away the sand that had formed in the corners of her eyes. Slowly but surely last night returned—Isla, the castle, the paintings—and Mairead perked up, swinging her legs off the side of the bed and getting to her feet.

She searched the dresser in the room, quickly finding a hairbrush and a hand mirror. She ran the former through her hair, checking the latter until she was certain she looked presentable. She walked to the door, grasped the handle, and pulled it open.

Isla stood on the other side, eyes widening with surprise. "Oh!" she squeaked. "Good timing! I just came to tell you that breakfast is ready!"

Mairead perked up. "Breakfast?" she repeated, mouth already watering at the thought.

The vampire's pearly fangs flashed as she grinned. "Of *course!*" Isla said. "I have to keep my model well-fed, after all!"

Mairead's stomach grumbled, and she laughed. "Can't argue with that."

Isla's dining room was bigger than the entirety of Mairead's old house. Much like the rest of the castle, it was coated in portraits of varying styles and hues. A gigantic, dark, wooden table spanned the length of the room, flanked by a dozen or so chairs. Isla sat down at the head of it, motioning for Mairead to join her at the nearest seat, a plate with food already set out for her.

"I had to guess what you wanted to eat, but I figured I couldn't go wrong with an omelet," Isla said. For herself, she grabbed a nearby wine bottle, uncorking it with her claws and pouring the very *non*-wine contents into her awaiting glass. "Omelets aren't my favorite, personally."

"You can *eat* this?" Mairead asked, sitting and staring down at her plate of food. "I thought vampires could only drink blood."

"Mhm," Isla confirmed, humming into her blood-filled glass

before taking a sip. "We can still eat human food just fine. It's just not very appetizing. Doesn't taste like it used to. It's the same with coffins and beds. We can do it, it just doesn't feel right. Human food … kinda tastes like chalk and seawater, if you ask me. But I keep human food around, just for occasions like this."

Mairead's face scrunched up at the thought, and she distracted herself with a welcoming mouthful of eggs. She swallowed before speaking up. "Do you have many models?"

Isla sank into her high-backed chair. "Not nearly as many as I'd like, I'm afraid. When I ask humans to model for me, they either scream and run away, try and kill me, or stay the night and leave the first chance they get because they think I'll suck them dry." She sighed, putting down her glass to cross her arms. "Human blood isn't *that* great, if I'm being quite honest. It's good, sure, but I think a lot of vampires only drink it to keep up the image."

Mairead frowned. "How many humans have you painted?"

"Successfully? Two. So, um …" Isla trailed off, pursing her lips and looking to the floor. "If you wanted to, I was maybe hoping you could … you know, stick around for a while. I'd love to try out different poses, different colors. I'd pay you extra, of course."

Mairead smiled, resting her chin in her hands. "I'd like that."

Isla looked up, amber eyes shimmering with surprise. "Really?"

"Of course!" Mairead said, nodding into her next mouthful of omelet. "I mean—you're really good at painting."

Isla perked up further, and Mairead was certain the woman might have blushed if the blood was still flowing in her veins. "Oh, well, that's only because I've had lots of time to practice!" she said, pointed ears flattening. "Even before I was turned, I always loved to paint."

"Still," Mairead continued. "All your practice has really paid off. Those portraits look so lifelike!"

"I only hope I can paint you just as well," Isla said, dipping her head as the corners of her sheepish smile reached her eyes.

"Well, there's only one way to find out, isn't there?" Mairead asked, quick to match the vampire's grin.

"I suppose so!" Isla agreed. "But finish your omelet first! I can't have you pose on an empty stomach!"

So she did.

Mairead knew in *theory* that portraits took a long time to sit for, but she never could have guessed they took *that* long.

She sat atop the throne-like seat Isla had chosen for her, back straightened and chin high like a queen regarding her subjects, entire body locked in place while the vampire painted. Mairead held her breath in short bursts, trying not to raise or lower her chest in any dramatic fashion in fear it would somehow mess with Isla's vision. Fortunately, she was no stranger to keeping still for a long time. Skill with a blade or bow was one thing, but one could not surprise a target by moving carelessly through the underbrush.

"You know," Isla said, poking her head out from behind the rectangular canvas, "you have beautiful eyes."

"I do?" Mairead asked, moving nothing but her mouth. Out of every feature, she considered her eyes the least striking. Brown eyes weren't nearly as attractive a trait as blue or green, at least as far as the townspeople were concerned. As far as she was concerned, however, the rest of her body made up for the plainness of her eyes.

"You do," Isla insisted. "They're so dark, and warm at the same time. Almost haunting." She returned her focus to her canvas, deep in thought. "I just … want to make certain I can capture that."

"You're welcome to try," Mairead said, smiling briefly before returning her expression to one of frozen neutrality.

"And try I shall," Isla said, that familiar laugh of hers ringing out, serving to stir the butterflies dormant in Mairead's stomach.

It took several hours and multiple breaks, but Isla at last declared she was finished.

Mairead emptied her lungs in a single breath, rising slowly to her feet and moving to the canvas. She clamped a hand over her lips, dark eyes widening at Isla's depiction. If she didn't know any better, she might have thought she was staring into a mirror. There she sat, domineering, regal, powerful, brown eyes burning and dark, like storm clouds ready to release rain.

"It's beautiful," Mairead said, voice muffled through her fingers. She dropped them and said it again, yearning for Isla to hear such praise.

"There is plenty more where this came from," Isla said, looking up at her model with a growing grin. "You are quite the muse. Now, how about we find a place to hang it?"

"Easier said than done." Mairead laughed.

They found a spot for the portrait relatively quickly—atop the castle's stony hearth.

"I rarely have an excuse to light this thing!" Isla exclaimed once the portrait was in place. "Vampires can't exactly freeze to death, so I don't need any warmth." With a flash of sparks from the flint the logs caught fire, crackling as the flames ate away at the wood. "Come," she said, motioning to the spot in front of the growing blaze. "It's been a long day."

Mairead sat down before the fire, warming her hands over the flickering flames. Isla sat beside her, careful not to ruin her outfit with the accumulated soot.

Now that Mairead was free to move and speak as often as she wished, the two quickly struck up a conversation. Isla gushed over the way Mairead wore her hair, while Mairead detailed previous scuffles with the undead, from the vampire child that tried to spirit away the older women in her town, to the admittedly handsome young bloodsucker whose otherwise intense charm failed to sway someone of her romantic leanings. Eventually, Isla revealed her age— a stunning one hundred and twenty-five to her meager twenty-seven.

"You look wonderful for one hundred and twenty-five," Mairead said.

"Blood works wonders for the skin," Isla teased.

Every once and a while, Mairead's gaze drifted upward, resting on the portrait of herself. She still couldn't quite comprehend the level of skill the painting possessed. The realism of the portrait ... it seemed wasted on someone like her, not noble, not rich. As far as the townspeople were concerned, she was pest control with a slightly inflated budget.

The feeling of Isla's head on her shoulder snapped her out of her self-deprecating funk. She looked down, smiling.

"If you would like, I could fill this entire room with images of you," Isla said.

"That would be very generous," Mairead said, chuckling. "But what about paintings of yourself? Do you have any of those?"

Isla sighed, lifting her head to shake it. "No. I cannot paint myself."

Mairead's brows knitted together. "And why not?"

"Vampires do not appear in mirrors. Therefore, I do not know what I look like. Or, well, I do not know each and every detail. The image of myself ... it's vague and abstract."

Mairead shifted in her spot on the floor, turning to face the vampire directly. "I'm no good at art, but perhaps I can describe you," she offered. "It will not be the same as a mirror, but it would be something."

Isla paused, considering it. "I suppose that could work, if it isn't too much trouble."

Mairead smiled. "In exchange for such beautiful pieces?" she asked, motioning to the portrait above the fire. "It is the least that I can do."

Isla's smile gleamed even brighter than the flames. "It's a deal, then!"

And so Mairead described Isla as best she could, from the waving locks of raven hair to the sap-like amber eyes that glowed in the light of the fire. She detailed her in lavish words—Isla's fox-like face, slender shoulders, soft lips, and sharp, dark nails. She described her through the night, only tiring when she could speak nothing more. She curled up in the vampire's lap as the moonlit dark outside pervaded, still desperately trying to string words together.

They fell asleep by the fire.

It took only a few days and a couple more paintings, but Mairead quickly came to discover vampires were just as hostile to each other as they were to the humans nearby.

The first one came in the middle of a modeling session. Mairead sat recumbent on one of Isla's many fainting couches.

"No self-respecting vampire doesn't have a *fainting couch*," Isla informed her. "What *else* are we meant to dramatically lie on when we hear bad news?"

An awful itch sprang up on the right side of her face. She dared not scratch it, in fear that Isla might lose whatever focus she currently possessed.

There came a loud crack, the splintering and buckling of wood. It was a sound Mairead knew all too well, ever since a couple of daring vampires attempted to take her in her sleep rather early on in her career. She rolled off the fainting couch, landing on all fours before scrambling to her feet. She pulled her blade from her belt, grip hard enough to whiten her knuckles.

"Mairead?" Isla asked, pointed ears twitching at the previous sound.

"Stay here," Mairead said, gaze narrowing in the direction of the noise. She moved toward the entrance with the short sword at her side, steps quick and feather-light. She wasn't in the woods, but that didn't mean that a misstep couldn't make enough noise to alert the intruder of her presence. The snap of a trod-upon stick and the echo of footsteps on stone possessed the same potential for damage.

She caught him by the entrance, standing over the ruined wood. His broad frame moved faster than his muscled, bulky body would have ever suggested, lips pulled back as he bared his fangs. He snarled, upon her in moments, swiping a clawed hand toward her chest.

"Human!" he growled, voice deep and booming.

She ducked the swing, swerving behind him as he fell forward. Mairead dug the tip of the blade into his thigh, carving it open while she spun to reach his back. The vampire howled in pain, black blood already spewing from the wound, sizzling at the silvered blade's contact. He turned just as swiftly as her, arm lunging out and gripping the sword by the blade.

His face twisted into a grimace as his grasp tightened about the blessed metal, and with a yank of his arms he wrenched the sword from Mairead's grasp.

She let it go as he pulled, sending the vampire backward and onto the cold, unforgiving floor, his injured leg preventing him from rising. Mairead clambered onto the vampire, straddling his muscled frame and pinning his clawed hands down with her feet. She pulled another blade from her hilt, dark gaze stormy and focused. It was a shorter one, the blade, but size hardly mattered.

With one hand she grabbed the vampire's hair, forcing the fistful to the floor to put his throat on display. With the other, she drove the blade into his throat, jerking it about until it hit an artery. She leaped up, not quick enough to avoid the spray of thick, inky blood that painted her face.

The vampire's arms lashed out, reaching to grab Mairead but going no further. The man gagged and sputtered, the geyser of sludge slowly lessening until it pooled around his still frame.

"Oh my god!"

Mairead's head snapped up, eyes landing on Isla standing at the end of the entrance hall. "Isla!" Mairead exclaimed, tracking black prints over the stone as she raced to meet her. "I told you to wait!"

"That was incredible!" Isla laughed, pulling the surprised huntress into an embrace. "You should have seen it!"

A nervous laugh spilled from Mairead's lips, but it grew more genuine the longer it lasted. "Really?" she asked.

"Yes, really!" Isla insisted. "I need to paint that! Ooh! Next time I paint you, you should pose with your sword!"

At last Isla let go, allowing Mairead to catch her breath. She lifted a hand, holding her head and sighing. She turned around to check on the vampire's body, already finding it shriveling away to ash where it lay. She looked up, eyes widening as she realized something else.

The black blood hadn't just hit her face, it had hit the nearby paintings, too.

"Oh no," Mairead whispered, heart sinking into her boots. "Oh no, no."

"Oh no what?" Isla asked, following her gaze. "Oh!"

"Your paintings," Mairead said, wincing. Vampire blood stained so easily- when the vampires attacked her in her bedroom it took her three entire days of washing to get the last of the blood out of her sheets.

Isla laughed, shaking her head. "Actually, I think a little black was just what they needed," she said, standing on her tiptoes and planting a kiss on the huntress's cheek. She just as quickly reeled back, however, as she got a mouthful of blackened blood. "Yugh. I think you could do without the mess, though."

Mairead laughed. "Yeah. I guess I could."

And so Isla started painting Mairead, weapons drawn and stance ready, glaring at some invisible foe. Portraits like that required far more breaks, however, as Mairead's arms got tired from holding up her sword or dagger or assorted knives. She hardly minded the breaks, of course. It meant she got to spend more time with Isla. They curled up together in front of the fire each night before retreating to their rooms, and each night that passed Mairead moved her guest room to be closer to Isla.

A week or so of 'battle portraits' passed before the next attack. It came in the form of two vampires this time, a man and a woman, both wiry and lean-muscled and impossibly angry.

The woman made the first move, propelled across the floor by invisible wings. Her sharp fangs snapped at the air, narrowly missing Mairead's nose as the latter retreated.

The male vampire caught her across the face while Mairead focused on his counterpart, his closed fist sending stars into her vision. She clattered to the floor, rolling instinctively onto her back as the man lunged, claws aimed for her jugular.

He was fast, but she was faster. She slipped her short sword from its sheath, slamming it into the vampire's stomach until his clammy flesh rested against the hilt. His jaw dropped open, black blood spilling from his mouth and onto Mairead's chest, viscous, stinking fluid clinging to the fabric. Within moments, the blessed silver did its work, eating away at the dead vampire's darkening, dissolving flesh.

A cry of horror ripped from the other assailant's throat, and with a flurry of wings she reverted into a bat, tearing through the air and toward the exit. Isla, alerted by the noise, blocked the path, transfigured as well. The two clashed, a writhing black cloud of squeaks and beating wings that Mairead did not dare interfere with.

At last Isla was ejected from the altercation, slamming into the floor and returning to normal, winded and scratched up. The other bat flew out the door, vanishing into the black of night.

"Isla!" Mairead cried, running over and falling to her knees, cradling the injured vampire.

"I'm okay," Isla said, melting into Mairead's arms. "I'm okay. Are you okay?"

"I'm okay," Mairead insisted. "I was worried she'd killed you!" The word *killed* almost didn't come out when she said it, almost stuck in her throat and choked her.

Isla laughed, entire body shuddering with pain thereafter. "It'll take a lot more than that to get rid of me, Mairead. I didn't reach one hundred and twenty-five by picking fights I knew I couldn't handle. I just … need to lie down."

Mairead carried the vampire to her room, setting her down in her coffin so that she could rest and recuperate. "If you need anything, call for me. I'll be in my room."

Isla nodded, curling in on herself. "Leave the door open."

She did.

Mairead cleaned herself of the blackened blood, burning her helplessly stained attire in the fireplace. She retreated to her guest room, putting on a nightgown before curling up and shutting her eyes.

The door creaked open and she tensed, eyes flying back open and softening once she spotted the source.

Isla stood in the doorway, glowing lantern in one hand. "Mairead," she whispered, entering the room and setting the lantern on the nightstand. "I … I was wondering if I could sleep with you tonight. In case that other one comes back."

Mairead lifted her head, smiling back and pulling the covers away so that Isla could join her. "Yeah. Yeah, you can."

Isla climbed into the bed, thankful smile wavering before shattering completely.

"Isla?" Mairead asked, voice barely audible. "What is it?"

"You are not safe here," Isla whispered. "So long as you are alive and as long as they know you exist, you are not safe in my home." Her amber eyes glistened with tears she attempted to blink away. "The others, they will hear that you are living in my castle. They will come for you. If you would like, you can leave. I can take you back to your town. I will not fault you if you do."

Mairead remained rooted in the covers, fingers lifting to hold the vampire's face. "You are worth every blade," she said, fingers threading through Isla's raven locks, "every claw, every fang that tries to strike me down."

Isla's smile returned, sad but certain. "Mairead," she whispered, wrapping her arms around the huntress's waist. "You are impossibly good to me."

Mairead rested her head in the vampire's shoulder, warm skin pressed against clammy flesh. Mairead didn't mind. So long as it was Isla, she would bear anything, discomfort, pain, or whatever rested in between.

A few weeks passed. Isla continued painting, but the sessions did not last as long as they used to. They only lasted half as long, and then the vampire retreated into her own room, instructing Mairead not to come in unless invited.

Mairead listened. She didn't see any point in upsetting Isla, especially not after all that she had done for her. It wouldn't be fair. It wouldn't be right. So she occupied herself in the stretches of time without her, wandering the castle grounds in the daytime, bundled up in Isla's attire to protect herself from the cold. Occasionally she would go hunting, setting traps and catching whatever wildlife fell victim to them. And whenever it got dark, she would bring the animals inside and she would help Isla prepare them for dinner.

The vampires still came, maybe once or twice every month for the next year. But each time Mairead met them in battle, and each time the vampire fell, until eventually the others nearby received enough of a hint to steer clear of the castle and its occupants.

Eventually, finally, and suddenly, Isla stopped spending most of the day in her room. And the day after that she pulled Mairead out of bed, dragging her across the hall and giggling all the while.

"I have a surprise for you!" Isla exclaimed, throwing the door to her room open and revealing the covered-up canvas not a few feet from the entrance.

"Another painting?" Mairead asked, cocking her head to the side.

Isla let go of her hand, beaming. "A *special* painting." With a mighty yank Isla pulled the sheet off the obscured canvas, revealing the picture hidden beneath.

Mairead gazed upon the portrait, falling to her knees with a soft, choking sound—part sob, part laugh, all joy.

Isla pulled Mairead to her feet, wrapped her in a hug so tight she feared Mairead would crumble beneath her, but she didn't.

"I hope I got it right," Isla said, smiling.

"You did, you did. I love you," Mairead whispered through her forming tears, voice wavering but audible as she deepened the vampire's embrace. "I love you."

"I love *you*," Isla repeated, louder, certain in her declaration, picking Mairead off her feet and spinning her around.

The painting was of them in Mairead's bed—in *their* bed. They lay there, frozen in the middle of their embrace, covered up to their chest in blankets and moonlight. They lay there, deathly pallor against flushed flesh, arms entangled and lips atop lips, the artist vampire and her warrior bride.

WANDERING

BY DEVAN BARLOW

The woods wore mist like armor, and the air was thick with the scents of loam and water, as Mordecai struggled to outpace his memories.

There'd been smoked fish at dinner, a type he'd never tasted before, and the conversation had almost been like conversations back home, except his brother wasn't there with him. More than one person had remarked on the absence of a local recluse, who apparently never joined no matter how often she was invited. The stories told about her didn't all add up, but he hadn't felt comfortable enough asking questions.

This was home now, he supposed, drawing his coat closer against the winds' ravaging. For as long as it lasted.

He was grateful that a friend of a friend of his grandmother had still been living here in Scotland, after leaving the shtetl a decade ago with her family. They'd taken him in, offering a place by the fire. Yet before half of the evening was winnowed away, Mordecai had been woken by his dreams, and he knew that if he stayed, he risked waking the others with his tears. The air would help, he believed, but even the air was different here, thick with the musk of damp wool and the berry-encrusted trees that grew so thickly, seeming to watch him like they knew he'd only just arrived.

Once, a dinner like this would have been made joyous by music, and he would have drifted asleep with his hands still thrumming from the vibrations of his violin. Now, though, he walked through the fog, hearing nothing but the scattered lowing of cattle. His violin was gone too.

Further off at the end of a long path, the laird's castle struggled upward from the sloping land as if the structure were frozen in the process of drowning. Its roofs sagged above the trees, both wood and stone made glaucous by the evening murk.

Mordecai couldn't pull his mind from the dream's claws, and before he realized how far he'd traveled he was along the riverbank. The trees loomed overhead, a judgmental audience. Yet with every puff of wind, they shivered as if forced to confront chilling truths.

Movement further along the bank caught his attention. He looked closer, expecting an animal, but found no more than the faint purl of the tide and a log partially submerged in the water, fuzzed with lichen. Yet there was also a face—

Suddenly the log was as large as a forest, gaining motion and detail until it blotted out the rest of the world. Mordecai cried out, twisting in a failed attempt to escape, and fell into the water. As air deserted him with impossible lassitude and his head pounded, he thought of his brother, of how he hadn't survived very much longer after all.

I'll make you a new bridle! cried out a voice.

Lights flashed as the sun shoved away the night. The world was reduced to splotches as a figure rose from beneath Mordecai, shoving into his midsection and upwards until at last water broke over him, ceding to night air a hundred times frostier than it had been before.

Hands dragged him through the thick mist, up the river bank which soughed with vibrations of unearthly sound. He struggled, desperate to rid himself of the river water lingering on his face, in his throat, along his skin, as if it hoped to make him its vessel.

What little breath had returned to him, fled when he saw what emerged from the water. It was shaped like a horse, but its coat seemed to be less fur than ragged dripping weeds. Its hooves pressed deeply into the murk, as if the ground was too afraid to rest underneath them.

The sound came from the horse creature. It lowered its nose into the water and blew out air, causing the water to thrash like the choppiest seas Mordecai had witnessed on the journey here.

Then the creature turned to stare at the person who, it seemed, had dragged Mordecai away. A woman, just visible through the mist.

"I've asked before," the horse creature spoke in a chthonian rumble, "and you've refused."

"I'll do it," the woman insisted. "Just spare him."

It was then that Mordecai realized she spoke Yiddish, if with a different lilt than that which came from his own throat.

"Before the full moon," the creature continued, "or his life is mine. And another of you will suffer."

She nodded so tightly it looked painful.

The creature blew another gust of air through its nostrils, and Mordecai shuddered at the odor of rot. "Don't think I haven't seen the one who followed you here. Still weak, but not for much longer."

Before the woman could reply, it sank beneath the water.

Ilana dragged the man through the mist back to her cottage, where he gravitated to the small, peaty fire. As chill and reaction subsided, his lips began moving. *It might be prayer*, she thought as she soaked up what little warmth remained, or it might be an attempt to voice the questions darting within his eyes.

"That creature"—he drew a breath—"what did it mean, 'the one who followed you here'?"

She flinched, wishing the fire could roar strongly enough to turn the entire river to mist. "The kelpie isn't the only thing waiting in the water to kill us." She pulled as far away as the cottage allowed, straightening her back as she rearranged spools of thread upon her table. "Make sure to stay inside during the full moon." Her hands shook, insistent on reminding her of what they could do. What she'd just promised the kelpie they *would* do.

"Or what, a horse will come out of the river and try to kill me?" His voice softened. "Why did you save me?"

"I imagine you've been through enough already," she said, without looking back at him. She'd seen this man the day before, walking through the village with the startled expression of one whose journey has just ended, amidst a family who'd been here for years. That told her enough, even without being able to place his accent.

"How did you know it wanted a bridle?"

"It's asked me for one before." She looked up as if the moon might somehow shine through the tenuous roof. "The laird." She hesitated, unsure how much she needed to explain, but his sudden alertness spoke of warnings conveyed by his hosts. Good.

"One of his ancestors bridled the kelpie. He's inherited the ability to command it. If the kelpie gets a new bridle, it'll be free."

"And the full moon?" he prompted hesitantly, scooting closer to the fire even as the smoke made his eyes water.

"The laird used to have a fiancée." She couldn't stop herself from slipping into the sort of tale-telling she'd grown up around, the cadence of story shaping her lips. "She was going to bring much-needed money to the estate. She herself wanted to be a violinist, not that anyone around her cared."

His mouth opened in surprise, but then he gestured for her to continue as if hoping she might not have noticed his reaction.

"The stories about him aren't exaggerated," she said. "Once he had her money, she was more useful to him dead than alive, so he could marry another fortune. And there was no welcome waiting for her back home. So she ran away. In the middle of the night, no plan, if she hadn't gone by … her cloak was all tangled in branches, hair going every which way. It was the full moon, and I … helped, the best I could." She wound her hands together to hide the physical reminiscence of calling down the moonlight, crafting a lantern before bidding the woman a rapid farewell. "This one's a lot less tolerant of us than his father was. And he was convinced we stole her from him. Every full moon he claims he hears her playing, and when he can't find her, he sends out the kelpie."

"To kill us."

She nodded. "Always followed by demands that we turn her over, as well as"—she sighed—"the treasure we're hiding underwater."

He stared at her. "Like in the vunder-mayses?"

"I used to believe those."

"So did I."

Their eyes met, crafting a channel of stillness athwart the flames' contortions, as they recognized they'd both been told variations on a similar story in the time before they'd come here.

Ilana said, unsure if she wanted the moment to be over or not, "I don't know who he misheard, or what he's convinced himself of, but he thinks we're hiding a treasure along with his fiancée."

It was no more, no less of an excuse than anyone ever gave for hurting them.

"This was supposed to be *over.*" She felt sickly invigorated by a wash of agonized rage. "Until you suddenly needed rescuing."

Except, she thought, *you haven't even really managed to rescue him either, have you?*

The vodyanoy had followed her, as steadfast as her memories and her guilt.

She didn't know, would never know, if the soldiers had made an agreement with the water creatures, or if the latter had just picked up on the currents of hate and suspicion and used those to target their own hunts. They could lurk in ponds, in tiny rivulets that might never even dream of tides.

The whole shtetl had fallen, between the soldiers and the creatures that had seemed to come out of the wood and water.

Except for Ilana. She'd been returning, unaware, triumphant, eager to tell everyone of her accomplishment. To craft garments from the very light of the moon, which no one else in the land could manage!

She had arrived too late to do anything but mourn, and see the remains, as well as one vodyanoy, caught between the disguise of a log and a form that still lurked whenever she closed her eyes. It had seen her in turn.

She'd fled. What else could she do?

The journey had been a string of places full of too many like herself, their fears and traumas all scraping up against one another, casting splinters of snappishness and alarm in every direction. There had been moments when Ilana *saw* something in the distance which looked like the creature, but she dared not speak of it. The worse fear was that she would say something and be deemed mad, have it turned against her.

Along the way, pity and scorn were visited upon them in equal parts, in a dozen different tongues. And there was no guarantee this new place, this island, would be any safer.

Ilana had hoped, desperately, that the vodyanoy would choke on the salt of the Channel. In case sheer distance wasn't sufficient to break this tether of pursuit. She'd thought once she got here, if she stayed away from the water …

But then she'd seen Mordecai, caught by the kelpie.

The kelpie, who did the laird's killing as the vodyanoy had done the soldiers'.

Mordecai was recalling the gossip at dinner, of the reclusive dressmaker. The only two who had come to her defense were Rivka and Miriam, who baked for the inn, though they had swiftly been talked over. But after everything he'd seen and heard since being pulled into the water, Mordecai wondered if one particular rumor about Ilana was true.

"Why does this kelpie think you can make it a new bridle? When there's obviously some kind of …" He sought for words, a lifetime of study and story not proffering exactly what he thought was needed. "Magic? Behind the laird's control of it?"

He noticed a thin shaft of light in the cottage, pouring through a crack near the top of the wall. It played around Ilana's hands, like an animal seeking affection, before quickly vanishing.

"I'm a dressmaker," she said.

"A dressmaker."

"Sewing a bridle—"

Mordecai wished the moon would come out from behind the clouds, suddenly convinced that luminous disc could confirm his suspicions.

"You can work with moonlight," he said quietly, wonderingly. "You … we heard about you back home, my brother and I—"

"And how much good does it seem to have done me?" she snapped, then pressed her lips together.

"Can you do it? Make the bridle?"

"I need the moon." She spoke as if to herself, hands twitching. "I need the moon, its light, if that will even *work*, and there's only five days until the full moon." She pressed her hands into her temples. For some time there was no sound beyond the wind outside and the fire's diminishing exuberance.

"Is your brother here too?" she asked at last.

Mordecai gasped as a chasm opened in his chest. He hadn't even noticed he'd mentioned Ira aloud.

"No," he whispered. It was the first time anyone had asked about Ira since he'd arrived. He wasn't sure his hosts even realized he hadn't left his home by himself. "We heard it was safe here, or close to, and that at least if you could play they'd keep you around for entertainment … I played the violin, he played clarinet, and we thought we could earn our way here."

Ilana's face tightened, anticipating what came next. She raised a hand, as if to lay it on his arm, then swiftly pulled back. He forced himself to keep talking, telling the story for the first time.

"We were run out of an inn. They said—" No, he wouldn't acknowledge the vile hatred of their supposed logic. "They broke both our instruments, and Ira … he didn't survive. I'm not sure how I did."

The two of them moved closer, though still didn't touch, sharing in the dying fire.

As the clock ticked toward the full moon, that heavenly body refused to show its face. Or perhaps the moon simply couldn't summon sufficient strength to appear. Thick masses of cloud ruled the sky for the following three nights. Mordecai looked out for Ilana as he went about his days, but she wasn't to be found.

He might have believed it all a fancy, except for the rain. It was relentless, unceasing, and every droplet reminded him of the river, as well as all the water both he and Ilana had traveled over to get here along its banks.

The water wasn't lying, and it wasn't a fable. Nor was the pronouncement that came on the second day, from one of the laird's toadies, voice orotund with privilege. The news of which spread through the village like plague.

Unless his fiancée was returned, they would all be turned out of their homes within the month.

The impossibility of the demand scattered down on the community like a further volley of rain. It didn't matter that it made less sense than a river monster tracking someone across an ocean.

Mordecai wondered, as the village swirled with fear weighted by experience, if all the creatures in the world's waters were actually hiding treasures. And only struck out to protect them from the same sort of pillaging and violence that had brought so many of them here.

Six mornings a week, when the moon could still be felt in the lightening sky, Rivka and Miriam could be found wreathed in sumptuous floury clouds in the inn's kitchen. Bantering in their shared Yiddish interspersed with scraps of one another's Polish and Russian, they made the most famous bread in the whole of the county, bringing in so much business the inn's owner contentedly looked the other way regarding certain things. Such as them receiving letters really meant for Ilana, and Ilana using unlet rooms for fittings.

There'd been no letters this morning though, and it was raining so vigorously, the sky so dark, that it seemed like midnight.

Every night had been painted in murk and cloud so thick the river itself might have been pressed against the sky to hide the moon from her.

As she struggled back to her cottage, a particularly harsh gust of wind sent her cloak whipping behind her and a deluge of rain onto the front of her dress. Her sleeve snagged on the branch of a rowan tree she could have sworn wasn't there a moment before. Several strikes of lightning collaborated to inscribe a shape against the sky that was simultaneously the kelpie and the vodyanoy that had followed her, and she screamed, the back of her throat tearing like the threads of her cloak.

No matter where she went, the water always followed.

The thud of her cottage door behind her was little comfort, faced as she was with the dead fireplace and her own still-dripping state.

Suddenly her door rattled, and on the other side waited Mordecai.

Before she could speak, he told her of the laird's pronouncement, unmoving until she finally dragged him inside. A wind slammed the door and Mordecai staggered forward and she reached out her hands to balance him. Suddenly they were touching.

They stayed there, and Ilana wondered if he too felt the curious sensation that the world beneath their feet was stable, even as the tempest upset all the world beyond the cottage.

He repeated the news more slowly, finishing with: "It won't matter if he controls the kelpie or not, or if your vodyanoy regains its strength. The laird will find a way to keep hurting us."

Ilana wanted to believe there were treasures beneath the sea, luminous rewards for the ones brave enough to seek them out, but there were only monsters, it seemed. Only hungry mouths, looking to drag them down.

Neither of them had moved from the cottage but to sit before the fire and, tremblingly, to light it. The full moon would rise that evening if the vault of the sky condescended to allow its presence.

Mordecai thought of his brother, of how he would join Ira this evening, wherever he was, thanks to the wrath of a kelpie. Shuddering, he thought of how many others from the village might suffer too, for the rage of a hateful man.

He thought of Ilana, caught by the creature which pursued her, and then he thought of something which caused him to cry aloud.

"If you can make cloth from the moon"—he jumped to his feet, startling her—"what else can you make? You said you gave his fiancée light to guide her way, when she escaped …" He raced through the plan spooling from his mind to his lips.

Ilana's eyes widened until finally she shook her head. "I am no luthier."

"And neither of us are vanquishers of water monsters," he countered, "but here we are."

Ilana rose and went to the door, opening it only wide enough to regard the sky with a perception Mordecai knew he couldn't understand.

"In that case," she murmured, "I have work to do."

When night finally fell, it was with a clearness sharp enough to flense. As midnight neared, they took their places.

Mordecai's peripheral vision flickered with the river's movement, but he forced himself to look toward the laird's castle.

He wasn't sure what the word of a kelpie was worth, but as the trueness of his own word had been questioned so many times, he thought he should extend the creature some trust.

He sat atop the kelpie's back, with Ilana behind him. It was the only way they could be close enough for the kelpie to access the water's power, without the two of them touching it themselves.

The weeds extending from the kelpie wavered in the breeze, etiolated and elegant and all too capable of pulling Mordecai under again. And Ilana wouldn't get him out this time.

The moon was high, and full. He clutched in his hands the instrument Ilana had woven for him, a violin and bow of gleaming, silver-white moonglow. Yet he feared holding it too tightly, for if it shattered then so too would their plan, and that he could not bear.

No more than he could bear to see such despair on Ilana's face again.

In her hands, she clasped the second construction she'd made, the bridle which when laid upon the kelpie's neck had seared the old one away with pure brightness.

Cued by some sense, Ilana whispered, "It's time."

Mordecai settled the moonlight violin under his chin, feeling almost as though he was home. He drew the bow across the first string, tension releasing minutely as the sound that emerged was … not the music of home, of his history, simultaneously closer and more distant. Yet he continued, willing the sound to reach the castle.

Ilana drew a startled breath.

Before, the moon had been reflected in water and subject to its sloshing contortions. Now the water became subject to the moon, drawn from the river depths to spread over the banks, bringing with it the creatures within.

On the bank a thickness of trees parted, letting through another channel of moonlight, within which was forced upon the air like ink scrawled on thick paper … a form … a face … as sudden as the one Mordecai had seen in the wood, but this one was *familiar*. Its outline trailed down to familiar hands holding the stem of a familiar clarinet from which trilled a counterpoint of moon-sound.

The water followed them everywhere, Mordecai thought as his chest squeezed and his eyes blurred and his hands moved as if compelled, but so did the moon.

Rain began, just as the figure of the laird appeared amid the trees, staggering and stumbling as though wading through water. The kelpie shifted, and Mordecai feared for the water's effect on the instrument, but the crafted moonlight in his hands only rippled, emanating grace notes.

The laird reached the edge of the bank, his expression confused but decaying steadily into anger. "Give her *BACK!*" he bellowed.

Ilana slid off the kelpie until she was in the water up to her shins, seemingly not noticing that she left a hand on Mordecai's back.

A *shudder* went through the water. Frantic ripples parted to reveal a creature that was simultaneously log and human and something Mordecai couldn't name, strong enough to block out the very moon, but still his hands moved along the violin.

Lightning sliced. Several trees shivered their last, scattering berries. Six branches flung toward them, falling upon each other in a hexagram that, for a moment, seemed to catch the moonlight and reflect it back thousandfold.

"You've hidden her!" The laird raged as he continued closing on them. "Just like you've hidden your treasure—"

His feet hit the water, and the vodyanoy pounced.

The moonlight faded, until there was nothing but a faint suggestion of light on Mordecai's face and his empty hands.

When she'd placed the bridle on the kelpie, before Mordecai had begun to play, the creature had stared into her eyes, and asked, "Your command?" with a bitterness like ancient, eroded soil.

"If I told you to never take another life?" Ilana ventured.

The kelpie snorted.

"Then never listen to that family again."

Now, though, the kelpie was gone, and only she and Mordecai remained. The rain had lessened to a thin, indecisive sputter.

"Maybe there is a treasure there." She gestured to the water, feeling as though her words were the only things keeping her from floating into the moon's domain. "But I don't think it will keep us warm. Aren't we cold enough already?" The wind picked up. She bent to gather some of the scattered rowan branches. "These will be good for the fire."

Supporting one another, trailing water, they wandered, but only a very little way further.

A Haunted Person

BY Ariadne Zhou

You live in an old house that is haunted with ghosts.

Or is it haunted by you?

No, that's not right, you've seen things from the corner of your eyes before, wisps of people just stepping out of view, cups and china moving through the actions of unseen hands, laughter from abandoned corners of the house.

You learned to dance and play piano from ghostly shades and have even taken photos, so, there must be ghosts here.

But you can't say that you aren't also haunting this house.

You should have left a long time ago.

Don't they say that once children grow up and turn into adults at the magical age of eighteen, they leave and set up their own home?

And yet, here you are.

Still here, after all these years, with the only home that you've ever had, not changing a thing.

You know you could leave, but—

You don't want to.

What would you do outside of here?

And this is your home, despite the echoing voices.

Or is it more precise to say that *you* are the one being haunted?

Your parents' expectations hang over you like the specters you see in the halls—*why aren't you married to a man yet? Why don't you set aside all these childish hobbies? When, when, when, will you finally grow up?*

You think you have grown up as you mop the wooden floors that stretch endlessly on, try your best to repair the leaky plumbing, take pictures of the ghosts, sort through the bills that pile up on the counter, and count the money from the ghost hunters and ghost tours that have come through your house.

But it's not enough, is it?

You've never seen your parents' ghosts. Those who haunt these halls besides you are long dead—people you've never met, yet you hear their voices all the same.

Why are you smiling? They sneer as you read your favorite fantasy book for the umpteenth time.

You're still watching that? That's for children, they scoff as you watch an animated show.

Why can't you just be normal? They demand as you spend yet another Friday night at home instead of out on a date.

You have no desire to go out on a date with a man, no matter how the voices echo in the empty house or how abnormal that makes you.

But what's normal in a haunted house anyway?

"It must be so fun to live here!" an odd bachelorette comments to you during her bachelorette party that she decided to hold here in your house.

You smile tightly, ducking your head.

Fun isn't the word you would use.

Still, there is some delicious irony to seeing these shrieking girls with penis-shaped confetti and champagne running around your house.

Your parents would have died again to see this.

Shameless, scandalous, they already hiss into your ear, but it's easier to ignore them with all these people around.

"But it's so big—you live here by yourself?" the bachelorette asks, glancing around. "All alone?"

You smile again. "It's alright."

(You're never alone. Maybe it would be better if you were.)

The bachelorette blanches a bit at your smile, and then quickly scrambles off to take part in the chaotic party.

But perhaps she wasn't entirely turned off, because a few months later, she's back again, her blonde tresses shining in the sunlight.

"Back so soon?" you ask with the same smile as before. "Would your husband like to see the ghosts?"

"Oh, I'm not married," the bachelorette says with a wave of her hand. "Caught my fiancé cheating on me with my bridesmaid, if you can believe it. The most cliché thing ever, I know. But! You wouldn't happen to need a social media person for the house, would you?"

You just stare at her.

(Social media?

The house manages to make money through mostly word of mouth and a tiny webpage you run with some of your favorite photos of the ghosts.

Most technology glitches in the house.

You're not sure if it's the ghosts or something your parents did— they never approved of things like that.

Godless, mind-numbing trash.)

You relay the technical difficulties to the bachelorette, but she seems unperturbed. "That's alright, there's a coffee shop down the street with Wi-Fi where I can set up."

"I can't pay you very much—"

"Oh, that's fine, I'm getting a lot from managing a bunch of influencer accounts anyway," the bachelorette says with a wave of her hand. "All remote work too, so I think there shouldn't be any issues with the location or hours!"

"If you're sure," you say doubtfully.

"Let's go to the coffee shop now, and you can show me what photos you have so far!" the bachelorette says cheerfully.

In some bemusement, you find yourself in the cheery little coffee shop, all the employees staring at you. The bachelorette doesn't seem to notice however, just exclaiming over the few photos you do have.

"These are quite good, you can see the ghosts clearly, and so it looks spooky, but also beautiful, with the sunlight spilling through the window here," the bachelorette says, examining the photo you have of the piano player. "I think the best strategy would be to only have periodic updates—keeps up the mystique, you know? Unless you want more business—I could invite some influencers over?"

"I think we're doing alright," you say as you fold your hands in your lap, a wry smile tugging at the corners of your mouth.

Your parents would *loathe* influencers perhaps even more than the occasional ghost hunter or odd party—but you don't want to do that to your ghosts. It seems so peaceful for them to be stuck in time, without having influencers intent on mugging for the camera and more followers getting in there.

"The historical society gives a stipend for some of the upkeep, and my programming job pays the bills," you say simply.

"Oh, you're a programmer, love coding and stuff?" the bachelorette asks, wiggling her fingers.

"Not so much," you say honestly, stretching your hand out over the photographs. "I prefer ghosts and photography."

"You took all of these?" the bachelorette says with wide eyes. "Wow! You're really good!"

You blink, not sure what to say.

(The closest thing to a compliment you had ever got on the photos was your mother's sneer that *that would look nice if it weren't for that ghost.*)

"It's the contrast between the ghosts and the sunlight and elegance of the house that really makes all the photos pop," the bachelorette chatters on, looking at your favorite photo of the ghostly piano player at her daily noontime recital. "It's what made me convince my maid of honor to throw the bachelorette party here!"

"I am very sorry about your wedding," you tell her earnestly.

The bachelorette grimaces and waves her hand. "All in the past, I don't want to dwell on it. So—your website's layout isn't terrible, but what do you think of adding a photo reel? And maybe a Twitter?"

So, begins your professional relationship with the bachelorette, filled with days at the coffee shop poring over photos and the design of the tickets, and later with her coming over to dinner at the house and laughing as you tell her stories of the ghosts.

"She really taught you how to play the piano?" she asks, nodding over at the piano bench where notes are fluttering forward and a wisp of hands can be faintly seen through the rays of sunlight streaming in through the window.

"In a way." You nod, sipping your tea. "I watched her hands until I figured out how to play what she plays."

(And then your parents yelled at you for wasting your time on such frivolous, ghostly pursuits. Still, they couldn't always keep an eye on you, and now that they're gone, at least you can create this ghostly soothing music yourself as well.

Sometimes you can even duet with the hands.)

"Wow, it's just like *In the Halls of Mars!*" she exclaims.

You perk up. "You've also read the Haunted Planets series?"

"Reread them—I've read *Shadow of Venus* about ten times now!" the bachelorette laughs happily.

You had never met anyone else who had read this series in real life—just online.

She really is pretty great.

"Play something for me," she urges you, and with a smile, you oblige.

The house begins to get more guests, you bond over books and music with the bachelorette, you don't have to fret quite as much at the end of the month as you did before about how to pay the various utility bills, and even your parents' voices seem quieter.

Then, she kisses you.

You draw away almost immediately, your hands flying up to your mouth as you stammer, "I—I'm not—"

The bachelorette winces, rubbing the back of her neck. "Oh god, did I read you completely wrong? I'm so sorry—I thought—I really should have asked first—I'll just—can we just pretend that didn't happen?"

(But how can you just forget that that happened?

It's both the most beautiful thing and the most terrifying thing that has ever happened to you.

Just another way that you're wrong and disappoint your parents even when they're gone.

Why are you always like this, it's just typical, you can't do anything right, why can't you just be normal—)

"Hey, are you alright?" The bachelorette has crouched down and is touching your shoulder. "You—does your head hurt? Uh— why are the lights flickering around here, are the ghosts mad—"

"Because I'm wrong," you say, looking down at the ground, practically hearing your parents' footsteps coming up the stairs. "I'm messed up and not normal and a disgusting shut-in—"

"You're someone who takes the most beautiful photographs that I've ever seen while single-handedly keeping this whole place afloat," the bachelorette cuts in, her hands gripping your own. "And if you're wrong, I'm even more wrong, so we can just be wrong together, right?"

You look up, staring at her. "You—together?"

"If you'll have me," the bachelorette says, ducking her head shyly.

You just stare at her even more, the ghostly wind whipping around both of you, and the footsteps loud on the stairs. "Even with —all this?"

"I like all this," the bachelorette says stoutly, and then looks over your shoulder, narrows her eyes, and calls out, "And I like her, and you're not scaring me away from her, and even more importantly, stop trying to scare her! She has nothing to fear here!"

(That's right.

What's the worst they could do to you now?

They are nothing but ghosts now, and ghosts are always stuck in the past, living in a loop.

You, on the other hand—

If you want to haunt this house, that is your choice, but you don't have to keep listening to their voices.

You may be haunted, and you can haunt this house, but you can't be the ghost of your own life.

It's your life, and you're not alone anymore.)

You stand and turn to face the looming darkness behind you. The whispers are still loud (*wrongwrongWRONG*), but you grab the bachelorette's hand, hold them up to the dark, and say simply, "I'm going to live my life, whether you like it or not."

The wind stops, and the darkness seems to retreat upon itself, the whispers fading away, but still there.

The bachelorette looks at you and asks, "So—should I take that as a good sign?"

"Yes," you say firmly, then lean forward to hesitantly kiss her.

She kisses you back, and you smile as you hear ghostly piano notes drifting around the house.

THE FEAST OF DEAD MAN'S HOLLOW

BY DESIRÉE M. NICCOLI

Fog rolled off the standing water, curling its wispy tendrils around the leatherleaf and stunted black spruce that jutted from vibrant red mats of sphagnum moss.

Theodore sloshed through a partially submerged area in his waders, using a walking stick to test the bottom—soft but holding firm. Enough to hold his weight, anyway. And as he trudged, wafts of slowly rotting peat—all at once earthy, dank, and slightly floral—plumed the air.

There was a cluster of sundews ahead, their brightly colored rosettes tipped with dewy, sticky filaments, sweet to the taste but designed to hold on and never let go. The digestive enzyme they excreted broke down trapped prey, the unlucky insect languishing four to six days until completely digested.

Bending to examine the carnivorous plant, Theodore was mildly disappointed to see it hadn't caught anything in its embrace—stems still unfurled and reaching, to hold and to feed.

He always loved the pretty, vicious things.

Theodore had been sneaking off to Dead Man's Hollow since he was a kid. The peat bog was a dangerous place to explore, for child and adult alike, its many hazards fodder for grisly tales—of people getting lost and swallowed by the bog, never to be seen again, of murder and ghosts and eerily well-preserved bodies dredged up from the murk. But he'd always had a sixth sense for firmer ground, and he'd never found a body. Not a human one at least.

The peatlands he knew were rich with blueberry and cranberry patches; the former he'd eat by the handful, the latter collected for recipes. He'd catch and release frogs or find a fallen log to sprawl across, basking in the sun. Sometimes he brought a book or a bit of paper to draw on.

No one else dared venture inside Dead Man's Hollow, so it was a quiet place, *his place*, all to himself.

Or it was.

Theodore stared down the mud-splattered ditcher parked on a solid stretch of ground, unguarded but ready to dig the trenches that would drain the bog dry. To make the land "optimal for development."

All so big-tech billionaire Leon Marks could dabble in real estate and build a secluded lodge for the ultra-rich deep in the Maine wilds—accessible by small chopper only, an exclusive experience. What was good enough for the Rockefellers and Vanderbilts on Mount Desert Island wasn't good enough for Marks. He had to pillage precious, untouched land farther north.

Theodore had always been so careful and safe in his explorations. Even with three decades of peatland familiarity under his belt, a network of firm ground vividly mapped out in his mind, he still carried a long stick equal to his height to perform depth tests. Poking here, poking there, but never quite stepping a foot out of line.

And now Theodore was about to do something very stupid.

Kneeling next to the machine, he slipped off his backpack, filled with wrenches, cutters, and other tools. For the past week, he'd studied online diagrams and equipment manuals, learning how to best break a ditcher and delay development without hurting the bog itself.

What he called activism, others called sabotage. Or worse, eco-terrorism.

A cold sweat trickled down the back of his neck, and he paused to push his glasses up the bridge of his nose, a thick, black plastic pair that made him look especially "nerdy", as his friends liked to tease. Glasses that were usually paired with crisp button-down shirts, woolen sweaters, and corduroy trousers. Not the "destroys private property" type, whatever that was supposed to look like. If tattoos were required, he supposed the tree line cuff inked on his right arm could count, although it wasn't very intimidating.

He wasn't very intimidating.

The fog thickened as he worked, hands stained with grime and grease. Overhead the sky darkened, and the temperature dropped, heralding a brewing storm—a storm his weather app hadn't warned him about today.

Every ghost story he'd ever heard crowded his thoughts— stories he'd ignored in the face of a beautiful, bountiful ecosystem. Shadows crept in, making him feel watched, and when water splashed nearby, he nearly jumped out of his skin, certain cold, clammy, dead hands would seize him from below.

"Just a frog," he breathed, watching the creature's long legs kick out before disappearing beneath the murky water.

It was because he was doing something illegal. Nothing haunted or supernatural, just nerves.

Leaving his walking stick behind, he shuffled around the ditcher to better reach and mess with the engine. The sooner he got this done and over with, the better. But as he stepped down, a little wider than he meant to, the ground gave out beneath him, and he plunged backward into a pool of cold mud.

Panic made him flail and kick, thirty years of experience out the window in a single instance. The struggle made him sink deeper.

Stupid. Stupid. Stupid.

Overconfidence and complacency were deadly.

And Theodore had just made a fatal mistake.

A horse whinnied.

Theodore's first thought was that if Leon Marks and his land development team caught him, he'd go to jail, but the second was that he hoped they did and fished him out. His third thought was spent puzzling out why a billionaire would ride a horse into a bog. Sure, the filthy rich did all sorts of bizarre, eccentric things, but this was particularly strange and stupid.

Slowly turning his head, mud up to his ears, he was going to shout a warning, but instead watched with growing terror as a white horse thundered toward him with impossible ease, as if there wasn't treacherous, sucking mud beneath its hooves.

And astride it was a woman clad all in black, from tattered long coat and riding leathers down to gloves and boots. Her clothing was old, but not like the vintage styles Theodore tended to wear. For all he knew, she could've been fresh off the set of a spooky period piece or a late 1700s reenactment. She was riding hard, her gaze pinned on him, dark brows pinched in fierce determination.

Just as he thought she'd blow past him, she withdrew her foot from the stirrup and slid bodily down the saddle in the most astounding feat of trick riding he'd ever seen, and before he could process that she'd reached into the muck and grabbed him by the scruff of his collar, he was already being hoisted out and into the saddle.

Next thing he knew, they were galloping out of the bog, weaving in and out between the trees, his rescuer perched snuggly behind him. Cool air whipped against wet skin, an unflattering recipe for chattering teeth and a runny nose. He eyed his shirtsleeve, covered in a thick layer of bog muck, and sniffed back hard instead. That was the best he could do for now.

Too amazed by the circumstances to speak, he snuck a glance over his shoulder.

She had curly, raven-black hair cut chin-length on one side, undercut on the other, and brown eyes so dark they were nearly pools of black. Her skin tone could've rivaled moonlight, and if it was anything like his, no amount of sun exposure would tan it.

Unlike her roughened, old-timey clothing, her makeup seemed quite modern—smokey eyes and dark purple lipstick—but the combination wouldn't be out of place in a Tim Burton movie.

He glanced back again, hoping to glimpse recognizable features.

A green ribbon was tied in a neat bow around her neck, a lovely pop of color offsetting her fiercely serious expression and attire.

He tried to parse her features further, considering if maybe he'd seen her on the cover of an entertainment magazine with Winona Ryder or Christina Ricci. But then his thoughts jumped to how much taller she sat in the saddle than him, how her broad shoulders and solid arms framed his body, and that perhaps she was the lady goth version of Henry Cavill.

He liked that. A lot.

With her arms pressed around him, holding the reins, and her leather-clad thighs squeezing his, radiating warmth he desperately wanted—no, *needed*—to soak in, he tried not to focus on every flex of muscle or how the horse's undulating motion rubbed their bodies together. The combination was wreaking havoc in places that made him grateful for his waders and being covered in cold mud.

Of all the things he could've said to this gorgeous woman, what came out of his mouth was, "How'd you lift one hundred and sixty pounds out of bog mud? Is that even humanly possible?"

His cheeks flamed with the force of a thousand suns.

"Hmph." *Not human,* thought Ardruina.

Her companion went beet red. "Sorry, that was rude, but that was seriously a cool move. How'd you do that? Are you a power lifter?"

This shivering, mud-covered slip of a man was rather verbose for someone who'd just nearly died.

"Momentum." Ardruina leaned away sharply when he craned his head to meet her eyes, just barely avoiding a streak of mud across her chin. *Going to strain your neck if you keep doing that.*

The look he gave her was cutely skeptical. He was short enough that she could easily rest her chin atop his head, and if it weren't for the mud, she might've done so, just to feel like she was the hero in one of those romantic fairytales. The kind she'd never star in.

Beneath the mud, she caught glimpses of light brown hair cropped short along the sides, but parted at the left, a longer section combed across the top. Very 1950s in style, if her memory served her. Blue eyes, square jaw. The barest hint of scruff.

"Well, however you did it, thank you for the rescue. Name's Theodore, by the way. Though you could call me Teddy for short."

She snorted. "I'm not calling you Teddy."

"Even though you're holding me like a ..."

"Do not finish that sentence," she warned, though a smile threatened to overtake her face.

"Teddy Bear."

"I can put you back where I found you."

"Sorry, I talk a lot when I'm nervous, and you're really pretty, which is no excuse for badly flirting, but I think almost dying is making it worse. Just ignore me. Or better yet, I'll shut up."

The words "pretty" and "flirting" danced circles in her head, rendering her speechless. Usually, people ran away from her screaming. They deserved it, but still.

"All my friends call me Theo, no one calls me Teddy, but I always thought it would be a cute endearment, you know?"

"Theodore?"

"Yes?"

"You're still talking." *Dammit.* That was meant to sound teasing, but it came out all wrong, even to her own ears.

He shrunk in on himself, cowed like a kicked puppy.

This is why she'd hidden herself away and left him alone all these years. She wasn't by nature the benevolent sort, but even she drew the line at puppy kicking.

Solitude made her socially inept, and this sweet, shy man didn't deserve to feel her conversational snarls, not when he'd been a friend and ally to the bog all his life. He'd even tried to protect it in his own clumsy way, and it had nearly cost him his life.

"My name's Ardruina." It wasn't much of an olive-branch, so she gave him a bit of a hug, and Theodore perked up right away, bringing his back flush with her chest. "Just Ardruina, though," she added, before he could get any clever ideas. "I don't like nicknames."

"Never heard that one before, but it's beautiful. Wouldn't dream of shortening it."

The way he sunk his weight into her arms just then, relaxed and perfectly at ease … *blast it.* She laid her cheek against his temple, mud and all. If he liked her touch, he could have it.

She should leave him at the edge of the forest, where the wilds met civilization, but she wasn't ready to part ways with her endearing companion. Besides, she had to ensure he properly recovered from his ordeal. To go through the trouble of rescuing him, only for him to catch his death—wet and shaking like a leaf—just wouldn't do.

Was that another sniffle?

Yes, really, just concerned about his health.

With an encouraging kick to her mount's sides, she rode them deeper into the forest.

Kidnapping, but for a good cause.

"Is this your home?" Theodore stared at the structure, a certifiable log cabin.

The mysterious horsewoman named Ardruina nodded as she helped him out of the saddle, her leather-gloved hands enclosed around his waist, steadying him as he swung down. He already missed the feel of her, pressed up behind him, directing the horse with each flex of her sturdy legs.

"We can go inside after we've washed up."

He swiped a hand down his front, a clump of mud falling away. "Good idea."

The horse would need tending to, but when he turned to help, it was gone.

"Um."

He scanned the trees, trying to spy its white hide in the fog, but the creature had vanished without a trace, quiet as a ghost. Not even hoofprints marked the dirt where it stood.

Clapping a hand against his back, Ardruina said, "Come on. Don't worry about Lady Crane. She'll return in the morning."

Weird. But if she wasn't worrying over the horse, neither would he.

Theodore followed Ardruina around the cabin to where there was a steaming hot spring and a small storage shack.

"Go ahead. Strip down and hop in. I'll bring soap and towels." Ardruina opened the shack door and disappeared inside.

The waders took the brunt of the mess, so by the time he'd peeled off all his layers, naked but for his glasses, he was just a shivering slip of cold, pale flesh, streaked with mud. Not his best look. Casting nervous glances at the partially open door, he eased himself into the hot spring, feeling out the bottom with his feet, but he couldn't help but exhale a sigh of relief as the heat seeped into his limbs.

Cold bits shrinking up into his body? Not the first impression he wanted this jacked woman to have about his naked physique.

Setting his glasses aside, Theodore vigorously scrubbed mud off his face and out of his hair, wanting to look a little more presentable when Ardruina returned. For no other reason than he was wildly attracted to her, and if she bestowed upon him an ounce of attention, he'd die a happy man.

By the time Ardruina exited the shack, carrying a stack of towels and two bars of soap, he was lounging in the spring, arms spread wide, and only slightly squinting. Overall, he was going for cool but would settle on relaxed.

"Where's your glasses?"

He lifted them to his face, clear one moment, fogging the next. But in that split second, he noticed that the mud stains he'd left on her clothes were gone. She must've cleaned up inside the shack.

"They don't do me a lot of good in here." He shrugged, affecting a carefree grin. *That sounded smooth, right?*

Nodding firmly, Ardruina strode toward him, and he jolted at her sudden, rapid approach, covering his junk with a startled splash. *Shit. Shit. Shit.* While the steam provided a little cover, the water itself was clear, and modesty prevailed over the cool bastard act.

A little smirk lifted the corner of her lips as she set a towel and soap bar beside him—bending so close he could tilt her face and bring those plush, purple lips to his.

"Thank you." His voice came out a little breathless.

"Mind if I join you?"

He gulped, cupping himself tighter. Without his glasses, he wouldn't see much. That had to count for something. "I don't mind."

Everything would've been fine if she'd moved to the other side of the spring, but as brazen as a wood nymph, she yanked off her boots right beside him. Then her coat. Then her gloves. Then, oh God, her shirt and trousers.

Bare as can be, she slid in next to him, divested of everything except that pretty, green bow around her neck. Tilting her head back with a soft moan, she asked, "Isn't this nice?"

He bit the inside of his cheek to keep his thoughts respectful. To not think about the sleek, rippling muscle and sheer power beside him. Or that she could crush his windpipe with a single hand, and he'd thank her for the privilege of her touch. "Mhm."

Folding her arms behind her head, a motion that did nothing to obscure her chest, she cracked open one eye. "You have enough room over there?"

His cheeks were on fire, and dear God, he hoped she'd think it was the steam. "Plenty." *Too much. Too little.*

"Good." She smiled and closed her eye. "We can go back for your tools in the morning if you want. Finish the job you started. Just thought you might want to rest."

After almost drowning in mud.

"You'd do that?"

"Protect the bog? Absolutely."

"What I'm doing is illegal."

She shrugged. "Draining the bog should be, too."

That was why delaying development was so important—to buy enough time for a key bill to pass that would block the project altogether. But once construction was underway, it would be too little too late.

Peatlands like Dead Man's Hollow were essential terrestrial ecosystems, mitigating climate change and stabilizing the carbon cycle. Even though the known ones only covered about three percent of the world's land surface, they stored at least two times more carbon than all the standing forests combined.

Leon Marks could not, and would not, succeed. Not if Theodore could help it.

"I don't want to get you into trouble."

"You don't need to worry about that." Her tone was too serious to be a simple, reassuring platitude. When she said, "I'm the trouble that finds people," he believed her.

Ever since she'd joined him in the hot spring, Theodore had been a constant shade of pink. And yet, at every opening she offered him to back out, to bathe separately, to ask for more space, he declined.

The sweet, shy man tried so hard not to look down, and mostly succeeded, but she could see that she was torturing him. And she'd brought him back here for a reason, hadn't she? Even if she didn't know it at the time. When it came down to it, she'd been starved of companionship and of touch for an ungodly amount of time, and he seemed interested in both. A few centuries spent relentlessly haunting a remote stretch of forest, and making sport of scaring away people, was fun for a while, but it did her no favors in the romance department.

In hindsight, she'd maybe gotten a little too scary for her own good.

Holding out a bar of soap, Ardruina asked, "Wash my back for me?"

"I don't know if that's a good idea." Theodore averted his gaze.

That gave her pause. She'd tease and he'd blush, but this was the first time he wouldn't meet her eye. "Is everything okay?"

He sunk deeper into the water, angling his body away from hers. "Um, yes, but I have an, uh, erection," he finally answered, wincing, as if admitting that cost him.

Maybe it had. Not only had his rosy color deepened, he'd also tensed. Either he feared her, or how she'd react to that knowledge.

"That doesn't bother me," she said gently, "But if it bothers you, I can leave, and meet you inside whenever you're ready to come in."

"Oh." He lost the frightened deer look. "It really doesn't bother you?"

She shook her head. "You said you thought I was pretty, and it's a natural reaction, right?"

"You are pretty. Really pretty, but I didn't want to be a creep."

"You're not. I'm inviting you to touch me."

He finally relaxed, taking the bar of soap from her outstretched palm. "Alright. Turn around."

Fighting back a smile at her victory, she complied and listened to him work the soap into a lather.

Slick hands dragged up her arms, and as Theodore's ragged exhale tickled the base of her neck, her skin erupted in goosebumps. He was so warm at her back, close, but not quite touching his body to hers. Cupping one shoulder, he moved his other hand in tight, slow circles, massaging away her riding aches.

Scooping water into his palm, he trickled it down the length of her back, repeating the process over and over, before lathering his hands once more.

The smooth glide of his palms, the unhurried, savoring touch.

This. This was what she'd been missing, what she needed.

And then his fingers skated along the base of her neck, light as a feather, but also teasing the skin just below the ribbon, trekking too close to perilous ground.

She flinched.

"Don't knock the ribbon loose," she warned. "Whatever you do."

Neither of them would like it if he did.

"I'll be careful," he promised.

Nipping the lobe of her ear with his teeth and newfound daring, Theodore washed her front instead.

She leaned into him with a pleased sigh.

The darkening sky that had threatened rain, finally opened up, and they rushed inside, naked and laughing. Kicking the door behind him, Theodore backed his tall beauty against the wall, hands at her hips.

He'd been so afraid of making her uncomfortable, of being too greedy for touch, but there wasn't an inch of him that she'd shied away from, didn't ask for under heavy, panting breaths.

Brushing away a rain-soaked curl that had fallen into her eyes, Theodore cupped her cheek and rose on the balls of his feet to kiss lips still perfectly, and miraculously purple, no matter how many times he sucked them into his mouth, so sweet and full like slices of plum. Every needy sigh and hitched breath between them were music to his ears. And just because he was the shorter of the two didn't mean they didn't fit well together, their bodies notching in all the right places.

Snaking an arm around his waist, and holding him flush, Ardruina broke their kiss to say, "I grabbed your glasses." She presented them in offering. "Thought you'd like to see."

Grinning, he accepted the frames, pushing them onto his face.

"So handsome," she purred, leaning in for another kiss, but a flash of green caught his eye.

"Wait, wait, wait!" He held her steady, and she stiffened, her hurt expression cleaving his heart.

He didn't know why she asked him to be careful around her green ribbon. Whether it was purely cosmetic, or sentimental, or hiding something she was self-conscious about, but he promised to take care wherever it was concerned.

And right now, it was coming undone.

They must have jostled it loose in their romantic enthusiasm.

"Shh, easy sweetheart. Your pretty ribbon's unraveling. Want me to fix it?"

She froze, the first time he'd seen fear in her eyes. It took him a second to realize she wasn't even breathing.

"Sweetheart?"

A tear rolled down her cheek. He barely knew Ardruina, that was true, but in their short time together, she didn't strike him as the type to cry, much less let someone else see it, but she didn't even try to wipe the tear away.

"Please," she whispered, barely twitching a muscle.

"I've got you," he soothed, and gently pulled the sides that would tighten the base knot first. Once that felt secure, he pinned it in place with a pinkie, then looped one side, then the other, and tied them together snugly, but not so much that the fabric cut into her skin. "There, how's that?"

Touching a hand to her throat, she sucked in a relieved breath, and hugged him so tight, the air whooshed out of him. "Thank you."

He smoothed his hands over her back, mapping her topography, where every hard muscle met soft valley. "I'm sorry for the nickname. 'Sweetheart' kind of just came out."

"Don't be, you earned it." She tucked her face into the crook of his neck. "And besides, I think I actually like it."

Theodore didn't know what had just happened between them but setting the ribbon to rights was important to Ardruina, and he didn't need to understand the finer points of her relief and gratitude to appreciate the weight of it.

The horse, Lady Crane, was waiting for them outside the next morning, saddled and bridled, just as Ardruina had said, but it still shocked him to see the creature. His clothes, too, had been cleaned.

"How?"

Ardruina's smile was sad as she helped him into the saddle. "I don't think you'd believe me if I told you." She swung up behind him, fitting them neatly together, and clicked her tongue, spurring the horse into a canter.

That morning, while he brought up food from her root cellar to fix them breakfast, she donned her riding leathers again, the same ones he met her in. The way she layered and tucked and tied, it was like watching her put on armor. And it made him wonder why.

Everything about Ardruina was a mystery. Why she dressed the way she did and lived a simple life without modern conveniences deep in the woods and had a horse that was more ghost than domesticated animal. Why she spent five minutes checking the green ribbon in a mirror and had enough superhuman strength to pull a full-grown man out of sucking bog mud and seat him on the saddle of a moving horse. Why he'd never seen her before.

Too many unlikely and impossible things combined. Maybe he wouldn't believe her if she told him. Or maybe he already knew something preternatural was afoot. Something out of a fairytale or folklore. But he wasn't scared, just sated and happy and ready to save Dead Man's Hollow, because the sooner he did that, the sooner they could continue exploring one another.

Theodore was naturally curious—years of visiting the bog, turning over rocks, picking up critters, nurtured that—but preservation and conservation shaped him, too. Knowing when to leave something be. To not take what wasn't freely given.

"You don't have to tell me anything you don't want to," he began, threading his fingers through hers, the leather of her glove warm and soft. "But if you did tell me, you might be surprised by what I'm willing to believe."

She tilted his head back, kissing him slow and deep, and smoothed a hand under his shirt, across his belly. "I like you," she murmured against his lips.

He reached to cup her cheek. "And I like you."

All his tools were right where he'd left them. His walking stick, too.

But Lady Crane was sidestepping irritably, her ears laid flat. Theodore didn't know much about horses, but he knew enough to be worried. Something had her spooked.

"Something's wrong," Ardruina said, looping a protective arm around him.

A branch snapped behind them, and the horse reared, kicking out her legs. The moment Theodore felt himself sliding, he squeezed his legs and clung to the saddle, Ardruina bracing around him. When they returned to the ground, Ardruina's sharp cry pierced his ear, her weight and warmth disappearing.

"Ardruina!" he yelled, twisting to see if she'd fallen.

Rough hands yanked him off the saddle. He landed on the ground with a hard smack, pain blooming in his shoulder. Lady Crane reared again, and he rolled away to avoid her flailing hooves.

"Uh, uh, uh. Where do ya think you're going?" He was seized by the front of his shirt and dragged, mud and groundwater soaking the fabric, rocks scraping his skin.

The man above him was ridiculously muscled and wore a black T-shirt two sizes too small, mud-spattered jeans, and ass-kicking boots. Also, he was gruff, bearded, and had never seen moisturizer in his life.

Just as a broken branch cut a wicked, painful slice into his back, Theodore was hauled to his feet, arms jammed behind his back. The force of it was very nearly enough to dislocate his shoulders, and a pained, breathless whimper rushed out of his lungs. He hated how a man such as this would see it as a sign of weakness.

Heart pounding a million miles a minute, he observed the scene before him, his brain trying to catch up and assess the mess they'd landed in.

Two other men with similar builds had also pinned Ardruina's arms, though they strained to contain her. She fought their combined grasp, eyes dark, glittering pools of rage, too strong and fierce for either of them to handle alone.

Watching it all from the sidelines was Leon Marks. He looked just as douchey in his designer aviators and bougie hiking gear as he did in a bespoke suit on the cover of *Forbes*. The smug bastard was chewing gum with his mouth open, flashing a too-white smile.

"Got us here two meddling weirdos playing at eco-warriors," Leon laughed.

"Let her go," Theodore demanded. "She's got nothing to do with this."

"You rode in together." Leon gestured blandly to Lady Crane, the agitated horse snorting and stamping her hooves. "Looks like aiding and abetting to me." To his goons, he added, "Get rid of him first, then his goth girlfriend."

"Get your hands off her! Don't you touch her!" Theodore thrashed, but the man had an iron grip.

A fist collided into the side of his face.

"Theodore!"

It hurt, but not as much as it could've. And when he looked up, he saw Leon dabbing at his knuckles with a tissue, which he then deposited on the ground with a careless flick of his fingers.

The fucker sucker-punched him.

But as Theodore was dragged to the water's edge, a cold certainty washed over him. He knew what they intended to do. What they'd force Ardruina to watch, what would befall her next.

Once shoved to the ground, he wrestled his arms free, clawing and punching, but the goon had him by the shoulders, pushing him back and back and back, cool water lapping at his scalp. He was engaging in the hardest crunch of his life just trying to keep his head above water.

"Let him go, or I swear you'll regret this!" Ardruina shouted.

Leon ignored her, expression bored.

Adrenaline was on Theodore's side for now, but he couldn't break free, and he couldn't keep this up. The crash was coming.

If only he was stronger. If only he'd insisted on coming back here alone.

If only, if only.

Ardruina met his eyes then with a strange, distant calm. "I'm sorry, Teddy," she said, and with a rough yank, freed one of her arms and ripped the green ribbon from her neck.

Her head tumbled to the ground. And her body with it, her shocked captors letting go.

Theodore screamed.

Theodore clawed and thrashed and choked on water as Marks's goon tried holding him down.

He didn't know how it was possible, to just lose one's head like that, but what mattered most, what hurt the most, was his Ardruina was dead.

Every nerve ending screeched agony, cried for blood and vengeance. If only he'd the strength to enact his will.

His captor's hold on him loosened just enough for Theodore to come up sputtering for breath.

"What the fuck?"

Ardruina's head still lay on the ground, her face thankfully turned away.

But her body sat up, and rose from the ground, a gleaming sickle in hand.

What the fuck indeed.

There was no hesitation. She slashed right, and then left, lopping off the heads of the men who'd held her—one brutal stroke each—as if she was born to do it. Before they could even process what was happening. Before *Theodore* could process what was happening.

Chest squared, and arms tensed for more slashing, she cut a rage-fueled path along the ground. He didn't need the benefit of facial expression to know she was out for blood, and that the one holding him did not have long to live in this world.

"Don't come any closer," the man stammered, pulling a knife from his boot. "Or I'll slit his throat."

Fuck that. Expending the last of his energy, Theodore grabbed the man's wrist with one hand and jammed the heel of the other into his nose, jerking his head back. Abdomen on fire and utterly spent, he collapsed, water rushing over his mouth and nose, gravity and the weight of the other man working against him.

A silver blade flashed overhead, and a spray of blood hit the water's surface, just above his face.

The man, and his hulking weight, were wrenched away.

Then, a headless, leather-clad figure came into view, visage distorted by a rippling, blood-speckled surface. It plunged a fist into the water and hoisted him up.

Theodore sucked in a great gulp of air. Whatever enabled this nature-defying feat, the timing was excellent for his screaming lungs, but maybe not his neck ...

"It's still me, Teddy. Don't be afraid. You're safe now."

It was Ardruina's voice but thrown funny, as if she were twenty feet away and not right by his side, cradling him to her body. Her headless body. It made no damn sense, but he believed her.

An engine revved.

"Leon's getting away," he croaked, pointing.

The asshole had an ATV.

After situating him somewhere solid and mostly dry, Ardruina stood and whirled around, her tattered coat sweeping out behind her. In one fluid motion, she mounted Lady Crane and raced after Leon.

Scrambling to his feet, Theodore followed on foot. He had to see, had to know.

Through the trees, he saw Ardruina riding down the fleeing billionaire. Arm raised high, she swung with vicious force, decapitating him in one blow from behind. Leon's head rolled and bounced to the side, fancy sunglasses flying, and without a living driver, the ATV crashed into a cluster of boulders with a sickening crunch.

As Ardruina circled back, riding at a steady gallop, a voice behind him said, "I wanted to tell you, Teddy, but this is obviously a lot to confess."

He spun around.

Ardruina's fallen head, laying cheek down on a mat of pine needles, gazed up at him apologetically.

Shit. Damn. Fuckity. Fuck.

Get your act together, Theo, she needs you.

Breathe in. Breathe out.

"Are you okay?" he stammered, crouching down. Talking to an animated, decapitated head was not on his list of things he thought would be happening today. "Do you have a concussion from the …?" He motioned the falling off part with his hand.

"It doesn't feel good, but I'm alive in my own way."

Right.

Her body reined in beside him and jumped down, retrieving its head.

"I know this is asking a lot, but could you help me with the ribbon?" She blushed, a cross between shy and embarrassed, as she aligned herself neck to … neck.

Theodore found the green ribbon near where her head had been, and after brushing pine needles from her cheek with a trembling hand, wrapped the ribbon around her neck and tied it in a neat, tight bow.

God, how's that gonna stay on? He wrung his hands, certain they were both in denial.

When she let go, he shot forward, palms outstretched, ready to catch her head, but she just stretched and cracked her neck, full motion returned.

Thank Jesus. He never wanted to see her head fall off ever again.

"Better?" He meant to sound composed and suave, but the question came out in a mousey squeak.

"Much." She nodded, casting a look about, taking in the carnage.

They'd have to clean this up.

Bending down, Theodore lifted one of the decapitated heads. "Oh gosh, I forgot how heavy these things were," he gagged, almost dropping it. Everything was weird and clammy and if he looked at it, he'd hurl, so he didn't.

Ardruina smirked, joining him in body disposal. "You do this often?"

"Well, no," he replied, chucking goon #1's head into the bog. *Splat.* Sucking mud pulled it down with a loud, ugly belch. "I meant the trivia."

"That seems truer to character."

"You look like you've chopped off heads before."

"Only those who deserved it." And then after a moment, "I'm not going to chop your head off, Theodore."

Cool.

"So, um, I don't mean to sound rude or ungrateful—you did rescue me twice in two days, which wow, I'm shaping up to be a real damsel in distress, aren't I?"

"Theodore," she said softly, cutting off his rambling. "You can just ask. It won't offend me."

"What ... who are you?"

"Have you ever heard of The Wild Huntsman? Or the Dullahan?"

"That's Irish folklore, right?"

She nodded. "Mm. But the first one's German."

"Oh, I forgot about that. Like in the Legend of Sleepy Hollow."

"Just like that." Her answering smile was playfully impish. "I was heading north, on my way here, at the time."

Oh. *Ohhh.*

A bona fide, supernatural legend. He'd already known Ardruina was way out of his league, but this defied comprehension.

Piece after piece, they fed the bog their feast of misdeeds, knowing Dead Man's Hollow would hold onto their secrets and never let go. *To hold and to feed.*

Sabotage gone wrong. Murder. Almost dying, *again*. A centuries-old, sometimes-headless girlfriend. There was so much to process, but one thing stood out, one feeling that outshined them all.

"I can't tell you how glad I am you're not dead."

When Theodore took Ardruina's hand, she smiled.

Ribbon of Blue Poison

by Agatha Andrews

Every town has that one house, the kind with dark stories that drip off the tongues of neighbors to frighten children. Such houses are often ghosts of former grandeur, veiled by overgrown gardens and sad histories. I'm a living phantom that lurks in such a house, though I wasn't always like this. I used to meander joyfully through Port Lorraine, a pastel dream of a beach town, at least until all the deaths. Now, my name and humanity are lost beneath local legend. I hear what people say as they pass my windows. I'm no longer Laura Bell. Instead, I am known only as the Witch of Bell Mansion.

I am not a witch, though I am dangerous.

My home is the last Victorian house left in Port Lorraine, the lone survivor of a few brutal hurricanes. Our front garden was a thing of cultivated beauty, trimmed and shaped to sophisticated elegance. Now prickly roses and brambles grow wild, creating the sort of dangerous beauty that guards me from the outside world. The back of my house faces a secret beach, bordered by a fence and a jetty that divides me from the rest of Port Lorraine. I use the jetty to venture out at night, walking through the salty air on a path made of stone that cuts through the ocean. Sometimes I stand at the furthest tip, stare into the midnight horizon, and wonder what's out there. Other times I sit on the side, facing a town that doesn't want me. When I feel brave, I let my feet dangle over the edge, daring to take up even the tiniest space on their side of the divide. I never imagined I would live such an isolated life. Once haunted, however, it's hard to escape your ghosts.

One night, however, I tried.

I dreamt of my mother that night, a ghost who haunted us even while she lived. She was a Latin beauty—curvy, smart, and confident in a way that my father adored, and the locals hated. They whispered amongst themselves to all willing and jealous ears.

"Who does she think she is?"

"She doesn't deserve the Bell family or their money."

"Did you see her red shoes? Has she no shame?"

When my father died, their whispers transformed into a ceaseless, mocking cruelty against my mother's despair. They sneered at us when we tried to go about our business in town, threw rocks at our home, each weapon causing harm in equal measure. Kids I had always known shouted, "Let's peek at the freak!" while daring each other to climb our garden gates.

I was no longer human to them either. I'm not sure that I ever was. Sometimes I wonder, however, if this was deeper than simple hate. Her grief transformed her in a way that frightened them. It was strange and powerful.

It frightened me too.

Time froze in our house when we got news that my father's plane burst into flames on his flight home from a conference. Without a body, my mother never accepted his death or that life could march on without him. For ten years, she wore the same dress every day, the same hair style, the same smile, as if that could hold the truth at bay. She forbade any change in the house, which was fine for a while, but time has a way of showing itself on dresses, furniture, and children regardless of one's effort to preserve them.

In my dream, I relived my final day with my mother, the way she relived our final day before my father's death. It was like a curse I couldn't break.

"What are you doing, Mama?" I asked as I caught her, staring in horror at her reflection in her vanity mirror. For a moment, she didn't hear me. I asked again, gently touching her shoulder. "Mama, what is it?"

Her breath quickened as she struggled against the release of emotion, as if she had forgotten how to cry. Slowly, she reached up to touch her hair where a slender streak of silver had emerged. I thought it lovely, but this moment of lucidity shattered her illusion of time, and sorrow threatened to close in around her.

"I like it, Mama," I said with a smile. "It's enchanting."

She continued to stare in the mirror, and though her expression never changed, tears emerged and slowly trickled down her face like dew dripping from the petals of a rose.

"Are you alright?" I asked, at a loss of anything else to say. She closed her eyes and took a deep breath. As she slowly exhaled, her body changed. She sat up straighter and looked at herself again, this time with a slight smile on her face.

"Do you think your father will like it?" she asked.

I watched in horror as her grief morphed into a stronger beast. I wanted to scream, "He's dead! He will never see it!" Instead, I heard myself say, "I have no doubt he will," regretting the words as they fell from my mouth. I closed a rare window into reality, and I left her room, forsaking this morsel of hope. She resumed primping with a smile and her new happiness frightened me. In my dream, as in life, that was the last time I saw her. She wandered to the beach in the middle of the night and unraveled beneath the waves. She was found by a fisherman the next morning.

I awoke from this nightmare to a black sky veiled in fog, and all my sorrow and rage propelled me into it. Barefoot, wearing only a white cotton slip, I ran towards the beach, tired of memory, tired of the town's cruelty, tired of everything. I wanted the dark to swallow me whole, and I relished the fog's embrace as I forced my way through its thick clouds of salt. When I finally reached the shore, all my fire, all my anger escaped my body with a scream as I plunged full force into the water.

Though I was slow against the waves, I pushed forward, walking as far as I could before having to swim. The smooth barrels of the afternoon had become choppy and chaotic, like the water kept trying to spit me out. I was angry at it for its rudeness, so I did my best to kick against the undercurrent like a petulant child, but the waves easily silenced me with one foamy slap that sent me under.

My cotton slip billowed around me like Ophelia in Millais's painting. Though it was short and light, worn thin by use, my slip grew heavy, pulling on me as I moved further out. I was too angry at everything to be tragic, though, and for the first time in ages, I preferred a fight. I lived quietly for too long and I wanted to yell until my voice ran out. Blinded by water and night and rage, I thought I was alone, screaming into the void. Had I paid attention, I might have seen the shadow veiled in fog, watching me from the jetty.

A strong wave had just pounded me down, deep beneath the water, when large hands grabbed my waist and pulled me up. Before I knew what was happening, an arm wrapped around my body and dragged me back to shore while I coughed to catch my breath. It all happened so fast. We collapsed on the sand, and I sat there, stunned and breathless.

"Are you alright?" I heard him say with a voice that was deep and smooth. I couldn't see through the saltwater still stinging my eyes, but I felt his hands gently wipe the excess water from my brow and cheeks, a gesture of kindness and concern, gentle in an unfamiliar way. My loneliness slashed open like a wound festering beneath the skin. As isolated as I felt during my mother's grief-stricken madness, the last few years hurt worse without her. My eyes still closed, I reached up to feel his hands, my silence filled with both longing and fear. I ached at his touch since no one would dare come near me again. The town said men couldn't touch me without death, but those deaths weren't my fault.

The first time I had sex was with a tourist who wandered over to my side of the jetty one summer evening. I was twenty years old and filled with curiosity about sex more than desire. He was a young and handsome man that happily obliged me. We fucked right there on the beach because I didn't want to let a stranger in my house. He walked away when we were done, and I washed my virgin blood off in the evening surf. The newspaper reported his death the next day, an accidental drowning further up the beach. I recognized his face but hadn't known his name until I saw it in print.

Twice, I had sex with locals who ventured into my garden on a dare. They weren't strangers. We knew each other as kids, but I didn't let them in my house either. I knew why they were there. Each time, I could hear them laughing and jeering with friends before finally climbing over the fence. We fucked near the garden walls, where I could pin them against the brambles and prick them with thorns from my roses that grew furious and beautiful and wild. I wanted to penetrate them with a pain that mirrored my own, to get under their skin with a sharpness that felt like a curse. They called me a witch and a whore, which I relished because those are women in possession of their own power, something they would never understand. In the end, it didn't matter. They died anyway.

When they left my garden, bleeding and spent, they bragged to anyone who would listen. They got drunk and pranced like peacocks, telling story after story about fucking the Witch of Bell Mansion, at least according to the police that questioned me. They crashed their cars while driving in an alcoholic haze. It wasn't my fault that they died after visiting my garden, but the town blamed me anyway.

"Sweetheart, are you alright?" this man asked me again. I could see him clearly now, his beautiful dark eyes filled with worry.

"I don't know ... I ... I ..." My breathing was faster, my lungs more aware of how little air had been in them in the last few minutes.

"It's okay. As long as you can breathe, just take your time," he said as he checked my arms and legs.

I didn't know what he was looking for, but I let him proceed as I watched him glisten in the moonlight.

"I'm Diego Salvatore, the new doctor in town. What's your name?" he asked.

My breath caught in my throat. In a town that robbed me of my name, this question felt like a gift. "I'm Laura … Laura Bell."

He smiled in acknowledgment, with a slight nod. When he looked satisfied that I was alright, he relaxed and sat facing me in the sand. "Well, you're lucky the man-of-war didn't get to you," he said with breath of relief.

"The what?" I asked turning to look around me. I had run with so much purpose through blinding fog that I missed the wretched creatures.

"The man-of-war," he said with a smile. "I thought you were screaming from being stung or wrapped in one of their tentacles." He gently touched my foot with one hand while he pointed with the other, and it took me a moment to tear my eyes away from the warm reassurance of his touch to look at the undulating line of blue venomous blobs that stretched down the beach. "There's a bunch washed up on shore."

"It's like a ribbon of blue poison," I said, just above a whisper.

He looked at me a moment. I saw him glance at my body beneath the wet, white cotton that clung to me, translucent and teasing. The delicate tips of my breasts hardened as the breeze kissed my skin and I saw the gulp in his throat as he tore his eyes away. "That sounds like a story waiting to be written," he said as his eyes met mine.

A black, wet curl fell over his forehead. It was as enticing as his smile. "I've already written it," I said, letting him in on my secret. "I've just never shared it with anyone."

"What's it about?" he said softly, the sweetness in his voice soothing my anger and sorrow still bubbling beneath the surface.

I looked out at the dead gelatinous blobs on the beach and wondered how they got there. Were they dead before they washed ashore, or were they cast there against their will, unable to return? I sighed, my eyes fixed on them to hide my vulnerability.

"The story is about a girl whose mother tied a blue velvet ribbon around her neck that she could never remove. Her mother thought the deep shade of blue so beautiful that she ignored the poison in the velvet that seared to her daughter's skin, choking the joy of life from her, but not the life itself. She lived a half-life. She could know love but not be loved, have a garden but not beauty, could know pain but feel no relief. Her mother wore a ribbon from the same spool, laced with the same poison. When a tiny thread unraveled from it, she tried to tuck it away, but she unraveled the ribbon completely and died from the shock of its absence."

I could feel him looking at me, giving me space to continue, and I realized I hadn't taken a breath since the beginning of the story. I fought back tears as I looked into his beautiful brown eyes, holding his gaze to keep from drowning. "Her daughter saw the choice before her, death or a half-life."

"What did she choose?" he asked quietly, reaching for my hands.

"She wanted at least one thing in life she could control," I shrugged. "She looked in the mirror, found a string and unraveled her ribbon. At least death was on her own terms."

He looked at me a moment, then said, "I wish she'd found the antidote instead."

I stared in shock, my mouth open as if to speak, but I couldn't form words.

"It's your story and it should end the way you want. I'm just a sucker for hope," he said with smile that made me want to press my lips to his.

I sat quiet a moment, digesting the concept of hope. It had been a while since I thought I was allowed such a thing.

"The daughter deserved happiness," he said, giving my hands a reassuring squeeze.

"How do you know?" I whispered, struggling to believe him.

"The poison was thrust upon her but that doesn't make her wicked," he said. "Unless you haven't told me the whole story," he added with a wink.

I laughed. It was small, little more than a giggle, but it was enough. This morsel of joy tasted delicious, and I wanted more.

He stood up, facing sideways, and removed his shirt. As if in slow motion, a beautiful torso emerged, perfectly sculpted. I couldn't look at anything else. He turned slightly towards me, and that's when I saw a jagged, angry scar across his upper right chest.

I gasped.

He wrang out his shirt, his muscles flexing as the water fell away. "We all have our scars, Laura Bell. I walked out here tonight trying to escape my own bad dream, trying to clear my head." He smiled warmly at me. He knew my story was more than just a fairy tale.

"I know it's still wet," he said as he handed me his shirt, "But it will at least be an extra layer for you if you're cold."

I reached up to take it, not sure whether to smile or cry. "Thank you," I said. "For the shirt, and … and for saying my name." I slipped his shirt over me, the weight of it like an embrace. "It's hard to know how much you miss a thing when it seems gone forever."

"I didn't realize who you were when I pulled you from the water, but now that I know, I confess I've heard a story or two" he said. My heart sank, but he offered me his hand. "I ignored them, of course. Never give other people the power to decide who you are." He held my gaze, as he helped me to stand, then said, "Make them say your name."

I looked at him a moment, contemplating what he said, feeling a tingle of power emerging. I reached up to lightly trace his scar with my finger. "I want to hear you say it again."

A slight grin curled on his lip as he reached up to slip my hair behind my ear before he leaned in, his cheek brushing against mine, to whisper, "If you're not afraid of my scar, Laura Bell, I'm not afraid of yours."

His lips found mine. His kiss was warm and full, letting me decide what I wanted from the moment. I probed further and felt his tongue ready for me. It was the first time a kiss didn't feel like a fight, and I could feel all my sorrow melt into an unfamiliar happiness. His hands cupped my face and, instead of removing salty seawater, this time his thumb wiped away a salty tear.

"Savior," I said as we pulled apart. "Salvatore means savior. Seems fitting. You're very good at it."

He shook his head. "I didn't save you from anything." We started walking towards the jetty, neutral territory between me and Port Lorraine. "I thought you were running from someone, then you started screaming in the water and I thought the man-of war got you. Since that wasn't the case, it looks like all I really did was bother you," he said with a lighthearted laugh, reaching for my hand as we climbed up the rocks.

"I don't know." I shrugged as we started walking on the leveled path. His question brought everything back. Anger and fear propelled me from my home that night, and I ran because I had no idea what to do next. "Maybe you saved me from myself."

He looked at me, without judgement, and asked, "Do you want to talk about it?"

"Not really." We walked in peaceful silence as he allowed me space to gather my thoughts and feelings. "Thank you," I said as we reached the end of the jetty. I looked down at the water splashing against the rocks, not wanting to meet his gaze. "I must have looked crazy running in the water like that."

He shrugged. "I'm just happy you didn't get attacked by man-of-war." He gave me a sideways glance, then added "I think you know a little something about how much poison can hurt."

I stopped walking, realizing what he risked to help me. "You could have been hurt going in after me! I'm so sorry."

"I'm fine," he said, lifting my chin with his hand. "We both are."

He leaned in to kiss me again, soft, slow, and delicious. Though my eyes were closed, I could sense the sun slowly emerging from its slumber, ribbons of color rising through the darkness. Standing on the edge of this rocky border, we turned to watch them unravel into the beautiful blue of a new day.

AS TWILIGHT FALLS ON SANDTHORN HALL

BY A. R. FREDERIKSEN

My Dear Agnes,

Do not fear for my health.

I am in perfectly capable hands with Ms. Iversen. Truthfully, this has been the case in all the months since the misfortune of my wife's passing. I will not bless her wicked soul, as you know, but I will lament her parting from our world. You are most welcome to visit Sandthorn Hall and appraise the family heirlooms at your leisure—for which I will gladly arrange the transportation— but you must not come because you fear for my health. If I worried you with my last letter, I will speak no more of ghosts and curses.

As I said, I am in perfectly capable hands.

Yours sincerely,

Vidar

"Overly capable hands." I spoke my fear aloud, huddled in the sandy dunes.

Rubbing the letter with restless fingers, I studied the stains of orange berry juice smeared across the page. They were a testament to how many times I had sat out here, with this exact letter, among these salt-crusted and prickly sandthorn bushes. In front of me, below the rolling dunes, the ocean nibbled at the coastline. Behind me, the presence of Sandthorn Hall pressed down on my neck, demanding that I return in time for dusk, in time for Ms. Iversen to apply her ointment to Vidar's lesions with her capable hands—the lesions that he believed to be the ghostly curse of his recently deceased wife.

I believed differently.

Tonight, I would prove it.

Pocketing the letter with trembling fingers, I pulled my skirts up above my knees and trod back through the orange-and-black bushes, approaching the old manor house where I had spent the last month trying to match what Vidar had told me in his letters with what I had observed in person. Holding my tongue all the while, as I grappled for the truth.

It began after his wife died of illness in the spring, half a year ago.

We had kept up correspondence throughout his marriage, although it had waned in comparison to when we were younger, before he had inherited Sandthorn Hall after marrying Isabella. After her untimely death, however, the correspondence changed.

He changed. His letters became harried. Hurried. Haunted. Hunted.

And now I was here, trying to reclaim the man I cared for from the life that had engulfed him, knowing it wasn't my duty, knowing that I had turned him away many times before. I had ended up here regardless, leaving us both to lick each other's wounds.

Love made pitiful creatures of anyone who dared to love wholly.

I stopped outside the entrance to the Hall, my pulse drawing a tight string around my throat. When I stepped inside, the solemn curves of the Hall folded around me like a fitted kidskin glove, guiding me towards the kitchen.

Just in time, as I had planned it, to catch Ms. Iversen puttering about with her preparations for Vidar's daily skin treatment.

She stood by the sturdiest table, wisps of her graying hair falling around her face as she prepared the customary tray that she would take to Vidar's bedroom with fingers perpetually stained orange from the berries that haunted my days and nights.

Even now, standing here, far from the windswept dunes, they haunted me.

The green-tiled kitchen reeked of those sweet-smelling berries for which the Hall had been named upon its construction so many decades ago. They were the same orange berries that peppered the windswept seaside of the north. Berries that smelled as sweet as candy, but tasted as sour as wine gone bad, clogging your throat with every swallow. Much like the housekeeper herself, I suspected.

I tipped my chin higher and cleared my throat. "Excuse me?"

"Miss Thorsen!" The housekeeper touched her chest with one surprised hand. "Are you back from the doctor already? I thought you would surely spend the night in town?"

"It was only minor indigestion." I wafted her worry aside with a lie.

"Well, that's a relief to hear. We have enough ailment around here, as it is."

"I wish to assist." I gestured to the tray with my healthy hand, taking care to hide the other one that carried the proof of my suspicion and the real reason that I had gone to the doctor today. "I will bring the tray to Vidar's room this evening. I will administer his—treatment. I am quite confident I know the procedure by now, after all these weeks."

Ms. Iversen's lips lifted in a faint smirk that looked nothing like the smile she had worn until now. Her hand fell to her cocked hip. "You will what? Pardon me?"

Vidar had always been vain, for as long as my daft heart had known him, but never to the point of folly where he refused to see a licensed doctor for the lesions that speckled his back. Instead, he'd rather rely on his housekeeper and her homemade berry remedy.

This wasn't the Middle Ages, for Christ's sake.

Neither was it the home of a vengeful ghost, for that matter.

It was the home of a gullible man, first warped by grief, then warped by anger. A man who had been taken advantage of for reasons that were still unclear to me, yet obvious enough that I had to act on the nagging suspicion that clawed at my gut, making bloody ribbons of my insides, peeling and pulling, bit by bit.

"I said"—my hands clenched in the fabric of my skirt, matching my tone of voice—"that I will assist Vidar with his treatment this evening. In your place, of course."

"Oh, no." Ms. Iversen shook her head. "No, no. That will not do. You are here to appraise the family heirlooms as a favor. Not to act as a nursemaid. Not only will that be poor hospitality, but it will also be highly improper. I will take to the task as usual. It is no extra burden on me, I assure you. A mother's touch does wonders for ailments such as these."

She might be a mother for all I knew, and I saw no reason why she would lie about that of all things, but she was not Vidar's mother. Of that, I was sure. And there was no reason for her to bring motherhood into our negotiation—because that was what this was: a negotiation.

Frustration burgeoned from my chest to my throat, pressing against my eyes and ears. But I would never prove my theory if I showed my hand too soon, in the figurative sense as much as the literal one. "And you believe it is proper for a *housekeeper* to deny the request of an invited guest? A family friend of old?"

"I believe you invited yourself, miss." Grabbing a hold of the tray with the orange-tinted ointment in its crude glass jar, Ms. Iversen caught my eye. "And it didn't sound much like a request to my ears, but I am prone to mishearing." A pause. A sting. A moment that escaped me too quickly, leaving me thoroughly eviscerated. Defeated. "Was there anything else, miss?"

My breath swirled like hot tar inside my mouth. I shook my head, unwilling to open my mouth lest all that tar spilled loose and flooded the floor by my feet, showing my hand too soon.

"Very well." Ms. Iversen stepped away from the table as if she was beyond reproach and shame. Beyond me. "Do find me if you think of something later, shall we say?"

I waited in the kitchen, rooted to the spot, until I could no longer hear the tinkling of Ms. Iversen's tray. Then I retreated to my room, the corners of my vision colored in flaming red. It was all I could do not to slam the door behind me. I paced the room, my lungs bellowing like a set of colicky babies, robbing my breath from me.

It was true that sandthorn eased skin irritation.

It was also true that hogweed sap burned holes in the skin.

Slowly, I came to a stop. Raising my left hand to my face, I studied the palm I had taken great care to hide from Ms. Iversen. The lesion on there was small, but there was no mistaking that it was a lesion. It had happened by lucky circumstance, truth be told. Or unlucky, depending on how one chose to look at it.

Three days ago, I was bitten by a spider out among the sandthorns. Upon returning to the Hall, I found Ms. Iversen's ointment unattended in the kitchen. On a whim, I applied a bit of her renowned homemade remedy to my irritated skin, directly on top of the spider bite.

The next day, yesterday, I woke with a blistering lesion on top of the bite.

Today, back in town, the doctor confirmed that hogweed burns had been particularly prevalent this year, in an unforeseen amount, due to optimal growing conditions that were rarely found this far north, causing hysteria in parents and spouses alike.

There was no hysteria inside Sandthorn Hall.

No ghost, no curse, and no coincidence.

There was only Ms. Iversen.

I waited until nighttime, when I knew she would be asleep. Then, on bare feet and with a single candleholder in hand, I made my way through the house long past midnight. Sand had a way of getting into the damp crevices of the floorboards no matter how often they were swept clean, all throughout the house, and tonight was no different. The longer that I walked, the more sand accumulated between my toes, grainy and merciless, urging me to walk faster until the flame of my candle sputtered when I turned a corner.

Vidar's door was closed.

I hadn't expected differently, but it still made me pause.

It still made the inside of my body bloom hot and wild.

We had toed a painstaking line, Vidar and I, for so long. There had been a time before Isabella, and then there had been a time with Isabella, and now there was a time after Isabella. Time was fickle.

I stood there, in front of the door, long enough for the candle to spit wax at me, a mere hairsbreadth away from the lesion inside my palm. I dropped the candleholder with a hiss. It fell to the floor like an anchor at sea, knocking against the bottom of Vidar's door. The flame went out instantly. Every muscle in my body stretched tight.

The door slid open. "Agnes?"

I stood very still, hoping for the dark to swallow me.

The door opened further. "Are you sleepwalking again?"

"Again?" I sputtered, my spine snapping straight. I could make out his outline in the shadowed doorway. "That was one time. And I was fourteen years old. I do not sleepwalk."

"Right." Warmth ringed that single word; the kind I could've dozed off to under different circumstances. "You're here for a reason, then?"

Rubbing my brow with clammy fingers, I managed a strangled, "Let me inside."

When he didn't move, I added in a voice more strangled than ever, "I realize this situation can be misconstrued. Especially given our history. But my purpose is ... biblical, if you will. This time. I would not be here if it was not. I am not heartless."

A beat of a pause. Then, softly, in the dark: "More's the pity."

When he shifted aside to let me pass, the sweet smell of sandthorn berries shed free from his skin like a fine mist. My tongue pulled back down my throat in a reflexive gag. To think I used to love that smell; now it brought me cold sweat and a caged bird's heart.

Once inside the lightless room, I kept a hand against the wall to maintain my sense of place, asking with lips that felt numb, "Will you light a candle?"

"No." His warmth from before was gone, replaced with a cold needlepoint of a word.

It took me a handful of seconds to compose a reply. Specifically, it took me a handful of seconds to decide how far I could push this newfound Vidar who refused to see a licensed doctor and who believed in ghosts and curses.

"I didn't come here to gawk at your back in the middle of the night, Vidar." I pushed away from the wall and fisted my hands by my sides, mindful of my palm. "Besides, I assume you put on a nightshirt before opening that door. If not, feel free to do so now, but you have to light that candle. Please. You won't believe me unless you can see me."

The air close to me shivered with movement. "Believe you?"

"Yes." I squinted at the faint outline of him, now closer. "Believe me."

When he finally lit the candle on his nightstand, the flame flickered weakly before catching on with a fervor. I pressed my lips tightly together to stifle my gasp. He wore no shirt, after all. His lesioned back faced me for half of a second before he twisted around, burnt-sugar eyes catching mine like a stiff crop would lash across a horse.

"You were saying?" he pressed, the words striking my calves, weakening my knees.

Pulling myself up straighter, I stepped forward, braving the scent of Ms. Iversen's foul misdemeanor that clung to Vidar like the scent of a corpse. "Here. Look at this."

I held out my left hand in the space between us, turning it upwards until my fingers pointed to the ceiling above us. The restless flame of the candle accentuated the single lesion in the center of my palm, creating shadow and light that made the inflammation look alive.

Drawing a slow breath, I remembered the speech I had practiced all day, but my preparation died when Vidar grabbed my hand and bent his body over it. His breath tickled my palm, threatened to rip open my congested heart then and there, but I stood still and bade my time. This was a Vidar I recognized, if nothing else.

Then, ever so slowly, Vidar's face tipped up to meet mine. His eyes skittered down to my mouth, and then back up to my eyes. "She always envied you. Envied us."

I swallowed, my hand twitching in his grip. "Ms. Iversen?"

"What?" He let my hand fall abruptly. "Of course not."

I held my hand to my chest as if he'd spurned it, my mouth working wordlessly. Eventually, I managed to say, "I don't understand."

"Isabella." He spat the word into the corners of the room, making them shudder. "She has cursed you like she has cursed me. I should've known. I shouldn't have let you come here. You must tell Ms. Iversen. You must use her—"

"It is no remedy!" My voice was lightning, slipping free from my grasp, lashing out with destructive precision. "There is no ghost, and there is no curse, and there is certainly no remedy. In fact, there is quite the opposite. You used to be a man of science, so listen to me now. Did you know I went to the doctor in town today? Your old colleague, for that matter? And do you know what he told me?" I twisted my hand in the air between us. "About this?"

Vidar leaned away from me, as if my hand was more offensive than the ripe-sweet ointment lathered across his back. "No. Of course, I don't. How would—"

"Listen to me." Stepping forward, I placed my lesioned palm against the hot flesh of his shoulder, splaying my fingers out across his collarbone. It stung, but the pain made me brave. "Ms. Iversen is not treating your lesions. She is making them worse. That ointment you proudly carry like a cure? It's more than just sandthorn berries. She has laced it with hogweed sap. I used it on my palm, for a spider bite yesterday, and the doctor confirmed it today. You must listen to me, Vidar. Your housekeeper is not helping you. Far from it. She's even been purposely stopping me from helping you. And I think you already know this. Why would she wish you ill?"

"If what you say is true ..." Vidar fell silent, his eyes straying to the dim outline of the window. Several heartbeats passed. Then his eyes slid back to mine. "If that is true, then I have something I must also show you. But not now. It is too dark. It will have to be at dawn."

Tight-laced tension spilled over inside my chest. "Dawn?"

"Will you do that for me? With me?" His arm lifted until his fingers encircled the wrist of my hand pressed against his naked shoulder. "Will you meet me at dawn by the gatehouse?"

His fingers released my wrist just as I pulled back my arm. I cleared my throat, pressed my heels together, stood taller, and raised my chin. "Yes. I will."

Nothing more was spoken between us, but plenty was promised.

I left the room with those promises pulling a long and delicate thread behind me, between the two of us, that no closed door could snip apart.

Time would tell if the rising sun could.

Hours later, the sun tugged itself up above the horizon with none of the urgency that had pebbled my chest ever since leaving Vidar's room. I hadn't slept at all. Now, standing by the gatehouse with curlicues of fog by my feet, shrouding the orange-and-black sandthorn bushes like ghostly soup, I was ready for those pebbles to fly free, their aim tried and true.

Vidar approached from the Hall, stiffly, with his hands in his coat.

"Here we are," I announced loudly. "And we're going where, was it?"

"To Monk's Dune." His voice was subdued. Partly by the morning mist, but also partly by the collar of his coat. And perhaps the manner of his mind. "Follow me."

Biting the inside of my cheek, I fell into step behind him. "Monk's Dune? Where—"

"Where Isabella jumped into the sea, yes." His eye caught mine over his shoulder. "If only she had hit the sea, of course, and not the beach." He turned back around and resumed our walk. "After what you told me, I'm afraid I've made a wrong calculation."

My head spinning, I tripped over a wayward root and steadied myself with a hand to his back. At his hiss of pain, I retreated as if burnt. We stood still once again.

"You're being very obscure," I said, filling the silence.

"I have to show you," was his reply. "Like you had to show me. Words will not suffice. And any warning I give you ..." He drew a long breath that painted black swirls in the fog upon its release. "I'm afraid you'll leave me if I do."

I fought for an answer. "It is my right to leave."

A smile tugged at his mouth, but it was impossible to tell whether it turned upwards or downwards. "And so can you blame me for wanting to minimize that risk?"

Monk's Dune was a ten-minute walk past the gatehouse, making it a fifteen-minute walk from the Hall. It was a dune like any other around these parts, except the sea had eaten away at the sand, creating a dune that was less like a rotund leaf pile and more like a cliff in terms of height and steepness. And in terms of the lethal impact upon landing, rock or no rock, of course.

I breathed through a throat fat with nerves as we approached the edge, forging our way through gnarled sandthorn bushes. I ripped my skirts over and over again, but I didn't dare stop; I was afraid I'd never start again if I did. My sweat made my palm sting.

"Vidar," I began, "I don't think—"

"Here we are." He gestured with the sweep of an arm towards a tangle of sandthorns. It would've looked like any of the bushes we had just passed, if it hadn't been for the fact that a pair of garden scissors had clipped a concave space in the middle of it.

And then there was the skull.

My skin sucked so tight to my bones that I couldn't move.

The skull sat in the middle of that hollow space, like the token of an altar, encircled by orange berries and black wiry branches. Berries rested in the empty sockets of its eyes, stains of orange berry juice coloring the cheekbones, dripping down like tears.

"I thought it would make her stop." Vidar's voice almost didn't reach my ears; the rush of blood in my head was too loud. "I thought if I put her back here, she would stop. But if what you tell me is true, and it sounds like it is, and you have no reason to lie, then …"

I swallowed, tasting the rush of blood on the back of my tongue. Turning away from the skull, I focused on his face. "Then you dug up your wife's skull for nothing."

"Did I?" He removed his hands from his pockets until they hung limply by his sides, as if he needed the weight to keep him grounded. "Did I dig up her skull for nothing?"

It was too much. "Yes. Vidar. You did." Far too much. "You know you did."

He raised both hands to rub them across his face, groaning into the fog. The movement was so abrupt that my knees buckled with alarm. "I am so confused."

I locked my knees, flattened my tongue against the sour roof of my mouth, and reached for him with my good hand. "I know," I began. "Vidar, we need to—"

The cock of a pistol cracked a clear path through the morning mist.

"You've desecrated my daughter's grave." Ms. Iversen sounded like her normal self, but the pistol in her hand was new. "And here I thought you had only desecrated her memory." The housekeeper laughed, shaking her head. "Hogweed seems so simple now. Too simple. I suppose that is why I have brought this." She jiggled the pistol in the air. Then she aimed it at Vidar with an accuracy that jabbed fear through my heart. "Is it not?"

"I don't understand." Vidar's words were slow, but steady. "Your daughter?"

I didn't care to understand. I only cared to get rid of this. All of this. The pistol. The skull. Ms. Iversen. The strange conviction that had ensnared Vidar, making him believe in ghosts and curses to the point that he'd dug up his dead wife's skull to make it stop. At that thought, my eyes zeroed in on the skull. Not only was it nearly close enough for me to touch, but I was the one who stood the closest to it.

My breath snagged in my lungs.

"Isabella was adopted." Vidar's voice was faint to my ears. Unimportant.

"And I birthed her," Ms. Iversen answered primly. A mother's touch. Motherhood. I was brought back to the kitchen with Mrs. Iversen. Suddenly, it made all the sense in the world. She wasn't Vidar's mother. She was Isabella's. Her mother's touch had not been aimed at Vidar, but at Isabella. A mother's touch protected. A mother's touch avenged. She hadn't lied to me back then, after all. I just hadn't understood at the time. I did now.

"That just means you orphaned her," Vidar told Mrs. Iversen as he shifted beside me, but I had eyes only for that horrid, horrid skull. "And if you orphaned her, why do you care about her grave or her memory?"

The sea was quiet this morning. So quiet I had almost forgotten we stood at the edge of a dune tall enough to be a cliff. But I could hear it now. Gentle, welcoming waves. What Isabella had heard, too.

"I am here now," Ms. Iversen said with a cold, wet sheen to her eyes. "That is all that matters. I failed at loving her in life and so I can only love her in death." Finality steeled her voice. "And love her, I will."

I didn't wait to see where that finality would lead. Instead, I listened to the blood that pumped through my body. I was no mother, but a mother's touch had nothing on a once-lover's. A would-be lover's. If she could use her touch, then so could I.

So would I.

My vision blurred at the edges. Darkened. Zeroed in on that grisly skull.

Kicking out my leg, my boot connected with the sphere of white-yellow bone. Victory burst on my tongue, sweet and hot. The skull shot free from the bushes as if it had waited for this moment, for my foot, for my judgment, heading straight for the edge of the dune where no plants had enough purchase to grow.

It went over the edge, promptly, dropping like a bird's egg.

And Ms. Iversen—perhaps shockingly, perhaps not—went with it.

Her outraged cry shredded the air, followed by a flurry of her skirts, and then the dull thud of a pistol hitting the sand. The shot went off, burrowing into the ground. Grains of sand went everywhere, flying into my face, obscuring my view. When they settled, I saw Ms. Iversen's feet dip below the dune. Then I saw no more. The horizon was clear. Undisturbed.

It happened all too quickly. Too easily.

"Agnes." Vidar's voice reached me. "Agnes?"

"Love her in death." My voice was frail. I blinked and stepped closer to the edge, stretching my neck. "I didn't think she'd actually ..."

Vidar's rigid hands grabbed my waist, bringing me away from the edge I had been inching towards for a better look. "We're going back inside. Now. And then we're calling into town."

When I laughed, the world spun, forcing my stomach up my throat until I gagged on my laugh. Gagged on the world that had gone right, but still somehow wrong. "That's the most sensible thing you've said to me in weeks. Maybe I finally got through to you?"

Vidar's smile was grim. "I should think you did."

"What did the doctor say?" I asked the following day. "About your lesions?"

We were alone inside the westward lounge, bathed in an orange sunset after the authorities had questioned us most thoroughly on yesterday. Ms. Iversen hadn't fallen to her death, unlike poor Isabella, but it was unlikely that she would ever walk without assistance again. Or that she would ever work for anyone again, convicted of the crime of digging up her daughter's skull in a fit of mad grief. It was the only way. Vidar and I had agreed.

"He said you were right." Vidar rubbed a quick hand across his mouth where a smile played at the edges that I suspected he'd tried to hide. "Naturally, you were right."

I nodded resolutely. "Good. That settles the last of it. Thank heavens."

Ms. Iversen had confirmed as much herself, before she had jumped, but I was primarily elated that Vidar had sought out licensed expertise at long last. My heart could rest easy.

Vidar cleared his throat. "It's not the last of it, I'm afraid."

I stared at him, my chest churning slowly. "What else is there? What did I miss?"

When he leaned forward in his chair, he rested his elbows on his knees and folded his hands together in the empty space in-between. It was a posture that sparked every nerve in my body to life. A familiar posture that prefaced danger. Not to my body, but to my heart.

His broiling eyes latched onto mine. "I would like you to stay with me, Agnes."

Desperately opting for humor, I answered, "I will not be your new housekeeper."

"But would you marry me? In time?" He wouldn't have my frantic humor, of course, but he would have my heart. It was nothing new—and yet it was, somehow, this time.

I folded my anxious hands in my lap. The air was thick enough to wrap up and eat. Wetting my lips, I said very carefully while looking out the window, "On one condition."

Vidar shifted in his chair, no doubt seeking my wayward gaze. "Which is?"

"Hack down all those sandthorns outside." I slashed my gaze across his, cocking a firm brow. "Once you've done that, we can have this conversation again."

"Hack down—" His laugh was a hot tickle in my sternum, an itch that wouldn't be scratched no matter the number of years and wives and housekeepers. "I am an injured man! Have some mercy!"

I shrugged, smiling faintly. "Then I suppose I will have to stay for some time."

His laugh died down to a smile of his own. "I suppose you will."

Until then, he would be in perfectly capable hands.

My hands.

SILVER-PLATED PROMISES

BY REBECCA E. TREASURE

Beyond the worn velvet curtains of Mrs. Humfreys' boarding house, the Wyoming prairie fell to darkness. A lingering echo of *thieves, thieves, thieves* in my mind faded, leaving me in the comparative silence of rain hammering on the roof and wind whipping at the shutters. I smoothed my blue linen vest over my red gingham gown—the very best in pioneer fashion—and smiled to the rancher to my right and the prospector to my left.

These would be my neighbors, these rough types at the empty edges of the nation and during the nights—when the voices gave me peace—I could at least pretend to be one of them. I met the striking brown eyes of the solemn woman across from me for a brief moment, glancing away before a blush could fully form on my cheeks.

Calla Remany always wore gray gingham and a serious expression. Despite my predicament, she fascinated me. We'd scarcely spoken, and yet I anticipated our every meeting, delaying my departure with excuse after excuse. Another reason, among many, it would be better for me to continue my journey sooner rather than later. And yet I stayed at this last refuge of civilization, the entry into the wilds of Montana. I'd paused there, delaying my cursed familial quest into the great northern plains.

The front door creaked open and the table hushed as a man in a wide-brimmed hat dripped into the room. Beyond his towering figure, the open door revealed an evening so windswept and torrential it was a wonder he'd seen the building at all. The worn rug absorbed the runoff from his long coat, the dampness giving the reds and oranges a hint of their former glory.

He swept us all with such a look of disdain my fingertips checked my lips for stray crumbs of their own accord. The old thought tumbled through, worn so smooth by time it barely disturbed my mind by its passage. *Could he be the one?*

For a long moment, no one dared move. Something about the man stilled us. The uniformity of his dark gray clothing, made black by the rain? Perhaps. Or the barest hint of a shadow on his otherwise smooth chin, tanned by sun and weather. Or the way he carried himself as though braced for an assault.

The landlady unfroze first, naturally. Having run the boarding house during the Civil War and the disruptions of the Indian Wars and now into a new century, this stranger flustered her only a moment.

"Well? Close the door, man, and come in out of the rain." Mrs. Humfrey bustled past him, her face perhaps more pale in a flash of lightning than the flickering oil lamps revealed, and closed the door. He did not move out of her way. When she turned and eyed him up and down, still he did not move. Finally, just as her narrow lips opened, likely to release something sharp enough to goad him to action, he moved with such rapidity I jumped in my seat.

Sweeping the hat from his head, showering my cheeks and Mrs. Humfreys with cold discarded droplets, he bowed. "My name is Samuel Hiram Garfield." He said it 'gah-field', making him seem quite the fancy gent for a boarding house such as Mrs. Humfreys ran. "The first."

Calla, across from me, stirred, her eyes narrowing. Only she of the table had not turned to stare at the stranger. While we were all still blinking at that pronouncement, he thrust a wad of paper money at Mrs. Humfreys, stomped over to the table, and settled at the only open seat. Two seats down and across from mine, as it happened. Calla leaned back and I had the fleeting impression she wanted to stay out of his eyeline. I couldn't blame her, at that, for the man gave such an impression of wild danger.

Mrs. Humfreys had just served her most excellent turnip casserole, the salt-rich steam still lingering amidst the sugared crisp hint of the cobbler coming from the kitchen. Every gaze fixed to the newcomer, and he seemed to know it, for a twinkle passed into his eye like an approaching train in the night. In a slow gesture reminiscent of a snake oil salesman pulling out his bottle, the long fingers reached into the voluminous coat and thunked an oyster fork down upon Mrs. Humfreys' well-washed silk tablecloth.

My breath caught in my throat as though a wine cork had been hammered past my tongue. The low light glimmered on the curves of the fork, the three sharp tines stabbing accusingly into the breathless silence. The impression on the handle, though too far for me to be certain, had the right shapes, the familiar curves. I reached for the pocket in my vest, my cheeks aflame with sudden excitement, my skin sizzling like fatty bacon.

All the many rehearsals of what I would say should the moment arrive fled my memory, leaving me with only the most basic manners. "Excuse me," I murmured.

Everyone's eyes turned to me, but I kept my gaze only on the man now peering at me with one eyebrow arched. He reminded me of the old Generals with a broad mustache well kept and an arrogance in the twist of his lips. I'd never have guessed it would be such a man.

I withdrew my oldest companion—the four-inch oyster knife with the wide silver handle and the narrow-pointed blade—and the sparkling in his eyes shifted to something closer to astonishment. I flipped it in my hand and offered it to him across the span, my eyes now drifting back to his oyster fork. "I've found you at last," I said.

Now moving as a man in a fever dream, his right hand closed upon my knife while his left scooped up and offered me his fork. A glance was all I needed—it had the same pattern of milkvetch flowers along the handle as my knife. Our eyes met over the silverware raised for inspection.

Without needing to speak, we rose from the table in synchronized motions. I held the oyster fork, he the knife. I turned to Mrs. Humfreys and half-smiled. "The gentleman is an old friend. May I speak to him in the parlor?"

Her left eyebrow became so angular it resembled Pike's Peak for a moment, her lips compressing into a thin line of preserved propriety. Then she nodded once. "But leave the door open."

"Of course," I murmured.

When at last we were as alone as Mrs. Humfreys would allow, I looked him up and down. "You're not at all what I expected."

He snorted. "Serves you right for having expectations at all."

"Pardon?"

"You heard me." He threw himself upon the chaise lounge under the painting of a herd of buffalo. "You're no work of art yourself."

I scowled. Not at all how I pictured the meeting going. I pressed on. "How did you come to find me?"

He laughed again and my scowl deepened. "They didn't tell you either, I suppose."

"Tell me what?"

"Hold up the fork. No, flat in the palm of your hand. Point the tines toward me. That's right. Now, turn away."

As I turned toward the empty fireplace, the fork twisted of its own accord, keeping the points aimed directly at my new friend.

Or rather, at my oyster blade.

My scowl transferred from him to my parents and grandparents, may they rest in peace. "All along? I can hardly believe it. Does mine as well?"

He shrugged, held up my knife, and twisted at his hips. A grunt. "It doesn't care for my fork, but"—he wobbled some more —"it's pointing somewhere. North again."

I glared at the silverware, annoyed. "How did I never notice? I've held it in my hand for hours, I've—"

"I know. It might have some kind of distance trick. I only discovered it in Denver and have been following it north ever since. When did you arrive?"

"I've been here for several weeks."

"In the boarding house?" He looked around at the worn velvet furniture, the faded painting, the patched curtains.

"Well?" Despite myself, a flush came into my cheeks, my eyes darting to the dining room. Why I should care what this man thought escapes me even now. Despite having berated myself over the lingering—malingering, if we're to be totally honest—at the precipice of a decision, the inability to ignore my longing, I owed him nothing. Especially since he looked more rough and tumble than the worst of Mrs. Humfreys' patrons.

Embarrassment shivered along my spine and I turned away, pacing to the window. The black night flashed now and there with lightning, otherwise the glass reflected my silhouette back at me. "I'd given up hope of ever finding you," I finally said. "I had resolved to attempt and complete the journey on my own."

"If it weren't for the whispers, I'm sure I would have," he said.

I nodded. Damnable things. Really a wonder either of us were sane enough to speak at all. Thank heaven they wore themselves out at night.

"Well then." My reflection in the window disappeared into a near flash and I turned back to him. "My name is Sadie Margaret Wilson. What now?"

He shrugged. "We follow the blade, I suppose. Perhaps I was always meant to find you, and together we find the end."

Forced to face the moment, I found myself eager to begin. Only the smallest of pangs pricked my heart for what I would leave behind. "North tomorrow? I can be ready by morning."

"Before dawn," he said. "I like to be moving before they begin yattering away."

"Agreed." I offered him the oyster fork atop my palm. He hesitated, his fist closing around the knife. I understood the reaction. I'd been searching so long for the mate of my silver, I found it difficult to release the moment. Yet the thought of not having my blade tucked in my vest disturbed my thoughts as well.

He arranged a room with Mrs. Humfreys for the night and we parted ways. My thoughts raced, marveling at having at last found the partner promised from my cradle, the culmination of my family's hopes and promises. I did take my time over dessert, bravely pouring coffee for Calla. She smiled, briefly, when our hands brushed and I fled the table, knowing I would leave her behind.

We should have set off at that moment. Likely would have if not for the storm. I packed, and then paced. Settling for a moment on the bed, and then up again to light on the edge of the bureau, back to the bed, on and on. I thought of the woman's brown eyes, wondering if I could return to Mrs. Humfreys free of my burden and pursue the unthinkable. I thought of Father's eyes if he could have known I'd finally found the matching silver, my companion, to finally absolve our family's debt to the silver mine.

Perhaps if this worked, if we finished the job, the madness would leave Father and I could tell him. I thought of Mother's frown of disapproval—and fear for her only daughter—when I left to travel west. I finally settled myself enough to drift off for a moment just around two in the morning.

I awoke an hour or so before dawn by instinct—like Garfield, it was my favorite time of day—and found him waiting in the front hall.

He rocked onto his toes. "Morning."

I nodded to him, not quite awake enough to converse, and led the way into the cool predawn. Mud clung to my boots, rainwater still pooling in the center of the puddles. We collected our horses from the stable behind the boarding house—his a large black and mine a roan mare—and set off toward the top of the world.

We said little. Unsurprising given our whispering passengers. Pleasant to share companionship with someone who would understand why my brow would tighten and my own words cease as soon as the sun broke the horizon. Despite his prickly approach, I found myself smiling at the empty prairie ahead. I'd found him and now we'd return the silver to where it belonged—the last of it—

and rid our families of the burden our grandparents had unwittingly given us.

I turned to my companion just as the dawn threatened to break and fill my head with yammering voices. "You've no idea where we must go?"

He spread his hands. "My father was just a boy and lived at many mining camps. My grandfather died of a bullet to the ear when I was just a babe." He clicked at his horse and came alongside. "You?"

I shook my head. "Father ..." I frowned. "Your father told you stories?"

He blinked as though remembering something. "Not in the last few years, of course. Not since it really took him. But when I was a boy."

I nodded, disappointed. "I see." For a moment I'd dreamed of a respite for my father, a return to normalcy, to the man whose laugh once echoed round the neighborhood like a church bell. I'd have given a great deal to hear that laughter again.

"Perhaps, when we finish our journey ..." He left the question hanging and I nodded.

"Here it comes," I said, and it did.

Come back to us, bring it home, come home, bring us home, I want to leave, I need to go, We are lonely, We are alone, We are many, come to home, bring thee back to us, you're the last to us, come along home, run, rush, thieves, thieves, thieves.

On and on the voices went. I settled into the mare's back, trusting her to carry me safely. She swayed beneath me, our spines shifting in rhythm, her mane tickling my fingertips. In the boarding house, I'd hidden in the room during the day, not forced to think or consider or make conversation while the whispers rushed around my mind. It took all my will and concentration to keep the mare's nose pointed north, to eat the hard tack at midday, drink alongside her wet nose as the sun settled into a downward path.

My companion's face stayed grim and still as we rode. Every hour or so I'd take out the blade and hold it flat on my palm, adjusting our path a few degrees there or here. He said nothing. I found my head filled with questions now that speaking would be near impossible, or at least terribly unpleasant—as I knew all too well. Did his voices say the same as mine? Had they started just as he came into his growth? What stories had his parents told him of the mines and the whispers, of the search and the final pieces?

Out of sympathy and respect I kept these thoughts to myself, content to at least have new considerations. Midday, he shocked me with a sudden flurry of movement and the *crack* of a rifle shot. He hopped from his horse and retrieved a fat hare from the brush.

I found myself ashamed. Here I wallowed in my misery and he fought through to have the wherewithal to provide more than hardtack and tea for our meals. I'd surrendered to the voices and now had a new hope breathed into me by this strange man.

Evening crept around us, chirped into purpled-gold by the crickets. The birds settled with the sun, and I heaved a sigh of relief.

"At last," he said. A smile broke his face. "I am grateful for the last glimmers of light left to enjoy in peace each day." His gaze lingered on the last yellowing edges of the day, a surprisingly gentle smile on his cheeks. The expression contrasted with his demeanor, adding a dimension I had not expected.

I shared the moment of peace—surprised the thought hadn't ever occurred to me before—and then turned to the task of making camp in the dark. We split our chores amiably, without much fuss or debate, and eventually I sighed and rubbed my belly.

"Many thanks for the stew. However did you manage to keep your mind clear enough to aim?"

In the flickering firelight his face rippled through a number of emotions before settling, it seemed to me, on a carefully blank expression. "Many years of practice. Had to keep my belly filled, didn't I?"

"I suppose. My parents always warned me against getting too complacent in our security. Even when I left, though, and came to the west to escape the press of people, I've found it easier to manage my affairs in the dark."

Again, his face twisted for a moment. "I've had no such luxuries."

His words left me embarrassed again. Foolish to assume that just because my family had other resources but the wealth of the stolen silver, others had similar circumstances. "Hopefully we both find ourselves in better situations."

He grunted, all comfortable companionship gone. "Long day on the morrow. Best get some rest." And without another word he rolled into his horse blanket and began to snore.

I admit to some disappointment at being left holding my bag of questions with nowhere to set them, but my mother's face in my memory glaring down her nose at daring to even mention our position in society kept me from any outward reaction. Who knows what other hardships the man had endured alongside our shared curse? I resolved to be a more considerate companion in the future and rolled into my own rest.

We awoke at nearly the same moment the next morning and packed up the camp. The dust of the prairie mingled with the predawn mist and the ever-present musk of grass. Thinking of his shared moment of peace from the previous evening, I mentioned the scent—one of my favorite things about the west—but he only grunted. More disappointment, alas. We swung onto our horses and were about to head along the blade's path when hoofbeats from the path we'd taken disturbed our precious silence.

We shared a glance—rueful, frustrated—and silently decided to turn and ride. If the riders were for us, well then, they could very well catch up. We'd not waste our few moments of serenity.

When Calla Remany and a Marshal resolved from formless figures in the golden light just before the whispers would begin, we shared a new glance, this one full of suspicion and doubt of the other. He clearly thought the same as me—a cheat? A fraud? A wanted person?

The Marshal rode up careful, hand poised near the low-slung holster. "Mornin' folks. You Garfield and Wilson?"

My companion tilted his head. "What of it?"

"Well," the Marshal said slowly, "the landlady at a boardin' house in town said one of you passed her some bills that turned out to be not quite legitimate. This lady here claimed to know you, offered to help me sort the situation."

Those warm brown eyes found mine, solemn as ever. I shifted on my horse, flushing furiously and avoiding her steady gaze. So, Garfield was a forger. It made sense—he'd needed resources to get out to the west, to find me. Without Father's luck and Mother's family, I might have been forced to play such loose games with the law.

Calla kept her eyes on me. Despite our never having said more than a few meager words between us, her presence had a kind of nostalgia to it, a comfort. The Marshal's gaze never left Garfield, hand ready to grab the pistol at his side. A standoff, no one speaking or moving.

Deciding, I rocked forward, drawing the eyes of all three to me. "I'm sure it was an error, but"—I held up my hand to forestall the arguments brewing all around—"I'm happy to pay whatever debt is owed for my companion."

"Now, wait a moment," said Garfield.

Calla's eyes narrowed and Garfield blustered.

I glared at him, then tilted my head to the ever-lightening eastern horizon. "Nonsense. Our business is too urgent to sort out what is, I'm sure, an honest mistake. Please, Marshal, how much?"

"Two dollars."

"Done. Please take five and apologize to Mrs. Humfreys for me. She was very kind."

The Marshal grunted and turned his horse away. I had the thought that the broad man was disappointed he hadn't gotten to draw his weapon after all. Calla eyed me for a moment longer, her hand fiddling with something in the pocket of her gingham. Garfield's eyes were on the Marshal's back, full of suppressed anger.

After a moment, Calla clicked her horse forward. "As it happens," she said, her voice like the sharp blade of a yucca spine. "I am riding this way as well. Do you mind the company?"

I winced. Garfield snorted and turned his horse. I gestured toward the path and she rode ahead of me. I exhaled and turned north, bracing myself for the whispers.

They did not disappoint, joining me just as we crested a ridge overlooking a long valley, perhaps eight miles wide from hill to hill. A herd of antelope numbering in the hundreds, even thousands, thundered across the low grasses. If it weren't for the whispering, it might have been an idyllic view, a view rapidly vanishing from the American landscape as mines and railroads and civilization pushed ever outwards.

Calla proved to be an amiable companion, speaking not at all during the day, whether because Garfield and I kept our peace or through some ingrained habit of her own I didn't know. Atop the ever-present musk of grass, she brought a hint of dried roses and lilacs to the air whenever the breeze moved through her hair. If nothing else, she ensured I took note of my surroundings more often than typical.

That evening, Garfield rolled into his blanket as soon as darkness silenced our silvery hauntings and we'd consumed some meager rations. Calla brought out a harmonica from her pack and, with a wink, breathed music into the night. Helpless against those brown eyes, lit only by muted flickers from the coals, I spent my night as captive as my day—no less haunted, but much more content.

We pushed for many days, riding north and then west until the west overtook the north and we wandered through hills and then mountains. Calla, when pressed about her destination, only looked at me and shrugged. "I'll know when I get there," she said. We moved ever closer in the dim light of our evening fires, until we sat with the cloth of our clothes brushing, until I could feel her breath in my ribs.

Garfield said nothing during the day and little at night. He'd been raised in New Orleans, he said. When I asked about his accent, he said his mother insisted he sound upper class. His father had spent all the money the family ever had.

Strange stories followed, sometimes contradictory. His father had been a miner's son from the west, but his grandfather owned a shipping company on the Mississippi. His grandmother was New Orleans born and bred, but she'd met his father in the Montana camps working as a seamstress. I decided the whispers left me confused at times, too, and let him have his stories. Calla told no such stories, keeping her words to the immediate. And yet, I felt I knew her far better than I did Garfield.

The further north we traveled, the more my anticipation grew. Freedom for me and my family could be over any horizon. Nine days after departing Mrs. Humfreys' boarding house in Sheridan, we found ourselves gazing into the black opening of an abandoned mineshaft.

'Granite Mine', the broken sign over the door read.

"At last," I said, glancing back to where Calla waited by our horses, out of hearing. "The knife points directly in." The last rays of sunlight faded from the hillside behind us and the world fell to still darkness.

"Tomorrow," said Garfield. "Let's rest tonight."

I wanted to argue—to be so close to the end and wait felt like torture, and I didn't know how he could face another dawn—but I'd gone along with all his other suggestions, and he'd kept us fed by hunting each day we rode. To fight now felt foolish, so I turned away from the mine.

He had his rifle pointed at me. The fading dusk light glowed golden along the barrel. "Very good," he said. "Now just hand over that knife and I won't have to pull this trigger."

"What are you talking about? You just said—"

"It doesn't matter what I said," he snapped, his northeast accent thicker than I'd heard it yet. "Hand over the blade."

I stepped back, closer to the mine's entrance. "Why?"

He shook the rifle and I twitched, fear punching into my chest as I realized he meant it and the violence in his eyes was no dream. "Just hand it over."

"You're going to go in alone?"

His eyes glistened. "Sure. I'll go in alone."

"And put the silver back?"

"Right. No need for both of us to go in and risk ourselves. I'll take care of everything."

Calla stepped from behind a juniper, a sleek pistol raised. In the fading light, her eyes glistened with a hard, cold hatred that transformed her lovely face. Her voice carried past me into the mine and echoed. "He's lying."

Garfield spun to her. I sank, trembling, into the dirt in front of the mine's entrance. My knees refused to support me anymore, and I could hardly blame them in a world that made so little sense.

"You must be the sister," Garfield said in a conversational tone. "I wondered."

Calla kept her gun up. "You killed my brother in cold blood."

"I've killed a lot of people's brothers. None of them were stupid enough to follow me."

"Yet. Besides, I have other reasons for being here," she said, and patted her vest.

I raised my head, realization striking me. "My parents said only the fork remained. My father thought he'd found them all." Before the madness, at least he'd had that.

Calla nodded. "And mine thought it was only our two, a spoon for me and a fork for Matthew, but didn't know where to return them." She tilted her head, a flash of sunset turning her smile golden. "I suppose I should thank you for bringing me here, in the end. Never would have found it without you."

"You're both dead," Garfield said. "Gimme what you got."

She laughed at him, brittle as burnt bread. "Not a chance. I will free my family."

I must have reacted because she sighed. "Your father, too?"

"Yes. Slowly over the years, the words and logic just left him." She nodded. "So, Garfield. You'll have to take us all into the mine with you."

He shook his head. "You leave your gun."

Calla laughed again. "You leave your gun."

I pushed myself to my feet. I'd been carrying the voices my whole life, and this man wanted to ensure they never left me, that they continued to haunt my father and prevent me from living my life? "Do you even hear them?"

He grinned and shook his head. "According to her brother"— he jerked his head at Calla—"only the families of those who stole the silver hear it. Figured I'd help myself. Pile of silver, already cast, just waiting in the mine."

My skin crawled at the callous mention of Calla's brother. "Fine. We'll all three go down. I'll carry a light and you two can carry your guns. Much good may they do you."

I lit a lantern and, pretending that the rifle that swung between Calla and I bothered me not at all, led the way into the mine. At first the walls were wide apart and well braced, but the further we descended into the damp and dark the more broken the boards and the frame holding up the ceiling. At last we came to a half-caved-in stretch. My heart hammered in my chest, the weight of the mountain above me bearing down on my spirit, but with two angry gun-bearing folk behind me, I pressed forward.

Another stretch had only enough room to crawl through, but onward and down we went, the press of earth and the smothering scent of dirt pressing into my nostrils and my lungs almost drawing tears from my eyes. Still the cavern went on, down and deeper into the earth. I focused on the hope that, somehow, we would stop him and the torture of my family would at last be ended and I would tell Calla how I couldn't bear to be parted from her side.

Whatever entity demanded the return of the silver, I wanted to be rid of it and move forward with life. We had not deserved such punishment—the families of mine owners and miners struggling to make a life for themselves in a new country. The unintentional damage the few dozen grandfathers had caused to the colony or the group or whatever awaited us had surely been repaid a dozen times over by the insanity of our fathers and their fathers.

We stopped at a dead end, the silence so complete I could hear my heartbeat. Most people would cringe from such emptiness, but something in me embraced it. Peaceful, quiet, alone. Life had been none of those things for me. Ahead of us, glistening tarnished in the weak light of the lamp, was a pile of silver. Forks and spoons and knives and pins and buckles and watches and bars and lumps and lamps and blades tossed one by one as each generation paid their debt, made the pilgrimage to this place.

We were the last, us three. The whispers promised. We were last.

Garfield exhaled. "Look at it all." He had his back to the wall, the rifle still clutched in his hand.

I shook my head. "You'd condemn so many to insanity and yourself, too, you know."

"Hey," he said, casting his voice to the broader cave as though the silver would listen, "I didn't steal it. I'm just here to make sure it doesn't go to waste."

"They've always insisted it all had to come back, completely." I reached into my vest and tossed my blade on the pile. A pulse of warmth went through me like a summer wind and I shivered in the cold absence of its passing.

Calla tossed a little silver spoon onto the pile. "Now you," she said.

He shook his head. "No."

"Oh, you can take the silver after," she said. "But first, free us. Put it all back. Then we won't care a bit for what you do."

I closed my eyes, hoping. I rather suspected the vengeful spirits wouldn't be so understanding, since we'd brought him along, but said nothing. I'd lived with the voices my whole life. What would it be like to suddenly have them start whisper-screaming into your very thoughts as a grown man? He wouldn't last a day.

Unfortunately, Mr. Garfield had paid better attention than I hoped. "No chance," he said. "I will put it back and release your families, but"—his raised finger stifled the hope sprouting in my chest—"you must carry this wealth for me until I can sell it."

I shared a glance with Calla, my skin sizzling with fear. "We'll lose our minds."

He shrugged. "I will not, and that is my concern." He shook his pistol. "It's that or I can bury you here with the treasure."

I shivered at the coldness in his voice. My father would be freed, but I would take his place. I thought of the fear in his eyes each dawn, the drained exhaustion when the sun at last dropped away. My grandfather had taken the silver without malicious intent, but I knew the cost. Shouldering the family burden, releasing my hopes and dreams of Calla, I met Garfield's eyes and nodded. Calla did as well. Garfield grinned.

"I'm not a cruel man." He tossed the little oyster fork onto the pile. "Just a poor one." He bent, reaching for a silver tea service.

The metal coalesced, sliding seamlessly, a river of silver in the dim light. Any tarnish vanished, the reflection so bright I blinked in the sudden illumination. A scent like overcooked cast iron teased my nostrils, my eyes watering with the power of it. The ground trembled.

"We are returned," said a slippery voice in my head. Slippery like teeth glancing off an open wound. Garfield shrieked, his hands on his ears. Calla and I stood still, eyeing the creature.

Vaguely man-shaped but only because it had limbs and a lump on the top that could have been a head, the creature had no discernable eyes or mouth—just a body. It took a thundering step forward, the dust shaking from the ceiling. Then another. It paused, expanding. "We are returned," it boomed aloud. "At last we are whole."

I took a deep breath. "I'm sorry."

Without moving, its attention shifted to me. "Sorry? For tearing myself from myself? The pain"—it hissed, twisted, screeched and all three of us squirmed away—"was unbearable."

"They didn't know," Calla said. "They couldn't have known."

The voice continued, scratching at my ears and within my mind. "I could take your parts from you, scatter them across the land. I've lived in your spirits and I know you would not survive it."

It expanded again, enormous and hulking. Waves of heat came from the creature, burning at my skin like a high noon sun, while in my mind the heat came from anger. Hot, intense fury.

I forced my body to stay still, to not cringe away from it. It had every right to be angry. "But we brought you back. We did everything we could. Once we knew, we returned."

It hesitated. Stopped growing. A cold wave rippled over the glistening surface. Within my mind, I heard a whispered, "Go. Now."

Distantly there was a cracking and then a crash and I whirled, eager to leave the mine behind. What an irony it would be to die just as I finished the job. Calla obviously had the same thought and abandoned the mine.

Garfield cried out. "No! The silver!" But the mountain rumbled and his bootsteps fell into place behind me. Calla ran just ahead of me, ducking under the trembling mineshaft ceiling, hands outstretched. We erupted into the valley just ahead of a great cloud of dust, Garfield on our heels.

I eyed the lightening sky to the east, setting the lamp down at my feet. "Now we find out."

"We returned it all," said Calla. "It said …" but she knew as well as I that liars abound. So we waited. Garfield sat with his head in his hands, muttering about lost wealth. I figured he'd have a story to tell, but nothing more. As foul as I found the man, we'd finished the job despite him.

The sun broke the eastern ridge. Braced, I closed my eyes and listened. A meadowlark in the distance. Wind in the aspens. A shifting rock beneath, deep in the mine. A sigh of relief, and then the sound of someone laughing, nearly hysterical. Not until the gunshot punctured the morning did I open my eyes.

Garfield stared at the hole in his chest with an open mouth. Calla stomped over to him and kicked the rifle from his trembling fingers. "Now my family is free," she said. She turned toward the dawn, her silhouette glowing in the silence. After a moment, she extended her hand to me. "Coming?"

I took one last look at Garfield's corpse. Then I stood and, my life ahead of me, kissed Calla in the quiet dawn.

JACARANDA HOUSE

BY SAMANTHA LOKAI

It wasn't long after my arrival at Jacaranda House that I began to wonder about Esmerelda Sorzano's real intentions for having me there. There was no tangible reason for this sudden onset of doubt, except for a feeling that seeped into me in the middle of the night. Whatever I had been dreaming of had faded from memory, but my body was slower to follow—breathless, heart pounding, and the lingering urge to run.

Esmerelda walked into my art studio almost a year to the day after I moved to El Cerro, and with her came a chill on that sweltering afternoon. Her greying hair was coiled into a tight bun in an effort to lift the years from her face, and her perfume—bitter and stale with age—burned my eyes and nose. She sauntered around, regarding my artwork, and ignored my attempt for conversation. Although we had never crossed paths before, I knew of the reclusive Sorzano woman and her son, and the elusive Jacaranda House.

The view from my window was of their house, isolated on El Cerro's peak and shrouded by low lying fog. It overlooked the village with a melancholic disenchantment and I developed a fascination for the place. There was something haunting about it; an allure that proved irresistible when Esmerelda Sorzano returned with a proposition.

Within days of our arrangement, I arrived at the Jacaranda estate. Although the main village was a mere few miles away, on the hilltop dense fog and slate grey clouds blotted out the Caribbean warmth. Jungle bordered the edges of the grounds, and its murky silhouette swelled with menace under the weakening daylight. Royal palm trees lined the pathway like stoical watchmen with their fern tops nodding in the strengthening wind. The air carried an oppressive intensity that was more than humidity—it held a gloominess to it that hung heavy over the house and land.

Night was closing in, ushering me forward with haste, and the way behind me fading fast with the last of the light. It was at that point I felt an urge to turn around and leave. I wondered if animals felt this fleeting burst of dread, an inner warning, right before they were trapped. And then, like those ill-fated creatures, I was lured by the sight suddenly before me. The Jacaranda House.

I couldn't help but regard the Sorzano's villa with awe. Without any recent images to be found, my curiosity had led me to paint my own. I contemplated the villa's appearance with the same reverie as I would with an original composition at an art gallery. Being an old cocoa estate, the villa was a mix of European architecture adapted to Caribbean climate and style. Two floors high, dark wooden jalousie windows, and lavish wood panels beneath a pitched gable roof made it stand out from the houses in the village. The ornate balustrading was entangled in vines of Heartleaf climbing across the stone walls and steps, their heart shaped leaves blackened and wilting from blight.

Jacaranda trees adorned the front of the villa with wide spreading branches stretching toward each other to form a sort of canopy. They had been the inspiration behind the house's namesake years ago when the estate was thriving. Throughout the passing of time, the trees had continued to flourish even after the demise of the Sorzano's land.

Esmerelda's struggling finances had been the reason I was invited to their house. Her need for money had forced her to consider auctioning the family's art collection. Unfortunately, some of the pieces had been damaged after being stored away and neglected. Esmerelda requested my services to restore the paintings. As much as I was happy with my decision to move to El Cerro, I wasn't earning enough with handmade greeting cards, portraits and the odd painting. She offered me a fair wage and I was eager for the opportunity to work with art of such caliber.

I must confess, it was also the house or rather my fixation toward it that lured me into accepting her offer. All of those nights spent looking at it from my window. Beguiling, under El Cerro's moonshine. Unaware I was being gazed upon too. Something was drawing me to Jacaranda House long before Esmerelda had made her offer.

I paused underneath the canopy of branches, the Jacaranda's violet blossoms glowed with the same purple and pink hues as the fading twilight sky. I was unsettled by its ethereal vibrancy against the dismal surroundings—a ruse to deceive me—one of many as I would learn in the coming days.

Each night I was tormented by the same dream. I dismissed it as anxiety over an unfamiliar bed and the eeriness of the place. It wasn't long till these night terrors stopped fading from memory. Instead, they were more like glimpses behind a veil, one that grew thinner the longer I stayed at the villa. A force was manifesting itself and I was aligning with its desires.

In these nightmares, I was in bed unable to speak or move my arms and legs. Something pressed hard against my chest, heavy like a stone slab, squeezing the air out of my lungs. I lay there choking for breath, my screams stifled to a whimper, beneath a blanket of coldness. Floating above me, a haze of black mist hissed and sighed with the wanton craving of a wild animal stalking its prey.

Sebastian and I met over a series of fleeting moments–glimpses of him exiting rooms as I approached, or gone by the time I reached the bottom of the stairs. Sometimes while I worked, I sensed a presence. I would look around the room for what I felt and couldn't see, but there was only the fluttering of curtains and the lingering of him. The rooms downstairs each had a doorway to the hallway and another to the next adjoining room. It often left me disoriented; a maze that allowed our game of hide and seek to continue.

One evening while working, I heard his footsteps linger at the doorway.

"You know, I'm beginning to think you're avoiding me," I said and continued to work my paintbrush without looking at him.

"I was beginning to think the same."

The hint of mischief in his tone made me smile. By the time I turned around, he was gone.

The next night, he stopped by the doorway again.

"Checking in on my progress again?" I asked him.

"It's fascinating to see the damage reversed and the paintings returning to their original form."

"It's a satisfying feeling, especially with pieces like these with so much history attached. Of course, that makes it more difficult in a way, the risk of messing it up."

"You're doing a fine job so far. It's an admirable talent."

"Well, I'm only following the original painter's vision. Besides, the damage is only minor."

"Still, it takes some skill to be able to do that."

"I have to admit, I feel a little like I'm deceiving people. It may look the same as the original after I'm done, but without the original artist, will it ever truly be? Maybe we should accept the cracks and discolorations of time rather than creating a delusion." I joked.

"So much of life is a delusion," he said lightly.

"That, I'd have to agree."

I desperately wanted to look around and meet his gaze. The brief silence that followed carried an intense anticipation. My heart pounded and my cheeks flushed.

"Good night, Sabrina." And with that, Sebastian Sorzano was gone.

On one particularly humid morning, the mugginess had filled the room until it was impossible to breathe. My sleep had been disturbed with the same dream again and I was exhausted and nauseated. I went for a walk in the back garden to get some air and stumbled upon an old greenhouse. It was surrounded by tall weeds and wild vines creeping across its frame. I should have been deterred by its decrepit appearance, but instead I was charmed by the building's pretty Victorian design and its whimsical presence against the wilderness.

Much to my curiosity, the interior was a contrast of well-maintained flower beds and plants neatly arranged. An enchantment of colorful blooms with delicate petals and sweet perfume.

I paused at a bouquet of burgundy black roses with tears of dewdrops weeping from their velvet petals and reached for one. Before I could pinch hold of a stem, a hand closed over mine.

"You can hurt yourself if you're not careful." Sebastian pointed to thorns under the rose's leaves. Dark eyes held mine, as enigmatic as the night sky and just as impossible to look away. His auburn hair curled in the humidity and under the mid-morning light his tanned skin shimmered with a sheen of perspiration. "It's easy to be lured in by their beauty only to suffer pain from their sharp little daggers." He smiled.

"Well, for these, it would be worth it."

He plucked a rose from the bunch, careful to avoid the thorns, and offered it to me. "Then, you deserve one."

The flowers in the greenhouse weren't your typical variety. Sebastian grew rare hybrids. I recalled it being mentioned in the village and would sometimes see the florist visit the estate every few months to make a collection. The flowers were left in crates at the entrance and payment was left in the post box. Sebastian always avoided the exchange and never went down to the village. It fueled gossip about his reclusive nature and many theories, some unsavory, as to why he avoided people. None of which were obvious to me, at least not yet.

After that day, we met at the greenhouse every sundown after I finished my work. Sometimes we talked for hours, other times we tended to the flowers together in quiet, stealing glances at each other. I looked forward to our time, and the greenhouse became a solace away from the gloominess of the villa, and his mother.

We kept a distance between us in the house. Although he never said it, he was weary of his mother and I suspected she wouldn't approve. She kept to herself and we barely spoke when she brought me my meals. Those brief encounters were enough to sense a strangeness to that woman and it made me uneasy. Sometimes I caught her staring at me or heard her footsteps pause at my bedroom door late at night. She seemed to begrudge my presence at Jacaranda House, and it made me wonder why she insisted I come.

I might have left had it not been for the change happening within me. My passion for art was alive again and I couldn't lose it. Each piece I worked on rekindled my love for painting. After losing both of my parents in a car accident a couple years ago, my desire to create art had been lost—along with a part of myself. El Cerro kept coming to mind during those dark days, calling to me. My happiest memories were the summers spent here with my parents. I craved the comfort of those times and hoped by returning, I would recapture my passion again. Restoring the artwork had ignited my desire to create.

At nights, I stayed awake for hours sketching ideas on paper. When I mentioned this to Sebastian, he joked that it must be the Jacaranda trees for they were known to represent rebirth. It was true, my spirit had awakened and as my creativity blossomed, so did my feelings for Sebastian. Unknown to me, however, there were things stirring within Jacaranda House that threatened to destroy everything.

I was up late in my bedroom, sketching by moonlight when I overheard arguing between Esmerelda and Sebastian. Even though I couldn't make out what they were saying, I got a feeling it was over me. Earlier that evening she was waiting for us when we returned from the greenhouse. She didn't say anything, she didn't need to. Sebastian's whole demeanor changed around her. His posture stiffened and he was suddenly cold toward me, avoiding my eyes as he excused himself. I was left wondering what happened to bring on such a switch in his personality. It wasn't the first time he reacted this way with me when his mother was close.

Their voices grew louder, footsteps stormed out of the house and the front door slammed. Sebastian was hurrying across the back yard toward the greenhouse. I went to him, slipping out quietly and keeping hidden in the shadows. The air was potent with the Jacaranda's sweet scent and the petals showered down on me, clinging to my nightgown as I meandered through the dark. Sebastian was pacing around the greenhouse, wild eyed and frantic upon seeing me.

"You shouldn't be here."

"I-I'm sorry. I didn't mean to intrude."

"No, I mean you can't be here at the villa anymore. You need to leave, Sabrina. While you still can. If you don't …"

"Sebastian, slow down."

"Listen to me, Sabrina, you have to get away from this place. Tomorrow the florist will be here to make a collection. You can get a ride back to the village."

"What? I still have a couple more days of work to do. Why are you acting this way? You don't want me here?"

"It's not that." He shook his head.

"Is it your mother? Is she not happy with the paintings? Why hasn't she spoken to me about it herself?"

He held me by the shoulders. "You need to get away without her knowing."

"Sebastian, you're not making sense." My cheeks burned. "If I've done something wrong …"

"Once you return to the village, don't ever come back here … it's not safe." His tone was solemn.

"Not safe?" I searched his face.

"You have to trust me."

"Then leave with me tomorrow. If you had an argument with your mother, we can talk about it away from here. I'm sure you're overreacting."

"I can't come with you." He faced away from me.

"If you're that worried, why aren't you driving me away from here right now?"

"I wish I could, but I can't." His bowed his head.

My voice was unsteady. "Can't or don't want to! Are you having doubts about what's happening between us? Is that why you want me to leave? Is it because your mother doesn't approve of us? You could try being honest with me instead of being a coward!"

Sebastian grabbed my hand and spun me around as I was leaving. He stared into my eyes; his expression pained. "That's not it. I wish I could go with you far away from this wretched place! But I can't. The moment I walk beyond this estate … my heart stops. I can't ever leave here, Sabrina. I'm bound to remain here forever. I would die if I left."

"Wh-what? How can something like that be possible?"

"My mother." Sebastian's face reddened. "She can't bear the thought of me leaving her or Jacaranda House." His posture deflated and he looked away. "Mama wanted me to take over the estate after Father passed, but I refused. My dream was to be a journalist. I was offered an internship with one of the big newspapers in the main town and planned on moving out of El Cerro. Mama was hysterical. She made all sorts of threats and even got it in her head that I was doing all of this because of a woman. I didn't know how far she would go to stop me."

Dread filled my stomach. "What did she do?"

"She worked Obeah over me. Now I'm bound to this place forever. My heart weakens and stops beating whenever I set foot outside of the premises."

El Cerro carried a mystic undercurrent I always felt. Hushed whispers of things that couldn't be explained circulated around the village from as long as I could remember, including Obeah–the Caribbean's oldest, darkest magic. I believed Sebastian was telling the truth and as his words sunk in, I sensed there was much more to me being here.

"Sebastian, there has to be a way out of this. We can figure it out."

His eyes darkened. "I meant what I said, Sabrina. You need to get away from here."

"Why? Is she planning something?" Whatever it was, I wasn't afraid of Esmerelda.

"I don't know for sure. But she knows I have feelings for you and I'm afraid of what she'll do."

"You have feelings for me?" My heart skipped a beat.

He paused and his face softened. "From the moment I saw you."

"You barely said a word to me when I first arrived," I arched my eyebrows.

"It was long before you came to Jacaranda House." His cheeks flushed. "You were at your place in the village."

"In the village? But how were you able to leave?"

"One night I was at my lowest, the torture of being trapped here with my mother for the rest of my life was unbearable. I went beyond the estate into the jungle, prepared to die." He lowered his eyes.

"Sebastian." I whispered and cupped his face.

"I tried escaping in the past and it was always the same when I approached the end of the property–my chest tightened with twisting daggers of pain and I struggled to breathe. That night, I found myself walking further and further away without my body rebelling. The jungle was bathed in the full moon's silver light and I was compelled to keep walking. Whenever I stumbled into shadows, the curse took hold until I moved back into the moonlight.

"It must be true what the villagers say. El Cerro's full moon holds a strange kind of magic." I looked up at the sky peeking through the moss-stained glass of the green house. There was no full moon tonight much to my disappointment.

Sebastian clasped my hands and pulled me closer. "The trail through the jungle led me to a clearing across from your place. That's when I saw you at your window painting by moonlight in the midnight hours. Each time, I was drawn to walk that same path and at the end of it there was always you."

I thought back to those nights when the moon was full and how I would gaze upon Jacaranda House on the hill, and my compulsion toward it. "I think I felt you on those nights."

"You were the reason I kept on going, even from afar. When you came here to the house, I thought it had to be Fate." He clenched his jaw. "Until I realized my mother must know. And it's why you must go, Sabrina. You're in danger."

"I'm not afraid of your mother." I said through gritted teeth.

"This is all my fault." He pulled jacaranda blossoms from the strands of my hair. They shimmered in the moonlight and fluttered to the ground.

I hushed his lips with my fingers and he kissed my fingertips. We fell silent, our eyes lost in each other's. I slid my other hand up his chest and around the back of his neck into his tousled hair. He pulled me closer until our bodies were pressing against each other. Hot breaths caressing each other's skin. I brushed my lips against his neck, tasted the salt on his skin and inhaled the sweet scent of rose. He resisted, until my mouth found his. He was mine and I was his.

We lay on the floor, tangled in old blankets and each other, the smell of newly bloomed flowers clung to our bare skin. Gusts of wind whipped outside, rattling the doors and glass panes of the greenhouse with urgency, a reminder that it was time to part for the night. We got dressed and ran through drizzling rain back to the house and Sebastian bid me goodnight at my bedroom door. He was terrified of what his mother was capable of. He pleaded with me to consider returning home tomorrow with the promise that he we would come to me in the village when the moon was full.

The next day, I woke up feverish and barely able to move. I drifted in and out of consciousness with the sound of tinnitus ringing in my ear. The air hummed with a rising turmoil that I felt across my skin and in my gut. Dragging myself out of bed, I stumbled out of the house and into the yard, calling to Sebastian.

A hush had settled over the estate. Clouds of sea mist hung stagnant and every leaf and flower were subdued into stillness. As still as an image on canvas. Above me, black clouds gathered across an ashen sky and a flock of corbeaux circled with menace. These large black vultures preyed on animals that were on the verge of death, ready to swoop in and feed on their dead carcass. My flesh prickled with goose bumps.

The ground was littered with fallen Jacaranda flowers and as the petals melted with decay, their scent turned foul and bitter. A lone gust of wind rushed past and a wooden swing swayed and squeaked on rusty chains. Except, it wasn't the wind. It was the shadow that had tormented me in my nightmares. Was I asleep now? Was this a hallucination? The corbeaux cawed and scattered into the jungle where the black mist descended into the foliage.

My body convulsed, my vision blurred, and my will was no longer my own. I was compelled by an unseen force to walk into the jungle. Wild branches scratched my skin and tore into my nightgown. My limbs twisted and twitched and I felt like they would snap and mangle if I tried to resist. The pressure of my trapped screams made my eyes and head feel like they would burst.

I came to an abandoned hut once used by the cocoa workers to shelter from the sun on their breaks. It had a crooked roof on four trunk posts and only one wall at the back. I collapsed onto the dirt no longer propelled by whatever had brought me there. Flambeaus made from glass bottles filled with pitch-oil and old rags were lit and arranged around a circle of stones. Esmerelda was standing in the middle holding one. Her face was hardened like stone and her pupils large and black like coal. In her other hand were various talismans and herbs all tied together with twine, including a lock of my hair that she used to control my body to come to her.

"What have you done to me?" I sat up.

"Stop resisting child. Close your eyes and let your body surrender to sleep. It will be easier if you do." She started sprinkling a mixture of powder and leaves. "It's time."

"Time? What are you planning to do, you crazy old hag! It was never about the paintings, was it? You tricked me into coming. Why did you bring me here?"

She bared her teeth in a callous smile. "I never wanted you at Jacaranda House. I had no choice. There's things about this place that outsiders wouldn't understand."

"You mean things like the Obeah you worked over your own son. How could you do that to him? Keeping him here with you like a prisoner!"

"He belongs here with me. I did it to protect him."

"What you did was cruel!"

She lowered her head in silence for a moment.

"I couldn't let him throw his life away back then and I won't let him now either. When Sebastian suggested we restore and sell the paintings, I wondered how he came up with such an idea so unexpectedly. Then I saw you at your art shop one day and my suspicions grew. I saw him cross over into the jungle one night. I suppose it was only a matter of time he worked out that he could leave under the full moon's protection. I followed him to the edge of the jungle to your place and it suddenly all made sense. Stupid boy, it was a hasty suggestion he never really thought through and I doubt he expected you to come work here at the house."

"Why didyou really bring me here? I didn't think you'd want me anywhere near him."

"It was a small price to pay if it meant getting rid of you for good. I couldn't risk his infatuation controlling him that way. It was

Fate how it all came together. You should be happy you're doing this for us ... for Sebastian."

"Doing what?" My eyes darted around me.

Esmerelda stared out at the estate. "We need more than money to upkeep this land. It's hungry." She lowered her eyes.

Her tone unsettled me. What other horrors had this woman inflicted.

"Working an Obeah spell for a curse that powerful proved to be more complicated than the harmless charms for luck in love and money. I had to draw upon the darkest of magic and in doing so, summoned an evil spirit into our home. For the curse to be upheld, this malevolent force needed to sustain its power by drawing off a source, so it took hold of the land. I regretted what I did, but by then it was too late and couldn't be reversed. It drew from the estate's life-force to maintain the curse over Sebastian, until there was nothing left."

It had never been disease or blight that devoured the Jacaranda estate of life, but a force far more sinister. "But there's nothing left of this land. It's barren of life?" The look on Esmerelda's face told me everything I needed to know. An icy chill snaked its way through me.

"Now you understand why I brought you here. The land is gone and the spirit needs a new source. I can feel it taking hold of me. If I don't find a way to stop it from using me, I'll perish like my plantation."

Its poison was already running through her, slowly rotting away her sanity. Someone else needed to take her place and she intended for that person to be me. I thought of my night terrors and of the dark shadow, and how it had been stalking me. Waiting for its next prey.

"N-no. You can't do this," my voice trembled. I flinched at the stone circle where Esmerelda planned to sacrifice me, panic rising with my every breath.

"Sabrina!"

It was Sebastian. He was hunched over, clutching his chest and panting.

"Sebastian? Stop! If you come any further, you'll cross the boundary."

Esmerelda knew bringing me over the property line would keep Sebastian away from me.

"I won't let her hurt you." He turned to his mother "I heard everything, Mama."

"Then you know I did it all for you."

"For me? By keeping me here trapped like an animal and inviting evil into our home? You damned us to hell after you meddled in this ... *Obeah* thing! You had no business messing with that kind of black magic."

She shook her head. "Don't you get it, boy! Maybe evil was already here. This house has always had something running through it. We all felt it."

"Mama, what you're doing is wrong. Let her go." He panted.

"I can't do that. Our land won't survive ... and neither would I!"

"Then so be it! This has to end now. What happens in another few years when this spirit needs another source to sustain itself? You can't keep sacrificing innocent people."

Esmerelda lowered her head. "It's all we have. I can't let it go to ruin. I've kept it going after your father passed. Don't you see? Everything is just like it was when he was here ... it's like he's still with us. As long as I keep things the same ... he's still with us." Her voice was hollow.

"Open your eyes and look around you, Mama!" Everything *has* changed! The estate is in ruins. And so is my life! The land has deteriorated ... and so have you." Tears rolled down his cheeks.

She bowed her head and began to sob. Sebastian's words were reaching her. For a fleeting moment her features softened. Esmerelda seemed to be surfacing out of the darkness that was controlling her. She tried to resist, until it was too strong, and with a guttural wail that echoed through the jungle, she was lost to it.

Her pupils enlarged to cover the whites of her eyes as she began to whisper in a different language and work the string of objects. My body convulsed and moved into the middle of the stone circle against my will. The force was too strong and I couldn't fight it. The smell of kerosene burned my nose as Esmerelda sprinkled it along the stones.

"Mama! Stop! Please!" Sebastian shouted.

"Sebastian, your mother's gone!" I shouted in between sobs. "It's taken possession over her."

He dashed forward toward the hut, but once he crossed over into the jungle he started wheezing and pain pierced his chest. I could see the veins bulging along his neck and reddening across his eyes.

"Sabastian! Don't! You can't!" I begged him.

Esmerelda no longer cared what happened to her son and continued in her trance-like state. She was nothing more than a vessel now. She touched a lit flambeau onto the stones and flames encircled me. Sebastian was on his hands and knees, crawling toward me, his heart slowing with each move forward. I fought against my paralysis but it was useless. The flames strengthened and the heat burned my skin. Strong winds rushed around me and a shadow settled over my head. My body was growing weaker as the life force syphoned out of me.

Sebastian was on his stomach, unable to come any further. He grabbed a stone in one final attempt and threw it at Esmerelda. It hit her on the back of her head and she fell. The pause in her chanting broke my paralysis and I collapsed as the flames lowered to a flicker. I stumbled upright and stepped over the fire. Sebastian was motionless on the ground. Before I could get to him, Esmerelda grabbed my ankle and I tripped over.

She reached for the chain to resume her control over me. I dragged her backward and retrieved it, then tossed it into the fire. Enraged, she began to summon the spirit with an incantation and I knew I was in grave danger. I looked around the hut in frantic desperation for a way to stop her. The can of kerosene she had used earlier was behind me and I drenched her with it, knowing what I had to do. When she came toward me, I pummelled into her with everything I had, and pushed her into the ring of fire. Esmerelda cracked her head against a large stone in the middle of the circle and then burst into flames.

Sebastian wasn't breathing and I couldn't find a pulse. He was gone.

I cradled his head while repeating his name, tears flowing while I wept. My heart ached knowing that he sacrificed himself in trying to save me. I wished I never came to this wretched place. If I hadn't fallen for Esmerelda's wicked tricks, he might still be alive. We would never have met and I wouldn't know the unbearable agony of losing him. Then, the moments we shared flashed through my mind and I remembered how he made me feel. Although our time was short, I cherished the memory of us and I was grateful to have had it than not.

"I love you, Sebastian," I kissed him. As our lips touched, gusts of wind rustled the tree tops and fallen leaves whirled around us. The corbeaux swarmed out of the jungle, peppering the sky, and shrieking. It was nearing twilight and the storm clouds were parting.

Sebastian's eyes fluttered opened.

"Sebastian?"

It took him a moment to fully wake.

"I thought you were ..." I wrapped my arms around him.

"Sabrina!" He coughed. "Thank goodness you're safe. Where's mother?"

I shook my head and looked down, tears streaming down my face. "She's gone. Sebastian, I'm so sorry."

He squeezed my hand. "She was already gone." He mourned the loss of his mother, but accepted she had been lost to him for a much longer time.

Esmerelda was right, there was always a darkness imbedded in their home. When she practiced black magic, she lifted a veil and invited it in. Her malice had been the catalyst for it to take root.

Had she not fostered such a dark heart, the spirit never would have manifested.

"We need to get you back behind the boundary. Hurry!" I said, remembering the curse.

He paused. "I-I don't feel it." He stood up. "I think it's gone, Sabrina."

"You can't be sure. We have to get you back," I pleaded, not wanting to risk losing him again.

He walked further away. "I don't feel it anymore!" He started laughing. "The curse is gone. It's over, Sabrina." He lifted me off the ground in an embrace.

The death of Esmerelda brought an end to the curse. Or maybe it was true love's kiss. Sebastian was no longer bound to his mother or Jacaranda House. She had been the conjurer of the spell and now that she was gone so was the debt to the dark spirit. Without the curse to uphold, the spirit no longer needed to sustain itself from a source.

We paused at the Jacaranda trees—new buds formed which was unusual for the time of year.

"It's incredible how these trees have withstood the disease and blight. They somehow survived against the odds." I paused to admire them.

"Behind its delicate beauty, the Jacarandas have a strong core. I think that anything with such light and resilience can overcome all darkness. Some people too." He winked.

I held his gaze. "You've proven that to be true."

There was still so much we didn't understand. Things that were not of our world could never fully be explained or understood. Only time would tell if the dark entity was truly gone for good or was it merely waiting to manifest itself again. Sometimes I wake up in the middle of the night and I think I can still feel it, a quiet stirring, within the walls of Jacaranda House.

DESIRE SO FULMINANT

BY GERALDINE BORELLA

I rode out for Grimsheath as soon as I received the letter from Dr. Percy Foster. I was to be his second-in-charge, with a view to taking over the practice upon his retirement, which I hoped was as imminent as he proclaimed. Ambition in a man, my father insisted, was admirable, and I don't mind admitting that succession drove my desire above anything else. Certainly above living in Grimsheath.

I reined my horse in, perched upon a rise approaching town, and looked over my new home. The desolate day helped little—the grey clouds so low I could reach out and pocket one—but despite the weather, I could tell Grimsheath was named with apt consideration. It was not my preferred place of existence, and decidedly different to the descriptions provided by Dr. Foster.

Still, I was there for work, and sick people abound in all sorts of towns, whether gay by appearance or grim.

Dr. Foster's residence was on the edge of the village, which was one consolation. At least I might gaze over woodland, albeit foreboding and dark, instead of broken-down huts, grotty stores, and muddied roads. The house was large, with a weatherboard exterior, numerous sash windows, and one chimney stack projecting from the roof. I hoped it would be warm but feared it might not, noting the temperature drop considerably on my way into the valley.

"Ah, Dr. Wood!" said Dr. Foster. He greeted me at the door, instructing a servant to attend to my horse. "I hope you travelled well."

"I did, thank you." I nodded at Dr. Foster, while removing my hat. The man gestured to a young lady standing by. "May I present my daughter, Isabella. Isabella, my new charge, Dr. Kingsley Wood."

I bowed and she nodded. An attractive young lady of rosy complexion, intense violet eyes, and shining raven hair swept up in the latest fashion, she was nonetheless dressed in a rather sombre black taffeta dress with lace collar. It struck me as mourning attire, though I felt it too impertinent to enquire and confirm it so. There was no mother in attendance and I wondered if perhaps Dr. Foster's wife had passed recently. It would certainly explain the matter of her dress.

"Dr. Wood," she said. "I'm pleased to make your acquaintance, and I hope you will enjoy your time here in Grimsheath."

"I'm certain I will. Thank you, Miss Foster."

"Please," she said. "If we are to live together, I should like you to call me Isabella."

I nodded, despite the impropriety of the request.

"And I shall call you?" she asked, eyebrows raised.

"Dr. Wood," I replied. One side of her mouth twitched as she failed to stifle a somewhat facetious smile.

"Indeed," she said. "Dr. Wood, it is then."

Dr. Foster cleared his throat, then said, "Well then, come along, Wood."

After a tour of the house and surgery, I was shown to my room and allowed time to unpack. It occurred to me, as I sat on the bed in my attic room, bouncing up and down to test the acceptability of the mattress and springs, that perhaps Dr. Foster expected more from me than I'd thought. Perhaps he wanted me to take up the position of son-in-law as well as second-in-charge. I can't say I was too happy about the notion.

At dinner, Dr. Foster detailed his current area of research—respiratory medicine.

"I had a cadaver delivered this morning and I plan to investigate the lungs."

I pressed my napkin to my lips and tried not to choke on the forkful of peas I'd just swallowed. "A cadaver, you say?"

"Yes, indeed, and fear not, man. It was procured by legal means, an unclaimed body from a workhouse. No grave rob or body snatch has been carried out. And I have an anatomist licence as per the Warburton Anatomy Act. It's all above board, I assure you."

I glanced at Isabella, who chewed on her roast potatoes, unaffected by the rather grotesque dinner conversation. It disturbed me, I must admit, making me even less receptive to her. My mother and my sister, Lucy, would be horrified to hear such a topic discussed, especially whilst dining.

Noting my attention, she set down her cutlery and gestured at the tureen of roast turkey. "More meat, Dr. Wood?"

"No, I've had more than enough, thank you."

Dr. Foster smiled at his daughter in obvious adoration and pride. "Isabella is a tremendous help. She's knowledgeable in many aspects of medicine. A steady head in the toughest of crises. I expect you'll find her just as valuable, Wood."

I nodded, but did not reply. Never a man to be pushed, especially not in matters of the heart, I took exception to the attempts they were making in the hopes of leading me to a matrimonial match. Mother had oft remarked upon my picky and independent nature, calling me far too stubborn for my own good. I suppose it's those qualities that made me take steps back from Isabella Foster. The more I felt her forced upon me, the more I demurred.

Dr. Foster broke the uncomfortable silence. "We shall be visiting Lady Clementine at Ashthorne House tomorrow morning. She suffers from a particularly bad case of emphysema. I visit her second daily."

"For dry cupping?"

"Indeed, and to administer an emetic."

I nodded. So far we were on the same page with regards to medical treatment. That was heartening.

"She's the wife of Julian Ashthorne Esquire, recently deceased."

"Oh, I see."

"He was killed in a hunting accident. Shot in the head."

"Tragic."

"It was. He's survived by his wife and their daughter, Emelia."

"She's rather odd," said Isabella, leaning over the table and saying the words as though she knew she shouldn't, but couldn't help it anyway. It did not endear her to me in the slightest. Decent folk know little can be gained from loose tongues with spiteful intent.

I refused to reply and she mistook my silence for interest.

"Though she did see her father fall and suffer that self-inflicted gunshot wound."

"Self-inflicted?" I said, despite my intention to ignore her.

"Yes," said Dr. Foster. "He fell from his horse as it jumped over a log. He lost his gun in the doing and it went off."

"That *is* an awful business."

"Indeed," said Isabella. "And it could explain her strange behaviour, I suppose."

"Hmm," I said. My mind raced, opening doors to the imagination and heart, as I pictured the tragic Emelia Ashthorne and was swamped by an overwhelming sense of sympathy. It's safe to say I was smitten before I'd even locked eyes upon her.

Dr. Foster and I rode to Ashthorne House in the morning as planned, a good ten minutes south of town. I don't know what I thought I'd find but it certainly wasn't the dark port-wine coloured brick manor I came upon. It had turrets, peaks and arches, and many a window for a servant to clean, though servants appeared to be lacking. Everything was highlighted in black brick, the shingled roof also of a dark colour. I would call it grand but in no way inviting. My tastes—if ever I should own a country manor—erred towards light sandstone with fountains out front, a hedged maze and pretty flower gardens, but the gardens of Ashthorne House were choked with goosegrass and thistle, and the dark house did little to inspire. It overlooked a pond, a rather unattractive body of murky water filled with hyacinth and pondweed.

"It's gone downhill since Lord Julian died and Lady Clementine took ill," noted Dr. Foster, as he handed his reins over to the stable boy. He'd obviously seen my concern and felt it necessary to explain.

"I see," I replied, feeling all the more sympathy for the young lady discussed last night. *First the death of her father and now she contends with a sickly mother and a decaying estate.*

"The patient's disease state I'd classify as fulminant. It came on rather suddenly and has escalated quickly."

"Sounds very serious."

"Yes, I'm doing all I can to keep her alive."

I handed the reins of my horse to the stable boy as well, and glanced up at the house. A young lady peered down upon us from a third storey window, her complexion so fair as to be ghostlike and her hair the white-blonde of a dove. Was it Lady Emelia? I couldn't say but she wore a pink dress, not the uniform of a lady's maid or sensible attire of a housekeeper.

We were met at the door by the butler, Roberts, and shown to the drawing room.

"I shall see if Lady Clementine is ready to receive you," he said.

"Thank you, Mr Roberts," said Dr. Foster.

We'd brought our doctor's bags and clutched onto them, waiting in awkward silence. The room was lined in equal part with walnut panelling and deep magenta wallpaper, the wide floorboards also of dark walnut. Brown leather furniture sat upon large Persian rugs in magenta and navy, and thick curtains guarded the windows, blocking the light like valiant soldiers. The fireplace was ornately moulded in curlicues, the mantle inhabited by holy crosses alone, and the ceiling painted with a skilful reproduction of Rubens's *Massacre of the Innocents*. An amazing piece of artwork, but the slaughter of mothers and infant sons, bodies run through with blades, felt disturbing in a room of reception, a place meant for polite discourse.

Not a touch of femininity was displayed, which made me wonder at the character of Lady Clementine Ashthorne. I imagined a pious, matronly woman who paid little attention to frivolity and cheer. I wasn't far wrong.

When we were shown to her bedroom, a space not dissimilar in decoration and atmospheric gloom to the drawing room, she was in bed propped up on pillows, attended by a maid. She breathed fast and shallow, in obvious distress. Her light brown hair, streaked with grey, was pulled back into a severe bun and she had the downturned mouth of a woman who's seen little pleasure in life and expects the same for others.

"It's getting worse," she said, in between breaths, bypassing greetings and introductions. That, at least, was to be expected. Most emphysemic patients conserve energy and breath for conversational necessities alone. She was in the midst of opening mail, an ornate silver letter-opener at her side. Her maid removed the items, stepping back, and the letter-opener clattered to the floor. I picked it up, noting the intricate metal rook at the base of the handle.

"Thank you, sir," said the maid, as I handed it over.

"I'm sorry to hear your suffering is worse," said Dr. Foster, replying to Lady Ashthorne. Then, he gestured at me. "This is my new offsider, Dr. Wood."

"Pleased to meet you, Lady Ashthorne," I said.

She grunted in reply and Dr. Foster and I set to work, her maid, Lottie, assisting.

"Hand me the infusion of digitalis, Wood. I'll give her some to calm the heart."

"Indeed," I said, and he took this moment to instruct— unnecessarily I might add—on the correct administration of digitalis given its narrow therapeutic window and propensity for toxicity. I'd seen enough digitalis poisoning in my years of practice— mostly by those who knew little of the drug and extracted it from foxgloves in the garden for every malady under the sun—to know its deleterious effects. Still, I listened to show respect to a more experienced colleague.

During the dry cupping procedure, a loud banging could be heard upstairs, as though someone hammered upon a door with the palm of their hand. I glanced at the ceiling.

Lady Clementine huffed, frustrated by the commotion, and before long, a young lady dressed in pink—the white-haired waif I'd seen in the window—burst into the room carrying a small Pomeranian puppy.

"Mother, you're being attended to. Good," she said.

Lottie stiffened and scowled, appearing to become almost proprietorial of her mistress, stroking her hand.

"I am," said Clementine, portioning words and struggling to breathe.

The young lady met my gaze and said, "I'm Lady Emelia Ashthorne. And you are …?"

Dr. Foster spoke in my place, before I could muster a reply. "This is Dr. Kingsley Wood, my new charge."

"Pleased to meet you, Dr. Wood. It's nice to see a fresh face around here." She smiled. "A handsome one at that."

Lady Clementine coughed, almost choking, and glared at her daughter. In response, Lady Emelia pleaded, a sincere desperation reflected in her sea-green eyes.

"Please tell me you can do something for my dear mother, for she suffers so."

"We're trying, Lady Emelia," said Dr. Foster. "Doing our utmost best."

"I couldn't bear to be all alone in this monstrosity of a house. First my dear brother, Myles, then my father, and now Mother too? It's all too much for one person to contend with."

Her brother, Myles?

Clementine Ashthorne managed to yell, in between coughing and spluttering and dragging air into her lungs with a frightening wheeze. "Do not ... speak of your ... brother!" Her face went a dreadful shade of purple-red, spit spooling from her lips.

"Now, now, madam," said Dr. Foster, trying to calm her down. Lottie continued caressing her mistress's hand, while shooting evil glares at Lady Emelia.

Lady Clementine pointed at the door. "Get her ... out of here!" She turned and begged her maid. "Lottie ... do what you must."

The utter sadness on Lady Emelia's face pulled at my heartstrings as Lottie hustled her to the door, grabbing her roughly by the arm and leading her away. I heard footsteps on the stairs and on the floor above, and a door slammed.

Has the maid wheedled her way into Lady Clementine's favour, taking the place of her daughter? I'd seen such a thing happen on deathbeds before, the wealthy patient swindled by a close friend or servant hoping for inheritance, and I resolved to watch Lottie with keen scrutiny thereafter.

When the treatment was complete, Dr. Foster and I took our leave and rode back to town.

The rest of the day was spent tending to sprained joints, injuries of the eye, and a case of dysentery. Late afternoon we were in Dr. Foster's surgery, elbow deep in human vivisection, examining the lungs of the recently delivered cadaver. The poor fellow had worked in the mines, by the looks. We could see from the black stains and diminished lung capacity.

At dinner, I enquired about Emelia Ashthorne's brother, Myles.

"They've dealt with their fair share of death, the Ashthornes," said Dr. Foster as he dished green beans onto his plate. "Myles died at the age of six, drowned in the pond on the estate."

"How dreadful."

"Indeed. He was found by Emelia, and fished out by his father, but it was all too late by then."

"Lady Clementine turned to religion for solace. She's very devout," added Isabella, as she passed the bowl of beans to me.

I wasn't surprised to hear it, after noting the religious iconography on display in Ashthorne House—the artwork throughout and holy crosses mounted over every doorway.

"Did you meet Lady Emelia?" asked Isabella.

"Yes, we became acquainted, but only for a short time."

"Lady Clementine did not want her in the room," explained Dr. Foster.

Isabella gave a small laugh—an uncharitable reaction to the young woman's plight. "They've always had a fractious relationship, those two."

I held my tongue, wondering how she might respond to others passing judgement on her own familial relations. Indeed, her cold heart—given she herself had no mother and *should* be in a position to empathise with someone on the brink of losing theirs—astounded me.

"Lottie hunted her out," said Dr. Foster, as he cut up a chunk of leathery beef in his stew.

"Good old loyal Lottie," said Isabella. "I must catch up with her sometime. See how she's coping with Lady Clementine's sorry state. She'll be terribly upset."

I focussed on my meal to hide my astonishment. The utter disregard of a young lady in emotional distress, in favour of her scheming servant, froze my heart towards Isabella Foster more than any matrimonial coercion ever could.

When I retired to my room that night, I lay in bed and pondered the tragic situation of Lady Emelia. All alone—in physicality and spirit—in a dismal manor house, surrounded by nothing but space and cold indifference. How could I not feel sorry for her?

A flush spread across my face as I remembered her remarking upon my looks. Her comment was immodest, though touching, and I couldn't help but imagine us striding the long corridors and staircases of Ashthorne House, she on my arm, gazing up with desire: her protector, her guide, her love. Such were the peculiar, though ardent, machinations of my mind, leading to surprisingly vivid and heated dreams.

I arose after one in particular, my body acting in wanton ways, and made for the kitchen to slake my thirst. As I stood at the sink, gulping water and groaning, I was startled to see movement to my left. It was Isabella, seated by the hearth, dressed in her nightgown, the glow silhouetting her body and leaving me in no uncertainty as to what lay beneath. I'm ashamed to admit that the sight of her womanly curves sparked my desire anew.

"I'm terribly sorry," I mumbled, bowing my head and averting my gaze.

"You have nothing to be sorry for," said Isabella. "I couldn't sleep, just like you." She nodded at a chair. "Why don't you take a seat and tell me all about your family home in Cornwall and about your siblings?"

"No, I think it's best I leave," I said, making for the door.

"There's no need, really. Not on my account."

I chanced one last glance in her direction, against better judgement, and noted that vexing twitch to her mouth again, as she stifled a knowing smile. It hastened my departure; I did *not* wish to be caught in a compromising position with the scheming woman, for my own sake as well as hers.

My next trip out to Ashthorne House was solo, Dr. Foster entrusting me with the care of Lady Clementine whilst he continued his research with the cadaver. I must admit to a level of excitement at going there on my own. I'd like to think it was due to the trust Foster had placed in me, but secretly I knew it was more to do with the prospect of catching another glimpse of Lady Emelia.

I treated Lady Clementine as per my previous visit with Dr. Foster, her maid Lottie once more in attendance, and then was shown to the door. Disappointed not to see Lady Emelia, I wondered where she might be. Was she alright?

Mounting my horse, I urged her forward into a trot, but reined her in as soon as I saw the young lady in question, sobbing by the banks of the murky pond. She rocked back and forth on her knees, holding something to her chest. What it was, I could not say, but I leapt off my horse and hurried over.

"Lady Emelia, whatever is the matter?" I asked, approaching from behind. When I got close, I gasped to see what she clung onto. It was a puppy, lying dead and bloodied in her hands, Lady Clementine's rook-handled letter-opener speared right through its tiny body.

"Oh my," I said, sinking to my knees beside her. There was little I could do for the poor creature. Its body was cold and stiff, its soul long departed.

"My precious Jasper," she sobbed, still holding the pup close to her chest. The blood of the small creature stained the front of her dress. "Who could have done such a thing?"

"Someone with access to this letter-opener, I suspect," I said, unnecessarily.

"It's Mother's," she cried, swiping at her tears. "She's never liked Jasper, hated him yipping and scratching her floors, but to do something like this …?" She shook her head. "No, but it can't have been her. It doesn't make sense. I can't imagine her having the strength or stamina to complete such a dreadful task."

"Would she have instructed her maid to do it perhaps?" I ventured.

Emelia tilted her head and thought on it for a moment, then said, "It's possible. When I'm unable to leave my room, Lottie collects Jasper to relieve himself outside. She could have done it then."

She began to sob again, then fixed her glassy sea-green gaze upon me. I offered her my handkerchief and she accepted it, wiping her tears. "Mother keeps me locked up, you see, away from sin and temptation, so that I may repent and cleanse my soul. I have free time to stroll around the grounds each day though, for an hour or two."

I thought back to my first trip to Ashthorne House, to the hammering I'd heard from above. Had she been locked in her room then? I frowned as I thought on her words: *"To repent and cleanse your soul?"* I couldn't possibly imagine a person more pure of heart and spirit than Lady Emelia Ashthorne, and to see her mourning over her puppy, an innocent being snatched away in a horrific manner, angered me more than I can express. Whoever had committed such an evil deed needed purification of the soul, not Lady Emelia Ashthorne.

"I shall go and confront your mother and her maid immediately," I said, the fire of my outrage burning bright.

"You must not!" cried Emelia. She shook her head in a panic, her white-blonde curls bobbing. "It will only cause more harm to come to me. You don't know what they're like, the evil things they have done." She shuddered, her face a mask of absolute terror; I could only imagine the awful deeds alluded to. She stroked my cheek with the back of her hand. "Please promise me you won't intervene, dearest darling Dr. Wood."

I swallowed my rage, and desire swiftly took its place. *She called me her darling!* Taking her hand, which was still at my cheek, I kissed it tenderly.

"Please, call me Kingsley. And know that you have my word. At least for now, sweet Emelia," I whispered. "But I'll not stand by and see you tortured so. Not forever."

She got to her feet, dead dog in her hands, and said, "I shall go find Mr Roberts. He'll know what to do with Jasper."

"No, give him to me. I'll take him there," I said. She handed Jasper over and I carried him to the house. Emelia stayed by the pond, minding my horse.

"Not again," said Roberts, when I presented the dead pup to him. He grimaced and shook his head.

"I beg your pardon?"

"Nothing," he said, his face set in a stony mask. He took the dog and walked off towards the stables, presumably to pass the grim task of burial on to the stableboy.

When I returned, Emelia handed over the reins of my horse and thanked me. She squared her shoulders and lifted her chin. "Someday I'll have this place all to myself. Only then will my world be devoid of nasty surprises." She turned then, and walked back towards the entrance of the house.

When I spoke about the events of the day at dinner, detailing my suspicions, Isabella frowned and shared a concerned look with her father.

"Lottie Johnstone is not the type to harm a puppy, Dr. Wood," said Isabella.

"No, indeed not," said Dr. Foster, a grave expression upon his face. "I delivered Lottie Johnstone into this world and would swear upon the Holy Bible that she'd never do such a thing."

"I suggest you take care in making such allegations, Dr. Wood," said Isabella. "It wouldn't do to ruin a working woman's reputation so cavalierly."

I finished my meal and begged off to bed as soon as practicable, determined to get away from the Fosters' judgemental gaze. *Ruin a woman's reputation so cavalierly?* Isabella's comment rankled, and was laughable when reflecting upon her own licentious behaviour, parading around in her nightgown with a gentleman under her roof.

Awake once more in the middle of the night, I decided to put my mind to work in the hopes of tiring it out. I'd tossed and turned until falling asleep, imagining the terrible acts Emelia had alluded to—

committed by her mother and that deceitful maid—while reliving the events of the day and the stinging comment from Isabella Foster. I worried over how I could help the young lady. I'd come to realise, with no-one else prepared to act on her behalf, I'd need to do so myself. When I finally slept, my dreams proved even more fitful, filled with skewered puppies, drowned children, gunshot wounds to the head and fervent religious torment. To busy the hands and calm the mind, I decided to check on what Dr. Foster had discovered so far with his research.

An early morning visit with a cadaver isn't everybody's idea of fun, though it was better than lying in bed staring at the ceiling. But as I descended the stairs, I heard a carriage pull up outside and noticed lantern light shine through the windows. I met the caller at the door, expecting it to be the husband of the seamstress who lived out of town—she was heavily pregnant with her third child. But it was Mr Roberts from Ashthorne House.

"You must come," he said. "Lady Clementine is much worse."

I nodded, raced upstairs to change and grab my doctor's bag, then met Roberts outside. By then, Isabella was there, dressed and ready to come along to assist.

"Better me than Father," she said, explaining he'd woken her in the night with fever and sore throat. "He needs his rest."

I nodded, none too pleased to have her with me, but preferring not to argue at this point, time being of the essence.

She gestured to my doctor's bag. "I refilled your supplies yesterday afternoon, so you should be well stocked up."

"You did?" I was surprised; it was a task I'd normally attend to myself.

"Yes, I was checking Father's, so I took the liberty to fill yours too. Topped up your digitalis infusion mostly."

I helped her onto the carriage and then climbed on; Roberts set the horses to run. I was confused—I'd used little of the digitalis— but now wasn't the time to comment, and besides, she was no doubt confusing my bottle with her father's. When we got to Ashthorne House, Roberts let us in through the servant's entrance.

A mass of excitable Pomeranian puppies—just like Emelia's Jasper—rushed up, yapping and licking, and wagging their tails.

"Oh, goodness," cried Isabella, squatting to pet them. "Aren't they adorable."

"Yes, a litter from Lady Clementine's favourite bitch, Esmeralda."

"Lady Clementine's?" I said, confused.

"Dog breeding has always been a passion of hers," said Roberts, before gesturing for us to follow. "Please, come this way."

Lottie Johnstone met us at the door of Lady Clementine's room. "Thank goodness, you've come, Bella," she said, grabbing Isabella's hands and grasping them tight. "She's been vomitin' and is real bad with the dysentery. I fear for her life, I do."

I rounded on the maid, annoyed by her overt display of false emotion. "Where's her daughter? She should be here by her mother's side. Locked in her room, is she?"

The maid frowned. "Locked in her room? Whatever would we do that for?"

I scowled at the lying witch and grabbed my stethoscope to examine the patient. Her pulse was extremely slow and her breathing constrained.

"What have you given her?" I demanded of the deceitful wretch. Incensed, I grabbed her by the shoulders and shook her hard. "Tell me, woman!"

"Dr. Wood!" exclaimed Isabella.

The maid cried out, "What do you mean? I ain't given her nothin'."

My mind raced. Lady Clementine looked to have been given digitalis, and a rather large dose of it. Had Lottie Johnstone taken it from my bag while I tended her yesterday? Had she decanted it for later use?

At that moment Lady Emelia turned up, dressed in a nightgown, her long white-blonde tresses freed and flowing. Her attire—much the same as Isabella's only a few nights ago—was unseemly, though I felt more disposed towards her. The realisation jolted. Why wasn't I outraged, embarrassed for her impropriety? Instead, I found myself wanting to offer my jacket to ensure her warmth.

"Isabella," Emelia said, her voice as cold as the early morning air. She lifted her chin and stared down her nose.

Isabella gave a stiff nod. "Lady Emelia."

Then, like the sun emerging from a bank of storm clouds, her dark visage disappeared. She turned to me and smiled wide. "Dearest Kingsley, thank you for coming, though I fear you may be too late. Mummy is looking rather dreadful, isn't she?"

Isabella flinched, no doubt from Emelia's use of my first name and from the strange tone she had taken. She'd sounded cheery, in complete contrast to the direness of the situation her mother was in.

Right then, a puppy scampered through the door, and Lottie said, "Oh, Jasper, you little blighter. Come on, out you go." She scooped him up and took him away.

I frowned at Emelia. "Jasper?"

She giggled and shrugged, then glanced elsewhere.

Isabella said, "Dr. Wood, the patient."

I turned to check on Lady Clementine, but she'd already taken her last breath.

"Oh, is she gone?" said Lady Emelia, in a tone one might use to enquire about the weather. "Dear me … never mind." She turned on her heel and skipped out of the room, as merry as a young child at play.

I realised then who else might have gained access to my medicine bag, and turned to gape at Isabella.

"I did tell you she was odd," she said, and she leaned forward to slip Lady Clementine's eyelids shut.

"And that is my honest and full account," I said, sitting opposite Sergeant Davies in the Grimsheath Police Station.

"That is rather disturbing," he said, rubbing his chin. "We had our suspicions concerning Lord Ashthorne's death, and there's been wild conjecture around town for years about the drowning of Myles Ashthorne—"

"Conjecture?"

"Yes. Rumours abound that the young lad died at the hands of his twin sister, Emelia. They say a gardener found her standing by the pond, drenched and bedraggled, laughing and pointing at her brother's floating body. I'd thought it all poppycock, gossip you might say, but perhaps there's truth to the rumours after all."

I drew in a sharp breath, the clench in my stomach tightening.

"Don't worry none, Dr. Wood," said the sergeant. "I'll look into it, and if you could get those blood and tissue samples seen to, I'd be much obliged. We might have a chance of conviction if we collect some real evidence."

When I left the interview room, I was pleased to see Isabella waiting. She'd urged me to report my suspicions on the ride back to town. What a fool I'd been, mistaking her capacity for scientific enquiry for callousness, and regarding her as unladylike and coarse. In truth, she was level-headed, open-minded, capable and forthright. I admired those qualities immensely, and now saw her in a far different light.

"We must return to Ashthorne House," I said.

"Now?"

"Indeed. Sergeant Davies wants us to collect blood and tissue samples of the deceased."

"To examine for evidence?"

"Yes." I hung my head and rubbed a hand down the length of my face, upset by the whole sorry business. She grabbed me into a strong embrace, which I welcomed, regardless of any ridiculous societal rule that might suggest impropriety.

"Let me come with you, Kingsley," she whispered, and the use of my first name, so tender in delivery, filled me with warmth. I nodded, resting my forehead against hers, then she took my hand and we walked home to saddle the horses.

Despite the grim task ahead, the ride to Ashthorne House proved exhilarating, Isabella proposing a race. She grinned across at me, and the fire in her cheeks resembled the fire in my heart. I needed the distraction—the touch of merriment—as a diversion from dark thoughts. How did she know this? Was it innate, a woman's intuition?

I'd developed a sudden deep affection for her. An intense desire to always be in her steady and calming presence. Though, given my last case of desire so fulminant—of which I'd had an acute case indeed—I reminded myself to take more care this time.

When we reached Ashthorne House, Roberts received us and led us up to Lady Clementine's room. He left us with Lottie, who was red-eyed from crying.

"We're here to take samples," I told her. "Of blood and tissue."

"But she's dead!" cried Lottie. "Why stick needles in my poor mistress now?"

"We've been instructed to by the police."

Before any more could be said, Emelia Ashthorne entered the room and held a pistol to Isabella's head.

"No, no, no, Miss Emelia," screamed Lottie. "Not Bella too."

"Sit down, Lottie, and shut your mouth," said Emelia. She turned to address me. "You'll not touch my mother. I expressly forbid it."

"You have no choice in the matter, Lady Emelia," I said.

"Oh, I think I do." She cocked the gun, and Lottie sobbed.

"No, not Isabella, Lady Emelia, please!"

"It's okay, Lottie," said Isabella, trying to calm the maid down. "Everything will be okay."

Emelia laughed at that—a terrible, sinister sound; it told me nothing would ever be okay again.

Propelled to act and save Isabella, I raised the doctor's bag slowly while looking at Emelia and pointing. "I shall set this down."

She nodded, and I put the bag on the bedside table behind. With my back turned, I picked up a small brass clock. Praying my aim was true, I spun and pitched it at Lady Emelia. *Crack!* It hit her on the forehead and she slumped to the floor. As she fell, the gun discharged with a deafening boom. Lottie screamed and clutched at her right shoulder. She'd been hit; blood spurted from the open wound.

I raced over to Isabella and Emelia. Emelia was out cold, and I took Isabella into my arms.

"My darling, are you okay?"

"I'm fine. See to Lottie. She needs your help, not I."

I wanted to kiss her in that moment, for her level-headedness and compassion, for her strength and heart, but as she'd pointed out, I needed to attend to Lottie and also restrain Lady Emelia.

With the rushing arrival of Roberts—Isabella explaining what had happened—Lady Emelia was delivered to her room and detained within. I tended to Lottie as best I could, then instructed Roberts to ready the carriage—she needed transporting to The Royal Berkshire Hospital—and asked him to send for Sergeant Davies as well. In the meantime, I collected samples from Lady Clementine, accompanied by the sounds of loud hammering and screams from above.

"You did well, darling husband. I'm so proud of you," said Isabella, six months later in front of the Magistrates Court. She kissed me on the cheek. I'd just given testimony in the murder case against Lady Emelia Ashthorne.

"As I am of you, my dear," I said.

We set off for home, sitting snug in the carriage. I held her hand, and she rested her head upon my shoulder. Suffused with warmth and tender joy, I now classified the fulminant desire I had for my wife as more chronic than acute, and of a nature considered entirely incurable.

THE COTTAGE

BY FATMIRE MARKE

Few things unsettled Lira's spirit the way the howling wind of the Black Forest could. It whipped around the trees and cut through the darkness from every direction, rising and falling, the sound of a woman wailing in anguish. She gripped the strap of her bag tighter, stepping through the tall grass. Something slithered past her, brushing her ankle. She shivered but kept her eyes forward; it would be worse if she looked. Things were always far worse than she imagined. The irony of being fearful of things that lurked in the night as she prowled through the encroaching darknesswas not lost on her. In the distance, a howl echoed. Lira flinched. Most would think it a wolf. But she knew better and picked up her pace.

Through the blackening leaves, Lira caught sight of the cottage, its thatched roof sagging and gaping in the parts she had attempted but failed to patch. *Her talents were not for repairing things*, she thought. Her talents were for destroying and so it was no wonder this is what awaited her. The last time she'd woven the reeds through the roof slats, she had faced a threat in the shadows of the forest. In her haste, she had failed to prepare the cottage for her inevitable return. As she made her way around the perimeter, she felt relieved to see that none of the windows were broken. Lira bent down to smell a rose bloom still clinging to the last glimmer of life. At the touch of her fingertips, the petals fluttered to the ground. She smiled at the way the rose fell apart because of her. Lira liked when things, especially people, fell apart because of her touch.

Lira plucked a dry hydrangea stem as she stepped up to the door, the scent of decay permeating the cold autumn air. The jangling of keys disrupted the sound of rustling leaves and creatures hidden in the trees. Lira felt the familiar ache that accompanied her as she entered the cottage alone. The ache for him. She wondered if the promise she made was enough to lure him here again. It wasn't her usual way of hunting and it had been a risk to assume her prey would follow her twice, let alone a third time. But she had to finish him. A heavy scent of decaying wood hung in the air the way it always did when returning to the cottage after an extended absence.

Before opening the shutters or pulling the sheets off of the furniture, Lira went into the bedroom and flung open the wardrobe. Her hand reached for a sweater, deep inside, and she felt the familiar texture of scratchy wool. A navy-blue fisherman's sweater he wore often and seldom washed. She slipped it on and inhaled the scent. It still lingered even after all this time. The smell of burning wood and cologne.

The ache in her stomach traveled up to her throat, threatening to deprive her of the air she breathed as she thought about the prospect that this would not go as planned. The dread she felt if he did not come to her. She needed him. A sacrifice would be hard to come by after the summer season with less opportunity. The summering city folk had all long since left their manor houses. It would be too risky to take another local. The last time was still fresh on their tongues. Her own undoing would come from her lapses in judgment, her mother had always said. Lira glanced at the fireplace, stained with black soot and a single handprint above the mantle, the bricks hiding the bones of previous years.

Never again, she thought.

The locals would believe the rumor of a runaway only once. That story would not be readily accepted a second time.

Lira lit several candles around the cabin and a single kerosene lamp at the window seat. The darkness outside loomed. A thick fog swirling in the black of night. She wondered if Jack sensed her desperation the night she had invited him to the cottage. She hoped this would not end up being another lapse of judgment. Another mistake for her mother to criticize her for. She would not fail this time. She was in control.

"Jack, I am waiting for you," she said, her voice echoing in the empty cottage like a broken lullaby. "I have something for you."

She turned toward the fireplace, flicking her wrist. Flames roared to life, the wood from last autumn serving as a charred bed of amber coals. The fire wasn't enough to warm her. She needed Jack. Remnants of a shoe could still be seen. Another reason she could never let anyone stay here. The cottage harbored too much and Lira could not begin to unbury it all for strangers. Jack had been the first guest who had been able to leave, and when he left, she felt hollow. His easy laugh had filled the walls and her.

The window howled louder at night, calling to her to go out and hunt. Her skin prickled and stung, her bones ached and the hunger overwhelmed her. Maybe leaving London was a mistake, she thought. Hunting in London had become almost too easy. The men were eager and had the means to solicit her. She led them to their death like horses to water. Lira licked her lips—the taste of the last one still lingered. She hadn't expected him to be a challenge, yet he was. When she had finally ended him, the reward proved to be worth the trouble.

All the while, Jack clouded her mind. The only one she'd allowed to leave her grasp. The way their bodies molded together—the way she felt overwhelmed by his touch—still simmered under her skin. Lira shook her head, knowing if she continued to ruminate about him, he would feel it, wherever he was.

How could she have fallen for it? His smile had been enough to weaken her resolve. There was something about him that made her lose the steel grip over her thoughts and emotions. The cold-blooded work she did, the grinding of bones to dust after luring her prey, compromised by the way he looked into the bleakness of her soul. He awakened something long dormant within her and so she had endeavored to treat him as something more than a meal to be devoured.

Just then, the door shook. Lira rose from her chair by the fire, reaching for the poker without breaking her eyes from the door. It had to be the wind. But one could never be certain. Moments passed but the door stood still. She shivered, glancing at the weakening flames. The fire within her still burned. A moment later, the door burst open and a gust of wind blew through the cottage, extinguishing the fire and knocking things to the ground.

"Hello, Lira," Jack said, his voice low and flat, a glint in his eye and the corners of his lips curling just enough to make her whimper.

She stood up, trying to hide the weakness she had come to have for him and turned to reignite the fire. When she turned back, he was standing close enough that she could smell whiskey on his breath and a mix of sweat and cologne. She closed her eyes. The memories flooded back, of seeing him in Notting Hill below a cherry blossom tree. Of strolling Kensington Gardens and the first time his lips met hers under the shade of her parasol. The steady build up within her of a desire to love and be loved she had once convinced herself she did not possess. Lira realized in that moment just how hungry she had become for his affection, her desire awakened by the sound of his deep throated laugh. It danced in the air like a song and his touch soothed and spread like a balm over her long dead soul.

"Jack," she said, her voice barely audible.

"Lira," he said again, her name lilting like a song whenever he said it.

Oh, how she missed it.

"I am so pleased you accepted my invitation."

"I thought it would never come," he said, his green eyes undressing her. "Do you always carry a knife?" he murmured, flashing a wicked smile.

Lira wondered how he knew. She'd hidden the blade under her petticoat and made sure to not so much as glance at her dress, let alone reach for it. The sharp tip pressed against her thigh and gave her an oddly satisfying sensation. She watched as Jack ran his fingers through his black hair, noticing the veins bulging on his forearms. She wanted him to slip the knife from its place and press it against her.

Lira bent forward, untying the laces of her boots, ensuring her dress exposed just enough of her thigh for him to see the glint of the sharp-edged dagger she would use on him. He leaned against a table and smirked. The air between them thickened and the room grew suddenly hot despite the freezing temperatures in the cottage. She kicked off the boots and slipped off her stockings, then sauntered over to him ensuring that their eyes remained locked.

"I always do. One never knows when they may need to slice an apple … or someone's throat," she purred.

Jack leaned in closer, tilting his head to the side and exposing his neck. The veins pulsed and her breathing quickened.

"Is that so? Do tell me more," he said.

Lira stood close enough to him to smell the rust scent of blood on his breath. Her mouth watered imagining the taste of his lips.

"I can show you," she said.

"The way you showed Thatcher?" Jack asked, his brows raised ever so slightly. "Poor chap. He had no idea what he was walking into or who he was walking into it *with.*"

"We all have a job to do, Jack," she said. "It isn't my fault that yours is so very dull while mine—"

"Have you considered the possibility that one day, your deeds will come back to haunt you?"

The danger of letting Jack in, really letting him in, meant she had to take a look at her own reflection and what looked back at her was a wretched creature masquerading as a siren of the city. She steeled herself and looked at him again with more fortitude.

"That's enough lecturing," she said, her voice low and angry. "It's time for your lesson."

Jack reached up and touched her collarbone, letting the tip of his finger trace it and slowly move over her skin until it reached the rim of her neckline. She tried to steady her breathing but her chest rose and fell quickly. Jack's eyes undressed her, seeing through the fabric of her dress. He licked his lips the lower his gaze went. Lira shivered.

"Teach me," he said, his voice a low growl that made her feel faint.

She felt the heat rising between her legs and knew any effort to resist him would be a waste of time. They both wanted this. They both *needed* this.

"Sit down," she said.

He grinned, raising his eyebrows and cocking his head to the side. Lira gave him a look—a warning—to obey. Finally, he sat down and tilted back, spreading his legs and placing his hands behind his neck. The way he looked at her made her weak, her knees threatening to turn to mud. Lightning lit up the cottage just then as thunder struck close by. The sound of a tree cracking filled the room.

"Perfect," she said. "A loud storm to hide the sound of your screams."

"What makes you so sure you can make me scream?"

Lira let her mouth slowly curve into a smile, her eyes blazing. She effortlessly lifted her dress to pull out the knife from its sheath. The sharp edge glinted in the firelight. She stepped forward and lifted his chin with the tip, pressing just hard enough to cause a speck of blood to run down his neck before bending down to clean it off with a flick of her tongue. He groaned.

"This is just the start. When I finish you off, you won't be able to scream anymore."

Jack's eyes smoldered and he swallowed hard.

"Teach me," he said again. "Teach me everything. Finish me. I am yours."

Lira reached over her right shoulder and pulled the string keeping her dress on. A slight tug and it tumbled to the floor. All that she wore was the knife sheath and a ribbon around her neck the color of crimson. *Hunting was fun*, she thought. *But this? Complete submission. This was intoxicating.*

The lesson began as the storm raged. Flashes of white illuminated the room, casting shadows on the walls. The cracks of thunder hid his screams and hers too as the cottage shook and the trees, like dancing skeletons, stood watch over their demise. The rain danced on the roof. The candles flickered and the fire blazed beside the one they created between them. By the end of the night, only one of the fires would be extinguished.

DRACULA IN EAST END

BY THERESA TYREE

Wanted: Reliable and attractive girl to serve as assistant to visiting noble man. Must be neat and tidy. Must not ask questions about the habits of the household. Must find evening hours agreeable. Required skills: cleaning, note-taking, conversation. No cooking skills necessary. Applicants should submit their credentials to R. Renfield at Carfax House in East End. Be advised: blood will be drawn to make sure applicants are in good health.

Kaliyah's first impression of the house was that it belonged to someone who was in love with power. Bold black and deep red were employed in broad straight lines to emphasize the gothic grace of the structure. The hard wood of the entryway gave way to plush carpeting at the beginning of interior halls that Kaliyah felt she could get lost in. A gilt-framed portrait of a handsome man with an aquiline nose and an all-consuming stare stood in the center of the double staircase that led to the upper floors.

But the most striking feature of the house was the display cases.

Every wall had one. Whether standing or mounted, they were fit into the house like puzzle pieces, elegantly slotted together to create a portrait of a warrior. Spears from Africa populated racks like ladder rungs—easily spaced and high enough to scale the wall. Bronze gladius swords sat like gems behind glass, so green with age that one would be a fool to doubt its import and authenticity. Whip swords from India. Curved blades from Arabia. Maces, hammers, stakes, and even a few poles that Kaliyah recognized as for impaling were modeled in these cases.

But it was the guns that took her breath away.

She hadn't known that she would be working in a house with guns when she had taken this job.

"Does my collection frighten you?"

Kaliyah started and turned, pulling her eyes away from the guns in the parlor display case.

The man with the aquiline nose from the portrait she'd noticed when she'd first entered the house lounged with easy grace in one of the doorways opposite the parlor.

"Forgive me," he said. "I didn't mean to startle you."

Kaliyah looked between the man and the display case with the guns. "I was just noticing that the weapons in this case aren't like the others, sir."

The man smiled. "A sharp eye. What good fortune I have that Mr. Renfield chose you for this position."

Kaliyah smiled gently and dropped her eyes back to the floor demurely.

"Well then, as this is our first meeting, let's go over your role and responsibilities, shall we?" The man stepped forward and began to circle her. "I am the master of this house. You may call me either 'master' or 'sir'. Either is acceptable at any time. We won't stand on ceremony too much, though, despite the titles. Consider them a formality, as your duties will extend from cleaning to sometimes cover conversation and companionship during meal times and occasional outings. What I need you most for, my dear Miss Devi, is your compassion and kindness in understanding my unique lifestyle."

He stopped in front of her and smiled, lips together and charming. The warmth in his eyes was the sort one saw when a collector took possession of another worthy addition to his hoard.

"Is all of that agreeable?"

Kaliyah nodded her head gently, looking up at him through her dark lashes. "Yes, Master."

The man laughed genteelly and extended his hand.

Kaliyah placed her fingers daintily in his hand. But where many men might have kissed her knuckles, he turned her arm and rolled her sleeve up to her elbow. Kaliyah allowed the gesture and waited as he examined the inside of her elbow.

"This is where your blood was drawn for your interview, yes?"

"Yes, sir."

The man nodded approvingly. "It has healed beautifully." He closed his eyes and took a long breath in through his nose, then replaced her sleeve. "You'll forgive me. I do wish to make sure that none of my staff is mishandled, and your perfume is ravishing so close to one's nose."

Kaliyah blushed becomingly. "But, Master ... I'm not wearing any perfume."

He chortled and he kissed her knuckles. "Then it must be that you are naturally charming, my dear."

Her first night, the master gave her a tour of the house. He guided her through the winding hallways, introduced every display case by its contents, explained his liquid diet (but clarified that he didn't expect her to adhere to it), and finished the evening by showing her to her own quarters—which he said were completely at her disposal.

"And I do mean entirely, Miss Devi," he insisted. "It would be completely outside my power to enter these quarters unless explicitly invited in."

Stalemate in the South and Scarcity at Home:

News from the front of the South African War has continued to be poor. Despite the superior edge in weaponry, due to the terrain and the weather, troops have continued to only hold ground. Meanwhile, the surplus of women without husbands continues to plague our society. With many women taking on even more of the careers that their natural mates have left behind, there is confusion as to why our government continues to pour resources and lives into the war.

Kaliyah found herself once more in the entryway parlor, gazing at the large mounted display case full of guns.

This was the most public room in the house. Of all of his weapons, it was these that the master chose to highlight for his guests; these that he was proudest to display and wished to converse on the most.

Kaliyah tilted her head to one side thoughtfully and examined them again. Her inert feather duster framed her face and she tapped it with a finger as her eyes moved over the guns.

"Taking in the sights?"

Kaliyah didn't jump this time. She'd gotten used to his way of creeping up on her over the passing weeks.

"I was just wondering why, out of everything in your collection, it's these specific weapons you choose to keep in the room where you receive company."

The master smiled from his place leaning against the doorframe—close-lipped and cordial. "I'd love to hear the conclusions you've come to so far."

"For the sake of your entertainment, then, sir." Kaliyah tapped her feather duster twice more and then folded her hands neatly in front of her. "Your collection is so vast. And so well organized. One might think you had been there yourself, you have such an extensive number of pieces from each period of war. Even the British Museum would covet your trove." Kaliyah giggled. "It's almost like you hoard them, like a dragon."

The master smirked a little. "I'm sure it's not the only quality of mine one could compare to a dragon's."

Kaliyah laughed loudly then, coving her mouth with one hand and dismissing the master's words with a wave of her feather duster. "Oh, sir, you do jest."

The master inclined his head enigmatically. "Go on, then, what else?"

Kaliyah turned back to the weapons on display. "Well, of all the eras covered in your collection, this case seems to contain the most recent entries."

"Well spotted."

Kaliyah sighed nostalgically and touched the glass of the display case gracefully. "Weaponry has come so far since the old days."

"It has."

Kaliyah looked back towards the master and gave him a coy look. "Now that I've explained why I think you keep these pieces in the parlor, will you honor me with the true answer?"

The master grinned, seemingly pleased to have Kaliyah ask for his true answer, and stuck his hands roguishly into the pockets of his fine suit trousers. "I suppose that would be because they're being used to fight the war in Africa at the moment."

The smile faded from Kaliyah's face and she turned to give the guns a new hard look.

The master came into the room and pointed to one of the guns. "That there was the first machine gun invented by Hiram Maxim in 1884. It differs from the Gatling gun in the library in that it uses the force of the recoil to expel the cartridge for the bullet so that it can continue firing without the need for a crank to expel and load. All this model needs is a simple spring. Four short years after, he licensed production of the weapon to Great Britain. I've made rather good use of being the one responsible for that deal." He gestured to the rest of the case. "We've developed several other models, added some exciting features, and modified the design for ease of use. Every soldier we have is trained in their use and equipped with them these days."

Kaliyah looked the case over, looking to each gun in its stage of evolution. "I see."

"When entertaining in the parlor, it does help to have the selection on hand. Both for business partners and for company concerned about the news from South Africa."

"I imagine you have many guests to console then, sir, given the news is so poor."

The master took Kaliyah's feather duster from her and passed it lovingly over the case. "Sometimes a war doesn't have to be won to be worth fighting." He gave her one of his close-lipped smiles. "At least not for the right instigator."

Change on the Production Line:

Well-known Oil and Coal Baron Jonathan Harker, proponent of, and supplier for, the South African War, was found today exsanguinated in his office. He is survived by his cousin, Miss Lucy Westenra, to whom his property and assets fall to in lieu of any other living family. Miss Westenra says she intends to keep the business, with the help of her late cousin's secretary, who she says will be indispensable to her efforts. Changes Miss Westenra intends to make include updating safety measures of her mines and factories, a network of services and resources for those in her employ, shorter work days, and turning her company's focus away from the war and towards what she can do to better the community and the lives of those around her.

As the weeks passed, Kaliyah noticed the master becoming more familiar. He lingered when she worked, sometimes reading to her as she cleaned, occasionally absent-mindedly reaching up to move something out of her way as she dusted or lift something for her.

Other habits started to show as well. One evening he left her to dine alone because he couldn't abide the smell of the garlic she'd put into her methi dhokli. He excused himself as politely as possible, and when she offered not to use the herb again, he only asked that she warn him in advance so that he could avoid it, and that she perhaps dine on the veranda to help keep the smell out of the carpets and drapes.

His liquid diet was truly as strict as he said. Each of his meals was a deep red color, and quite thick. When Kaliyah supposed that he took wine for every meal, he gave her a playful look and said, "I do not drink ... wine," before taking a sip.

The way he delivered the line, Kaliyah thought he must have said it a thousand times before.

Sometimes when he was near her, he would pass close enough that his shoulder would brush against her own. It made Kaliyah watch him from under her lashes, considering if such advances were unwelcome or not.

The next time he did it, she let her fingers catch gently against his, and his eyes lit up like stars.

The next night, Kaliyah rose to her duties to find her master at her door. He was dressed for going out, and held over one arm a garment bag from one of the well-known tailors in the city. He extended it to Kaliyah, smiling roguishly at her, close-lipped and pleased with himself.

"You'll forgive me if I filched one of your dresses from the laundry in order to take your measurements," he said.

Kaliyah took the bag and opened it. A blood red dress of the finest silk sat inside. "Oh, but, sir … Where will I wear it?"

He swung his cape wide in the corridor. "Wherever you wish!"

Kaliyah laughed at the drama as he whirled back to face her.

"All jokes aside, though, I do have an evening planned, if you'd care for an adventure." He extended his hand to her, stopping just before the door frame.

She placed her hand in his—then shut the door in his face to change.

They attended the opera, then dined at a private restaurant that only the highest of high society knew about, then went to an auction where the master purchased a ruby necklace for Kaliyah that was worth more than ten years of her salary.

"I'll keep it in the box until we return home, if that's alright," the master said once the auctioneers had delivered the necklace into his hands. "Wouldn't want it snatched from your throat by ravenous thieves—and I admit to selfishly wanting to be the first to see it around your neck."

They retired to the parlor, where the master stood Kaliyah in front of the mirror and fastened the necklace for her.

The brilliance of the ruby was resplendent.

"More red," Kaliyah remarked, fingering the ruby gently.

"And more still," the master said, pouring two glasses from a decanter. He offered one to Kaliyah.

She eyed it. "I thought you said you don't drink wine."

"And I don't." He pressed the glass closer to Kaliyah. "Special occasions call for a special drink."

Kaliyah took her glass and inspected it. "What is it then?"

"Blood."

Kaliyah stilled and watched the master.

The master went to his display case full of machine guns and took a sip from his glass. "Long ago, there was a warlord who believed that he could absorb the power of his enemies through their blood. He bathed in it. He drank it. He made their life further his own." He turned back to Kaliyah and took another sip. "Some say it made him immortal. Others say it made him a monster. Whether it was the blood or not, something turned him great." He finished what was in his glass and laid it. He approached Kaliyah, his lips stained red. "But greatness can be lonely." He placed a hand on Kaliyah's waist.

Kaliyah only hesitated for a moment. Then, she moved her glass aside and stepped in, pressing her body brazenly against the master's.

He closed his eyes and sighed against her. "I had hoped you would answer this way." He lowered his head, his mouth mere inches from her neck—before he hissed in pain and shot back.

With a look of horror, he brought his hand to his neck. When he pulled it away, it was red with blood. He looked between his hand and Kaliyah, frozen with shock and the incongruity of something so soft turning so sharp.

"You even knew my story," Kaliyah crooned as she wiped her mouth. "It's been centuries since I've had a fan as devoted as you, Mister Laurence Sutler." She licked off her fingers and smiled at him with teeth—fangs sharp and apparent between her lips. "Pulverizing your meals to take them as liquid was a nice touch—though the amount of tomatoes and red meat your chef goes through seems quite the expense. Real blood would almost be cheaper, if you weren't human." Her eyes gleamed, predatory and sparkling. "This is the first time you've had the real thing in quite some time, isn't it? Only for special occasions and the like, then?"

"But, the sunlight," he stuttered. "Your garlic!"

Kaliyah smiled almost kindly. "Oh, you didn't believe those stories, did you? Sunlight and garlic are just symbols—ones humans put a lot of belief into. It's not the bulb that's the problem for most vampires anyway, it's the holiness of the flowers—which you would know if you'd done any research. I say most, since it becomes a battle of wills when symbols charged with human belief fight against vampire magic. Channel your own will into a bit of blood, weave a spell with it, and poof; those symbols cease to hold any power over you." She snickered prettily. "Though I'd say your narrow-minded English taste is what let the garlic win over you."

Sutler scrambled back towards his guns, but bumped against one of the comfortable chairs in the room and went sprawling to the floor.

Kaliyah sauntered to him calmly and pinned him to the floor with the heel of her shoe. "Oh, don't go for your weapons. They won't do you any good anyway." She leaned over him, leering. "You know what I am."

The man struggled under Kaliyah's foot. "You can't be him! He … he was a warlord! A *man*."

Kaliyah's nose wrinkled distastefully at the word. "I find a lot of people these days throwing that word around as if it's supposed to mean something superior, when really it's just a title like any other." She flounced down in the chair next to her with a tired sigh, keeping her foot in place and the man below it trapped as she pouted. "And all the boring people throwing that word around are so stagnant and boorish. Like your great poet, Shakespeare, said, *'What's in a name?'* Not to reminisce, but back in my day wars were fought by the people who started them. Kings went to war with their troops. Bloodshed was active, not passive the way you politicians do it these days. The name I would have used for people like you is 'cowards.'" She looked down her strong nose at Sutler as he struggled and pressed her foot down more strongly.

He cried out at the force.

She leaned over the arm of her chair and leered at him. "And do you know what I have planned for you, my little worm?"

He shook his head, pleadingly. "Please ... don't!"

Kaliyah made a noise of disgust and snapped his back with a quick thrust of her foot. "Of course I'm going to kill you. You're fueling a war without end that serves no purpose. You refuse to listen to the new blood around you that cries for change. New ideas and powers die, crushed under the heel of your sluggish system." She angled her head prettily, adopting the demure close-lipped smile of her prior persona and looking at him through her lashes the way she had on the day she'd caught her fingers against him. She traced the shining ruby at her neck delicately with a finger. "The world turns on, Laurence. You need only to look at me and how much I've changed to notice that."

"But why?" Sutler gasped. His breath came quick and shallow from the pain, nerves and fear creating sweat on his pale skin. "You had power. You had status. You had everything. Why give it up to be ... to be ...?"

Kaliyah waited as Sutler's eyes flicked over her. "Well, go on," she prompted. She crouched over him and smiled with her fangs. "Tell me the silly mistaken titles you were going to lay at my feet."

Sutler huffed and looked wildly around him, still looking for a way to escape.

Kaliyah sighed and picked him up. He whimpered in pain as she positioned him in one of the chairs.

"I can't feel my legs ..."

"That is usually rather the point of breaking prey's back, yes."

He tried to fight her off one-handed, keeping the other at his neck.

Kaliyah broke his arm with a flick of her wrist and then knelt between his spread legs. She looked up at him coyly. At another time, Sutler might have dreamed of her there—but this was a nightmarish twist on the fantasy.

"You underestimate everyone who isn't like you. The young. The old. The beautiful. The ugly. The women. The children. The Blacks and the Indians and the natives of the Americas. That's what makes this form so perfect for destroying you. You're so sure you're right. Conquerors, you call yourselves, from your tiny castles in the great English city—where poor live in the streets and suffer in your factories and die in your wars. Such marvels you've achieved in your time, and still you can't be bothered to learn the one thing that divides people from monsters."

"And what is that?" Sutler huffed.

Kaliyah tore the leg of his trousers, exposing his thigh. She flashed him one more of her demure pretty smiles. "Mercy."

She lowered her lips to his femoral artery and drained him. He slipped away as the blood left him—weakness to dizziness to floating. Sleep and then death.

When she was finished, she wiped her mouth. She would arrange the body next. Make it look just as much an accident as the others. His assets would go to another—someone with a fresh perspective. Someone whose ideas would change the world the way she'd tried to all those years ago, when she had been the son of the dragon.

All the world needed was a little new blood.

West Ham Leadership a Sham! New Headmistress Instated:

A harrowing suicide and confession rocked the world of academia today when Arthur Holmwood, heir to both the Holmwood family fortune and Headmaster of West Ham Technical Institute, was found hanging outside his office window, blood drained from a cut on his neck and washed away by last night's rain. A suicide note was found on his desk, explaining the headmaster's sudden death as one of a guilty conscience. In it, Holmwood confessed to making his academic name through acts of plagiarism, all of which he took from his own students, many of whom attended classes via the school's women's department.

Professor Wilhelmina Murray of the women's college has been selected as his replacement for her indispensable knowledge of the previous Headmaster's filing system. She says she looks forward to helping the school reclaim its mission of being "a people's university" and highlighting the work of those who have been passed over previously. When asked for further comment, she had only this to say: "I've been asked how I feel about being thrown to wolves like this. If I think someone's only giving me this position to make a scapegoat or a sacrifice out of me. But, if I really am a virgin being offered to a dragon, I rather think I would fear the people offering me to the dragon more than I would the dragon itself."

Miss Murray has also joined forces with Miss Westenra to host a charity auction to create scholarships in engineering for the women's department. The headliner of the auction will be a sunrise ruby necklace donated to the auction by an anonymous donor who has identified themselves only with an ancient Wallachian sigil that appears to have belonged to The Order of the Dragon.

Kaliyah wore simple black clothes to Mina and Lucy's charity auction—a dress, a cloak, and a velvet bowler with a netted veil. A silver hatpin with a dragon motif was the only nod to her identity. The sun gleamed off of it, and Mina and Lucy turned their heads from their place on stage, sitting in two chairs like queens surveying a kingdom. It pleased Kaliyah to see the two of them so, united both in vision and in love.

Lucy snatched Mina's hand and pointed excitedly to Kaliyah in the audience. Mina beamed and waved. Kaliyah smiled under her shroud and raised her hand cordially, but kept the gesture small. Their tea plans for after the event were celebratory in nature instead of conspiratorial as before, but even so, Kaliyah survived hundreds of years by keeping a low profile.

The ladies rose to introduce themselves and the event. They took turns speaking of their hopes and dreams, encouraging those present to be generous so that vision became reality. All the while, their hands remained clasped, augmenting their words with passion and verve.

To the onlookers it was surely companionable; but Kaliyah knew how hard won the public display of affection was for the lovers. Even now, as they spoke of scholarships, careers, and a brighter future for the people of their nation, she knew they dreamed of the house they would have and the searing kisses they would share behind those closed doors.

All thanks to one who had once called himself the son of the dragon.

It felt good to use everything she knew of warfare to build something. To create a world where Mina and Lucy would live their lives as they wished. Where they were free.

Kaliyah had learned over lifetimes that there was no other cause worth fighting for.

To that end, she raised her hand as the ruby necklace she'd donated came up for auction, and doubled the starting bid.

THE MOSS-COVERED MIRAGE

BY DANA VICKERSON

The cabin should look like salvation, but all Mac can think is *trap*. She stumbles out of the dense knot of lodgepole pines into the circular clearing, the perfect geometry of the trees a neon warning sign. It's like a crop circle in a forest, with the little mossy building squarely in the center.

Roxy gasps in relief, but Mac clenches her jaw. Of course Roxy is excited. She probably led them right to it.

"A cabin," Roxy whispers as she loops her dirty arms around Mac's waist. "We're saved."

Mac's body goes rigid, aware of every place Roxy touches her. She drops their remaining pack to the ground, shirking off Roxy's embrace. With a thud, Mac sits and digs her fingers into the stalks of grass, so green they look painted, like Alice and the Queen's red roses.

Except this is not Wonderland.

The weight of her exhausted limbs and her gnawing hunger pin her in place. The trees raise their branches to the sky and bend into the clearing like imposing gods.

"What are you doing?" Roxy asks. "Mac, please don't shut down on me."

Mac can't form words, can't tell Roxy why they must turn back, keep looking for the trail, for some way out of this forest. It sounds insane, but she knows in her bones it's true.

Something is very wrong here.

Mac feels Roxy's long fingers around her waist like shackles and before she knows it, she's standing, one arm slung over Roxy's shoulders. At her back, she feels the wall of trees, imagines them knitting together. Closing for good.

A perfect curl of white smoke winds out of the stone chimney, inviting wary hikers in. A cedar porch bursting with potted azaleas wraps around three sides of the wood clapboard cabin, reminding Mac of every illustration she's ever seen in fairy-tale books. None of *those* stories ever end well.

The yellow front door is open wide with only the screen to keep the forest out.

Welcome, it says.

Come in.

Be saved.

After two days of aimlessly traipsing through the dense woods, the sight of such a beautiful respite should give Mac hope that all her fears of dying in this forest are unfounded, but she knows better.

This is a trap.

When she can feel her legs beneath her again, she plants her feet. "No."

"Mac, seriously, come on! This is not some unsolved mystery. This is not a conspiracy. This is a cabin"—her words slow down, as if Mac were a child—"where someone lives, who can help us."

Roxy's beautiful skin is shiny with sweat and the oily sheen of days without a proper shower. Her brown eyes are oceans of concern and compassion in equal parts, but Mac feels an undercurrent of secrecy. Roxy's hiding something.

Her hands are warm on Mac's cheeks. Despite the midday heat and the exertion of the hike, it chills Mac to the bone.

They cannot go inside.

Roxy sighs and lets her go, and Mac slumps into the not-painted-but-surely-painted grass.

She watches as Roxy walks onto the porch and calls for help.

The night before they got hopelessly lost, Roxy fiddled with the zipper of her bright yellow sleeping bag and waited for Mac to return to camp. She scratched the mosquito bites from when they'd spent the first evening of their trip sipping whiskey from a flask and catching up on the last few months. It felt good to be alone with Mac. Like old times. Not as intimate, though. Not yet.

The tent flap opened, and Mac slid in. Roxy watched Mac's face, a habit she'd developed over their years, first as lovers then friends. Gauging Mac's mood was something she did unconsciously, and so far, Mac had been in a very good one.

Until Mac noticed Roxy watching her, and her face hardened.

"What?" Mac said.

"Nothing." She'd imagined them calling back old jokes like when they used to get fifty cent beers at the karaoke bar. She'd pictured them laying exhausted side by side, hips and arms and hands touching, the heat between them rekindling.

But as Mac huffed and pulled her boots off, Roxy felt the opportunity slipping away.

"Everything okay?" Roxy asked, trying to sound light. Mac's back was tight with tension.

"Hm?" Mac said. Her eyes met Roxy's and she seemed to relax, which uncurled the tight knot in Roxy's stomach. "No, it was weird. I got the bear bag up fine, but when I was throwing the line, I heard the trees making these wild cracking noises."

"Yeah, the woods make some crazy sounds. I heard a bunch of animals last night."

"That's the other weird thing," Mac said as she slid into her sleeping bag. "I didn't hear *any* animals."

"Weird," Roxy said. She didn't want to talk about this, because she knew it could lead to a Mac-style rant about the unsolved mysteries of the woods. Bigfoot. Aliens.

"Yeah, what's weird is you picking this loop in the first place."

"Oh?" Roxy didn't know much about backpacking, but she suggested this portion of the Ozark Highland Trail because it was called *Lover's Loop*.

Mac stared at Roxy, as if she was trying to discern the real answers underneath Roxy's nonchalance. "Yeah, this portion of the highland trail is notorious. At least a few people disappear every year. It's like the forest eats them."

"Mac"—Roxy sighed—"you know that's just bullshit YouTube conspiracy theories. If that were true, don't you think the news would report on stuff like that?"

"You think *the news* tells you everything that goes on in the world?"

This was not how she wanted tonight to go, and she was ready to change the subject. She pulled her own shirt up just a little to expose the deep curve of her belly and the supple rise of her hip. Mac's eyes followed the slope of her body back up to her face.

"Hey," Roxy said when their eyes met. Mac's were bright green, like the top of a tree canopy as the sun shone through.

"Hey," Mac said. She blushed and looked down, clearing her throat. "So, a weird thing happened with Laura the other day."

"Ugh, Laura. Can we not? You guys have been spending way too much time together."

"Well, we are dating."

"Yeah, I know, but only for a few months."

Mac played with the snaps of her sleeping bag, not meeting Roxy's eyes. "She asked me to move in."

Roxy sat up, no longer worried about looking enticing. "Really?"

Mac kept her gaze down. "Yeah, when I was telling her about this trip, how you wanted to take me hiking, it kind of led to a fight. But we worked it out, and she asked me to move in."

"But she lives in Kansas City. You'd have to quit your job." Roxy tried hard to keep her tone neutral, but she felt like someone had poured ice water down her back.

"Yeah, I don't really see myself working at Delaney & Thompson forever. I hate that place. It's full of old white dudes. This could be my chance to make a change. There are plenty of engineering firms in KC. Big ones. And besides, I can't stay in Fayetteville forever. College is over."

"If it's so bad maybe you *should* leave," Roxy snapped. Mac was obviously ready to leave her behind. Roxy felt a sharp pinch in her chest.

"It's not all bad," Mac said, finally looking at Roxy.

They held each other's gaze in silence. Roxy's feelings pounded to be unleashed, to pull Mac into a kiss, to tell her how she really felt.

But she said nothing. She would find another time.

Their halted conversation hung in the air while they got ready for bed. Roxy's limbs hurt from the unfamiliar exertion of hiking, and though she had plans to stay up and talk, sleep took her as soon as she slipped into her sleeping bag.

When they got up the next morning, the bear bag–Mac's pack– was gone.

Mac holds her breath as Roxy knocks on the cedar door frame.

Everything about the cabin looks intentionally rustic, from the pine-needle-covered shake roof to the mossy coating on the stone. No major signs of decay, no indication that anything sinister is lurking inside, but Mac cannot let go of her suspicion.

There doesn't seem to be anyone around, yet the cabin is wide open and inviting.

While Roxy waits for a response, Mac fixates on reasons they should leave.

The clearing is all wrong. It's as if the forest opened a perfect spot of sunlight just for them. She knows it's an insane thought, but that's her brain. Her thoughts are a constant loop she must wade through. The mail man is a CIA agent. Her college professors conspired to flunk her. Her local barista puts the wrong sugar in her coffee, just to piss her off. Most of the time, Mac can discern what's real and what's not.

The danger in the cabin feels real.

And why is Roxy being so weird? Since the start, she's seemed nervous about something. Always watching. It's driving Mac nuts.

No one answers Roxy's calls, so Mac watches in horror as she pulls open the screen door and goes inside.

When she comes out, a smile is grotesquely plastered across her lovely face. Her features are twisted, covering sinister intentions. Like she read about smiling in a book and is trying it for the first time.

"Mac, come on," Roxy says. "There's food!"

Her rumbling stomach wars with her suspicious brain. She is lightheaded and exhausted, and before she can protest, Roxy pulls her into the cabin and deposits her on a plush blue couch. She blankets Mac with excited chatter.

Nervous chatter.

Mac stares at the clean interior. It seems inconceivable that an actual person lives here, so far removed from civilization. And why aren't they here? Where did they go?

A fresh-baked loaf of bread sits on the counter, filling the room with the disarming aroma of comfort.

Who baked the bread?

Time feels elastic, globby, like Mac's world is doing loops inside a lava lamp. How long have they been in the woods? How long since her pack was stripped from the tree? Mac can't remember.

No claw marks, no torn rope. The knot had simply come undone or been untied. Her pack gone. And the food. And the map.

Mac doesn't doze off, how can she? But when her eyes focus again, the light from the large picture window is golden. She can see the line of trees ringing the clearing through the glass.

Her eyes burn like she's been crying.

"Mac," Roxy says softly, treating Mac like a broken thing. It's infuriating. She is just exhausted. Hungry.

Roxy holds out a plate. Bread slathered with butter and jam. Fruit. Glistening and plump. It looks like a painting. A simulation.

It looks like the kind of thing an alien would try to give a tired, hungry human.

Meant to look enticing. To put her at ease.

Mac doesn't want to look at Roxy, at the food that is probably-not-food. So, she stares out the window at the trees.

"Mac," Roxy repeats, more firmly this time, but Mac stands, knocking the plate out of Roxy's hand.

"Sorry, I," Mac starts, but she never finishes. She is out the front door followed by Roxy's calls of alarm.

There *is* something wrong. The trees are closer to the cabin.

The morning that Mac and Roxy got hopelessly lost, a futile search found no trace of the missing pack, so they gave up and broke camp.

The mood of their trip was spoiled. Roxy watched Mac's back as they retraced their steps, choosing to go back the way they came since they didn't know the way forward.

She wanted to berate Mac for leaving the map in her pack, but Mac already seemed to be doing a good job of taking it out on herself.

The air was hot and heavy, and while it was a relief to hike unburdened—Mac had taken her pack—she felt guilty allowing Mac to carry all their supplies. The guilt wasn't just about that. She'd been on edge since Mac's mood had gone sour.

During their first day of hiking, she'd been fascinated by how lush the summer greenery was, but now it made things confusing. Everything looked the same.

Mac halted abruptly and Roxy, still looking up at the hazy sky, slammed into her back.

"Jesus, watch out," Mac muttered.

Roxy hated that tone. It usually made her overcompensate with niceties, which seemed to make Mac worse. "Sorry. I wasn't watching. Silly me." Her tone felt forced even to her own ears. She wished she hadn't said anything.

Roxy peered around Mac's broad back. The trail forked, and the trees were unblazed.

"Damnit," Mac said, louder this time.

"Do you remember which way we came?"

"If I did, do you think I'd have stopped?" Mac didn't turn around.

Roxy trudged through the dense underbrush to stand beside Mac, inspecting each direction. To the left, the trail dropped off into a steep valley, running alongside a stream. To the right, the trail climbed. Roxy's legs wobbled at the sight.

Mac started down the path toward the stream without further discussion. Roxy wanted to object. She wanted to push Mac to weigh their options, but instead she followed.

It stung that Mac didn't feel it warranted a conversation. Maybe Roxy had some insight into which way they came. But she didn't. She didn't even remember this portion of the woods, which surprised her, since they'd just come through the day before. At least, she thought they had, since they were still on the trail.

The trees knotted together, tangled tight against the sky, though she knew it was only a trick of perspective. It made her shudder to think of the trees holding hands, bearing down on them.

They hiked along the stream for what felt like hours, stopping to pump water through their charcoal filter, topping their Nalgenes off with cool spring water. Roxy's stomach grumbled, but she didn't dare mention it.

All the food had been in the bear bag.

The repetitive motion of the hike was a sedative. Left foot, right foot. She watched dust motes dance through the sun-dappled air, fixated on the back of Mac's head, dirty purple bandana wrapped tight around her short, soft curls. Thought about all the things she would eat when they found their way out.

By midday, they left the trail without noticing. By the first blushes of sunset, they were completely lost.

Mac stands in the clearing, the cabin to her back. She feels in her bones that the trees are closer, that they'd taken one giant Red

Rover step toward the moss-covered cabin, but now she isn't sure. Roxy must think she's an idiot.

If the woman in there is Roxy.

Mac turns back to the cabin, focusing all her fear on what's waiting inside.

Roxy sits on the sofa, picking food off her plate, a large mug resting between her knees. The smell of coffee winds up through Mac's nostrils, and her brain screams for caffeine. That's what she needs. She's sleep deprived. It's making her think strange things about this weird cabin and the freaky trees and her friend.

Her friend. Roxy is her friend.

"What?" Roxy says, looking up. She doesn't have her chipper facade on. Something is wrong. Tendrils of anxiety weave their way back down Mac's neck, sending ice rolling across her body like river rapids.

This is it. Roxy is caught. In what, she doesn't know, but she's about to find out.

"Why did you bring me here?" Mac says, her tone too brusque, her voice quivering. She doesn't like confrontation. She prefers to analyze, try the pieces in different configurations until something fits.

Roxy looks affronted, like it was out of left field for Mac to ask her such things, even though she is obviously hiding something. "What do you mean? Camping? Jeez. I can't ask my best friend out for some good exercise and outdoor fun?"

Mac stares. Roxy sets the plate down and rearranges the large nature photography books on the wooden coffee table. Roxy tried to babble at her earlier that a photographer must live out here. Seemed a convenient detail. One Mac doesn't believe. This isn't a real cabin. No one lives here.

"No, Roxy. Not the camping trip. Why did you bring us to this cabin?"

Roxy looks honestly confused by the question, and Mac is astounded by Roxy's acting skills.

"The cabin? We found it together. We are lost in the woods, Mac. You're starting to scare me. You haven't been making sense all day. First, you're out there raving about the trees and now you're in here accusing me of, what, taking you to an isolated cabin? Pulling your pack out of the trees?"

That is exactly what she's accusing her of, and Mac feels elated that she's found her out. The pieces fall into place. Roxy must have gotten up in the middle of the night. She wasn't sure how, given the size of the tent. She must have gotten her to pick the wrong way back, though Mac can't remember if she led the hike back or if Roxy did.

"Mac, you're spinning. Talk to me. You're freaking me out."

Roxy stands up and steps toward her, but Mac recoils. Roxy hates the outdoors. Would never have suggested this.

"Mac," Roxy says, voice calm and measured, "you should sit down."

Mac's entire body feels electric. Her fears find validation and explodes into a roaring fire.

"I brought you out here," Roxy says, but Mac's ears are ringing, and she can't focus, "because I love you. I know that now. I can't lose you, and I guess I got scared when you started hanging out with Laura, so—"

Mac stops listening. This isn't the real Roxy. Roxy broke up with her years ago, has held her at arm's length ever since, has been her friend but nothing more.

No, this is a trap.

Mac takes three long steps to the kitchen and pulls a knife out of the wooden block, but Roxy isn't watching. She is staring out the window.

"Holy shit. The trees *are* closer."

After a terse argument about who lost the trail, Mac and Roxy made camp in the dark. With no food to eat, they settled into their sleeping bags, silence hanging in the air like a third companion.

Roxy squeezed her eyes shut and tried not to think about Mac's hip pressing into hers. This trip hadn't gone at all as she'd hoped.

She needed Mac to see that maybe they could be something more again. She rolled onto her hip and rested her hand across Mac's belly.

Mac's eyes snapped open. Roxy hoped to see intrigue and desire, but behind the confusion was the familiar look Mac had given her so often toward the end of their relationship.

Suspicion.

"What are you doing?" Mac asked, her voice dry.

Roxy shrugged, pulled the sleeping bag open so Mac could see the curve of her breast under her thin T-shirt, the supple skin above her underwear. "Mac," she said, slightly breathless. "I miss you."

Mac recoiled, actually recoiled, and it sent waves of shame through Roxy, igniting her temper. She pulled the sleeping bag shut and turned away, curling into a ball. She could feel Mac watching her, but she didn't want to be seen. This whole thing was a mistake.

Neither of them spoke as they broke camp in the morning and began their trudge in search of the trail. They were both lightheaded and dazed, stumbling through the forest.

Midday, they found the cabin.

Mac follows Roxy onto the porch, down the steps, and into the clearing, knife still in hand. Three steps off the porch is a line of impenetrable trees.

Towering over the cabin, the canopy blocks out the sunlight. Roxy whimpers, and she reaches for Mac's hand, finding the knife. Their eyes meet, and Roxy's are a torrent of fear and hurt. She holds Roxy's gaze and sees her for the first time in days. The real her. Her friend.

Roxy looks down at the knife, her face a silent question of Mac's intentions. Mac drops it, hearing the soft thud as it hits the grass.

They lunge for each other, gripping tight, as the trees stand watch. Mac is right about this place, but she is wrong about her best friend.

So wrong.

All her confusion and inaction melt away, and an overwhelming urge to see Roxy safely out of the wood kicks in.

Mac pulls them into the cabin and grabs the pack, which lies discarded on the clean floor. She opens the cabinets and starts jamming in whatever food she can.

"We have to go. We have to go now," Mac says softly, like the trees outside can hear them.

Roxy nods in a daze.

Mac slings the pack over her shoulder and grabs Roxy's hand, leading her toward the front door, but it is too late.

The door is gone.

The floorboards creak, dark green roots winding up through the cedar planks.

They are trapped.

It *was* a trap.

Somehow that makes it better. That she did understand some part of what was happening. That she's not crazy.

Glass pops as branches shatter the windows. The wooden beams groan as the trees push down on the roof.

Mac turns to Roxy, this time no longer afraid of what she'll find.

"I'm sorry, Roxy. I think I knew why you brought me out here, and I didn't want to face it. Didn't want to risk trying again."

Roxy nods. "I love you, Mac. That's the only reason I brought you out here."

Mac squeezes Roxy's shoulders and pulls her closer. This is real. The cabin, the woods, and Roxy. Roxy has always been real.

And now they will always be together.

As the walls bow and break from the intrusion of gnarled roots and branches, the clawing tendrils of doubt unwind themselves from Mac's brain. The relief is foreign and unmooring, as though she's just dropped a heavy pack after days of hiking. Like she will float off the floor. She doesn't know if she's ever felt like this.

So sure.

Mac puts her hands over Roxy's cheeks, tears and sweat sliding along her fingertips. She looks deep into Roxy's eyes, something she's been afraid to do for days. Too afraid she'd see a monster lurking underneath. All she finds is love.

The last thing Mac says before the trees envelope them is, "I know that now."

THE PHANTOMS OF WILDRIDGE HALL

BY MARIANNE HALBERT

The fog clung to Wildridge Manor like a shroud. In the waning light of day, the scent of the sea drifted to me as I walked the garden path. I was making my way across crumbling flagstone when I heard the distinct sound of a carriage. The steady unhurried *clip-clop, clip-clop* of a single horse, and wheels crunching over a lane. Through the mist and beyond a row of trees, I could make out the faint outline in the gloom. No, not a carriage—*a hearse*. My chest tightened and I quickened my pace, the crunch of shells and pebbles beneath my steps as I moved away from the garden and on to a small path leading to the mansion. *Was I too late?* Wildridge Manor loomed before me.

The doors were massive, fitted with two brass knobs in the shape of squirming fish. I reached for one, the metal cold under my trembling hand. I heard waves crashing against cliffs. I thought of the tales my friends had told—their warnings about Wildridge Hall, about what lay beneath the surface just offshore. Perhaps I'd made a mistake. It wasn't too late to return. I could walk back to the road, find a good Samaritan to take me to the station, and escape the draw of Wildridge. But—that note in my pocket; that *hearse*.

I raised the door knocker and clanged it once. Twice. Thrice. The waves continued to crash rhythmically in the distance, mocking the pounding of my heart.

The door swung open and paused as though the opener were assessing me. Then it opened more. A young woman stood silent.

Dressed in a servant's uniform, wiry brown hair peeking out from her bonnet, she looked beyond me as though expecting to see someone else.

"Yes?" she said.

The chill of the evening had seeped beneath my clothes. I shivered. "Trella DuMont. I've just arrived from Bibury. Lady Odessa is expecting me." A shaggy gray dog approached me and began to sniff the hem of my cloak. A smaller hound hung back, wary.

"Trella DuMont?" There was doubt in the servant's voice as she studied my face.

"Yes," I confirmed.

The woman's chest heaved, and she stepped back, opening the door fully. "I'm Lethia." A young girl peered out from behind her skirts before covering her eyes with Lethia's apron. "Don't mind my Poppy. She's shy of strangers."

I stepped through the threshold and into the entryway. Lethia closed the door and took a few steps toward a hall.

"And Lady Odessa is …?" I asked, loathing the tremble I heard in my voice. My thoughts were consumed by the hearse that had passed me on the shell-covered road and in my mind's eye it carried Lady Odessa's corpse, still and gray.

"Resting in her chambers." Her voice sounded so at ease I found myself relaxing. "Your things?" she asked, glancing at my empty hands.

"At the roadside. The driver refused to approach the house. Wouldn't even enter the grounds. Warned me away from it, in fact." *Why did I say that? What must she think of me?* "But of course, I paid him no mind," I tried to assure her.

"Ah, no surprise there. Townsfolk fear the Wildridge Phantoms." She chuckled, tousling her daughter's wild curly hair. "I'll send Mr. Parsley for your things." She was looking at Poppy as she said that last and raised her brows. Poppy scurried off, in search of Mr. Parsley, no doubt. Lethia then took my cloak and made a face. "Why, it's soaked through with the fog. We'll see the madame and then we'll get you near the fire." She hung my cloak on a hook near the door. "Please," she said, walking toward a large staircase and beckoning me forward.

I placed my hand on the railing, trying to steady myself. I sensed eyes watching me and looked down the dim hallway. An imposing figure stood there, candlelight from the hall sconce reflecting in his dark eyes, but otherwise he fell mostly in shadow. I took a few steps and turned to look at him once more, but the figure had vanished.

I followed Lethia up several flights of stairs and then we walked toward the east wing of the mansion. Lethia slowed her pace as we approached an open door. She spoke softly as we entered the room.

"My lady, Miss DuMont has just now arrived—"

The room was grand, as expected. Intricate floral wallpaper lined the room, heavy red drapes lined the windows, and precious curios filled shelves and cabinets. I hadn't seen Lady Odessa in nearly a year. She had needed a companion while visiting a distant cousin just outside of Bibury and had selected me through a common acquaintance. Some of the girls in our quaint village whispered about the curse at Wildridge. But I wasn't going to Wildridge, at least not then.

Now she lay before me, dwarfed by a massive four-poster bed. A young man sat by her bedside holding her hand, worry lines evident across his young brow. She struggled to sit up as soon as she saw me and he assisted her, placing an extra satin pillow behind her back. He rose from his chair, straightening his broad shoulders. He was tall—very tall. I knew from her descriptions—"eyes as blue as the morning sea, and he has his father's hair ... thick sandy waves dusted with gold"—this must be her younger son, Emory Quintrell. He turned from her and looked directly at me for the first time with those deep blue eyes, startled upon seeing me. He collected himself, then motioned toward the chair he had just vacated.

"Please, miss." His voice was so humble, placating.

I nodded and accepted the seat. Lady Odessa immediately enveloped my hand in hers. Her skin felt papery and delicate as she squeezed.

"Opal," she breathed.

I looked to Emory, confused. He opened his mouth as though to say something but refrained.

"It's Miss DuMont. From Bibury," I said gently.

She studied my countenance and her familiar broad smile lit up her face. She squeezed my hand more firmly. "Oh, my dear Trella. The doctors say I need a dryer climate, that Wildridge is too laden with fog and mist for my lungs to heal. But I know what I need, and I certainly have it now." She reached one hand toward Emory and pulled my hand into his. "Show her around and help her feel at home."

A servant entered the room carrying a tea tray and set it down on the sideboard. Lethia joined her and began to prepare a cup.

Emory hesitated, watching Lethia pour the tea. His mother sat up straighter and shooed us away good naturedly, her hands flapping like a bird's wings as she grinned. He escorted me into the hall.

He held his arm out at the top of the stairs and we descended, arm in arm.

"Wildridge is charming, once you get to know her. Mother's wing is to the east, as you saw. My brother and I have our quarters to the south. Yours are to the west, overlooking the gardens and the dark woods beyond. Lethia can acquaint you with your quarters. You can get lost if you're not careful. It was apparently easier when it was simply Wildridge Hall. But my father continued to build, adding room after room, floor after floor, wing after wing, until it became the Wildridge Manor you see now." We stopped on the landing below the fourth floor, and he pointed to indicate the layout. "On the third floor there are many sitting rooms, reading rooms, libraries and music rooms." We descended another flight. "On the second floor we have the parlor, the dining hall, the tearoom, and the ballroom." The foyer was ahead of us, and the doors leading to the garden beyond that. He glanced down to the lower level and a dimly lit hall. "You needn't ever go below. That's just the servants' quarters, kitchens and pantry."

I recalled Lady Odessa's description of the sea and asked if he could show me. We walked out through a large glass door at the end of the ballroom onto an enormous terrace on the east side. I approached the edge, resting my hand on a stone wall. Night had fallen. Moonlight pierced dark clouds and reflected on the water. The sea churned below, angry and smashing into the rocks.

A lone figure stood on the rocks along the shore, oblivious to the ocean spray, his long jacket and scarf billowing in the wind.

"Magnus?" I inquired.

Emory's shoulders slouched. "My older brother is a bit solitary. He prefers to spend his mornings scavenging for sea glass rather than spend time with me, or Mother. His days are devoted to work. And his evenings," he looked at his brother and gestured with his hand. *Like that.* "I used to admire him so, followed him, wanted to be him. Now, we barely speak, each finding ways to escape each other within these halls."

"I'm so sorry. Is there no hope of repairing the bond?" I asked. He hesitated and I hoped I hadn't overstepped. His only reply was a weak smile and a shrug. We stood in the moonlight, the air thick with the scent of the sea, whitecaps breaking against the shore. After a minute I broke the silence.

"Can you escort me down there tomorrow? I've never been to the coast."

He paused. "I would, but … I don't go to the shore. I'm probably destroying any image you had of me, but the truth is, I'm deathly afraid of heights. And there's a portion of the path that gets very narrow," and he said it again under his breath, looking queasy, "*very* narrow."

Lethia stepped on to the terrace. "Miss DuMont, I've prepared a supper tray. Bangers and mash. You must be hungry after your travel. I could take it up to your room or arrange it in the dining hall?"

I smiled at Emory. "In my room, if that's all right? I am tired."

"Of course," he said. "Goodnight, Miss DuMont." He tipped his head toward me in a farewell, and I followed Lethia to my chambers.

The room was furnished lavishly, a scallop-shaped canopy over the bed. Curved windows lined one wall. Ornate décor, from the armoire to the vanity table filled the room. A golden fainting couch sat near the windows, and I wondered what I might spy that would make one faint.

"It's stunning," I said.

"It was hers." Lethia set the dinner tray on a marble-topped cherrywood table.

"Hers? Lady Odessa?" I asked.

"Oh, no Miss Trella. This was Miss Opal's quarters during her year-long engagement to Magnus. It's strange to think, if things had gone differently, they'd be married by now." She moved to the bed to turn down the covers. Perhaps a broken engagement explained Magnus's sullen disposition.

The mirror at the vanity was outlined in the most beautiful stones I'd ever seen. Shades of aquamarine, seafoam, and deep blue. Candlelight sparkled off them and through them, casting rays across the room.

"Those stones—" I began.

"Ah, that would be Mr. Quintrell. He scours the shoreline looking for his precious sea glass. If you ask me, he takes after his father. Obsessed with the lost souls off the shores of Wildridge. Spends more time with the dead than the living."

"Where does the path begin? The one that leads to the sea? I thought I might explore in the morning."

She looked up from fluffing the pillows. "Off of the east parlor. But you must manage Sorrow's Ridge. If you lose your footing there, there'll be one less place for dinner." She laughed a little uneasily. "Stay to the path so you don't get off into the brambles. It's an S-shaped trail. Curve to the left and it swings back to the lower ridge—Sorrow's Ridge. Then curve to the right and it curls down to the shore. Not much sand below, just the rocks and tidepools."

The bangers and mash were comforting. After unpacking my belongings, I went to the window. I looked out over the garden where I'd been when I heard the hearse. I thought of my mother. Of how, even after she was in the ground, I would perceive her. A shadow in the corner of my eye in our little parlor. The whiff of lemon cakes baking when I entered the cold kitchen. Her low humming coming from the other side of the wall. It was comforting sensing her so close yet heartbreaking knowing she was so far. The most I could hope for was a fleeting hint of her *almost there*.

I slept fitfully and arose at dawn. I bundled up and set out for the path to the sea. I followed Lethia's directions, veering to the left, and back to the right. I nearly stumbled when I heard something up ahead—a small giggle—and then Poppy jumped out from the tall amber grass.

"Did I frighten you?" she asked, pleased with herself.

"You certainly did," I said, feeling my heart racing. Behind her, through the thick scrub, I made out a spire.

"What is that?" I gestured.

She leaned in slightly toward me. "That's the Dead House. We're not allowed to go there." Her tone was somber. She moved her head casually, making sure no one else was around. Her mouth turned into a smirk as she held her hand toward me. "Would you like me to show you?"

Squawking seagulls swooped nearby, then hopped on the black rocks far below, pecking at their lunch. We rounded a bend, the ocean to our left, the scent of the sea briny in my nose. Tucked along the cliff was what appeared to be a small open-air chapel, with a curved entryway on the seaside. White stone seahorses and long brass torches flanked the entrance. I turned back to Poppy, and she nodded, encouraging me.

I stepped in. It took a moment for my mind to understand what my eyes were seeing. The torches were lit around the room. In the center lay a glass coffin with gold-plated edges. The cushion was the deep pink of a conch shell. But what shocked me to my core was the woman motionless behind the glass. She was young and slender, and her golden hair lay in ringlets over her shoulders and draping her waist. Her hands were folded neatly across the swell of her chest. A delicate string was tied to the index finger of her right hand. My gaze followed the string through a tiny hole in the lid of her coffin, where it led to a thin brass shepherd's hook. Dangling from the end of the thread was a dainty brass bell.

I looked back again to her form, to her face, to her hair. I saw my own reflection in the glass. She could be me. Except that her skin was a pallid greenish color. Her eyelids were not quite sealed closed revealing just a slit of white. A foamy crust had formed over her parted lips. We were so similar in appearance I felt like death had just walked over my grave and whispered in my ear. I thought of the hearse the day I arrived. I heard a low humming, and I stumbled back, stepping into the daylight.

"Who?" I managed to squeak out.

Poppy was cutting bunches of the bright pink flowers that grew wild in low clumps around the chapel. She didn't turn as she spoke.

"Mistress Opal, silly. Who else?"

Mistress Opal. "She was betrothed to Mr. Quintrell?"

Poppy nodded, her face suddenly solemn. "His father had the shrine built to honor the dead. Magnus keeps the torches burning."

I softly spoke my thoughts out loud. "It's no wonder you're not allowed to go here."

Poppy shrugged as she continued to cut and study the flowers. "There's a lot goes on at Wildridge that's not allowed. You'll get used to it. We all do."

Waves crashed and I felt my chest tighten. "How, how did she …?" My mind thought of Sorrow's Ridge, but she looked so unbroken.

"No one knows. She went to sleep one night, and never woke up. In the same bed you sleep in. I wonder if you'll not wake up one morning." Poppy giggled. She brushed the dry grass from her hands and put her small scissors back in her pocket. She gathered her flowers and held one bunch out to me. "Sea thrift?"

I accepted it absently and tucked it into the waist of my coat.

She took my hand, and we started back up the path, but I paused when I saw the figure near the shore. Magnus.

"You go ahead. I'll be up shortly."

Poppy nodded and skipped up the trail.

I stepped forward. Within a few feet the path narrowed drastically. It was dizzying, Wildridge looming above me, the jagged rocks like a maw below. My head swam for a moment, but I took in a deep breath of sea air and carefully continued. Before long the path widened again, and I'd made it to the shore. I approached Magnus. He must've heard my step and turned.

"Miss DuMont." Was that a hint of annoyance?

I maneuvered carefully over the crags and tide pools, little sea creatures darting and squirming. I stood near Magnus and looked out over the ocean. It was so vast, so endless, so wild. I caught him watching me.

"I'm sorry, it's just, I've never been to the seaside before. We have a gentle river and lazy swans in my village. I've never seen the ocean until Wildridge …"

He grinned. "I've heard my mother's tales about the incomparable Miss DuMont of Bibury. Let me see if I recall correctly. You are fluent in French and Italian, the reigning champion at Forfeits, the only person who knows precisely how Mother prefers her afternoon tea, though we shan't mention that to Lethia as she prides herself with that skill, and you can lasso the moon, but only on Tuesdays."

I felt my cheeks blushing. "Well, I've heard of the unparalleled Mr. Magnus Quintrell. That he's a highly esteemed solicitor, that he shares his father's deep love of the sea and her mysteries, and he creates handsome displays from sea glass."

He opened his palm and nodded. "According to my father, many years ago, two schooners carrying goods from the East got caught in a terrible storm off these shores. He said Poseidon himself cast up the tempest so that the ships would sink to the ocean floor and the treasure would be his. Glass bottles in all shades of blue and green and more shattered, then scattered along the coastline, polished over the years by the unyielding waves washing over them again and again."

In the daylight, I could see that his hair was a shade darker than Emory's but his eyes were a shade lighter. While Emory might catch a young woman's eye first, there was something in Magnus's demeanor that was intriguing. He seemed like an old soul.

A gust picked up then and toppled me off balance. I let out a small shriek startling the seagulls as one foot left the rock and I began to fall. Magnus didn't hesitate. He reached for me, his steady arms around me, pulling me toward him. In reaching for me he'd emptied his hands, the precious sea glass falling into the waves. I clung to him, shivering.

"We should get you back to Wildridge." I wasn't going to argue. In the distance I saw the steeple of the shrine just a faded outline behind the tall grasses in the hazy morning sun and thought of the decaying corpse of his fiancée. Of the things that weren't allowed—but happened anyway.

Magnus scooped me up into his arms, carrying me across jagged rocks until we reached the path. He set me down, yet my arms still drooped around his neck. I raised my gaze to meet his. His stormy eyes focused on mine and I was keenly aware of his hands around my waist. I found myself wondering how it would feel to press my lips to his and sensed a thrill deep within me. Blushing, I released him and began the winding walk to the top of the ridge at a brisk pace, sensing him right behind. I expected a word of warning as we approached Sorrow's Ridge, but he said nothing.

I passed by Lady Odessa on the stairs. She put a hand on my arm and stared at the bundle of flowers in the waist of my coat. I'd forgotten they were even there.

"You mustn't bring those in the house, dear."

"But, why?" I asked.

She looked confused. "I ... well look at that, I can't recall. But leave the sea thrift to the sea. Join us in the music room?"

I nodded and continued up the stairs. I changed out of my walking clothes which still smelled of the ocean—a scent I was coming to associate with Magnus.

Lady Odessa sat on a divan in the music room, nodding along as Emory played the viola, the rich tones filling the room. I caught myself watching his strong bow arm, the precision and control it took to create the music. Poppy snuck in and snuggled up against my side. She cupped her hand to my ear and whispered, "Don't tell Mother." Then she looked from Lady Odessa to Emory and smiled, enjoying being part of the occasion.

Lady Odessa bragged about my proficiency at the piano and Emory insisted I play. Then he and I took turns reading poetry to our small audience and I couldn't help noticing the way he looked at me as he read Lady Mary Wortley Montagu's "A Hymn to the Moon" as though it had been written for us alone.

At one point, I noticed Lethia had entered the room. She asked if we'd seen Poppy, but Poppy had disappeared, and we all shook our heads innocently. There was more than annoyance in Lethia's expression; she was nearly seething. Emory stood, stepping away from me and placing the slim volume back onto the shelf. Lady Odessa retired to her room to rest, and I went upstairs to dress for dinner. Later, Lethia braided my hair as a plaited headband as I sat at the vanity, letting my long blonde curls flow over my shoulders and down my back.

"So, they were very in love?" I asked, hoping it sounded casual.

"Opal and Magnus?" Her tone sounded dull, distant.

I wondered if she'd found Poppy. I nodded, looking at her reflection in the mirror.

She hesitated. "It was an arranged marriage. Some say Opal was secretly in love with another man. But they were both committed to it. Lady Odessa won't rest easy until she knows there's an heir to Wildridge."

"Love seems so complicated."

Lethia cracked a knowing smile. "It certainly can be." She put the final pins in my hair.

"Lethia? Are you …?" I smiled. *Was she in love?*

"No point speaking of it. I don't think the madame would approve."

I turned to face her. "Surely, she wouldn't stand in the way of your happiness. Or of providing a father for Poppy. She's so generous of spirit. When I heard she'd fallen ill—when I saw the phantom hearse in the fog …"

Lethia stiffened, a pallor spreading across her face. "A phantom hearse?"

"The day I arrived, just before you opened the door."

She was shaking. "Oh, no no, Miss Trella. That's an omen for sure." She turned to me before fleeing into the hall. "Wildridge is warning you away."

I entered the dining hall. Lady Odessa was at the head of the table. Emory sat to her left. The seat to her right remained empty.

"Magnus, is he …?" I asked.

She waved her napkin. "Who knows. He marches to his own beat. Please sit."

Lethia and the cook brought out a large bowl of prawn bisque and a fish pie. Lethia still looked pale and wouldn't look me in the eye. Emory stood, took a carafe of wine, and poured about half a glass for his mother. She scolded him and he added a splash more.

"May I?" he asked. I lifted my glass toward him, and he poured.

Magnus entered, watching us for a moment as our hands touched. He took his seat, brooding. Emory moved to pour some wine for him, but Magnus lay his hand over his glass. Emory took a seat.

"Trella," Lady Odessa said, "you must tell me what you think of our little Wildridge Manor." She had a sparkle in her eye.

"Little!" I laughed. "It's so grand! The gardens, the manor house, the ocean. It's just as you described but even more so."

"I wish you could've seen it in its glory. It's a bit run down since Phillip passed, but I'm hopeful a new generation will restore it. I'm still so grateful, my dear girl, that you came to see an old woman in her hour of need. I don't know how you sensed it, but you were always sensitive."

I raised my glass to take a sip of my wine and paused. "Well, I hardly had to sense it. I came as soon as I received your note."

Lady Odessa looked puzzled. "My note? My dear, I didn't dispatch any note." Then she looked to Emory for confirmation. "Did I?" The confusion in her countenance pained me.

He raised his eyebrows. "Not that I'm aware of, Mother."

Magnus seemed agitated. "What note?"

"It was on Lady Odessa's stationery. I recognized it from when I was her companion in Bibury."

"Well, dear," she said, "it is fortuitous. We've tragically lost Opal, but you're so like her in some ways. Perhaps another match could be made." She glanced at Magnus, then back to me.

Magnus was horrified. The look he gave me cut me to the core. The allure I'd felt earlier in his arms evaporated and I felt foolish, ashamed. He stood, trembling with rage. He looked around the room like a man frenzied and cornered. He gripped the edge of the tablecloth in both hands and yanked, a cry of anguish erupting from within him. Everything shattered to the floor. The bisque, the fish pie, the wine, my pride. The dogs came in and began to lap up the dinner.

"Magnus!" Lady Odessa said, shocked and offended. She began shaking and Lethia insisted on helping her upstairs.

I escaped to the garden, and Emory followed me.

"Am I?" I asked. "Very like her in some ways?"

He chuckled, then became more earnest and began to study me. I felt self-conscious under his gaze. "Physically, there's no question." He gently touched my hair, studying it in the moonlight, the sound of the waves crashing against cliffs in the distance. "Both young. Both fair. I don't know you well enough to know if you share other characteristics."

"What was she like?"

"She was rich." His eyebrows went up, questioning.

"I am not."

"She was self-indulgent." He didn't sound judgmental, simply acknowledging a fact.

It hurt to hear that after being compared to her. "Is it true that she loved someone else?"

He looked pained for a moment. "She meant to marry my brother. Whatever you may have heard."

"I'm sorry, I shouldn't give heed to idle gossip."

"Mother is determined to see a wedding and a new union to take over the estate. If Magnus is too consumed in mourning to consider matrimony, I fear it won't be long before Mother attempts to unite the two of us." His voice sounded resigned. He took my hand. "I'd do anything to please her."

"Us? No," I said, pulling away and trying not to sound dismissive but I couldn't ponder the possibility.

I awoke in the night, forgetting for a moment that I was no longer in my little cottage. A breeze blew in. I arose from bed and moved to shut the window when I heard a sound—a low moaning. I slipped into my nightrobe, the silk blue-silver in the moonlight that streamed into the room. I lit a single candle in a brass holder and made my way soundlessly down the stairs. All else seemed hushed, no stirring coming from the south or east wing. I crept down to the second floor. I peered down the dark shadow of the servants' quarters and made my way across the ballroom.

Once on the terrace, I leaned over as far as I dared, the wind whipping at the flame of my candle. The dreadful moaning grew more pronounced. I lifted my candle, and my heart nearly stopped when another sound was added to the mix—the light yet distinct tinkle of a bell. My thoughts went to Opal in her eternal slumber in the Dead House, that delicate string tied to her slender rotting finger *just in case* ... The thought was too horrendous to contemplate.

A gust of wind tossed my hair and snuffed my flame just as I glimpsed a phantom shadow in my periphery. I screamed. I raced inside, through the ballroom, across the foyer, and flung open the door. I bolted down the steps and into the garden, keeping Wildridge between me and the ocean. Between me and the Dead House. That's when I heard it—the *clip-clop, clip-clop* of a horse and the trundling of wheels. Disoriented by my terror, I couldn't tell which direction it was traveling. Was it coming toward me or moving away? A hand fell onto my shoulder. In my fright my knees buckled, and all went dark.

Magnus laid a blanket over me, then added more logs to the fire in the parlor. I'd just told him what I'd experienced between waking in my room and fainting in the garden. He turned toward me, the flames casting shadows across his face. He took a seat in a wingback chair near me.

"You say you heard moaning."

"Yes," I answered. "Coming from my window. Then below the terrace. But worse"—I shuddered—"the sound of a tiny bell."

He leaned forward. "That's impossible." He seemed angry, yet terrified. "You put too much stock in the rumors and myths surrounding Wildridge. If there is a phantom, it's not the souls of lost sailors or the specter of my departed betrothed. It's the shadow of my father and his obsession with those souls lost in the shipwreck. It's my mother's mourning and the way she's only half present much of the time. It's the vast chasm between my brother and I when we brush past each other. Our *brokenness* is the phantom that haunts these halls. Someone who knows only quaint village life feeding the lazy swans along a gentle river is bound to see ghosts in every shadow rather than what's right before her eyes."

I was aghast. "You know *nothing* of me or my life. I would never trouble your mother with my own tragedies. I certainly would not divulge them to someone who flies into a fit of rage at the idea of marrying me, but do not presume that I don't have my own sorrows." The sting of tears threatened to form in my eyes, and I forced myself to remain calm. His face softened and his voice was gentler when he spoke.

"Of course." He stood, looking uncomfortable, almost humble. "Forgive me, I shouldn't presume. On my honor, my behavior at dinner was not driven by the suggestion of a match between us. The last young woman in that position lost her life. I couldn't bear the thought ..." His voice broke slightly, quivering. Daylight was arriving. Magnus took his leave.

Lethia's eyes grew wide. "You've seen it again?"

I'd found her in the dining hall laying out breakfast. "Well, not seen, exactly. But I heard the hearse in the night."

She grabbed a pinch of salt in her right hand and threw it over her left shoulder. "It's a portent for certain, miss. I fear you'll meet the same fate as Opal if you don't get away."

"But I can't just abandon Lady Odessa."

"I know how fond you are of her, but she wouldn't want you to risk your life, or your soul. You've lifted her spirits. Let that be enough."

"That sound. That *bell*. I need to know." *Could she still be alive somehow?*

Lethia seemed flummoxed. "Fine. If I agree to go with you and we see that Opal remains dead, you'll agree to quit Wildridge?"

I acquiesced.

We made our way down the path. Opal lay unchanged.

"She was beautiful," Lethia observed. "She should have married Magnus. But we saw the way she looked at Emory. And the way he looked back." Her tone was strange, resentful.

"Emory?" I asked.

"Upon their mother's death the estate is to be left to the eldest, unless the younger is married and the eldest is unwed. If Emory and Opal had married it would all be his. But even if I married Emory, it would all go to Magnus if he and Opal were married, since he's the eldest. It would all be lost to us. I couldn't allow that."

I heard a small chuckle coming from outside the Dead House. Emory stepped forward.

"Us?" he laughed more heartily. "My dear Lethia. You've been a loyal servant and quite entertaining during our rendezvous, but you can't believe that I would marry you? As you said, my father wanted to carry on the family line. That requires breeding. Thus, why I wrote to Miss DuMont upon Opal's death. Trella comes from good stock. And Mother had described them as looking so alike. One is as good as the other."

I spied Magnus storming up the path from below. He must've heard.

He looked horrified. "Then you weren't in love with Opal? You didn't kill her to keep her from me?"

"No," I said, realizing the truth. "That was Lethia." I thought of the flowers, the tea. Opal and Lady Odessa. The terms of the will. "She put the sea thrift in her tea. And meant to do the same to your mother once Lethia and Emory were married."

Lethia's face was contorted with rage, matching the turbulence of the swells against the cliff. Seafoam sprayed up. She grabbed a torch from its casing. Magnus instinctively put himself between us, shielding me. Lethia refocused her fury where it was really directed. Running at Emory, she rammed the flaming torch into his chest. Shoved backward, his arms pinwheeled for a moment before he plunged off Sorrow's Ridge to his death on the rocks below.

"You," she seethed, turning on me. "You did this. If you'd never come here, he would have wanted *me* again." A moaning sound carried up the cliffside, grasses blowing in the wind. Lethia turned back, uncertain. "Emory?"

She looked over the edge of the cliff. She turned and her haunted eyes met my gaze. "Oh, heaven. Their souls! How ragged. How rotten. The undertaker has come for Emory and now he comes for me!"

Magnus reached for her, barely allowing *"No,"* to escape his lips before she stepped into nothingness and plummeted.

Magnus turned to me and took me tight in his arms. We moved toward the cliff to see the lovers below, the waves rolling over them, leaving their broken bodies but claiming their souls.

We couldn't bear to tell Lady Odessa or Poppy the truth. What point would it serve? We told a more palatable tale. Lethia was picking flowers and lost her footing. Emory tried to rescue her but in the end they both perished. Lady Odessa accepted it. If Poppy had her doubts, she never revealed it.

In the music room one day, Poppy divulged to me that "A Hymn to the Moon" was actually Magnus's favorite poem. Emory'd stolen it, she'd said, to make women swoon. She asked if I enjoyed the prank she and her mother had played on me. Lethia told her I enjoyed a good scare and so they went out the back kitchen and made moaning sounds beneath my room, then below the veranda, deepening their timbre to sound like sailors. She giggled recounting that it was she who got to ring the little bell.

Opal was buried on her family's estate. Now we stand in the Dead House, Magnus and I, surrounded by an arch of sea glass, leaving flowers for the dead. I cannot help but wonder what apparitions Lethia beheld in those final moments that haunted her so. The parson and Lady Odessa await us on the veranda for the small ceremony. Magnus turns to me with a smile and brushes a light kiss across my cheek. He takes my hands in his and softly recites "A Hymn to the Moon."

"By thy pale beams I solitary rove,
To thee my tender grief confide;
Serenely sweet you gild the silent grove,
My friend, my goddess, and my guide."

We walk the path hand in hand, on the verge of being joined in marriage. I glance back at Sorrow's Ridge and hear my mother's soft hum on the breeze. We are haunted by our sorrows, but we can sometimes find comfort there as well. I squeeze Magnus's hand, my heart aflame and my entire being thrilled, pondering the days and nights to come.

THE BLACKBURNE LIGHTHOUSE

BY ANN WUEHLER

The moon bounced over the restless waters of the Atlantic as I fled my cousin's tiny cottage on the shores of Blackburne Bay. My tolerance extended far and wide, but hands grabbing at my ankles from beneath the bed crossed a line even for an "on the shelf" grump such as myself.

I saw Eustacia's elderly rowboat.

Before my good sense could kick me harder than my cousin's ancient, fat pony, I clambered into it and pushed off into the surf. I looked back at the shore and several shadows stood there. They gibbered and danced on the sand amid the broken shells, driftwood pieces, and flotsam tossed there by the waves. It did not seem fair or right that my cousin's cottage be infested so with spirits, with ghosts, with whatever malicious nasties. They tormented me more and more with every visit here.

Eustacia herself they left alone. She never spoke of ghosts. She was the most practical, realistic person I've yet to meet. Ghosts had no place in her cozy, small world of painting seascapes so sedate I used them instead of warm milk to fall asleep. She took up sewing to supplement her small income inherited from her father.

Even now she probably slept in dreamless slumber beneath sheets she washed like clockwork every two weeks. She boiled them with Queen Elizabeth root, a habit her mother had handed down.

I realized, as I bobbed and swayed on the unruly back of the Atlantic, that I did not have paddles. I drifted far too rapidly for my taste, caught in some sort of unseen current. The dark outlines of the lighthouse reared up like a raised arm, perhaps a mile down or so, the light flashing out with lazy regularity. I gulped but perhaps I could seek a bit of shelter there with Edgard Stivers before a long, cold walk back to Eustacia's haunted domicile of timbers, tile, and stone.

However, seeking shelter with Mr. Stivers left me quite perturbed and excited in my mind. The last time visiting my cousin, I had gone into the post office to mail a letter. By accident, I had bumped into him in my rush to avoid getting soaked in the squall that had developed in seeming moments. As usual, I had forgotten my umbrella. My hand had gripped at the buttons of his waistcoat, his person solid and warm against my hand. His cap had fallen off, his hair wild and unkempt but lush as a thicket of secret tangled bushes.

Perhaps that is how they greet each other in Boston, the bad-tempered gentleman had growled at me, *but even you have better manners than that.*

And he winked at me, as if we were friends or he meant to confuse me. I must admit little pangs sounded in my belly. I must confess I could only nod for a moment, my face as hot as Eustacia's teapot.

My lips flapped out that someone with manners would not have said that to me.

I have no manners, miss, the wretch replied before handing me his own black umbrella for my scurry back to the cottage.

The shadows followed along with my absurd flight, as if I were Moses floating down the Nile. I could not think of another story to parallel my own at the moment. The old rowboat began to leak. My bare feet flinched from sea water trying to cover them. I heard the boom of the surf against the big rocks that marked the place old Abel Crooks liked to fish. He told stories of sailors returning to the shore, years dead and counted among the lost. But everyone who lived against the ocean had such stories.

I lifted my cotton night skirts to my knees to avoid too much soaking, though to rescue myself, I'd have to fling myself over the side, make for the sand bar that lined the shore here or drift out to my death. Caroline Brinker had fallen asleep in a small skiff. She had yet to return forty some years later.

Ridiculous to be so caught out, to flee from perchance imagined fingers wrapping about my ankle as weird moans drifted to my ears from the walls around me.

I tried to paddle nearer the shore but something brushed my hand. Something slimy, soft, nefarious. Maybe it was the back of a great fish. Maybe it was something unnatural. Either way, I kept my hands in the boat after that. The current tossed me toward the lighthouse, the comforting light telling me Mr. Stivers at least would be at home.

I ignored the small thrill at meeting the man again. I had already doomed myself to being the silliest of halfwits by leaping in a ratty rowboat without checking for oars. A ratty rowboat riddled with leaks, at that. I'd either be a funny tale, my cheeks hot with shame at my night antics or a tragic tale with everyone quite sure of my watery fate.

I saw my chance as the sandbar loomed to my left.

I sped by the lighthouse, leaped over the side, the cotton of my nightdress immediately soaking up half the Atlantic. Down under I went, flailing to get topside again. I fought to get to the edge of the sandbar, the sands shifting and treacherous beneath my feet even when I could stand upright again, the cloth tugging me toward the open waters.

Something else seemed to be tugging me under as well.

Hands all over me as I churned toward the dark shore, my teeth locked against screaming to be left alone. A single shriek escaped me as I turned to beat at the hands trying to drown me. "Leave off, you drowned savages!"

I saw sailors, a host of them, rising from the depths, festooned with seaweed, their faces bloated horrors. I saw water-ruined flesh nibbled by fishes and their fingers stretching out to make me one of their own company.

My hand found a thin slippery stick and I brandished this at the host moving toward me through the surf. "Get away," I yelled. "I'll change your sheets!" I had nothing much to threaten them all with except my nursing skills. My mind kept filling with images of me trying to strangle ghosts with hospital sheets. Maybe I could use seaweed or a broken shell. How did one fight off dead sailors roving about on a late summer night?

Arms locked about me just under my arms. A smell of tobacco, rich and aromatic. A solid male body fitting to mine as the man dragged me to the sands without much effort, his strength like a balm and yet alarming. The drowned men became bits of mist, drifting off toward wherever their graves must be along the sea bed itself.

I saw one of the ghosts linger before it faded. A dark-haired one with a single good eye left.

My spine settled against a very broad, ungiving chest. Rather like leaning back against sun-warmed rocks on a cool spring morning. I shivered, in my soaked clothing, the fear and absurdity that had chased me into having to be rescued even a tiny bit almost unbearable in the presence of this confusing man. I needed yet to return his umbrella. He must think me a clumsy, forgetful old frump, indeed. Or did he forget me the instant I vanished from his sight?

"Forgive me. I lost the oars, sir." I stepped away from the man, trying to control myself and not care that I stood there in a wet elderly nightdress, my hair plastered to my face in wanton strands, my person kept too long against the man's body. A rather highly enjoyable meeting, a confusing swirl of muscle, tobacco fumes and my own wayward wish that he put his arms about me again. I did not wish that, of course.

I had had a most disturbing night, that's all this was. A stray hound would have sufficed to comfort me after the rowboat and ghosts. Of course.

"Lost oars, of course," said Edgard Stivers from behind me, just behind me, his voice drifting over my head. "Best come inside before you freeze."

A strange moan rose from the sea. A whale? I could almost hear a name within that moan.

"I do not need your help." I sneezed in a most pitiful way, negating my words entirely but I turned to stomp back to the cottage, despite its nightly inhabitants.

"What you need …!" And he stopped. I heard his throat cleared.

I dared turn. Our next to last meeting had not gone well, either. I had bumped into him at the general store while buying Eustacia some yellow ribbon for her summer hat. I had bounced off him, as he had the same stability as a mountain. Nothing would knock him off his frame, so to speak. He had growled most unpleasantly at me about being clumsy. I had called him a wild beast that other beasts avoided but I am rather tart and harsh.

At least I am not clumsy, hehad rejoined, before tipping his hat at me with a tiny grin that declared he had won this round. I had lost the battle at the post office, too.

"What I need is none of your concern. It's a long walk back, my cousin's rowboat is lost and I have no wish to argue with such an unpleasant man. Good night!"

His hand caught my arm but I had not yet stormed off. Something held me still, as if I wished a good, hearty fight to clear my head and remind me ghosts were but products of badly cooked stew.

I barely came to his shoulders, which seemed like wings this night. He should be swooping about like a powerful bat. His fingers encircled my arm. I shivered but I had gone for a swim in my night things while fighting off sailor ghosts and whatever strange beasties had been drawn to a lone woman in a sinking rowboat. A glow in my belly, a delight in my blood told me to be careful with how careless I was being. I was not some young thing or some flirt. I had never really been young and I could not recall ever flirting with anyone.

"All of this to get me to kiss you," Edgard Stivers said, and I was glad the moon did not quite reveal my astonished face. The scar along his face made him seem a pirate crept onto the quiet shores of Blackburne Bay, to steal all the gold at the lighthouse.

Did pirates steal gold from lighthouses? My mind seemed full of strange fancies, questions I could not answer and an outrage that he somehow saw into my head a little bit.

I did wish to kiss him. I did.

But so did every female about who had seen the stranger come to take over the duties of the lighthouse. Tall, with icy eyes that were sometimes blue, sometimes not, and a good solid build that was neither too skinny or too hefty. A thatch of curly brown-black hair with streaks of gold and copper that I longed to brush and tame, a beard I wanted to trim with scissors or yank at with my teeth or fingertips. I had such strange notions around this irritating man, this beastly unmannerly sort more suited to a children's tale of monsters than the sedate few inhabitants of Blackburne.

"That I or any other woman would have to resort to such antics to get a kiss from you proves such a kiss would not be worth it. That you are so leery of gentle affections does not speak highly of you at all," I said, tugging at the arm he yet captured.

"You wish a gentle affection from me? Very well." And oh, before I could form a riposte, he slid me upwards, my toes barely touching the sands. One arm lashed across my lower back, the other hand cupped the back of my head. Our lips met. My hands clutched at his hair, digging into the thick mass, toward the hard bones of his skull beneath. My belly met his. His tongue slipped into my mouth and I had never, ever been kissed so. And he remained gentle, the kiss slow and easy until it was not. But I did not wish a slow, easy kiss anymore. I wished a wild kiss that tasted of sea salt and tobacco, I wished his tongue wrapped around mine.

My arms locked about Mr. Stivers. My tongue met and played with his beneath the partial moon, with the surf in our ears.

"Edgard!"

The man erasing my good sense, my decency, my morals, pushed me backwards, his hand yet clutching at my arm, as if he had made it a sort of mission to keep me near. At least for now.

"Did you hear that?" His voice trembled. He seemed a man undone, truly so. I had seen hysteria in men and Edgard Stivers seemed on that verge. He trembled, his eyes had gone wide, his lips hung open as if he had trouble breathing. His hands shook like an old man with palsy. "I've never heard him speak so clear."

"Edgard!!"

I whipped about, searching the Atlantic. The sailors had returned. The host of dead sailors rising and falling with the waves, like strange misty human seals. And one drifting toward us, with a bloated face that the moonlight revealed to look a bit like the man clutching my arm in near mortal terror. The same thatch of unruly hair. The same shape to the square face, the same furrow that would not deepen any further on the dead man's forehead.

My eyes darted to the lighthouse. To the light sweeping lazily about.

"Mr. Stivers." I tugged at him to follow me.

He stumbled in the direction I wished. I noted the dead began to wade ashore, making no sound, creating no ripples, creating no splashes. A more eerie invading force I could not imagine. "Inside, sir."

The door made the appropriate rusty noises but the ocean hastened everything nearby into a damp, moist decline. I locked the door from the inside, but what door could keep out those already dead? I barely noted his bachelor fixations of a single frying pan, a hasty meal of eggs and potatoes waiting to be put away yet and a dish rag that needed replacing. I saw his pipe sending up ribbons of smoke.

"Cannot you clean up?" I attempted a bit of humor, a bit of poking a scared bear to snap him back into something useful.

His blue eyes focused on me, rather than the door which seemed flimsy, ready to fall and crumble the moment ghostly fists pounded on it for entrance.

"You will get sick living like this."

"I heard a woman shriek, I was having a late supper, a smoke before washing up," he said, blinking, breathing easier now, beginning to regain that snarling delightful way that did not scare or off-put me much. He doused the pipe, knocked the bowl clean of tobacco and ash. "My brother. I keep hearing him some nights but nothing, nothing like this."

We both looked at the door.

The slap of a palm against the other side. "You cannot hide from me, big brother," said the ghastly thing in a playful way, whispering it, yet we both heard it so clearly. "I have come home. Your light brought me home. Your light. Your light."

That was echoed by hundreds of voices, surrounding the base of the Blackburne lighthouse. I shivered in my wet things but the cold in me went so far deeper than mere chilled skin from an impromptu swim. Mr. Stivers absently placed a jacket about me. It did help.

"We either flee through them or flee to the very top floor," I proposed. "Where the light is. We wait until dawn. What does he want? Does he wish you dead as well? Did he drown?"

His eyes went to the ceiling. To the open door that led to the top floors of the lighthouse. We both shuddered at ripping open the front door to face whatever thronged out there trying to get in.

Edgard began the long climb up the rickety stairs toward the tippy-top where the big light revolved. Clockwork kept the lamps going in circles, the light bouncing against a concave mirror and out into the night.

We huddled on the wooden floor, the light like a poor shield against the night throwing spirits at us from the depths of the Atlantic. I put my head on his chest, trying to force myself to keep away but I knew I needed to warm up a bit before I could return to being a thorny, prudish cat. His rough woolen jacket smelled of his tobacco and something like ferns.

"Did he drown?" I repeated my question and heard the man sigh, felt him sigh, his arm about me as if we were kin.

"I was told, months later, his ship went down in a storm. He worked for a shipping company out of Boston, a small merchant fleet. He was returning from the Cape of Good Hope." Edgard caught his breath as I sat up, listening, my mouth opening like some ridiculous woman goldfish.

I heard the tramp of feet, when before they had made no sound. It was deliberate. It was meant to chill us and frighten us into hasty actions.

"What do we do, General Ellie Dinsmore? What do you command now?"

I met his wide eyes. I ignored his obvious ribbing. If I had to fight these damnable sailor ghosts and his dead brother, somehow, I would. Eustacia has always noted I am stubborn as the mold growing in her root cellar "We can stand in the beams of light. I hear ghosts do not like light. I do not think a shotgun, which I assume is below, will do much good. Or. Ask your brother what he wants. Maybe send him off to paradise, at peace, if you but …"

"EDGARD!"

"If I but go with him?" Edgard rose to his feet, as did I. I had left wet marks on his shirt. "I do not believe in ghosts. Yet here they are, every damn last one in creation."

"Only a few," I replied, taking his shaking hands, letting his fingers clutch mine as it seemed to help. "I will do the same with the one that keeps grabbing my ankles at Eustacia's. You must confront your brother. If that is indeed even him."

Edgard's drowned brother stood near the door of the top room of the lighthouse. He had appeared from the very air. Fish had nibbled an eye loose. His hair waved and floated as if he yet remained under the water. I heard Mr. Stivers give a small, choked sound, almost like a sob. He had loved his brother, that much even I could discern. I placed myself between the two as best I could. I had trained to protect those around me. To help them. To give them courage and strength when unthinkable horrors had to be faced.

I wished my cousin was there, with her twinkling eyes alight at how silly people could get, her refreshing pragmatism that all would work out as it should, why be fussed at all.

"Renny," Edgard Stivers whispered.

"You taught me to swim, brother," this Renny Stivers said, in a voice that ripped and clawed at my sanity. A drowned man spoke. It should not be possible. "I suffered so, trying to stay afloat. I suffered so finally having to give in. I suffered so."

"Please." Edgard moved back toward the big glass windows that let the light be seen by passing ships. "I told you not to go to sea. I told you!"

"You promised you'd come with me that last trip. You promised. I was to marry Maria, you did not like her. You promised." The ghost's hand reached out and out. He did not seem to see me at all, this ghost, his attention focused on his brother.

Something malicious and awful seemed to have infected the dead man. I moved so that I stood against Edgard, my hands up as the ghost drifted closer and closer. The other ghosts drummed their fingers on the door, some on the glass of the windows, floating in midair, peering in at this wretched scene. "Go back to the waters," I said, I ordered, I commanded. "You are not welcome here."

"She cannot save you, Edgard. The morning light cannot absolve you. You are damned, brother. Damned." Renny stood not inches from me, slightly shorter than his brother but not by much. I could smell the rot of him that no cleansing saltwater could cure.

"What do you want of me?" Edgard took my hand. I squeezed it, tight as I could. I pressed back against his still body, giving him what strength I had to give. "My brother loved me. I did not approve of Marie, that's true but she proved a most loyal, ardent girl. She mourned you for years. Years! Do you wish me to die? Am I to fling myself from the top of this old lighthouse to please you? What do you want, brother?"

The ghost of Renny Stivers moved backwards. And backwards. The one good eye did not waver as it fixed on Edgard. "Join me. Join us all. And we will never haunt these shores again." He moved that single eye to me. I saw worms and rot and lies in that single-eyed gaze. Whatever this was, it was not Edgard's brother. Whatever infested the dead sailors and others lost to the salty brine seemed malicious and terrible.

"Dawn will be here in a few hours," I said. I went right to the ghost, fearful yet incensed it demanded so high a price. "No one will die to satisfy you, spirit, whatever you are. This is not your brother, Mr. Stivers. Courage now. We sit and wait for the sun."

"You are not the Renny I knew," Edgard said, to my immense relief. His voice had a spark back in it. Good.

We sat, huddled together, our heads lowered, our arms about each other as if we were children, not grown adults. The dead tapped at the windows, the dead called out that Edgard should leap from the windows and end the suffering. That I leap, too. They called and called for us to leap to the rocks below the lighthouse, splatter ourselves to end the suffering, end the suffering, end the suffering.

I wept a bit at the soft exhortations that never let up.

Edgard shuddered all over as his brother cajoled and promised and threatened, as his brother knelt down by our huddled forms, whispering, whispering. Until the words began to sound like a tide coming into shore.

The glass broke on all the windows. The ghosts swarmed in. I felt myself being dragged toward the smashed new openings, I saw Edgard trying to resist, his strength no match for their will. I grabbed at Edgard's arm, I planted my feet. "I will not let you take the man I love! You cannot have us! Absolutely not, you wet demons! You are not welcome here! Go before I send my cousin after you. Go!" I yelled and shouted all manner of words, exhausted at all this, my fingers trying to dig into Mr. Stiver's arm to keep him with me, to keep him from death.

"I love her as well," Edgard Stivers shouted, our eyes meeting. We began to laugh. We laughed from our bellies, we bent over with mirth and merriment, the ghosts releasing us in their confusion and pain. I noted several of their ruined faces contorting into a rictus of grief and fury, as if laughter reminded them of everything they had lost far too early.

The last to go was the corpse of Renny Stivers. The single eye cleared, became soft and sweet as that perfect summer sky. That blue no artist can reproduce. I saw something like tentacles swirl out of his chest and drag him away into the last vestiges of the night. I heard Edgard give a sob as his heart broke all over again, as he lost his brother all over again.

The sun would rise in moments. The light had come back to the world.

Edgard stopped the clockwork, the lighthouse now just a singular building with windows that needed the glass replaced on the very top floor.

He looked properly scruffy. I used my thumb to absorb his few tears, his cheeks warm. I must have looked an actual fright with my ratty hair all about my face and shoulders, my cotton nightgown creased and stained and torn.

We said nothing, our eyes searching for those visitors that had so tormented us. My hand ran over the scar along his face. His hand traced my chin, down my neck and yes, lower. I nodded. I nodded my yes to him but I pulled back. "I have a call of nature," I said, flushing as he began laughing.

My belly hurt already from our former bout of cachinnations.

"I do as well. We answer that call and ..." He stopped, biting at his lips, drawing back.

"No need to think of my virtue now," I said. "You have a bed, sir?"

"I do. Meet me there in a few moments?"

I gave a great joyous laugh.

Our child did not arrive in the proper time after we were hastily wed by Judge Capers, with my cousin witnessing our nuptials and even baking us a truly terrible cake where she managed to burn the cherries and use too much salt. But we ate it in good humor. Everyone agreed that the obviously full-term child born to me had to be premature but politeness prevailed as long as a ring graced the fingers.

By mutual agreement, we settled in Boston, with Edgard going into banking and my nursing skills hired out on a private basis, to bolster our nest egg for our daughter and future children. We filled our small house with as much laughter as we could, as it seemed to work so well to keep the dead from visiting us on their nefarious missions. But Edgard loved to laugh, I discovered. I had thought him a dour, dark beast but he was a light-hearted man with feet of clay. What a grand discovery.

I asked Eustacia, when I could visit her again, about the ghosts in her cottage. I patted the small back of my daughter, waiting for my cousin to berate me for such nonsense.

"I've told them they can remain in my walls if they let me sleep a good eight hours every night," Eustacia said, daubing away at her latest seascape. Her eyes found me.

"I even suggested you and Mr. Stivers might make a handsome couple. Apparently that worked."

I bit at my lips, not sure what to make of this. Her lips quirked, her eyes twinkled with extra lights and she put down her paintbrush. I handed over Edwina to my cousin, who managed to get the last bit of gas from my daughter's small belly. "May I tell you of that night? I've yet to tell anyone."

"My darling Ellie, of course. But the shadows whispered some of it when I asked. What did happen?" Eustacia held my child as easily as any practiced mother as I confessed.

I noted a shadow that should not be there on her porch lingering by the open door that led into her kitchen. Perhaps it had paused to listen to my confession of that summer night. It slipped back into the cottage. I shivered and wished to be home, where no shadows wandered about willy-nilly.

"I must come see you in Boston. Perhaps later this fall?"

"Yes, of course. I even have a tiny guest room."

"I'll leave behind that lonely thing that enjoyed your ankles so. Another slice of cake?"

STAINLESS

BY JESSICA PETER

Angela leaned on her duffel bag, ignoring the graffiti on the seat in front of her as Iron Maiden pounded in her ears. The bus lurched to a stop. She stood, pulling her headphones around her neck and hitting pause on her Walkman. Thanking the driver with a quick word and a wave, she stepped out as the bus groaned and drove off, leaving her alone in an abandoned neighborhood. The sound of crickets was her only company.

Where were the families and golden retrievers, the white picket fences and all that shit?

The bungalows here were a uniform shade of grimy yellow, like nicotine-stained teeth. There were picket fences, but the once-white paint chipped and peeled. Broken and boarded windows leered at her like lascivious eyes. Above the houses, a tower belched thick black smoke and a lonely flame blazed against the darkening sky. She could smell the industry in the air, that familiar Rust Belt cocktail of smog and slag. In short, it looked like a hellscape of a suburb.

But empty. All empty. Angela had forgotten how badly it'd gone for the people who had worked the mills after the collapse of the steel industry. Only a skeleton crew kept the smoke pumping now. She shifted the bag with all her worldly possessions in it. Should she regret taking the housekeeper position? She immediately batted the thought down.

Angela had nothing else. No home, no people. The only way to go was forward.

Darkness had fallen as she stood and hesitated at the bus stop, and the November cold nipped at her nose. The burned-out streetlamps didn't help. She strode through the neighborhood, her long legs eating up the pavement. Then she turned the final corner to the street that would be her home and stopped short.

A Victorian mansion stood silhouetted against the clouds of smoke. Her stomach quivered with childhood-princess dreams, and then she noticed the decay. Like the abandoned wartime bungalows all around, the mansion was crumbing. One turret was nearly gone, held together by 4x4s that themselves had seen better days. The curlicued gingerbread details were stained with seeping darkness. But while the porch sagged, this front door wasn't blocked off, and there were lights on inside.

Home, sweet home. Angela shouldered her duffel and walked up.

Aidan paced as he watched his new housekeeper approaching. He'd told the agency that he'd wanted someone experienced, but what he'd meant was: old. Not someone who'd tempt him to leave his self-enforced prison. Not someone with thick auburn hair that he could picture untying from the ponytail and running his hands through.

He groaned and ran his hands over his own face instead, reminding himself of the ridges and furrows of damage that spoiled his face just as everything else in Vietnam had spoiled his mind.

The front door opened with a creak that he could hear all the way up in his third-floor rooms.

"Hello?" Her voice was muffled by the levels of the house but still clear. Young, strong.

Aidan didn't answer, of course.

Angela opened the door and walked into the foyer as the employment agency had directed, as weird as it felt. It was lit with a single lamp, and her motion through the room made shadows dance on the curling central staircase and in the corners that led to other rooms. Spooky.

But she'd known it'd be weird from the time she picked the position. The pay was good enough to forgive some sort of old hermit who didn't leave his rooms. At least he was a *rich* hermit. She could manage the house.

At least under the lamp was what she assumed included her next directions: a thick white envelope, her name on it in sharp black lettering. In the absence of a letter opener, Angela stuffed a finger into the corner of the envelope.

A horrible scream broke the silence. It seemed to come from everywhere at once. She dropped and crouched halfway underneath the table. The envelope fluttered to the ground beside her. She covered her mouth with both hands as her heart thudded.

She could run. But where would she go?

Pounding footsteps on stairs somewhere above her made her duck further under the table instead. A moment later, a door to the right of the foyer opened. Bright light silhouetted a figure in front of a different set of narrow stairs. Servants' stairs, Angela assumed.

"Are you alright?" The voice was deep, male. And far too youthful for the old man she'd pictured working for here.

"Mr. Carroll?"

"Yes," he said. "But call me Aidan."

"Aidan," Angela murmured. "You heard the scream too, right?"

He hesitated and she took the opportunity to squint at his silhouette. Tall and well-built, he'd evidently run down a couple flights of stairs, so he was clearly not the invalid she'd visualized when she took the position. She couldn't make out any other features. Curiosity and suspicion burned in her chest. What *other* reasons would someone have for not leaving their home? If only she could flip on another light.

"Yes, I heard it," Aidan finally put together, embarrassed at how distracted he was by her presence. All lush and warm and alive. He cleared his throat. "This house is ... well, just ignore anything you hear at night."

He regretted it as soon as he said it, especially with the skeptical look she gave him. Most of what *he* heard at night was the result of own guilty conscious. The flaws in his own brain. But if she'd heard the scream too ... he couldn't figure out what that meant.

She nodded and stood, dusting herself. Her tight smile and the little spots of red on her cheeks were the only indicator that disembodied screams weren't something she encountered every day. Despite the situation, desire shot through Aidan. It had been so long.

He clenched his jaw and reminded himself that she wasn't for him. No one was anymore. Instead, he made sure the light stayed at his back.

"The letter explains the rest. Your rooms are on the second floor."

"Rooms, huh? I like the sound of that." She gave a cheeky grin that cleared the tension on her face and made a dimple appear on one side.

Aidan's knees went weak for an instant. What had brought someone like her to a job like this? "Good," he said instead, his voice overly crisp. "I'll leave you to it." He closed the door before turning off the light behind him, then retreated up to his rooms alone. Like the monster he was.

Angela's first full workday was uneventful. She found the kitchen, laundry room, and other spaces, and set up her few belongings so that her multi-room space felt like hers. The old Victorian was creaky but mostly clean. Despite the business-like introductory letter from Aidan that explained how he only left the third floor for necessities, he'd evidently been coming down to keep things tidy between housekeepers. With Angela present though, that would likely end. The prospect of isolation stretched out in front of her, an image of the deserted, decaying suburb and the empty mansion haunting her brain.

But she'd make it here. She didn't have many other choices.

It wasn't until she sat propped in bed after watching the sun sink below the steel mills from the crack in her curtains, that Angela remembered the scream. Suddenly the isolation seemed oppressive. Who could that have been? Or what?

As soon as the questions came up in her mind, the fine hairs on her arms rose and the back of her neck tickled in that unmistakable feeling of being watched.

"Who's there?" she said aloud to the empty space, feeling stupid as she did it.

Had her employer installed peepholes? She rousted out bad guys at other places before. The thought gave Angela motivation and she flipped off her bedside lamp, and jumped up to prowl the room in the hopes that the darkness could illuminate any telltale pinpricks of light on the walls or ceiling.

It backfired.

Instead, the tickling feeling of being watched increased in the pitch blackness, the darkness laying on her thickly like a smothering quilt.

"You better not be fucking watching me!" It was supposed to sound strong, but her voice quavered and Angela cursed herself.

She saw no signs she was being watched. As she searched the room, she heard Aidan's footsteps above her—at the opposite end of the house.

Not him, then.

Angela's breathing came out in heavy gusts. She nearly ran to her bedside lamp, but before she made it there was a feminine whisper behind her.

Angela spun, but there was nothing.

Then another, younger, female voice issued from the other side of the room. Angela squinted in the darkness, but couldn't make out anything. As she reached for her lamp, the first voice came again from an impossible position: the opposite side of the room. If there was someone in here, they would have had to pass by Angela to get across.

She flipped the light on aggressively and blinked at the afterimages of the light. The room was empty. And Angela knew what was happening. Knew why the pay was so good and the position so often unfilled.

This house was haunted.

Angela climbed onto the bed, put her knees up, and hugged them tightly as the whispers started again. Unintelligible and feminine, with two distinct tones bouncing back and forth. Angela rocked and clenched her eyes shut, but after what seemed like forever, she realized it was *only* whispers and that tickling feeling.

She could drown out at least one of those.

Angela pulled out her Walkman, popped on her headphones, and hit play. Slayer screamed in her ears and she finally smiled. Tucking herself under the covers and stretching out, Angela began to drift off to sleep. She didn't turn off the light.

Angela blinked bleary eyes at the alarm clock. Her eyes were that grittiness you get when you keep the light on all night and Slayer was still pounding from the opposite pillow where her headphones had landed.

There was no more feeling of being watched. No more whispers.

Angela sat up and stretched, noticing something white under the door. Walking over, she found an envelope like the one Aidan had given her on her arrival. She smiled to see her name on the front in his bold handwriting. Somehow it lessened the fear from last night a bit.

As she unfolded the letter, a few bills fell out and she absentmindedly tucked them into her pocket to read.

Angela, it said.

Again, I apologize for anything you might have heard in the night. If indeed you heard anything in the night. This house is old and there is sometimes certain … sounds. The house settling, and other things. Angela snorted. Aidan was clearly trying to say the house was haunted without admitting the house was haunted. The house settling, her ass.

The letter went on to ask her to get groceries, included a list, and added a note that she could treat herself with whatever snacks she wanted. Angela nodded approvingly as if they were face-to-face. Not all employers would do that.

Then she flipped the paper over to dash off a quick response.

Aidan, she wrote.

That's generous of you—I mean it! And whose to say I wouldn't be getting all sorts of expensive snacks and eating you out of house and home.

Regards,

Angela

PS: I know the house is haunted.

She smiled as she tucked the letter back into the envelope, crossing out her own name and adding Aidan's. She'd add it to the breakfast tray she left by his door.

Despite everything, by the time Angela was heading down to cook breakfast, she was humming.

The acrid stench of gasoline woke Aidan from an uneasy sleep. He jumped out of bed immediately, his thin T-shirt clinging to the cold sweat across his chest.

Fear thudded in his veins for the person he'd brought here who'd evidently been sharing his nightmares over the past few weeks. For the *woman* he'd brought here. For Angela.

The charnel house stink of death lay heavily in his rooms, and only then did Aidan realize that this wasn't happening here and now. There was no gas, no fire, no burning flesh.

Not now, at least.

The rat-a-tat of automatic weapon fire and the pair of whispering voices told him the truth. This was his haunting, his guilt. And until Angela had arrived and heard it all too, Aidan had thought it was just in his head.

He thumped his fist into a table, but weakly. The whispers tornadoed into a fierce crescendo that nearly drove Aidan out of his head.

But Aidan knew he deserved whatever he got.

The problem was that he was verging on happiness now. He should have never invited someone, never run the risk that he would find someone that could matter to him, that could care for him.

He didn't deserve that.

But even though Aidan knew he should continue his self-imposed exile for what he'd done in that village in Vietnam, instead he sat at the table and started writing another letter.

Angela lay in bed with Pantera blaring in her ears. For the first time in the several weeks that she'd been here, she had turned the lights off. She couldn't help looking around the room as if waiting for the source of the whispers to reveal themselves, but thus far she'd seen nothing. It was an auditory spectre, and that was it. Or at least that's what she told herself.

The rest of the job was pretty enjoyable. She worked in the house, did the errands, kept her hands occupied … and then there were the letters.

Aidan stashed letters all over the mansion, evidently while Angela slept. The kitchen, the laundry, by his plate, outside her bedroom door. It had started with a request here, then a compliment there, and then the notes grew longer and it was witticisms and observations that made her desperate for daytime when she could see more, ghosts be damned. So she'd begun actively *flirting* back, possibly the least likely thing she'd ever done.

Now she was stupidly falling for an employer who clearly wanted nothing to do with her actual physical body.

But as she thought of the letters, she pictured his strong silhouette in the doorway that one time she'd seen him. The first night. Her hand drifted lower under her blankets.

A high-pitched scream echoed through the room. Angela tore her hand away from herself and ripped off her headphones, and sat panting, terrified and unsatisfied.

This wasn't the whispers.

"Hey, it's okay," she said. As if the ghosts cared.

The whispers were silent for a moment. Then her blanket was torn off her with so much aggression that it landed on the opposite side of the room. Angela was left shaking in the cold in her ragged pajamas, brain short-circuiting.

All this time, she'd thought they couldn't touch her.

Another scream and she was slapped across the face with sharp fingernails. She screamed herself, putting her hand to her face where it came back wet with blood that looked black in the moonlight.

The whispers in the walls started again and gained in volume until they drowned out her own thoughts.

Angela ran. She ran right up the stairs to the third-floor rooms where she'd dropped meals and clean laundry over the last weeks.

She barely had time to pound on the door when it swung open. Babbling about screams and ghosts and whispers in the walls, she stumbled into Aidan's outstretched arms, to silence and safety.

Aidan's heart echoed the pounding of Angela's against his chest. She shook as he held her. What the hell was he doing? He was about to unravel all the punishment of isolation he'd set for himself. Not only that, but if he let her in, she would see his face.

But he would have never brought someone here if he'd known the haunting wasn't only in his head.

"I'm so sorry," he murmured, kissing the top of her head. She stiffened and he cursed himself. What the hell did he think he was doing? The banter of all of those notes she'd sent were probably nothing more than doing a broken man a kindness.

He tried to pull away, but she wouldn't let go. Aidan looked down at her in puzzlement. Her shaking had slowed, and she slowly raised her head to look at him.

There was no escaping. A light was on in his room, so she would be able to see his ruined face. He waited for the gasp, the scream.

Instead, Angela looked thoughtful, pressing her lips together. "This is why you lock yourself away?"

Aidan swallowed, forcing himself to look away from her. "That and my ... brain. But ... all this time." He let out a long sigh as he looked toward the windows. "I thought I was hearing things. Turns out maybe I wasn't."

"Turns out you live in a goddamned haunted house!" She laughed, a big contagious guffaw.

"I guess I do." He couldn't help a smile.

Then her gaze sobered, and he waited for the judgment. "Vietnam?"

He swallowed past a lump in his throat and didn't trust himself to speak. But he nodded, voicelessly.

"Does it still hurt?" she asked, looking up at him. "Can I touch you?"

Aidan flinched and hoped she hadn't seen his reaction to the question. "Yeah." His voice was rough. "It doesn't hurt anymore. You can touch it. Me."

Angela raised her hands and trailed delicate fingers along his face. He could barely feel it on the most furrowed parts of his scarring but he leaned into it, knowing it was her.

Angela ran her hands over Aidan's scars, fascinated by the ripples and whorls that raised the entire right side of his face and across to the left, raising his mouth in a constant sneer and covering everything but his eyes. They blazed out at her, a pale blue or green that the dim light didn't let her see enough to tell, contrasted to the darkness of his hair.

"This is why you don't leave?" She still couldn't make sense of it. He had to be only around her age, in his early thirties.

"I don't want to scare children," he said, humour in his musical deep voice as he looked away, out the window across the dark grey lake. This was the man who'd left those notes where his wit shone through. The man whose silhouette alone was enough to make her want to touch herself earlier tonight.

"Will you kiss me?" she said it before she planned to.

Aidan looked down at her and doubt crinkled his expression. "You can't be serious."

"I am," Angela whispered it and ran one hand along his crisp jawline, another down his muscled bicep.

He bent his head and kissed her once, sweetly, the warmth of his mouth only brushing hers. Then he made as if to move away and take the warmth of him away from her.

"Aidan," she whispered. "Please."

As if that was all he needed to unleash himself, he bent back down and delved his tongue into her, and she gave back as good as she got. His lips were unscarred other than the ripple up to the right. She could feel it when he kissed her, and it just made her want him more.

She dragged him toward the four-poster bed and stopped kissing him only long enough to drop down backwards onto the bed, leading him onto it.

"Angela, sweet," his voice was measured but his eyes were wild, his chest rising and falling rapidly. "You don't think we're going too fast? And I'm your employer after all."

She scoffed and pulled him nearer to him by his collar. "I'm a big girl, I can make my own decisions." When he was close, she whispered into his ear, "And I've been dreaming about you every night since I've been here."

He chuckled, a dark sound that sent liquid heat all the way down Angela's body. He kissed down her neck, voracious.

"There's something *I've* been dreaming of since I first saw you outside," he murmured against her neck. "Can I go down on you?"

"Oh yeah," Angela said, then laughed at herself. She shimmed out of her embarrassingly ragged pajama bottoms. But his focus was one-track as he sunk to his knees and kissed his way all the way down her body. She revelled in the thought of how that ripple of scar on his lip would feel.

An angry buzz woke Angela and she squinted up at the dawn light. Alarm clock. Aidan sure woke up early for someone who didn't leave the house. Stretching with satisfaction, she looked around the room, at the items in the room: bookshelves full to bursting, exercise equipment, a desk covered in papers. Aidan was busy for someone who was, for all intents and purposes, a hermit. Then she turned to look at him, still sleeping and shirted. They hadn't gone all the way last night, but maybe this morning they would. She leaned over him, touching his shoulders.

Before she knew what was happening, she was flipped onto her back and her arms held with a vise grip. His face above hers was cold and inscrutable, like he was a stranger. Or she was. That painful grip made her whimper.

"Aidan, that hurts," she said, trying to bring him back to herself.

It took him a long moment but then he shook his head and collapsed beside her on the bed, putting his hands over his face.

"Last night was a mistake."

"Pardon?" Angela almost thought she'd heard the muffled words wrong.

He raised his head from his hands, and his expression was almost as cold as when he didn't recognize her. "Last night was a mistake."

"Because of this one panic attack? I can handle it." Dread rose in Angela's chest, and with it all her pleasant dreams of finally finding a place she belonged. She should have expected it would turn to dust like everything else in her life.

"Because of everything. This will never work," Aidan's voice was still so cold, so unfamiliar. "You don't have to feel sorry for me. Your paycheque doesn't include sex."

"Jesus, Aidan!" Angela sat up, anger running through her. "You know this is not what that's about."

But he refused to look at her anymore, and instead stood at the window and looked out at the angry grey lake beyond the steel mill, the waves white-capped with the crisp autumn wind.

"Just go," he said without turning.

Angela strode out of his room and slammed the door as if she was the one who was breaking it off. Because that's what this was, right? An ending. To something that barely had time to begin.

Only when she got back to the door to her room did she lean her head on the rough wood and address the fact that her eyes were moist. She refused to let the tears drop, and instead dashed them away with her hand. Aidan would be just like everyone else in her life, a presence that left her as soon as they got close.

So Angela would keep working, forget the letters and be the isolated housekeeper he evidently wanted. And she'd do her best to pretend this had never been anything.

The following days and nights passed in a blur. Angela spent the time cooking, cleaning, driving the old sedan for groceries, or walking the empty suburban streets, to only the chatter of squirrels and squeak of crickets.

No Aidan. No letters. No snatched conversations through the door. Other than that one glorious night together, Aidan had abandoned her. He'd acted against himself too, and left no opportunity to change his mind. Other than the odd time she'd hear his footsteps around the house, it was like she was in the mansion alone.

Except for the ghosts, of course. At nights the whispers in the walls still tormented her, but they didn't touch her again. They had something to do with Aidan, she was sure of it. As she ignored him, the ghosts were content. The whispers became as familiar to Angela as her own voice; not surprisingly, as she heard them more than she spoke herself. Angela though, she ached. For a brief shining moment, she'd thought she had a chance for something more here, but instead she was back to letting life pass. Just trying to keep surviving, and that was it.

Aidan paced his rooms, unable to focus on all the little things that had kept his attention in his long years alone. Everything had changed.

For one, his ghosts were real. He lived in a goddamned haunted house. The memory of Angela's turn of phrase made him smile, but then he pushed it down.

What she didn't know was that it wasn't the *house* that was haunted. It was him. Aidan always recognized the voices as the mother and child he'd accidentally killed in a Vietnamese village. Burned their entire village while the rest of his unit fired into it. The rat-a-tat-tat of the automatic weapons that haunted his nights even now.

They'd thought it was empty. And now the ghosts wouldn't leave his side, no matter where he went.

Angela didn't deserve the ghosts, but for some reason she stayed. The more he thought about it, the more a faint hint of hope lit in him. She was stronger than anyone he knew. And maybe, just maybe, part of why she stayed was for him. If she was strong enough to survive his ghosts, night after night, maybe she could manage him.

For the first time in weeks, Aidan's heart lightened. He smiled.

A rustle made him look to the ground. His belt stood on one end like a cobra.

"What the hell?" he said.

It leapt at him, and he tried to push it away, his biceps straining, but he was no match for the unseen hands that held it. The belt slipped around his neck and began to tighten.

Aiden fought to get his hands between the belt and his neck.

"Angela!" he yelled. He didn't know if she'd come, but she might be his only chance.

Heat rushed into his face as his body was lifted into the air and the belt looped around a ceiling beam. He scrabbled at the leather to try to find purchase again, get his hands in there, but there was no space. Again he tried to call for her, but he couldn't even summon the breath. Instead, Aidan kicked and thrashed, knocking down his dresser with a resounding crash.

His vision began to grey.

"Aidan?" Angela screamed it, after his cry of her name and the huge crash had echoed through the house, followed by silence.

She threw open his door to a freezing blast of wind. Aidan hung from a belt on the ceiling, his hands weakly pawing at this throat.

"Jesus!" She pushed through the thick, cold, air, but she wasn't tall enough. "Hold on, hold on, I'm coming." She set the big dresser back up and climbed onto it, then stood to unbuckle the belt from around Aidan's neck, unwilling to look at his bulging eyes and now-still hands. "I've got you, I've got you."

He came loose and slumped to the dresser top beside her, and she awkwardly held his too big, too limp body.

"Aidan, please, you can do this."

Aidan gasped, a ragged sound, and Angela's heart started beating again. He took several minutes rubbing his raw, red throat as Angela held him and looked around for the perpetrator of this violence. The room was still freezing and thick. It had been the ghosts. But why now?

"Angela, I was coming to tell you. I made a mistake. I want to try us. Being together."

She swallowed and had to push away tears that threatened. She'd waited for those words for weeks, but coming now with his voice ragged and his throat aflame it seemed more like a nightmare.

"How can I know you won't decide we won't work again?" she said.

"You came up here even though you knew what could be happening," he said.

"Of course," Angela replied. "You needed me."

"And you stayed. This whole time. You're stronger than anything. Stronger than me."

Angela shook her head, then something clicked. "Wait, were you coming to talk to me when you were hung?"

He nodded slowly and it dawned on her. That's what was different. That's why now.

"They don't want you happy," she finally said.

"What?" Aidan looked at her sharply. "You know who the ghosts are?"

"No, not directly. But I can guess."

"It's not the house that's haunted; it's me." Aidan hung his head into his hands. "God, what I've done."

The oppressive cold and pressure in the room lightened a bit. Was a confession all they wanted?

"Aidan, have you ever told anyone what you did?"

He shook his head slowly, and then tilted it, looking into the middle distance of his room as if he could see someone there. Then he started talking. He told of the war crimes his unit had carried out, and then the accidental death of a mother and daughter that were his fault.

As he spoke, the whispering began again, and Angela assigned the two voices roles in her mind: mother, daughter. She could almost distinguish them now, but the whispering grew louder and louder as Aidan spoke, until they layered on top of each other and drowned out everything.

"It's my fault," Aidan said through the whispers. They silenced and he spoke the rest to a quiet room. "It's all my fault, and I will never stop feeling responsible. I'm sorry!"

There was a soft woosh as if a window had opened. Warmth filtered back in.

"That's it?" Aidan said. Tears ran down the furrows of his scarred face.

"Maybe. For now." Angela walked to him, and they sat at the end of the bed as his shoulders shook with quiet tears.

Then he finally turned to her. "I can imagine you're not looking for someone so damaged."

"Don't you start with that again."

He laughed despite the tears trying on his face, and he cupped her chin. "You're beautiful. And even more strong."

Arousal stirred in Angela's body and she tried to squash it. This was about support first, not her own needs. But Aidan's gaze had heated too, and he ran a hand down the side of her body.

"Do you want this?" he said. "Me?"

"Yeah." Angela laughed, a throaty thing that was sultry even to her. "All of you."

Aidan picked her up as if she were light as a feather, carrying her to nest on all the pillows. Angela pulled down his face, and kissed him deeply, that scar above his lip once again reminding her of how much pleasure he could give.

Angela woke to sunlight streaming in the window, one of the first sunny days she'd had here. She turned to find Aidan beside her, already awake. Shirtless, the ripples of scar continued down part of his chest, but it didn't make his body any less alluring.

He leaned up to her and kissed her on the tip of her nose before gripping her in his strong arms.

"We're going to go back out in the world," she said suddenly. "Together."

He nodded against her hair. "Yeah, it's time. And I can do it if I have you. You're going to be my home now, can you manage that?"

Happiness flooded through Angela. "Always," she said.

You Transfix Me Quite

by Sasha Kielman

It was as if a great shadow had descended upon Thornfield Hall. Queer tales were told in the nearby village of strange happenings at night and blood-soaked sheets that even the most skilled and robust laundresses could not wash out. Ghosts were said to wander the broad, windy moors. These tales were once scoffed at by the hearty villagers but they had gained currency of late. The ancient house was said to be haunted, not just by the spectres of the past, souls that had not yet gone on to rest, but by the sins of the present and wounds that could not be properly healed.

The manor's mistress, the great Lady Fairfax, Duchess of York, was away on the Continent. She left managing her ancestral lands to her daughter, Eleanor, a decorated officer in her own right after abandoning her studies at Oxford to find her fame fighting against Napoleon. The village parson remembered the great lady's soul in his prayers each day, and exhorted the villagers to pray for her and her family at each Sunday service.

It was apparent that young Eleanor had returned from the wars not quite herself, with another commanding officer in tow. This mysterious elder gentleman called Sinclair was never seen in the village, but Eleanor generously allowed him to remain at Thornfield Hall.

"I do wish Lady Fairfax would return from the Continent," many in the village would say, only to be reminded by their compatriots of the enmity existing between the wise old woman and the mysterious figure who had taken Lady Eleanor under his sway. Many whispered further that Lord Sinclair was the cause of the supposed hauntings, that he performed gruesome experiments on wounded soldiers during the war, or that he himself was a ghost, a spectre of evil returned for revenge.

The two former soldiers lived alone amidst the ghosts and tragedies of years gone by, it was said, until Lady Fairfax returned from Paris, declaring herself retired, and her daughter placed an advertisement for a genteel lady companion for her mother. Her father General Windsor had gone to a watery grave in the Atlantic, God rest his soul.

Lady Eleanor's advertisement seeking a suitable companion, or secretary, perhaps, for Lady Fairfax was answered by a Miss Jane Elliott, who had been well-trained as a teacher and governess. She described herself as a hard worker, she could speak French, and her lack of familial entanglements was looked upon favorably by her prospective employer. Prior to her education, she came from an orphanage maintained by Mr. Ulysses Smith, who by all accounts was a strict master who often sent the children out as hired help.

The young lady's arrival in the village was greatly anticipated by all—many of the old matrons remembered her in their prayers at the local church on Sunday mornings. A young lady would do the old house—and family—some good, they thought. Perhaps the rumors were just that after all, they reassured themselves while they made the Sign of the Cross and looked over their shoulders. Tall tales and queer happenings were nothing compared to the modern age, or the Continental war with its own set of horrors caused by the emperor.

There were others in the village, however, who took it upon themselves to warn the young lady when she arrived. "The Fairfax family have a history of extreme and violent behavior," a wizened old crone told the governess, clasping her arm. "They've all been powerful, and brilliant, yes, and good-looking, but take care, miss. Something's not quite right up in that old house. Lady Eleanor hasn't been the same since she came back from the war with that older fellow."

Jane smiled graciously, and thanked the woman for her concerns, but put those thoughts far from her mind as she hurried along to meet her new employers. Surely, she had nothing to fear from a noblewoman her own age and two elder nobles.

Lady Fairfax received Jane Elliott warmly, welcoming her to Thornfield Hall and reassuring her that she was free to explore the entirety of the house and grounds and make herself comfortable, save the wing occupied by Lord Sinclair, about whom Lady Fairfax would say no more. In reply, Jane thanked her and urged her to call her simply Jane, as they would live and work on intimate terms from then forward. Having not grown up with courtly manners, her given name always felt more natural to her, and it was far better than being called 'girl' by her harsh former master.

And so Jane settled into her days at Thornfield Hall, grateful for the support of a genteel noblewoman and an opportunity to build her own life, though her own shadows and ghosts continued to haunt her. The loss of her parents weighed upon her heart. Whilst she knew they were gone to their graves, God rest their souls, she still longed for a family in which to belong. She eagerly hoped that she could build a life for herself in Yorkshire.

It was initially difficult for Jane to converse with Lady Eleanor, who was scarcely human before a morning cup of tea, and often spent long hours wandering the estate's grounds. She hacked away at dead trees and bushes with an ancient sword dating back to the time of the Conqueror, spending long hours upon the spacious land.

It was Jane's understanding that many young people who returned from the war on the Continent bore scars both physical and mental. It seemed Lady Eleanor was one such; she often cried out in the middle of the night, caught in yet another nightmare. She frequently suffered from migraines, rendering her incapable of leaving her canopied bed, the heavy draperies on both the bed and the large window panes drawn tightly shut to prevent the sun's assault on her weakened state.

It was a horror, one that a country governess turned companion, could not comprehend, though she knew all too well the tragedy of the orphanage. Her education and training was her sole pursuit and escape until she gained meaningful employment. Her heart would never be entirely full, however, due to the loss of her family and the abuse she had endured at the hands of a harsh master.

Yet Jane smiled over breakfast while her recalcitrant employer sipped her tea and slowly returned to the land of the living and the light. She offered her opinion when asked, and sought only to improve her employer's disposition and situation by kindness and compassion. Eleanor seemed intrigued by Jane's many drawings, often sketches of the surrounding countryside, or of her mother's profile while she read or answered her voluminous correspondence. Despite her demeanor, she found Eleanor Windsor to be a respectful employer and an intriguing study for her drawing pencil.

She spent her days often reading aloud to Lady Fairfax, who had been a great peer of the realm in her own right. She was wise, kind, and the sort of woman who could converse with anyone. Jane found herself smiling more often than not, certainly more than she ever had before arriving at the hall, at Lady Fairfax's wry observations and indomitable spirit.

To Jane, Lady Fairfax became the surrogate mother she never had and for which she had always longed. Yet Jane knew in her heart of hearts that her own mother had been no great lady, no astute woman of politics, nothing as compared to the kind, noble being who sat next to her before the fire and offered her the finest tea each day.

The house's west wing was occupied by Lord Sinclair, Eleanor's commanding officer. The Lady Fairfax and Lord Sinclair did not acknowledge each other; it seemed often to Jane that her employer's mother resented the interloper's influence over her daughter, though she would not deign to say so in her presence.

Indeed, Jane feared the old man—when he walked, he towered over her. His height approached six feet, and he cast a heavy shadow and walked with a loud gait wherever he went. When he appeared, it seemed as though the temperature in the room grew colder due to his haughty and condescending behavior. His words were cruel and harsh, and never complimentary, whether of the meals their cook dutifully prepared for them or of Lady Fairfax's efforts to improve the estate. He was dismissive of her and the servants, and so she avoided him during the day, as did Lady Fairfax. The two were never seen in the same room together.

Eventually, he began to ignore her presence when she dined with him and Eleanor. The lack of attention suited Jane fine; she was accustomed to such behavior, and had little to offer to his conversations with Eleanor about military training and battles overseas. Furthermore, he never called Jane by her given name or respectfully as 'Miss Elliott'—he only referred to her as 'child.' His disdain served to demonstrate his own lack of character, and as such Jane would not allow it to upset her.

Spring turned to summer, and summer to autumn, and Jane enjoyed her peaceful life at Thornfield Hall, interrupted only by the rumors of ghosts and Eleanor Windsor's mood swings, which were more pronounced after training sessions or meetings with Lord Sinclair. The two could remain in the library for hours, pouring over maps and charts, or history books related to various military campaigns. When the weather was fine, they were also often out of doors, seemingly practicing readiness or drills for a war long since ended.

The laundresses spent longer days toiling at their task after these grueling sessions, the water dripping red and staining their hands. The dark shadows languishing under Lady Windsor's eyes appeared more like bruises.

Over tea one morning, after the two had drilled for hours out of doors the previous day and Jane overheard a laundress bemoaning the state of Lady Windsor's clothes, Jane mentioned to Lady Fairfax that to her, young Lady Windsor seemed quite changeful and abrupt.

"She was even as a child," the lady replied, "though Sinclair's influence has made her short temper more pronounced."

Jane nodded in understanding. If Sinclair was as rude to Eleanor in private as he was to both herself and Lady Fairfax, an angry temper seemed likely to result.

Later that evening, as she headed for the library to select a volume to read after dinner, she overheard part of an impassioned conversation between mother and daughter. She stood outside the door, watching and listening without being seen herself.

"He's using you, and he will turn against you when he learns you cannot provide that which he requires."

"He is a wise leader."

"Wars do not make a man great. He cares only for your lineage, our family history and bloodline. He seduced you, but you can still save yourself."

Eleanor's face was flushed; Lady Fairfax's lips were pursed. Until that moment, Jane had only ever seen the great lady's kindness and diplomacy. Here, she could tell both mother and daughter had tempests brewing beneath the layers of their courtesy and intelligence.

Eleanor scoffed at her mother's words. "Says the great peer of the realm who married a war hero far beneath her own station, saying nothing when he left you alone for another of his reckless voyages."

Jane could see, rather than hear, Lady Fairfax's sudden intake of breath. She swallowed before speaking. "I am sorry, Eleanor, that both your father and I disappointed you so."

Lady Fairfax turned to take her leave. Both ladies hastened to their separate wings of the house, leaving Jane to select her night's reading with a pounding heart and shaking hands.

Despite her temper, and the abruptness with which she conducted conversations, Jane's heart was inclined towards Eleanor Windsor. Not only was she the daughter of the lady she so adored and a great war hero, who all hailed for her great courage and bravado, but she felt keenly for the loss of her father, being an orphan herself. Certainly, should Eleanor Windsor choose to withdraw from her relative solitude at the manor, she could be a great asset to the nation, or a respected country gentlewoman, or anything she chose to be.

Jane knew what it was like to have limited opportunities and resources, unlike her patron. It pained her all the more that Eleanor

Windsor limited herself by her choice to forego her inheritance. Sinclair reminded her painfully of Ulysses Smith. She trusted and believed that were she to escape Sinclair's influence, Eleanor would become acquainted with her true self, as Jane herself was.

With the changing of the seasons, the warm memories of the past six months seemed also to change, as did the character of Thornfield Hall itself. The nights became longer, the wind more vicious and severe, and the rumored ghosts finally made their appearance. A rich fall harvest soon became the uncertainty of winter, with trees casting shadows over the white snow-covered moors and weak sun and moonlight to play tricks upon the eyes.

But tonight was peaceful. Jane saw Lady Fairfax to her chambers, then retired to her own, relishing the luxuries of as many candles as she could possibly need or want and the hall's enormous library. She settled in to read, a cup of tea nearby and a blanket across her lap, when the air seemed to drop precipitously in temperature. No storm had passed by; the moors lay quiet and dormant, and all of the hall's occupants, servants included, had gone to bed.

It was altogether too quiet. Jane found herself awake and alert, as if waiting for something to occur. She could not concentrate on her book; the words passed her eyes as if raindrops.

A dark, malignant laugh echoed through the halls. It was no ordinary laugh, from no ordinary human.

Jane shuddered, and clutched her blanket more tightly about her.

There were footsteps in the distance.

Though she was certain it was but a trick of the light, Jane thought she saw a huge shadow pass by her door. It was at that moment that Pilot, Eleanor's black dog, began barking ferociously, and the shadow seemed to retreat, to slink back to whatever hell it came from. The sound of the footsteps faded as well.

Shaking, Jane scrambled into bed, and did not dare leave her chamber again that evening. Nor did she dare to mention the incident over breakfast with Eleanor the next morning. She seemed more exhausted than usual; dark shadows circled her eyes, and she hardly spoke.

The sun was glowing strongly when Jane went to Lady Fairfax's parlor. The elder woman too appeared fatigued, and when Jane sat down upon her usual chaise, the lady rose from her desk and approached, sitting next to her. Lady Fairfax took Jane's hand, clasping it to her and squeezing gently.

"Sinclair is evil," she said. "He's been preying on my daughter for far too long."

"What can we do?" Jane asked, looking into the eyes of a mother losing her greatest hope.

"I thought I would be able to help her. After the war, I begged her to return home, but it was too late. I had already lost her."

"If I go to Eleanor on your behalf, will she listen? Would she return your affection and affiliation?"

"I don't know," Lady Fairfax replied, shaking her head. "I have held hope she would. Perhaps, sometimes we need to create our own hope. Would you help me to write some letters today?"

Jane fetched the parchment and ink, and the two wrote to the lady's many allies: great peers of the realm, former Parliament members, and eminences from overseas, to advance her latest political project—and perhaps to invite other people back into Eleanor's life. To fill Thornfield Hall with music and laughter and dancing, might perhaps end Eleanor Windsor's isolation, and chase away the memories clinging to corners and hiding in the darkness like a thick layer of dust.

A few days passed, and the awaited reply letters did not arrive as expected.

It was not long thereafter that Jane heard the strange laughter in the night once more. This night, it was not just the eerie peal of laughter, but also the sound of something scratching. Fingernails, perhaps, brushing against the walls.

Jane sat upright in bed, trying to listen as carefully as she could over the rapid drumming of her own heartbeat.

Footsteps trailed down the hallway leading to Eleanor Windsor's chambers.

A door opened. A door closed.

She could no longer hear footsteps or scratching along the walls.

The shadow and the laughter disappeared. All Jane's senses were on alert. There was a darkness in the air, in the very heart of the place she longed to call home, a darkness fighting to penetrate Lady Fairfax's earnest, steadfast light. To Jane, it seemed to surround a young woman who sought to serve her country, learn the strategy of warfare, and returned home haunted by the blood she spilled in pursuit of that service.

As if called by someone, or something, Jane grabbed her heavy robe and a candle and quietly crept out of her room.

The heavy darkness was not a figment of her imagination, nor was it a trick of the light cast by the moon and the candles in the latest hours of the night; smoke emanated from Eleanor Windsor's chamber.

Moving as quickly as she could, she hurried to the door and thrust it open.

A wave of heat and the crackle of a fire met her.

Despite flame traveling up her bed from the heavy curtains, the chamber's only occupant remained sound asleep; in the moon and candlelight she looked peaceful and even younger than her nearly thirty years.

"Wake up!" Jane cried, attempting to shake her awake.

Eleanor merely murmured and turned; the smoke had stupefied her.

It was by the grace of God, perhaps, that she looked up from Eleanor Windsor's prone form to the bedside table where her water pitcher sat. Grabbing it, she doused the bed curtains as best she could and snatched a nearby blanket to attempt to smother the rest before running back to her own room and grabbing her water jug. Returning to Eleanor's chamber, she dumped the contents over her and the bed, and by God's aid, succeeded in extinguishing the flames.

Being drenched suddenly in water, along with the sounds of the commotion, finally awakened Eleanor Windsor from her stupor.

Her arms flailed as if reaching for an invisible, nonexistent sword or musket as she sat up in bed and flung her blankets from her.

"What happened? Jane?" she asked, looking about frantically.

"Your curtains were on fire, ma'am, and I was afraid you'd never awaken," she replied. "Somebody tried to kill you; you cannot find out soon enough who it is."

Eleanor shook her head, droplets falling from her hair, and grabbed her dressing gown and another blanket. She then stepped toward Jane, reaching for her hands to ascertain if she had been burned.

"Jane, are you alright? You saved my life."

Jane nodded, shaking from fear and adrenaline.

"I'll be back in just a moment. I must go to check on something. Will you remain here? Are you certain you are unharmed?"

"Yes, thank you. I shall remain here as you request."

"Thank you, Jane. Do not bother waking my mother. I will return shortly."

While Lady Windsor was gone, seeking to make herself useful, Jane refilled the water pitcher from the basin in her water closet and put the singed and smoke-scented blanket out to be washed. She examined the room closely, trying to discern any evidence which would give rise to the assailant's identity. There was no candlestick holder to be found, but melted wax had pooled on the floor beneath the heavy draperies. She sat down upon the unharmed bed, and considered all she saw and heard that night.

The servants and Lady Fairfax slept in separate quarters, on the other floors of the house. In this wing, only herself, Lady Windsor, and Lord Sinclair kept their quarters. There was no reason to suspect Lady Fairfax would want to harm her only daughter. It was her deepest desire that her relationship with her daughter be repaired and Eleanor devote himself to the family estate by accepting her position as heir. Nor did Jane believe there would be a motive for any of the servants to want to kill their mistress; she knew them to be hardworking, devoted, and well-paid for their labors and circumspection.

There was only one other person in the house.

Despite the residual heat in the room, ice crept down Jane's spine.

Thankfully, true to her word, Eleanor soon returned.

"I have found it all out, it is just as I thought. Have you heard queer laughter late at night before, Jane?"

"Yes, in fact I have. Lady Windsor—" she began, but Eleanor cut her off, taking her hands in her own.

"You just saved my life, for which I will never even begin to comprehend repayment. Please, call me Eleanor."

Jane looked up at her, startled by her earnest entreaty and plain words, and found herself captivated by her dark eyes. They were like her mother's eyes, and yet quite unlike, for she knew them most frequently to be haunted and encircled by deep shadows, like bruises marring her elegant face, the result of far too many sleepless nights and migraines preying upon her mind.

She nodded, swallowed, and continued. "Thank you, Eleanor. I could do no less. I must confess I do not believe either of us will have a deep, peaceful rest tonight."

"No indeed," she replied, turning away from her and releasing her hands. She rubbed her temples and pushed her sable hair away from her face.

"Please do try to get some rest tonight, however," she said, turning back to face Jane once more. "I will escort you back to your chamber. Please tell no one what you saw tonight."

Jane nodded once more, and took her proffered hand as she walked her to her chamber door.

After bidding her good night, Eleanor bowed and kissed her hand, then headed not to her own quarters, but to the library Jane so loved.

Retiring once more, Jane could not help but wonder why her heart was still racing, why she could still feel the press of Eleanor Windsor's lips on her hand like a brand that inflamed her entire body, her very soul.

She slept, dreaming of fire and entangled sheets and Eleanor Windsor's plush lips and raven hair.

The next morning, upon entering the library to select a new book to read with Lady Fairfax, she found Eleanor asleep upon the sofa.

She was thankful she did not gasp or make a sound when she saw her, for her deep, even breathing indicated she was finally getting the restful sleep she desperately needed. She tiptoed around the sofa, grabbed a few books at random, and crept back out of the library as quickly as possible.

Over breakfast, Eleanor did not mention being awakened that morning, much to Jane's relief, nor did she mention the terrifying incident of the night prior. She did, however, tell Jane that she was to be away for about a week; business in London called her attention, and she thought some time away might do her constitution some good. Besides, it would be difficult to head south once the winter set in.

Jane was pleased that Eleanor would be safe from Sinclair's pernicious influence for at least a week, and that she seemed eager to transact the duties expected of her as a landed gentlewoman. But Jane could not help but admit to herself she would miss Eleanor terribly.

A week had passed, and Jane not only kept her promise to Eleanor to not speak of what transpired to her mother, she also kept her promise to herself not to dwell on her budding sentiments for her.

There were no further incidents in the nighttime, and Jane did not see Lord Sinclair at all while Eleanor was gone. For the first time since she was a young girl, she earnestly prayed. Perhaps the old villagers influenced her in that regard. Thanking whichever deities were smiling down upon her, she had but a few requests. "When Eleanor returns, please let her be healed in body, mind, soul. Please help her fight what haunts her, and please let her be reconciled with her mother. Please let her see through Sinclair's pernicious behavior."

For herself, she asked nothing yet.

When Eleanor did finally return, she seemed well; some color had returned to her cheeks, and the shadows under her eyes were not nearly as pronounced. Lady Fairfax, too, was relieved to see her well again, and the three enjoyed a lively evening meal with a lovely French wine.

That night, after all had retired to bed, the horrors began anew.

Jane was started out of a deep and dreamless sleep by a quiet knock on her door. She opened it to admit Eleanor Windsor, holding a cloth to her face.

"Forgive me, Jane, but I could use your help once more. Are you afraid of blood?" she asked, taking her hand as she led her to her reading chair.

"No, Lady Windsor. I mean, Eleanor," she added hurriedly, concerned for her safety and health. "I am not afraid of blood."

"Will you help me?" she asked, removing the cloth to show a gash leading up her cheek.

"Of course," she replied, grabbing fresh cloths from her water closet. She brought them to her, urging her to press them to the open wound while she rinsed the bloody linens she removed. Eleanor sat in her reading chair, looking lost and forlorn, like a young girl who had lost her prized puppy rather than a distinguished former soldier and a member of the gentry.

"Will you go downstairs, into the quarters near the kitchen? There should be some herbs and potions down there. I can manage while you're gone," Eleanor asked when she stepped back into her chamber with the rinsed fabric.

"I can make a poultice," Jane offered, nodding.

"Thank you," Eleanor said, quietly. She took up a candle and was about to leave when she added, "If you see my mother or Sinclair, say nothing."

She turned back to look at Eleanor; her face was in her hands, blood starting to come through the new cloth. Her dark hair caught the candlelight as always, searing her heart once more.

Jane hurried downstairs to find what she needed, and saw no one. It seemed that her lady and the evil lord were deep in sleep. She dared not ask how Eleanor was injured; though her thoughts did not linger upon it, her heart knew the answer already.

She returned to her chamber to minister to Eleanor, and after about a quarter of an hour, the bleeding seemed to cease, and she suggested a walk outside for some fresh air, not long before the sun was due to rise.

After yet another night that seemed bleaker than most, and another spate of violence determined to end the life of one for whom she cared, Jane was eager to step out from the house's suddenly pressing confinement and into the orchard. It was chilly, but she knew the fresh air would do her well, and she was heartened to take a turn about the garden on Eleanor's arm.

"Jane, do you believe it possible that one may return from utter darkness, that even the worst can be forgiven?"

"I do," she replied. "If one's heart is true, if goodness still resides within, and forgiveness is sought, who are we to judge?"

"Would your answer remain the same if I told you a story of a young woman, who made a grievous error in a foreign country, turning her life from its intended course, and then continued to follow the wrong path through a dark wood? Even when she held the hopes of redeeming herself in her deepest heart, fighting against her own nature and wishing to enjoin herself in matrimony with an honest and moral wife, would she be justified in surmounting an obstacle of custom?"

"Such a person must do what is right, and look to make amends with those they have harmed." At this, she took Eleanor's hand, and pressed it gently.

"I am grateful, Jane," she replied, "for this and all the kindness you have done me."

"I am grateful too," she answered. After a moment, she added, "You are not alone." She surprised herself with the firmness of her conviction. Her emotions were in a flutter, her heart beating rapidly from the revelations with which she had been presented.

"Neither are you," Eleanor replied, and she kissed her hand once more.

Eleanor took her leave of her as dawn stretched her rosy fingers over their garden corner, the cocks beginning to crow and the sounds of the earth awakening from their deep slumber to begin another day.

As she sat with cheeks warmed and a faster heartbeat, Jane had to admit to herself that she had developed feelings for Eleanor Windsor, for which she scolded and castigated herself. After all, she was no one, born a nobody from the western reaches of the country. Eleanor, however, was the heir to a great estate, and daughter to a noble family dating back to the Conqueror.

She resolved quite firmly to put her feelings aside, though she felt her racing heart betrayed her when Eleanor once more took her hand and kissed it before bidding her adieu.

After her sleepless night and dawn sojourn through the gardens with Eleanor, the day passed strangely for Jane. She felt disembodied, as if she were the rumored ghost said to be haunting the Hall. She knew, however, that there existed no ghost, but rather a cruel and evil man who meted out violent punishment.

Jane did not see Sinclair during the day, but rather shadows in every corner, seemingly to match those under Eleanor's and her eyes. She could hardly concentrate on prayers, reading, or conversing with Lady Fairfax; her mind seemed clouded by a mist, like a fog indicating a heavy storm to follow.

That night, she retired early, taking care to lock and bolt her door. She did not dare keep a candle lit by her bedside, using only the moonlight to make ready for bed. She fell into a light sleep, only to be awakened by scratching along the hallway passage. A heavy foot accompanied it; she recognized the loud gait. The temperature in Jane's chamber seemed to drop while her heart rate rose precipitously.

It was Sinclair, as her heart had expected and feared all along.

She reminded herself she had firmly locked and bolted her door and though he was strong, a former military leader, he could not walk through walls.

Her doorknob rattled as he tried it. Jane scarcely breathed, praying earnestly that he would turn back down the hallway and return to his own quarters, sparing the rest of the household from whatever horrors he had planned.

Jane's prayers were not to be answered, as the oppressive presence at her chamber door continued down the passageway to Eleanor Windsor's quarters.

She flung off her blankets, grabbed her dressing gown, and unbolted her door. Her entrance into the hallway served as a distraction from the dark lord's nefarious purpose, as she had planned, but beyond that, she had not thought ahead to what she— or he—would do.

No ghost or malicious spirit come back from the dead greeted her, but Sinclair did.

His eyes were particularly cruel and vicious, menacing in the moonlight. Jane had not kept a candle lit for her own protection and peace of mind that night; now she lamented it, for she could have flung it at the evil entity present before her. She had no weapons, no manner of defending herself beyond her own wits and courage, those she had to rely upon when facing Mr. Smith's rage.

Perhaps the situation was not so different, she tried to tell herself, but Mr. Smith had never wanted Jane or any of her fellow orphans dead, nor had he ever tried to set one of his charges on fire in their own bed.

"You," he said, pointing a long, white finger at her. "You weak, pathetic girl. You distract her with your pretty prattle each day. She could be much more, and yet she remains here, bound to her mother and now to you."

Jane did not allow his condescension or her terror to sway her resolve, or weaken her spirit. She did not hold his gaze, but rather cast about her for anything she could use as protection. An ancient suit of armor, one to which she had never paid much mind, stood sentry in the hallway. As he approached her, she pulled the old sword from the knight's scabbard. It was heavy, but it felt right in her hands. She stood her ground as she had seen Eleanor do with her own preferred sword.

Sinclair only laughed at her.

Jane recognized his laugh. It was the same as she heard on those haunted nights. She would not allow him to daunt her, even if he had cruelty enough to attempt murder and strength of a younger man. In that moment Jane realized Sinclair too bore a heavy sword by his side. As she recognized his intent, she steeled her spine and gaze.

It was then that Eleanor emerged from her chamber, putting herself between Jane and Sinclair. Her appearance was that of an avenging guardian angel, by the grace of God.

"My dear, you know better than to challenge me. Don't make that mistake, like your pathetic governess here."

Eleanor looked up at Sinclair for but a moment, then back to Jane. Jane wordlessly handed her the sword she had claimed.

"Leave Jane out of this. You have no quarrel with her."

"Oh, but I do. She's a distraction we cannot afford."

"We?" Eleanor asked, raising an eyebrow. "I am not yours to command and obey."

Sinclair snarled. "You have always been weak and over-emotional. When I met you, I knew you had potential. You could have been a hero, a conqueror in your own right. But now, you are nothing, weakened by an orphan girl."

"I am not, and never have been, nothing," Eleanor answered. "Stand your ground for your insults to not just me, but to my mother and Jane as well."

"Very well, Eleanor. I shall give you no quarter." He raised his blade.

"Nor shall I," Eleanor replied, raising her own blade.

The deadliest dance Jane had ever, or would ever, witness ensued. She was uncertain as to how the clanging of metal on metal did not awaken every servant, even though their quarters were on the floor below.

She could hardly breathe, watching one feint or lunge, the other ducking or darting away. Both were clearly skilled combatants, though Eleanor had the advantage of youth, while Sinclair possessed height and experience.

Jane did not dare move or make a sound. What would she do if Eleanor fell, and Sinclair turned to her with his bloody blade? She would have to outrun him to the servants' quarters for help.

She was shaking as she watched their swords clash.

Sinclair grunted as he missed Eleanor's blade, below his own. While Sinclair's blade caught the air, sounding like a ghost moving through the hallway, Eleanor's blade struck true, ending her tormentor's life.

Jane rushed to her, to once more find blood covering them both.

It seemed as if a spell had been broken, for then the sun rose, bringing with it, servants and Lady Fairfax herself, at the top of the stairs to witness the gruesome tableau.

After cries and gasps from the assembled persons quieted, Jane soon found herself returned to her chamber, a heavy sleeping draught prepared for her and Eleanor both.

Eleanor spent a few days convalescing and recovering from her wounds, then requested Jane to meet her in the garden for tea one bright spring morning.

Jane was well pleased to join Eleanor; her presence in a room was more cheering than the brightest fire on a cold Yorkshire night.

However, she feared in the aftermath of her precipitous duel with her master, Eleanor would blame her for its cause or change her mind about continuing Jane's employment as her mother's companion.

"Jane," she greeted her, but before Eleanor could continue, Jane forced herself to speak.

"I will find another position," she began. "I entirely understand if you no longer desire my presence here at Thornfield Hall."

Eleanor shook her head. "Nothing could be further from the truth; I desire quite the opposite, in fact. Unless you prefer to leave," she hurriedly added. "I can understand if you came to despise and fear this place, and feel trapped in its net."

"I am no bird; and no net ensnares me: I am a free human being with an independent will," she replied, searching Eleanor's face for the blunt, tactless honesty she had always known her to possess.

"And you shall decide your destiny," Eleanor said, reaching for her hand. "That is why I will entirely understand if you do not wish to do me the honor of accepting my hand in marriage. I offer you my hand, my heart, and a share of all my possessions. I ask you to pass through life at my side—to be my second self, and best earthly companion."

Jane smiled, entwining Eleanor's fingers with her own.

"I will marry you, Eleanor. But you must ask your mother for her forgiveness, and I must ask her blessing."

The pair could have passed several hours or even days by themselves sitting in the garden, holding hands, but returned to the great manor house to attend their duties and start anew their life together.

Her heart full, Jane presented herself to Lady Fairfax, whose eyes twinkled in the sunlight.

"My lady," she began, sitting down on the sofa next to her. "Your daughter has had an unfortunate past, and made many mistakes. I told her she must find her own salvation and redemption, not depend upon another person. She allowed a cruel master to transform her heart and mind against you and against your teachings, morals, and bloodline. She must ask and pray for forgiveness. And yet, while I breathe and think I must love her."

The wise older lady, so like a mother to Jane, smiled and took her hands in her own. "I give you my blessing. It would be my greatest joy to have you as my daughter."

Jane's heart brimmed over with joy. The dark shadows had passed for both herself and Eleanor, and they could step out into in the spring sunlight with their greatest happiness. Her countenance was radiant, glowing in the fresh air.

Reader, she married her.

I am My Beloved's, and My Beloved is Mine

by Celia Winter

A white mist as delicate as a bride's veil and as haunting as a kittel, flooded Odesa when Golde arrived on the back of a wagon at dawn. The thick wet air filled her lungs with salt as birds she could not see called overhead. She wondered who they called to, what they called about.

She held a letter and a promise tight in her fist. She hadn't been able to pack the letter, hadn't put it in the pocket of her coat. She'd held it in her hand from the moment her uncle had pressed it into her palm and told her she would be going to a ship that would take her across the sea, away from all this.

"Is he a good man?" Golde had asked. She knew better than to expect much. Once she might have hoped to have a hand in who she married, but the goyim had taken that away from her when they'd taken her father and brother.

Her uncle's face had tightened, his eyes had grown guarded. "He is a good man." If not a lie, then it certainly wasn't a whole truth. He sounded just like her father when he was holding something back.

A good man, she'd repeated to herself over and over again. One who promised to take her across the sea to the new world. *One who takes my name for his own, rather than the other way around,* she had thought repeatedly on the back of the wagon from Oleksandrivka to Voznesens'k to Odesa.

The wind blew around her, and she crossed her arms more tightly over the little bundle of clothes she'd packed with her. It was cold and wet, and it clawed at her skin as if to say, *you won't get away from me, from here. You'll die here like your family, like everyone who came before you.*

I won't, Golde retorted to the wind. She would leave the old dying world behind. There was no future for her here but ghosts.

The mist muddled the port around her, making the clear-cut lines of the docks and ships seem more like spirits than wood. The mist made shadows of everyone she saw, turning people into ghosts. Would the dead claw at her like the wind? Would they bind her to this earth where so many had been slain, where it felt like even the possibility of a bright future was laced with the threat of death?

"You know where to find him?" asked the merchant gruffly. He had taken her on for very little coin and was clearly eager to be rid of her. She knew he hadn't liked taking her on her own without a man to accompany her, even if she was going to meet someone she was promised to.

She looked down at the letter in her hand.

When you reach the Odesa Port, call for Todros Rubin.

"I do," she lied.

"Good. Go on then," the merchant said, and he turned his back on her, like the door to childhood closing, leaving her locked outside forever.

The mists made even the mud glisten as she made her way towards the port. "Todros!" she croaked, the mist clogging her throat. A few shadows turned to look at her, blank faces staring at her. She couldn't tell if they were friend or foe, gentle or menacing. How would she ever find one man if she couldn't even see faces clearly? "Todros Rubin?" The whisper was more of a question than she wanted it to be. She wanted to boldly command this man to step forward—he who would be her husband coming to meet her. Instead, she was begging overly bright ghosts in the mist-flooded port to produce him.

"Todros Rubin?" A question again, but at least not a whisper. The wind blew behind her. This time it wasn't clawing at her; this time it sent her voice further, making it sound louder than it had before.

One of the shadows carried himself the way her father had, standing next to a boy a little younger than her brother in a long dark coat. For years, she'd dreamed of sailing to the New World with her mother, father, and brother. She'd dreamed that they would all live, that they would thrive together in a place where it didn't matter quite as much that they were Jews, that they would grow a garden full of vegetables and sweet-smelling flowers. But that dream had died with her brother and father.

"Todros Rubin?" What happened if she didn't find him? What if she got lost in this port forever? Her promised hadn't even told her what ship they would be departing on. He had given her a day and told her to call for him—hardly the wedding day she'd dreamed of since she was a girl. What if the ship she was supposed to sail on left without her, and the merchant wouldn't take her back to her uncle's house? What if she stayed here all day and night with nothing but strangers, nothing but ghosts?

"Todros Rubin!" She tried to be bolder, but her voice wasn't quite ready to command. At least it wasn't a question now. As she stepped through the glistening mud and milky air, a wall of shadows turned to look at her curiously. "Todros Rubin!"

The sounds of the docks were oddly muffled by the mist; the ghosts hummed and murmured to one another as they watched her go. Her heart hammered against her rib cage. What did the ghosts say?

They are not ghosts, Golde told herself. *They are people. They still live.* The ghosts were back home in Oleksandrivka, not in Odesa, not by the sea.

She had wept when they'd found her brother; she knew they'd found her father, but had been too numb to remember it. *I will get to America, then send for you,* she'd promised her mother tearfully when they'd said farewell. She'd tried to take more hope from her tears mixing with her mother's than she had when she'd wept over her brother's corpse as it lay in the spring snow. *I'll get us out of here. They can't have what's left of us.*

"Todros Rubin!"

Where are you, Todros Rubin? What did you do? Why do you need my name?

"He needs your name," her uncle had commanded. "Under no circumstances, tell anyone his true last name."

"I don't even know his true last name, how can I tell anyone?"

"You do," her uncle responded. "You remember little Todros, don't you? He used to play with" He swallowed. He didn't like saying his own son's name out loud. They kept each other company, his son, her father, and her brother—ghosts that forever would dance with the sabbath bride whenever she came to Oleksandrivka until Golde was long dead across the sea. It was fresh and raw; three months that had passed so quickly after the fires died, after the goyim laughed and made them dance to their own graves.

When she closed her eyes, she could still hear the laughter loudest of all.

"Todros! Todros Rubin!"

Yes, she did remember little Todros Fischel, who came to town every few months to help his father and learn how to service typewriters. He had been loud and annoying, and he and Shmueli had taken to each other like a duck to water. But it had been years since Golde had last seen him.

"He is a good man, no matter what he did," her uncle had promised her before he'd put her on the wagon. "And he'll get you to America. That's the most important thing."

That had been farewell.

And now, she made her way up and down the docks of the Odesa port, shouting, "Todros Rubin! Todros Rubin!" after a man she knew but didn't know and a future that would blossom across the sea if she could just find the seed that needed to sprout.

"Todros Rubin!" she called until her voice was hoarse. "Todros Rubin!" she begged the sea air and a future that would leave her father and brother behind, but might save her mother. "Todros Rubin!" she sobbed because he was nowhere to be found. She'd come all this way and for nothing, and now didn't even have the coin to get herself back to her uncle and her destroyed dreams.

"Golde?"

His voice was low and she stilled, trying to see which of the misty shadows was calling to her. She had spent so much time worrying about what would happen if she didn't find him that the reality that this man would be her husband had never quite set in. But here he was. She had found him at last.

Though not a big man, he was taller than her, and slender like a young tree. His face became more pronounced as he approached, a ghost returning to the world of the living. He was more handsome than she'd expected: he had a curly dark beard and a delicate nose. His eyes were pools of black fire against his pale face. They burned brighter the longer they looked at her. No wonder he had melted the mist away when he burned so brightly. Golde's mouth went dry. She could have done worse for a husband. Far, far worse.

She squared her shoulders. "Todros Rubin?" she asked, articulating carefully the name bestowed upon her family by the same state they fled.

He inclined his head and extended his hand to guide her towards a dock.

"How long have you been waiting?" she asked him quietly.

"Three days," he said. His voice was low and rich; it rumbled out of him like an oncoming storm. "I was going to board tonight if you hadn't arrived yet. The ship sails at midnight, and I must be on it."

"Well, I am here," she said. "My uncle said that we would be—"

"Married, yes," he finished for her. "I have witnesses and a ketubah ready. Then we will board."

She swallowed, wishing her uncle had come with her. No matter how many years she had dreamed of marriage, to be married without anyone from her family felt wrong; it *was* wrong— they were supposed to be there with her when the witnesses came.

She wasn't out of mourning yet—she shouldn't be marrying anyone at all. But it was now or Hashem knew when, and now was safer than a future when the goyim might be back.

There would be no festivities, no singing and dancing. It was just her and Todros Fischel in Odesa harbor with witnesses she didn't know, affirming that legally she was his wife.

It was quick—over with before it even really began. The two witnesses were old men she'd never seen before and would never see again. They gave her only a passing glance before turning to the man who would be her husband. She wondered what thoughts were dancing behind Todros's tense, dark eyes and unexpectedly fine nose while one of the strangers read the contract aloud. Two more signed the thing and handed it to Todros before Golde even had the chance to look at it properly. A shiver ran up her spine when he rolled it up and slid it unceremoniously into his bag. "We'll have a rabbi for the rest when we are across the sea," he promised her.

None of it felt real. She didn't feel married. There had been no vows; the only vow was the promise that there would be a vow later.

Todros extended his arm to her. "Wife?"

As if in a dream, she took it. The witnesses faded into the mist, into ghosts as they left them behind and made their way up the gangplank and onto the steamship that would take them to a new world.

The cabin they would sail in was cramped, smelled of stale saltwater and wet wood, and was lit with a guttering oil lamp that looked like it might fall over and burn them all if the ship rocked too hard. But the most disconcerting part was that they weren't the only people in it.

A pair of goyim were sitting in the second set of tiny bunks, chained to the cabin walls across from their own. They had been talking with one another but stopped, blank-faced, when Golde and Todros entered. The air in the musty cabin grew thick as the mist outside when the two men's eyes flashed with a hostility that made Golde's skin tighten over her bones in nervousness.

The Russian Empire was expansive, and there were many languages that flowed like rivers from the people who dwelled within it. When one of the goyim addressed them, he spoke in one that Golde didn't understand. Todros did, though. He responded in a tone that was as light as could be.

The two men were up and out of their bunks in a heartbeat. One of them spat before disappearing, slamming the door behind him and making the oil lamp creak metallically in their wake.

"What was that?" Golde asked. She wondered if she would get used to the moaning of the cabin walls as they bore the ship's weight on the waves. She wondered if it would get louder and worse when they were out to sea.

Todros' voice rumbled in his chest. "They said they didn't want to share a room with a Jew." The wooden cabin walls seemed to wail as they closed in on her like a coffin. "I told them to talk to the captain about it, then. We paid for our tickets as much as they did." He looked at her, then looked away, a flush creeping up from under his beard. He licked his lips nervously and Golde found she quite forgot the coffin walls.

They had not been married by a rabbi; there was no being sanctified to him, no sheva brachot. But now they were in an empty, if unguarded, room—just the two of them. The only thing that was as it should be after being wed.

She was alone in the cabin with her husband. Her husband. Todros Rubin. Todros Fischel who had become Rubin. A new Rubin in her life. It felt like a twisted exchange for the loss of her father and brother, but maybe one day it would be a comfort. Above them, the ship's bell rang out the hour. She wondered how many times it would ring before it brought them to a new life in a new world.

He shifted, his hand going into his pocket. "I picked this for you," he said, and her eyes dropped to his hand, which was drawing something she couldn't quite see from his waistcoat. He opened his fingers, though, and she saw a sprig of snowdrops. They were no longer fresh, but rather seemed to have been pressed together and dried out to preserve them. She wondered if he had actually picked them, or if he just said he had. She wasn't sure it mattered.

"Thank you," she whispered, taking the little dried flowers from him.

"I thought when we got to the New World, we would put them in a necklace—or something." He sounded so shy, and the flush on his cheeks only deepened.

"They are lovely," she whispered. She couldn't look away from his eyes. He had fascinating eyes, ones that danced brightly and flickered nervously and guarded themselves to unreadability all at once. "I don't know where to put them so they'll be safe."

"I can—" he began, but his voice trailed away, and she let him take the little snowdrops from her hand again. He crouched down next to his own bag and found their ketubah. He unrolled it, then rerolled it around the little white flowers, tying it tightly before carefully placing it back in his bag.

"I would have gotten you more," he said when he stood back up. "A ring, or a dress—something proper. But there wasn't much time."

"It all did seem ..." she paused, trying to find the right word, "rushed." She wondered if he would explain. *What did you do to make it so urgent?*

When he didn't, she asked, "What made it rushed?"

He wasn't a huge man but he loomed over her like a shadow as his intense dark eyes darted between each of hers, assessing, thinking quickly. "I needed to get my sister safely to Kyiv," he said at last. "She's to marry in the summer, so I couldn't bring her with me. That took more time and money than I would have liked. A blessing in disguise because it gave a matchmaker time to find you for me, but it also meant I wasn't as prepared for you as I should have liked to be." It wasn't quite the answer she'd wanted, but it was something.

He lifted his hand, his fingertips brushing the side of her arm and sending a jolt she wasn't expecting from her arm to her heart. Her whole body seemed warmer from just the briefest moment of contact. His hands were delicate, his fingers long. She was sure they were an asset to servicing the typewriters he'd worked on before he'd needed to flee. Her face had to be as pink as his when he'd given her the snowdrops.

Something in his face shifted, his eyes flickered a little brighter. How did his eyes burn like so many kinds of fire? First bright with a new log, then dancing when properly fed, and finally flickering with the dying hint of light from warm embers. She felt like she could lose herself in them if she stared too long. That the burning would eat her alive, but for some reason she wasn't afraid of that.

She felt suddenly cold as his hand left her arm. He turned away from her, sitting on the bottom bunk and patting the mattress for her to join him. It was made of straw, and crinkled and crunched under her weight as she sat at his side. It felt unexpectedly like her bed back home, the one her father had sung her to sleep in.

The ship continued to sway beneath them, the cacophonous music of the whining wood, the creaking lamp, and the ship's bell a crescendo through her body in time with her beating heart. She was sitting on a bed with her husband. It was not how she'd imagined it, but it was no less real. Her husband had fiery eyes and secrets he wouldn't speak to. Her uncle insisted he was a good man. Water dripped along the fogged portal, and the bunks added a clinking to the cabin's haphazard music as the waves rocked beneath them.

"Why did you need my name?" she blurted out. She hadn't meant to, but she'd been so distracted by his eyes, how close they were, how alone they were, how it was all right to be alone with her husband, that her lips moved without thought.

He stiffened, the bright flames in his eyes going duller for a moment, his face growing guarded. Somehow it seemed more shadowed than it had a moment before because his eyes were less bright.

"Some things are better left unsaid," he said quietly.

But there was power in a quiet voice—more power than in a shouted one. A shiver went up her spine. The groaning creaking ship danced with the silence that stretched between them like two separate circles at a wedding.

"What matters," he said after a long moment, "is that my sister is safe, and that we will be across the sea. Let the past stay here with the dead. There is a brighter future waiting for us."

She looked at him warily. In every interaction she'd had with him so far, he'd seemed gentle. It was the second time he'd brought up a sister he'd done all he could to keep safe as well. Her uncle insisted he was a good man, but even the fire in his eyes cast a shadow.

But despite the shadow, despite the nervousness of all of it, she wasn't sure she was afraid. She should be. Every instinct in her body told her that a man who wouldn't tell you why he was fleeing across the sea was the sort of man who would destroy for his own profit.

But he'd brought her snowdrops instead of nothing at all, and she found herself confused.

"I'm glad your sister is safe." Golde's voice was so much quieter than the ship's bell above them. If his sister was safe, then that meant he protected his family. It meant the man whose eyes shone like the sun could be the good man her uncle had promised her, even if she didn't know everything yet. Right?

Her fingers twitched towards his on the blanket of the bunk. His twitched back towards hers. This time, she was prepared for the jolt that went straight to her heart when the sides of their littlest fingers touched, dancing in counterpoint to the swirling questions that wouldn't quite fade away.

"So, the new world," she said. She curled her pinky around his.

"The new world," he replied.

She woke to the sound of the door closing and opened her eyes. The cabin was dark now. The little oil lamp that had flickered and whispered had gone out. She was alone in the bunk. The skin on her chin felt rough from Todros's beard and her swollen lips were full of the memory of the taste of his. She heard footsteps, then words in the language she didn't speak.

She pulled the blanket more tightly around her. She'd been glad that Todros had whispered they would wait for some of it until America. She was still fully clothed and very glad of it now that the goyim had returned. She was alone in the bed but that didn't worry her so long as Todros was in the bunk above her.

The stranger repeated what he'd said, more loudly and more slowly. Then a shadow that made the darkness even darker leaned over her bed, saying his words one more time.

Her heart slammed in her throat. Todros couldn't be there. He would have stepped in. He spoke the language and she did not, and he had driven the two of them out of the cabin earlier with such dexterity.

"I do not understand," she tried in German. She had been quick to learn German—it was similar enough to Yiddish. She spoke only a little Russian, and not well. Whatever these men were speaking, it was neither language.

"Where is your husband?" the goy asked in German without missing a beat. "Where did he go?"

"I do not know. I was asleep." She hated how ephemeral her voice sounded—gasping and faint the way it had when she'd begged the milky ghosts to produce Todros. She wanted some of that black fire that made Todros seem bigger and braver than any man in the world. How dare these men wake her and stand over her like this? What right did they have to do this? When they reached the New World, they wouldn't be the same.

The ship rocked beneath the creaking bunk; the bell clanged loudly on the deck above. It didn't sound like music now. Her skin was itching the way it had when she'd crouched in the spring snow, her breath a ghost in the air in front of her as the laughter died out at last.

Then the door opened. Todros was back, his jacket hanging open over his shirtsleeves. The shadow hanging over the bed retreated to the other side of the cabin.

When Todros spoke, it was in their language.

The argument that followed was brief. He lit the oil lamp again and stood firmly between Golde and the two men, his back neither broad nor tall, but it seemed stronger than the sea between her and the ghosts that followed her from her home. When it was done, he turned and knelt next to her, where she clung to the blankets. When he touched her hand, heat flooded her again as she knew it would. This time it didn't jolt—this time it burned. She hadn't realized how cold she'd been until he came back. Now she was trembling, but not with fear.

"Did they touch you?"

She shook her head.

He sat down on the bunk next to her, glaring across the cabin to the two goyim. They glared back at him and spoke again in the language she didn't understand.

"What are they saying?" she asked him.

"It doesn't matter," he said softly, not taking his eyes off them. "It doesn't concern us."

"What doesn't concern us?"

He stiffened, realizing his mistake. There were dark circles under his eyes. She had slept, but he seemed not to have. Maybe not for days.

"Someone was thrown overboard," Todros said calmly. "I heard someone on the deck talking about it when I went to check with the captain about why we hadn't cast away yet. It is past midnight, and we should have left two hours ago." *Did he refuse to sleep until we were out to sea?*

What did you do? Why are you fleeing?

"They're looking for the killer?"

"They've called in the army and are looking through the ship. Nothing that concerns us." He was trying to keep his face smooth as glass, but it was like the glass covering a silver-backed mirror. In his face, she saw her own nervousness, her own fear. They didn't need to find the killer if they found a suitable scapegoat. How long had he been out walking?

As if he heard her thoughts, the man across the cabin said in German, "He was gone many hours, your husband. Do you know where he went?"

She couldn't let herself be afraid now, so she shot him an acid look. It didn't burn enough, though, because he laughed.

She hated it when they laughed.

They sat there, wordlessly, side by side, the sides of their pinkies pressed against one another, but not quite daring to hold each other's hands. She focused as much as she could on the sound of his breath so that she didn't jump whenever she heard cabin doors opening nearby. *What did you do, Todros Rubin?*

Did you throw a man overboard?

Did you kill someone back home and that is why you flee now? Why you made sure your sister was safe when you couldn't protect her anymore?

Had he thrown a man overboard? He said he'd only gone to check with the captain when the ship hadn't departed, but she had been asleep. Her heart believed the fire in his eyes, but her head whispered that she had only just met him, only had the promise from her uncle that he was a good man. He hadn't told her the full truth; perhaps he was a liar who had duped everyone with those burning eyes of his.

It was another hour before the cabin door opened without a knock. Three soldiers stood there, carrying a lamp between them. When they spoke, it was in Russian. They spoke to the goyim first. They replied quickly to each question. Golde's skin prickled the whole time, waiting for the inevitable moment.

It came when the man, the one who had loomed over her like a shadow, pointed to Todros and said, "The Jew went for a walk and was gone for a very long time while his wife slept."

Then the soldiers turned their attention to the two of them. Todros continued to sit on the bunk, his back straight as an arrow, his face unreadable.

"Papers," the soldier barked, and Todros bent down to his bag to grab them. One soldier rifled through them while another stared for a long time at Todros. Todros stared back at him.

"You are from Liubashivka?" asked the one with the papers, rifling through them.

"I am," Todros said.

"When did you leave?"

"Two weeks ago. We were just married."

The soldier with the papers glanced between him and Golde. The soldier who was staring at Todros did not break his gaze.

A bad feeling pooled in Golde's stomach. She did not like those eyes. Those eyes were more than just appraising—they were comparing. They were the eyes of someone trying to piece together a puzzle.

"Congratulations," the soldier said, sounding bored.

"We are looking for a Todros Fischel out of Liubashivka," said the second soldier. "He killed our captain a little over a week ago."

Golde's breath caught in her throat, and it took all her fear and self-control not to look at her husband.

"You didn't know him, by any chance?"

Todros didn't respond. Time seemed to slow. She could tell from the way the oil lamp flickered against the wall. No flame danced that slowly.

He killed a man.

And may well have killed another tonight.

The silence now spoke louder than any of his quiet words. It was a knife held at his back, something to run from because it could —and would—kill him if he stayed.

Golde stared at the Russian soldiers in front of her and she remembered the way her brother had screamed for her to run, to hide.

Golde would let the coffin-cabin walls have Todros.

"My cousin used to play with Todros Fischel, and there were three Todros Fischels in his village to begin with. If you're going to search for someone, you'd better have more than just their name.

Names are common." Fischel wasn't though. That was a lie, but she knew these soldiers wouldn't know, and the ship would hopefully be halfway across the sea by the time they learned any better.

"Todros Rubin," said the first soldier, looking down at the ticket. "And Golde Rubin." He looked at her. "A common name, maybe. Or easily changeable. Your name changed when you married it. His could have too."

Golde let out an impressive huff of annoyance. Annoyance felt better than fear—if reckless. "Yes, because between our wedding two weeks ago, we had the time to celebrate with our families, make sure his sister was safely installed with his aunt as we prepared for our trip, kill your captain, change our names, and flee to Odesa. Quite precise."

Todros's hand tightened on her wrist. "Forgive my wife," he said quietly. "She is upset at being up so late. She forgets her manners."

He squeezed her wrist again. She wondered if it was to calm her down or to show her he didn't mean it. She didn't know him well enough.

"If they did change their names, it will be on their wedding contract," spoke the third soldier who had been so silent Golde had forgotten he was there at all. "They sign a wedding contract."

"It will be in their language though. I can't read it—can you?" asked the man holding the papers.

The thought of him unrolling their ketubah, of him dislodging the little snowdrops that Todros had dried flooded her with black fire. When Golde spoke next, the acid burned this time. "It also uses our names, not the ones you gave us. So if you are trying to find trickery, it's more than just a language that won't help you. Leave us be. Todros Rubin is not Todros Fischel. What description do you have? A Jew with dark hair named Todros? A credit to your dead captain."

She shouldn't have said that. She knew she shouldn't. All three soldiers stiffened and swelled with rage.

But Todros stood this time, and once again, his back spread out like the sea between her and danger. "My wife is grouchy when she is tired, I have learned these past two weeks. I am more than happy to provide you with what proof you need, but I am not a killer. I know no one on this ship but my wife, and while she may have a tongue like a whip, I have seen no reason to kill her just yet."

Perhaps under other circumstances she would have snarled at him too for the comments at her expense, but she was relieved, for once, when one of the soldiers chuckled. "Wives are more trouble than they're worth."

"So I am learning," quipped Todros. "Gentlemen, don't let us keep you. You'll find no killer here."

The first soldier handed him back his papers; the third soldier turned for the door. The second stared at him for a long moment, still trying to find his missing puzzle piece.

"Come on, Yuri," the first soldier said. Then the three were gone.

Todros sat down next to her on the bunk again, taking her hand and stroking it. His eyes flicked to the goyim across the way. "I must look like I'm chiding you," he snapped at her in Yiddish. "Because that was rude to soldiers who hated us." His fingers traced along each of hers, one at a time, thumb first, then pointer, all the way to her pinky. "But instead, I thank you. I didn't know what to say but you did. Thank you."

"I will appear chastened," she said, pretending to look meek. His eyes flickered in amusement. "But you owe me a story."

This time, his eyes didn't recede to ember. This time, they blazed brighter than they had a moment before.

"They came down on our town one night with fire and fury. We ran, we hid, we did our best to stay alive. One of them attacked my sister. It wasn't until he was bleeding in the snow that I realized he was a captain. And that two of his men had seen what happened."

A good man, her uncle had promised of a murderer. *You shall not kill,* but he had done it and she found she wasn't angry. Killing someone to save another was another law the sages had said was holy. If anything, the black fire in his eyes was spreading to her heart, igniting a righteous rage she hadn't known she could feel anymore.

"Thank you," she whispered. He had fought and survived, and she was glad to know that it could be done.

"Thank *you*," he replied.

"I would do it again."

"And I for you," he vowed.

They had said no wedding vows under a chuppah. There had been no singing, no dancing, no anything at all.

But I am my beloved's, and my beloved is mine.

Forever Home

by Vivian Kasley

The house was perfect. She was a Victorian, graceful with old but good bones. You could tell she'd had some work done over the years, but not enough to take away from her natural beauty, which was accented by tasteful shrubs and hedges, flowering plants, and well-placed trees. Wilhem and Claudia stood outside, juggling the last of their few belongings in their arms, and marveled as they drank in their new home. The three-story dark purple house with black-and-white accents had steep roofs, ornate shingles and gables and a wide decorated porch complete with its original spindlework. It was everything they had ever wanted.

"Would you look at those friezes and lace-like brackets? And that's just on the roof," Wilhem said.

"It's truly breathtaking, Wilhem," Claudia said, her voice barely more than a whisper over the whipping wind. Tears glazed her eyes, and before she could stop herself, they began to trace her cheeks.

"Hey. It's alright, love. C'mon, let's go inside before the rain starts." Wilhem looked up at the storm clouds racing above, tears of his own threatening to spill.

Most couples nearing their age began to think about moving to condos in a warmer climate, but they'd wanted to live a Victorian since they'd first gotten married over thirty-five years ago. Having never had children, they put any extra money they had away, hoping to one day make their dream come true. But even with their savings, they had to sell almost everything they had to make their dream a reality. Of course, it also didn't help that they were both retiring earlier than anticipated for reasons out of their control.

Other than their beds, the couple had sold all of their furniture, so both were thrilled to find out their new home came mostly furnished with the odds and ends of whoever had owned the home before. They were even more thrilled to learn that what was left behind reflected the Victorian era. Every room seemed to be crowded with lavish furniture made of walnut, mahogany, and rosewood. As they continued to explore, they were wowed by the exquisite floral wallpaper on the dark paneled walls, the plentiful iron candle sconces, the rich colored rugs adorning the gorgeous wood floors, and by the chandeliers hanging from the ceilings like glittering cobwebs. There was even a dusty grand piano in the parlor. It was an eclectic assemblage employing an aesthetic of excess and maximalism, so in other words, it was perfect.

Rain pelted the windows of the upstairs master bedroom as Claudia hung some of their clothes and put them away. She closed her eyes and inhaled the smells around her—wood, musty drapery, and other people's memories. It would be dark soon, and she wanted to make some iced tea and sandwiches for supper. The stove was gas, and they'd realized too late in the day that they'd forgotten to call and have it turned on. Luckily, the fridge worked okay, and the lunch meat and snacks she'd bought from the market that afternoon would do just fine. She promised Wilhem she'd make him roast beef with crispy potatoes and gravy laden Yorkshire puddings as soon as she could.

The stairs creaked as Claudia made her way down to the parlor. She went purposefully slow, enjoying the whine and groan of the aging staircase. She'd changed into a sheer pink nightgown, the bottom of the long silk robe she put over it softly trailing behind her. Before she entered the parlor, she smelled something burning. Panic flooded her senses for a brief moment, but then she heard the pop and crackle of a fire and realized quickly what it was. Wilhem smiled as soon as he saw her. He held an iron poker in one hand like a staff and the apples of his cheeks were flushed, letting her know he'd been at the bourbon.

"Did you pour me one?" Claudia asked.

"You know I did."

"Thank you, my love. Now, what kind of sandwich would you like?"

"Turkey and ham sounds good," Wilhem said, then he turned back to the fire, stoking it like it was something he had always done.

"That role suits you."

"Does it?" Wilhem didn't turn around, but kept stoking the already blazing fire.

Claudia's bottom lip and chin began to tremble uncontrollably as she watched him. His wide shoulders and the muscles in his strong back had always stoked her own fire. She turned to go before he could see her cry. He was having a hard enough time and he didn't need to keep seeing that.

Claudia's hands shook as she prepared their sandwiches. She was glad she'd forgotten to buy tomatoes earlier, because she wasn't sure—with her hands being so unsteady—she'd have been able to slice them. Nothing was fair. None of it. Here she was, in the home of her dreams with the love of her life, and neither of them would get to enjoy it for very long. They'd maybe have a few months at the very most, but that was wishful thinking with the stage of and type of cancer Wilhem had been diagnosed with. He'd opted out of treatment, seeing it as a hopeless endeavor. He wanted what time he had left to be uninhibited by the effects of chemo, radiation, and a cocktail of meds. The only thing he agreed to take was medical marijuana for pain and sleep.

When they had found out about his diagnosis, they made love several times, just like when they were newlyweds, then lay in the sweaty sheets afterwards discussing what to do next. She'd begged him to think about chemo and radiation, but Wilhem kept refusing, explaining how the doctor said it probably wouldn't do much considering the stage the cancer was at and where it had spread. "It would only make me feel horrible, and any time I do have left would be miserable. This's my choice, Claudia. Please, let me make one while I still can," he'd said.

After several sleepless nights, many tearful arguments, and even some begging on her knees, Claudia had conceded to Wilhem, but only after she'd convinced him to hear her out concerning her own decision. "If you're going to go, so then am I," she'd told him, her tone as blunt as a dull razor.

"What? No you're not, you're as healthy as a horse."

"I know. And that's why I must go too."

"Stop it, stop saying that. You're not making sense."

"No, you've made your choice, and now this is my choice."

"Claud, listen to what you're saying, it's selfish. Please ... don't make this even harder than it's already going to be. Accepting my fate and leaving you is the hardest thing I've ever had to do, but knowing you might hurt yourself because of it, I couldn't bear it."

"I am not being selfish."

"You are goddamn it!"

"Wilhem, I've thought this through. I'm gonna be sixty in a couple years. We have no children, no real close friends, and both our parents are gone. And our siblings have lives of their own, and couldn't be concerned with us unless it's about money. I have nobody *but* you. You're my whole entire world."

"And you're mine, but that doesn't mean I'd end it just because you ... well, if you were to pass. I know I once said I wouldn't remarry, but you? You could. Remarry, I mean."

"That's not a possibility."

"You're being irrational, Claud. You'll still be young by today's standards. And you're still beautiful. You always will be."

"I'm not changing my mind, Wil. You go, I go. There's nothing left to discuss."

"Claud, I … I don't know how to take this. You're hurting me. The thought of you—I can't even think of it …"

"Wil, if you'll hear me out, I have an idea. It might not make much sense at first, but just hear me out and if you still feel the same way after I am done telling you what I have to say, then I promise to stick around after …" Claudia's breath caught. "After you're gone."

Claudia set the plates of sandwiches down onto the table in the dining room, then poured some iced tea into a couple glasses. She called for Wilhem, and sat down across from his setting, picking at the crust of her bread and rolling the torn pieces into tiny balls. Wilhem was humming as he came to join her, and said nothing as he sat down and began to eat. The storm had passed, and the late sun's rays came through the bay sash window, turning the blue of his eyes into gleaming sapphires.

"Wilhem?"

"Yes, love?"

"There's no television. Do you think we should go into town tomorrow and get one?"

"Claud, I couldn't care less about a television at this point. I didn't even want to keep our phones, but I knew that'd be a stretch. I want all of my waking hours to be with you—talking, dancing, singing, and making love in every room of this house while I still can. Speaking of dancing, I brought our old record player."

"I thought you sold it?"

"Nope!" Wilhem winked at her and took a sip of tea, mischief evident in his eyes.

"Why're you looking at me like that?"

"Because I love you, and you're beautiful in your almost see-through nightgown, and I cannot wait to take it off of you."

"I love you, too, Wil." Claudia suddenly lost her appetite. She didn't understand how he was so calm about everything. *How could he want to make love during a time like this?* she wondered. Sure, selling everything and buying the house had been her idea, but she wondered if it had all been a terrible mistake. Maybe she should've been more persistent on him trying to fight for his life instead of giving it up. All of it had been a whirlwind, a fever dream, and in the moments leading up to the purchase of the house, there was nothing but happiness about their decision, but now, despair crept back in, the weight of it bogging her down.

After their early dinner, Claudia cleaned up, then joined Wilhem in the parlor as he set up the record player. She knew what he'd choose to play before he ever put the needle to the vinyl. Sinatra's velvety voice caressed her ears, and warmed her blood. As soon as Wilhem reached out his hand to her, she took it. They danced long into the evening, him brushing her graying honey hair away from her green eyes, their lips meeting more than once for kisses.

By the time they were ready for bed, Claudia was exhausted. Her bare feet felt rubbed raw from dancing on the hard wood, and her lower back ached from all the twirling. Wilhem brushed his teeth, then came into the bedroom with an obvious look of desire. He lit the candles he'd placed in the sconces, turned off the lights, and climbed into bed beside her. His fingers stroked her shoulder, then her neck.

Claudia smiled, but secretly questioned how he could be in such good spirits. She couldn't help but think of their pending situation all of the time. Sensing her apprehension, Wilhem crawled under the covers and lifted her nightgown over his head full of soft dark curls. He kissed her breasts, trailed his tongue down her stomach, then buried his face between her thighs. That was enough for her to lay back and forgot everything as he worked his magic.

His hands knew her body after so many years, and his touch was nothing short of electric. She could've come again just from him lifting her nightgown over her head, his breath warm against her neck and ear as he nibbled both. By the time he entered her, she couldn't help but cry out, and as they made love under the warmth of the duvet, she let her mind go blank once again.

They lay in the dark, staring at the candle's flames dancing upon the gilded ceiling. Rain tapped at the windows again, and distant thunder rumbled like a hungry stomach. Claudia's blood flowed like warm maple syrup, the area between her thighs satiated but still throbbing with greed. Wilhem rolled the nipple of her left breast with his thumb, sending shivers of desire down her back.

"Wilhem? What if there're others?"

"What do you mean?" he turned his face toward her own, and watched her delicate heart-shaped lips as she spoke.

"I mean, well, I hadn't thought about this until now, but what if there're others here who've died? What then?" Her own question made goosepimples rise on her flesh, so she pulled the sheet up to cover her breasts.

"Then we'll have guests. It would be one big happy family. The more the merrier!"

"Wil, I'm serious. Say they don't want more *people* hanging around?"

"I say, too bad. Besides, I'm sure people will buy this house once we're gone, so, we can't expect to be fully alone forever, can we? It'll be like that one movie. What's it called? *Beetlejuice*, that's the one. We can haunt people while they eat dinner, you know, make them do a little dance and then shove their faces into their shrimp cocktail. It'll be fun!"

"So, you really believe then?"

Wilhem sighed. "I don't know what I believe, but the fact that you believe it, makes me happy. And since we came to an agreement, I'll have to be okay with that."

"Can you repeat it for me? What you're supposed to do, I mean."

"Claud ..."

"Just do it."

"In the days following my departure, I am to move the note you place on the memory box and place it where we discussed. Satisfied?"

"Yes."

"And if none of that happens ... if I don't come back ... you promise to stick around?"

"I promise."

"Good." Wilhem yawned, then turned over. "Goodnight, my love."

"Goodnight."

The plan was a shaky one, Claudia knew that. She was never a big believer in the afterlife, but she had to hold on to something, anything, to make things easier. Because what if there was an afterlife? What if they could spend the rest of eternity, together forever in the home of their dreams? It would be worth it. Besides, with no children to look after her one day, and no family who gave two shits where she was, she felt it was the right thing to do. Wilhem was her life, her whole life. Her heart would no longer want to beat once his stopped. What she didn't tell him, was that even if he didn't move her note or caress her neck with his electric fingers, she'd still end it.

Over the next few weeks, the couple explored the house and all of its wonders. The spacious attic and basement were surprisingly mostly empty except for a few paintings, rusty tools, holiday decorations, and plenty of long-legged spiders. Claudia was sure with all the furniture left behind there'd be a treasure trove of things in either room, but alas, there was not. There weren't even any faded black and white photos where the people in them are staring blankly back at the photographer looking like they've seen some shit in their life and just want the picture taken already.

The house was elderly, having been erected in the 1860s, and yet Claudia felt no out of the ordinary cold spots or heard any strange whispers in the dark. At the very least she'd hoped to feel invisible eyes watching her as she roamed the cold dimly lit halls, or see a specter out of the corner of her eye that disappeared like smoke when she turned to greet it head-on.

But there was nothing. Not a peep. And that concerned her to great lengths.

As Wilhem became weaker by the day, Claudia decided they needed to do a séance. He was too tired to argue, and so he agreed. They turned their phones to silent, lit every available candle they had, and placed them around the parlor. The large throw rug was plush under their bottoms as they sat down in front of the table with the Ouija board she'd bought.

"So, we're going to attempt to contact spirits with a board game you picked up at Target?"

"Wil. Just be present."

"I am present, but I don't think anyone else will be."

"If this is how you feel, then why'd we agree to this, huh? Why'd you let me talk you into getting rid of everything, buying a house way beyond our means, and then waiting for you to …"

"Because I fucking love you, Claud, that's why. I want to believe the things you believe, can't you see that? And also, what you don't know is that I have a million-dollar life insurance policy that I took out through work months before we found out about this fucking bastard that's stealing my life from me. So, you'll be taken care of … you'll be okay."

Wilhem looked at her, and she kept her mouth shut. He'd lost so much weight, and the candlelight made his gaunt face seem creepier than it actually was. She didn't want to upset him further by telling him she knew about his policy; she'd found out when the insurance guy called the house looking for him and she told him she was his wife and could help if he needed. But knowing about the money wouldn't change her mind in the end. Money wasn't everything, but everything *was* Wilhem.

Claudia waited until enough time passed before she placed her fingers on the planchette, then she closed her eyes when she saw that Wilhem had closed his. She didn't want to ask if he closed his out of boredom or whether he was actually participating, so instead she focused all of her thoughts and energy, hoping it'd make a difference and that any other energy present would hitch a ride off her own. She wasn't exactly sure how séances worked, but she'd seen enough movies and read enough stories. The room grew colder, and even though she knew big old houses—including theirs—were bound to have random drafts, she took it as a sign to begin.

"Is anyone there? If anyone is there, could you please make yourself known?"

The silence in the room was deafening. Neither of them wanted to breathe for fear it would scare the other. After several moments of no movement, Claudia again asked, "Is anyone present in this house with us? Anyone at all?"

The candles flickered like crazy, casting sinister shadows on the walls. Wilhem had opened his eyes and was studying Claudia's face. His heart crumpled in his chest as he watched her. Her eyes were shut tight, and her mouth was set in a grim line. The planchette hadn't moved but for the minor half inch or two due to her twitchy fingers. She wanted this, and he wished more than anything that he could conjure up something—anything—to give her hope. He could join her, put his fingers on the planchette and maybe make it move a little, but he knew she'd know, and that would only hurt her further.

"Please … if you're there … anyone?"

"Claud—"

"Wil, don't ruin this, please."

Defeated, Wilhem closed his mouth and his eyes, hoping that something—anything— would come and give his beloved wife what she desperately wanted.

They sat in the parlor for what seemed like hours, Claudia almost in tears as she tried to summon the dead. She asked the same questions over and over in different ways until finally Wilhem couldn't take it anymore.

"I'm tired and my legs are getting numb. I don't want to do this anymore, Claud. Can we just go to bed, and maybe, fool around a little?"

"Fool around—are you serious, Wil? I have to do this. Can't you understand? I have to!"

"Yeah … sure. I understand. Stay down here and talk to the walls, but I'm going to bed."

"But I need you with me."

"Then be with me while I'm still here," Wilhem said, then he stood up and walked away.

As he climbed the stairs, the sadness he felt erupted into full blown tears when he realized she hadn't gotten up to follow him, and he bit into his knuckles to keep from screaming all of the things he wanted to scream at her. He could still hear her questioning the empty room, begging it to answer, as he opened the door to their bedroom. The joint he had left from earlier lay on its side in the ash tray on the bedside table. All he could do now, was hope that Mary Jane would hurry up and take him to dreamland.

Wilhem toked the tiny rumpled joint and immediately felt it work its magic. He buried his face into his pillow and wept, remembering the time when they were newly married and had gotten high together for the first time. Claudia had laughed and laughed, swearing that she would name their first child, "Puff the Magic Dragon."

"We'll call him Puff for short," she'd said.

"Him? But what if it's a girl?" he had asked.

"Well, we'll call her Jackie, as in little Jackie Paper."

"Or maybe Honah Lee."

"Oh my gosh, yes! That's perfect, Wil!"

They tried, oh how they had tried to get pregnant, but eventually they gave up when their savings began to dwindle. Neither of them wanted to go broke trying to have a child, so they filled their lives with as much love as they could.

He shoved the memory to the back of his memory bank, put the tear dampened pillow over his head to help drown out Claudia's desperate pleas from downstairs, and drifted off to sleep.

It was after two in the morning when Claudia stood up, her legs wobbly from sitting on the floor for so long. She'd eyed the planchette one last time before she blew out the candles. Nothing had happened. *How could a house be so old and not have one single ghost in it?* she wondered. *Because there are no ghosts, dum-dum.* "Shut up," Claudia whispered, her voice hoarse from hours of chatting to an empty room. "Shut up, shut up, shut up!"

Wilhem hadn't shut the bedroom door all the way, and she slipped through the opening without a sound. His pillow had slipped to the floor and he lay on his side, snoring softly. She carefully eased the pillow back under his head as she got into the bed and he stirred, rolling onto his back. She wanted to touch the soft stubble on his face and nuzzle her nose into the warmth of his neck to breathe his scent, but instead she lay her head on his chest and fell asleep to the rhymical thud of his heart.

Morning was more quiet than usual as one waited for the other to speak first. The scrape of the butter knife against Wilhem's rye toast and the slurping sound he made sipping his hot coffee caused Claudia to set her glass of orange juice down harder than planned, sending a pulpy splash onto the table. She sucked her teeth as she wiped it up with a napkin, feeling Wilhem's eyes burning into her as she did.

"Problem?" he asked.

"No. Why do you ask?"

"Because you're obviously upset about something."

"Does it matter?"

"Of course, it does, Claud, or I wouldn't ask."

"Well, for starters, you left me by myself last night. I was rambling on at a Ouija board like some kind of lunatic—"

320

"C'mon, Claud. That's not fair. I was tired, and we were getting nowhere. I'd began to get monkey butt from sitting there for so long, and it was clear nothing was gonna happen."

"Maybe it's because *you* didn't try hard enough. Your energy affected my energy. Ever think of that?"

"Sorry, Claud. I didn't mean to."

"Just say it."

"Say what?"

"You don't believe."

"Claud, you know how I feel."

"Yeah, I know, and that's what makes it worse."

"You're being unfair."

"Maybe, but you dying is unfair! This whole entire thing is unfair! Us buying a house that cost us everything because I thought … never mind. Just … I can't …" Claudia cried. She cried harder than she had since first finding out about his diagnosis. She couldn't breathe through her loud sobs. Wilhem got up from the table and encircled her into his arms. He had gotten so thin, and she could feel how thin, and it only made her cry harder.

"It's okay, baby. It's gonna be okay," he said.

"No, it isn't! It's not gonna be okay, goddamn it, Will! Can you please just stop pretending to be so accepting of what's gonna fucking happen? You're going to die, Wilhem. You're going to die and leave me all alone in this enormous cold empty fucking house and I can't stand it!" Claudia was panting, her face hot and wet with tears, strings of snot hanging from her nostrils. She felt like a rabid dog.

"I have accepted it, Claud. I have. And I need you to do the same. Please …" Wilhem finally broke and began to weep alongside her. They both collapsed to the floor, holding one another and crying until they ran out of steam.

"Wil?" Claudia lay beside him on the dining room floor, the waxed wood cool beneath her back.

"Yes?"

"I'm sorry."

"It's okay."

"No, it's not."

"It is. But can you please promise me something?"

"What?"

"Please don't do it, Claud."

"Wil—"

"Please. Promise me."

"Okay then, Wil. I won't."

"Good." He squeezed her hand.

Morning drained the both of them. Wilhem took a nap on the couch while Claudia did laundry and read a book in the cozy chair beside him. Her mind wandered as she read. She wondered if maybe ghosts only existed when something tragic happened to the person, like a murder or a sudden death. Or maybe they just needed one really good reason to return. Maybe they have unfinished business. *Maybe, maybe, maybe …*

She closed her book and watched him sleep. His breathing seemed labored. It reminded her of swells in a volatile sea. Her eyes wandered to his chapped lips, then to his clavicle, which jutted out like handle bars. Tears slid down her cheeks as she counted his ribs through his thin white shirt. It was only a matter of time now, and she knew that. She also knew she promised him she wouldn't do it, but sometimes promises were made to be broken.

The days began to go by the same. Mostly consisting of Wilhem sleeping on the couch and her watching him sleep. He had stopped eating, except for toast and a few spoonfuls of soup now and again. He stopped drinking his beloved coffee and only drank water. They'd attempted to make love once or twice, but eventually they gave up trying. He was too weak. So, she kissed him gently and massaged his thin cold limbs instead, telling him it was all alright. She hadn't brought up any more about ghosts or anything else involving their agreement since that day at breakfast. She only took care of him. He needed help to the bathroom, shaving, showering, and dressing.

She knew it was the day when she woke on the chair beside him and saw him staring up at the ceiling with glassy eyes. She tried to speak to him, but he didn't seem to notice she was even there. His breaths were raspy and few. Seeing him that way was painful enough to cause her to want to cut her heart from her chest to stop it from hurting, but she knew she couldn't break down right then. She needed to be present until he was no longer with her. She got up from the chair and knelt beside him, taking his stiff hand into her own.

"It's okay, my love. It's okay. I love you. I always will. Always. We've had so much together. And we've shared so many good memories. God, I love you so much, Wilhem ..." Claudia held his hand to her lips and wept.

Wilhem's eyes finally rested on Claudia's face. Her heart jumped when she saw him watching her.

"Wilhem?" Claudia hoped he'd be able to say something, anything.

He said what he needed to say with his eyes, then his fingers grazed her face, and he closed his eyes for good. Claudia rested her head on his chest until she heard the unmistakable rattle of his last breath. It was then she let loose a scream that echoed throughout the entire house. She knew she was supposed to call for him to be taken away, but she couldn't seem to move from his side. She pulled the blanket off of him and rubbed his mottled legs and feet, trying to warm them.

"Wilhem," she whispered. "I love you forever."

It wasn't real. It didn't feel real. How was she supposed to get up and call anyone? How was she supposed to go on? How was she supposed to keep her promise to him? She got up, moving on legs made of stone. A half empty bottle of bourbon sat on the counter in the kitchen. She pulled the cork from it and took a long pull. Then she took another long pull until it burned some sense into her. *Wilhem's dead. He's dead on the couch, getting stiffer and colder as I wander around the house like the ghost he probably won't be. You both made the necessary previous arrangements and you have to call, Claudia.* She moved her stone limbs to where her phone was, dialed the number she'd saved, and spoke in a voice that wasn't her own.

After she hung up with the funeral home, she threw her phone as if it were a venomous snake. It hit the floor and shattered the screen. She let loose another scream. In the other room the love of her life was already beginning to decay. The man who had made her body weep with pleasure just months ago was dead. He was never coming back. She refused to go back into the room. She couldn't. When the doorbell rang, she went to the door, opened it, and then walked away from the people standing there. She didn't want to greet those who came to take away her husband. As they entered the house, she stood near-by shaking with rage, and looked at them like they were all monsters.

It'd been a week since Wilhem's service. She was glad everyone was finally gone and leaving her alone as usual. His sister and her brothers came to the service, but didn't stay overnight. They didn't want to stick around long enough to find out if she might ask for their help with anything. She bet if they knew about the money, they would've chomped at the bit to help her wipe her ass if she asked.

The stillness and quiet in the big old Victorian were getting to her. She played all their favorite records, and drank bourbon and red wine, slow dancing with Wilhem's pillow, the scent of his head still clinging to it. And she wrote the note. Of course, she did. It was only a couple sentences long. *I'll love you forever. Come back to me,* it said. She put it on top of their memory box on the dresser, just like she said she would.It was only a sliver of hope, but a sliver is a sliver.

Claudia lay in bed, staring into the darkness, straining her ears to hear anything that could be a sign of Wilhems's return. But all she heard was the rain. The note still lay where she left it, untouched. The sliver of hope she'd felt the week before had dwindled down to nothing. Why had she believed in such nonsense? She rolled over and began to cry. And then she felt something. Like cold mist trailing the bare skin of her forearm. She yelped and sat up in the bed.

"Wilhem," she whispered to the dark room.

Nothing.

And then the cold mist returned, this time on her cheek. Claudia frantically pulled the sheets down, exposing more of her flesh. She closed her eyes and parted her lips, willing whatever was touching her to continue. It mapped her shoulders, her neck, and her upper back. Her nightgown began to feel damp, so she removed it. Then she lay naked atop the covers, shivering as the mist seem to engulf her, like a cloud. Her nipples hardened as the invisible coldness idled down the length of her body, slowly and deliberately, then it settled between her legs where it began a focused methodical pulsing of energy until she cried out.

After, she lay there, breathless. She smiled, then began to laugh and cry all at once. It was Wilhem! She knew it was. No one else knew how to make her feel that way. Claudia's head swam with what this meant. She reached for him, but her chilly lover had vanished.

"Wil?" She searched the dark, afraid to turn on the bedside lamp for fear the light would break the magic of what had happened. "Wilhem?"

She got up from the bed, turned on the light, and went to the memory box. The note still lay on top of it, untouched. Maybe he didn't see it? Did it matter after what he'd just done? Wasn't that all of the proof that she needed? She ran to the bathroom, knowing exactly what she was going for.

She'd been saving the bottle of sleeping pills for this moment. She'd take them all and wait for death to wrap her in its sweet embrace. She stared at the bottle, her lips quivering, tears streaming down her face. It wasn't a selfish suicide; it was her choosing to end her life to begin a new one. One where she and Wilhem could be together again. *Then why am I stalling? Because, you made a promise to Wil. And what if you don't come back, huh? What if you do it and then you never see Wil again? What if it wasn't him? What if you dreamt that?*

"I didn't dream it ... and it was him, I know it! It was real!"

Claudia twisted the lid from the bottle and looked down at all the little white pills. All she had to do was take them. No one would come calling and save her at the last minute, this she knew. She put one on her tongue. Her saliva gathered around the bitter tang of it. There was a lump as she swallowed. A lump of regret perhaps? *NO!* She indignantly put another. And just as she was about to put more, her phone rang. Startled, she dropped the bottle and the pills scattered everywhere. "Son of a bitch," she shouted.

Who the hell would be calling her at this hour? No one ever called. She trotted to the phone on the nightstand and looked at the screen. Unknown number. She tapped the screen to end call, then turned around to go back to the bathroom. Again, the phone began to ring. Claudia stomped back to the nightstand and picked up the phone, ready to chew out whoever had the nerve to disrupt her impending demise.

"Hello? Goddamn it! Don't call me again!" She turned her phone off and went back to the bathroom.

As she was on her knees gathering the pills, she heard music. It was soft at first, and then gradually louder. "Promises, Promises" by Naked Eyes. Had she played that record last? No. She'd played David Bowie. She stood up, and went for the stairs. The song's lyrics echoed off the walls, haunting her. It was freezing, colder than it normally was, and she realized she was still naked. Claudia wrapped her arms around her trembling body, following the lead of her billowing breath into the parlor. The light was already on. Hadn't she turned it off? *Yes, yes I did.* Her teeth chattered as she walked over to the record player. Beside it, she spotted a small piece of paper folded over that she hadn't noticed before.

Claudia picked the paper up and clenched her jaw to stop her teeth from chattering. She unfolded it and read the words scrawled on it.

"My love, you made me a promise. Please keep it. One day we will see each other again. This, I promise. Love you forever, Wilhem."

The note slipped from her fingers and fluttered to her feet. She gasped when the music stopped and the lights flickered. And then Wilhem's ghostly whisper seemed to come from everywhere and nowhere all at once. "I am home," he said. "And here I will stay forever."

Claudia smiled, and nodded her head. "I can wait, my love. I'll wait forever and an eternity if I have to."

THE DIE HAS BEEN CAST

BY MAKEDA K. BRAITHWAITE

"Hello, Judith." I greet my cousin as I enter her current room. I hold yellow sunflowers, her favourite, to refresh the dying ones in the vase. The yellow is the only thing that livens up this manor. She is as beautiful as ever, even after sleeping for over a year.

I pick up the old vase and set the new one down. They sit by the window; outside I see the berries and purple flowers that have grown there since my arrival. Fragrant belladonna, a pet project of Judith's according to the maid, since the plant wasn't native to the warm tropics. We had never been close before but I am the only unmarried cousin left that could come take care of her. Judith's family was far richer than my own. Her father struck oil in the late 90s before the turn of the century and since then, we hardly heard from that part of the family. At least until last year.

My mother had come running to my room to wake me up. It was Saturday, I remember because it was the Saturday after my last set of nursing exams. She fanned my face with a telegram and rancid urgency. "Julia. Julia. Your cousin needs *you.*"

"My cousin?" I couldn't remember any cousins but the one who lived across from us, on grandfather's land. "Roberto? Eustace?"

"Judith!" my mother hissed. That had woken me up.

I took the paper from her hand and read the telegraph. It was from my aunt, my father's sister. The telegraph detailed how ill Judith had fallen and how she had finally fell into a strange, deep sleep. They didn't want a non-family member caring for her. So, they requested me. I would be paid a stipend, given housing, all for taking care of my cousin. Had they asked me to, I would have done it for free.

Recently, I couldn't help but compare us. Where Judith was waifish with elegant beauty, I was shorter, more turns and twists. She modelled for Pears and was the belle of any room she glided into. Judith lived for herself and for the moment. I envied that about her, even if we rarely saw each other and barely knew one another. She went after things not really caring whose throat she slit in the process, even if it was family blood split. I was always too catholic for that.

Then came her marriage when I turned twenty-four and she twenty-three. Lars Randal came from a good family like ours. Except *his* had money, which made him perfect for Judith. There was a time when I thought he was perfect for me.

My heart had been broken when I found out they were getting married. Though, it's no secret why they were married, Judith was sporting a bump before it all and then mere months into the marriage she fell ill.

I set the dead flowers down and look at her carefully.

Judith had been washed and turned for the morning already. The IV in her arm gave her the required nutrients for the time. Technology in the city was far more advanced than the stuff in the clinic back home. I often thought of taking one back when Judith woke up. She would wake, that I was certain of. Whatever affliction cursed her seemed not to affect much else about her. The soft curls of her black hair grew still, the bronze of her skin was vibrant, and her lips pink enough to pluck. She was so young with such promise ahead of her.

Satisfied with her health, I kiss my cousin's cheek, pick the flowers up and leave the room. In the kitchen, I throw the flowers away and drain the water. They have a maid that can do this, but there isn't much else to do in the house until Lars comes home and I get some conversation. Patsy, the maid, is always busy and I hate to intrude. They have a phone too. In almost every other room! Mostly, I spend time in the greenhouse. There I plant flowers, herbs, and everything else I can get my hands on. I peek outside the window and realise there's no way I can make it there today. The rains have been miserable. Storms constant against the bleak endlessness of the Randal estate.

I find myself in her actual room a lot. That a married woman has her own room does puzzle me—I don't have room to judge.

The room her comatose body resides in currently is a guest room on the ground floor. The walls of *her* room are in her favourite sunflower yellow. It's the size of almost our entire home. I find my way into her closet and slip into the red dress. The red dress she wore early in her pregnancy, before the miscarriage from the accident that led her to be lying in bed. The dress is no mother's gown. On her, where there was space, I stretch it. I stand before her long mirror. The dress is delicate, red silk. Artfully, the cowl swoops over my chest. The silk is so fine. The red so lush. I close my eyes and relish in it. I picture *him* twirling me in it.

"Missus Greave, Missus Greave!"

The frantic voice throws me out of my thoughts, I don't even get to change out of the dress, I run downstairs to find its source. It keeps growing, until I find myself in the frame of Judith's door. The vase is knocked down, crystal shattered, flowers scattered, and water pooling on the hardwood floor. My cousin is awake. Her eyes follow the line of my face and her brows knit. The maid holds a glass of water and a nervous expression.

"Judith."

"Julia." She gestures with fingers for the glass, taking a mouthful as the maid fills her mouth. "That dress doesn't do justice for your breasts."

I grip the frame of the door.

"The dress." I repeat.

Her eyes drop to my bosom.

My hand feels the silk. I had forgotten the dress. "Oh, the dress! I'm so sorry, Judith. I hadn't meant to."

She raises a hand; I see that it takes great effort. "What's the date?"

"It's June 6th, 1966."

Judith cringes. The lost time bitter as it settled onto her face. "I see."

"Let me go … I'll call your husband and change."

"My husband?" She cocks her head to the side, dark hair falling onto her breasts. "Yes. Lars."

"I'll be right back." There isn't a phone in that room. And the next phone is in the kitchen, I go down the long corridor and dial Lars's number from committed memory. His secretary takes me to him.

"Hello—"

"Judith is awake."

"Oh."

I clear my throat and speak in monotone before hanging up. "You should come home soon."

Quickly, I change into the dress I had on earlier and try to scrub her perfume from my skin. I do this until red blooms beneath caramel. Judith is still bright when I get back to her. I hold a basket of my supplies, check her for anything I can. The mystery illness that had her like this was one thing, but for her to wake up and be talking …

"Mr. Randal is on his way."

She smiles. "Mister Randal?"

"Yes."

"I stole him. Did you know that?"

I had never dealt with anyone with her condition before, so I take it for delusions. She cannot yet separate the waking from dreaming. Stroking her forehead, I ask, "Who did you steal him from?"

She looks at me, lazy like a cat, smiling, all teeth, before speaking. "You."

Judith dies before Lars comes home.

I don't have the heart to tell him the insanity she was mumbling prior to her death. I suspect he would have agreed with her, I'm under no delusions that they married out of love but I knew of duty and the potential for affection to grow between them. Instead,

I tell him she was muttering all kinds of lovesick things. I let him think she died deliriously in love rather than just delirious.

Since she had become a Randal and no longer bore her father's name, the funeral was held at the estate. It's kept small, my aunt thanks me for caring for her. "Judith always thought of you as her favourite cousin."

That's a lie if I ever heard one, but I smile and nod. At the far corner, Lars stands with his parents, attendees pass by him and give their regrets. Our eyes meet and I don't think I can breathe; he passes his thumb over the ridge of his lower lip and looks as though he wants to say something to me. As if he wants to be reckless.

I turn to speak with my mother. I won't be leaving with her. Lars has asked me to stay an extra month. Grief for a couple so young is believed to be hard. Though I suspect this isn't Lars's issue.

When the last funeral guest has left, we sit in his study and share glasses of brown rum.

The record player is crooning something fierce but its weak against the rain. A thunderstorm fights the shingles of the roof and beats against the panes of the windows. I want to go back to the greenhouse. To dig my fingers in dirt and foster new growth. I don't mind getting wet for once but I am stuck to his side.

But Lars sits beside me. His large hand easily holds the tumbler that takes two of my own. He's on his third glass while I'm on my first. *I'm here to care for him not drink with him.*

Though I often wonder what the rum would taste like coming from his mouth. It can't be helped. I try not to feel like a whore, a traitor for finding him attractive. Lars is broad-shouldered, mature, and his face has a sublime quality that the grey-and-black beard do not hide. The maid has gone home too. It's just us and the groaning house.

"Judith and I were getting a divorce."

I spill rum on the muslin white dress I wore for the ceremony. Cursing, I try to find something to dab it. Lars hands me his handkerchief. "I'm sorry."

He waves his hand. "How often did you speak with your cousin?"

"Not often."

"Do you remember the afternoon I met her?"

Of course, I did. I had been staring at you all day. "No."

The rum loosens his lips. "It was a Saturday picnic. My mother had asked me to help with some items for church. I came down with the intention to ask for you and you were wearing a green dress with white linings. Your hair done up, real nice. A man was next to you, I hadn't known it was another cousin of yours until it was too late."

"Too late?"

"I asked Judith if you were courting him. She told me you were engaged." He rubs the glass against his forehead. "Such a fucking liar. Imagine my surprise five months down, when I see the young man and I ask him about you. He tells me, 'Julia? My baby cousin, is fine.' That afternoon I tell her it's over. Then I find her at the bottom of the stairs when I come home the next morning."

I down my drink and look away. Lightning snaps in the sky through the grey-black of the thunderstorm. "You were divorcing her because she lied to you? Were you doing it because of me?"

"I was leaving her because she deceived me. I was leaving her because I love you. I want you. I need you. I left her because the baby she was pregnant with wasn't mine. I was leaving her because I never loved her."

"I'm going to bed."

"Julia, please. Didn't you feel anything when we kissed so many months ago?"

The kiss. Yes, I remembered it. Hot August evening, frantic hands possessing curves of bodies and betrayal rotting the embrace. I had prayed for a fortnight for forgiveness. Avoided his gaze for months and whispered for penance as I washed Judith down with rosewater.

"Of course, I did. I haven't stopped thinking about it. I consider nothing else. You've rotted my lips to all other touches." Then I run out the room and hide.

In the morning, I feel an anger possess me like no other.

I go to Judith's bedroom and rip clothing off the hangars, throw jewellery across the room and toss shoes against the wall. I tear at the yellow wallpaper, until burgundy stands out. Halfway down the stairs, I've realised what I've done. I go back up to clean but find it in perfect condition. The windows are all opened wide, and the wind blows the curtains all the way up. Laughter rings against the walls in a pitch that rings my ears. Frantic, I slam each shut and lock them in place.

The windows had not been open since Judith's accident. My chest shakes from terror. My head is light, and stars dot my vision. Then a laugh tickles my ears.

"Are you packing up the room today?"

I gasp at the sound of Lars's voice.

"Julia?"

Lars's is holding me before I speak. Even with the windows closed, I feel a bitter wind encase me. It bites my skin. Like a live wire, pressed to every exposed part of my body. Am I losing my mind? Shaking Lars off, I turn and run to my room. Shutting the door.

In the following days, I hide from him like the coward I am but he doesn't seek me out. The front of my door gets lilies though. The occasional rose. The cupboards keep my favourite biscuit. And the greenhouse is always clean in the mornings.

Lars knows me like the inside of his favorite mug. He knows how quickly I warm. He knows the shaky handle he has to hold just right. He knows just how much it takes to fill me up. What tastes best inside the circular walls of my ceramic.

How dangerous it is, for someone you can't afford to love to know you like that. *You can love him, it's not like you ever stopped.* Right, I try to remember. Judith is dead and I am thirsty. The morning the levee almost breaks, is one of the few days where there isn't a horrendous rainfall. It's by no means bright. It's a Sunday, which means Patsy is at home and we're on our own. I must have fallen asleep in the library, because I wake up with the warmth of wool on my skin.

Eyes flashing open, I see Lars's face bathed by lamplight. He doesn't notice me staring yet. But in the softness of the yellow, I notice his long lashes, the cut of his cheekbones and the shape of his lips. Lars is a beautiful man.

Reaching a hand up, to curl it around his chin, I feel the prickles of his five o'clock shadow. His eyes flicker to mine. "I thought you were asleep."

"You're beautiful."

Lars smiles at the compliment and leans down, I turn my head and feel his lips at the corner of my mouth. I sit up, setting my feet onto the ground. He's still standing there, sweet and soft. "I should go start dinner."

"Okay."

He makes it very hard to be good.

"Should I throw this out?" A pair of green kitten heels dangle in my hand. Judith hardly wore shoes so low; I imagine it had been something she wore in pregnancy.

"The whole room can go."

I cut him a look. "She's gone. There's no need to be angry with her still."

"You don't get to tell me that." He snapped. "Not after she took *you* from me."

"Why didn't you ask me? Don't blame a dead woman for your faults."

"Why did she have to pick me? Couldn't the father marry her? She sacrificed us. Don't you think it was nefarious for her to pick me of all men? We slept together once—and I don't even remember it."

I had wondered this as well. Judith was selfish. Lars is rich and nice. Since she was pregnant before the wedding, I find myself sympathetic. My cousin did what she had to; I was just caught in the crossfire. I try not to be angry with a dead woman. I try to not to think about the wasted months and the shame from kissing him.

"I think women don't have the freedom of men. I think even rich women like Judith do things that poor women like me have considered. No one forced you to be with her. Not a soul."

Lars stretches tape across another box. "You're right. I've got a lot of making up to do and I will. I will be on my knees for the rest of our lives. But answer me, would you have done this to me?"

"If it was me, it would have been your child."

We don't speak again. The maid comes in and helps us take her things down. Lars brings down the last box to the truck, the driver will take it to her parents. The maid goes with him and we're alone.

The truck peels off into the distance. The birds coo in the thicket of trees. I lean against the right side of the doorframe and try to put some distance between us. He smells like citrus and tulsi. It's always when we're alone that recklessness fills me.

Turning to go inside, I hit his chest instead. Lars rests an arm at my waist and just stares at me. Not disturbingly, but like he was relearning every part of my face until his pupils dilated and rested at my lips. Lars closes his eyes for a moment, tongue poking out to wet his lips. Leaning towards me and pressing his forehead to my own.

Moments pass and he says, "Do you want a drink?"

We take a seat by the window of the study. It's not a horrible day. The rum burns my lips. I strike the silence between us down with one sentence. "I don't want to go home."

"Good."

"My mother is going to wonder why I'm not coming back home. Looking for a job with hospital." At this point, I'm just filling the air with something other than want.

Our thighs are touching, he doesn't respond to me but sets a hand on my knee. Calloused pad of his thumb tracing the flesh of my skin, I set a hand beneath his shirt, pressing a palm to the skin of his back. Lars ducks his head. "Do you want to work at the hospital?"

"I didn't go to school for nothing."

"You'd have to travel with me every day. It's a long ride down to town from here."

"That's stupid. What will people think of two unmarried people living together?"

"We wouldn't have to stay unmarried for very long. I'm a very stupid man if you haven't noticed."

I laugh. "Thank god you're so pretty."

"Not as pretty as you are right now. I like that smile on your face. I like the way your throw your head back when you laugh."

He presses his nose to my neck. Running it up to my ear. I don't think I had been this happy since—since Judith had announced their engagement. If joy could be kept, I would preserve this with the finest of salts, the sweetest of sugars, and the most acidic of vinegars. I would keep this forever.

Lars suggests that we go for a picnic by the creek on the property. I look up to the sky—it's never bright but it doesn't look like it'll rain soon which is new. He demands to pack the picnic basket. We set our blanket a few feet off from the water.

It's noon, but the sky doesn't seem to know it.

We nip at each other's skin. Our clothing lies beside us. This time when he kisses me, and I pull him close, shame is not the emotion that comes. Lars parts my legs and kisses my thighs, lapping at the honeyed curve between my legs conjuring a scream, and the crows leave the trees. We rut on top of the blanket the sweat glistens and we collapse alongside each other, braided limbs craving more of each other, the night falls and the cricket croaks.

A week down, he's in his study when I find the maid.

I had been coming from the library with a new book. The door to Judith's room—which I had not been in since we emptied it—is ajar. Curiosity makes me see what had happened. Her neck is twisted to the side, eyes rolled back, and tongue stretched from the outside. Fingertips and palms stained a strange purple. She is naked except for her feet. On them are a pair of green kitten heels. Judith's shoes. The wind carries a laughter in the swing of her hanging body.

When the police come, Lars speaks to them. He says *he* found her. He leaves out the fact that she killed herself in Judith's room.

The next day newspapers write about the house, first the model, now the maid. None mention the nakedness of the maid. Or separate rooms. Or stolen shoes.

Judith had never liked to share.

"She must have stolen it from the boxes," he suggests, lighting a cigarette when we're in bed. The maid hadn't seemed like the type of person to steal. Could it really be stealing if it was from a dead woman?

"Do you think its Judith?"

Lars shakes his head, leaning over to kiss me before he turns the light off. In the dark, he whispers. "Don't be ridiculous."

In the black I hear a laugh.

"You made tea?"

He looks up at me, swallowing a mouthful. "It was sitting on the counter. I thought you made it."

"I've been in the greenhouse the whole morning." I lean over to see his cup, the liquid is purple. "What kind of tea is it?"

"Some kind of berry tea."

"Is it Jamoon?"

"Too sweet for that." I go to the kettle, to smell it to see if I recognise it. A thud sounds behind me. Lars is on the ground, eyes at the back of his head and mouth agape. He looks like he's sleeping. The kettle drops and I feel the burn on the back of my legs as I fall beside him.

The laughter sounds again. It's louder this time. The sound comes from the walls. It's tickling, molasses thick and quicksilver fast. I try to shake him on my lap but at this point, I'm not even sure he's breathing. I follow the laughter, shaking in fear. The sound ends at the yellow room. I open it, it's just as if we had not cleared it out. In the shade of the closet, I see a silhouette.

Judith stands in moonlight, red dress over her slender figure with sunflowers in her hands.

Screams rip from my throat until the flesh is raw and my eyes burn. Then the sight disappears and the white of the ceiling swirls above me. For a while I just hear the sound of my screams and see the white. Then Lars appears above. He sits me up and realigns me to reality. Pulls me back to him being alive and well.

I snatch at him, pulling him over me until I find my breathing. I focus on the smell of his skin, the feel of his cotton nightshirt and sound the rain outside. The old house creaks in the night. "What happened?"

"I had a horrible dream … I … Lars we need to leave. We need to go somewhere."

"This is my ancestral home, Juls."

I cry. "Lars, please. Please."

"Alright." He strokes my back. "We'll leave tomorrow."

Lars pulls me down and holds me, we stay like this for a moment, and I try to find the words. *I love you* doesn't seem enough. I don't simply love him. The idea of losing him is tantamount to deathless death. Lars is as much of me as I am, I adore him. Words are petty to what I feel and this dream is too close. Arms around me let me know that I'm not floating in some treacherous outer space. He anchors me.

"I think she's punishing me."

"Judith?"

"She told me before she died that she stole you from me."

He kisses my forehead. "Didn't she?"

"She did. Judith was always selfish, but you let yourself be stolen."

"I wish you'd stop saying that."

"Why? Isn't it true."

"No. Well, no it isn't. I don't even remember sleeping with her. That night of the picnic, she invited me over for a drink. I was heartbroken so I went, I barely had a glass of brandy when I was knocked out. In the morning I was naked. So, no. It's not fair and I wish you'd stop saying it was."

"That wretch. Jesus, Lars."

Lars sighs. "She's dead. You're mine. We'll leave in the morning and whatever is haunting you will leave you. I promise."

We hold each other. His hands stay on my skin, calloused and stern, almost lulling me to sleep. I don't know how I've ever slept before sharing a bed with him. The way Lars easily snores with me lets me know he feels the same way. I want to hold him forever. He's mine now. I can protect him, I can love him. I will.

I'm almost asleep when laughter rings through the air. Jumping from Lars's arms, I scramble to slip on my slippers. I hear him huff behind me and follow. The laughter grows more.

"Aren't you hearing it?"

Lars says nothing, his mouth twisted to the side. We stop at the room again. Judith's yellow room. Despite me locking it, it's ajar. I push into it and it's empty, but the windows are open, and the wind blows rain into the room, wetting the beds and furniture. Lars pushes past me to close them.

I go to the closet and find something on a hanger that I was certain I had thrown away. The elegant red dress. I grab the dress and fly out of the room. Her laughter rocks me. I know it's her. Only Judith could get under my skin like this.

The rain pours on me, clouding my vision with grey shade so thick I can hardly see. The dress is over my shoulder. I open the greenhouse and take the shovel out and make my way to Judith's fresh grave.

Silk goes over her headstone—wife and daughter. The words mock me. *Wife*. How could she be the wife of a man she tricked into marriage? I dig but don't get deep enough—my arms burn, and my eyes don't stop crying. The wind blows the dress off, I crawl in the mud to grasp it. The shovel lies on the ground.

Lars pulls me back and the laughter stills.

"Don't you hear it?"

Lars kisses my head, and he picks me up and takes me inside. He sets the kettle, puts a record on, and prepares tea for us. He turns the stove on, slices bread and toasts it. A jar of unlabelled jam is taken out, and he spreads it across the bread for us. While the kettle boils, he brings the plate with two jam-covered slices over to us.

"I don't like grape. When did you even buy it?"

"Patsy made it before she ... c'mon, eat something."

I look at the thick layer. It smells good but my stomach can't take it. "No, thank you."

"Alright."

The kettle whistles, and he fills two mugs for us. I put my hands over our cups. "What tea are you using?"

"Darling, you're worrying the fuck out of me right now."

"The tea, Lars! Just tell me what you used!"

"Alright. Shit!" He slams the kettle down and shows me a box of mint tea.

My dirt-crusted hands cover my face. *I'm going insane.*

He rubs my back and I hear him pour the tea. "We'll leave in a few hours. I promise."

"You don't believe me, though, do you?"

"I believe that this house, perhaps the grief of losing Judith and misplaced shame has you spiralling. I believe that that may have an effect. I don't need anything else for that to be a reason."

"If it continues when we leave?"

"Then we'll find help."

"You'd send me to the asylum?" I push back the chair and stand.

"Hey." He raises his hands. "I would never do that. Listen, I'd never hurt you. I just got you. You think some dreams and hallucinations are going to keep you away from me? Never. There isn't a way beyond death for us to be apart, now."

I believe him and sit again, taking the cup. The tea has grown lukewarm but it's mint. The black liquid of my cup comforts me. We sip slowly. Lars reaches for the toast and takes a bite. On the second, he falls back out of the chair. It's my dream all over again.

The laughter rings again, low, and musical.

I touch the jam and try to smell it, there's a bitter note to it and a rash rises on my skin. I can think of only one thing that may cause this, the berries from outside the last room Judith occupied. Lars is still breathing when I check, I take the risk of going for my medical bag—left in the room she died in. Ransacking the space, I don't find it. My medical bag is not a small thing. I would have seen it in such a tiny space. I take the risk and go upstairs to the yellow room and see it on the bed.

The door shuts behind me as I enter. I put the bag on my shoulder and try to open the door only to find it closed. I jam my shoulder to it, and it doesn't budge. My fingernails scratch till my nails breaks and bleed.

Judith didn't share—her laughter echoes more. It fills my head like a stereo pressed to my ears, dialled up at full volume. It is a laughter that echoes against walls and chills my soul.

But Lars is dying and I will not take it lying down.

I go through her drawers for something that wasn't thrown out. A cigarette rolls around, matches, a broken perfume bottle, and mothballs. I grab the matches and throw the dress onto the ground—which was still around my neck—and light a match.

The windows fly open, rain and wind try to blow it out. I go back for the perfume bottle and throw the liquid onto the dress. It crackles and burns in magnificent destruction. Back to the door, I lean with barely any weight, and it pushes open.

Lars is still on the ground comatose.

I take the bottle. It reads Physostigmine, withdraw a dose with a needle and inject it into him. I stay there until it takes effect, until his speech stops slurring. The silence is noted. The house creaks on its own. The rain has no help in its fury. I hold Lars and know that he cannot be taken from me.

"Are we being very stupid right now?"

"More than likely." In the mirror of his car, I tap the kohl around my eyes—smudged by the drive. We didn't leave the house right away—instead, we stayed until Lars had healed. It's been a whole week since then. It hadn't taken him very long to recover, but I didn't want to risk it.

I suppose I also wanted to be sure the house didn't have the extra roommate as well and so far it had been silent.

Yet, here we are taking another risk. This morning, Lars had suddenly announced we'd be getting we'd be getting married and I couldn't argue it. Of course, I wanted to marry him and for once I didn't give a damn what anyone else thought.

"We don't have a witness." I point out as he exits to open my door. He's handsome in a sleek, dark blue suit.

"No problem. I rang my workmate."

Smiling, I slip my hand into his offered one. "I never knew you were such a planner."

"Oh, darling I'm not sitting and waiting anymore."

The small church is lightly decorated. It seems Lars had made call before this morning. Father Keogan stands at the pulpit with a well-dressed man by him. The ceremony doesn't take long and I sign my name besides his.

"I was surprised when you moved the wedding day up." The good Father says, after giving us his congratulations and blessings.

"Move the day up?"

I smile, turning my face to the mosaic art of the church windows. Jesus stands looking down at me. Purple and red in his robe, glinting in the shocking yellow sun. Something heavy sits on my stomach. Then I turn back to Lars and the feeling is gone.

"Well, Miss Julia—Mrs. Randal, had requested the ceremony for next week Wednesday."

A grin quirks on his lips. "Did she now?"

Father Keogan laughs, patting Lars on his shoulder. His workmate shakes my hand and leaves us alone, the priest strutting off somewhere and leaving two newlyweds to the hallowed walls.

"I would have told you if you hadn't beat me to it by a few days."

"Well, I've got more catching up to do." He wraps and arm around my waist and leads us forward.

In the months that follow, I personally scour the property. We find no other bushes but I scrub any traces of my cousin from the house—including having her body removed. That and the quick marriage hadn't been too welcomed.

Lars didn't seem to care so neither did I. Even when my aunt had come to collect body.

"You were probably planning it. Weren't you? Little low-life hussy. Not pretty enough to get your own husband so you took your cousin's? I bet you killed her. I bet you killed her!"

Sometimes I wish I had.

Lars, however, is able to respond. "Your daughter was the only schemer of the two. And I bet you that the little demon is burning in hell."

"She was the mother of your child!"

"If the child was mine, then I'm the Queen of England!"

We hadn't heard much from her after that. But according to my mother, my aunt was still furious. Lars and I stay in our manor that creaks and listen to records during rainstorms—and love without shame.

FIREFLY AND SPARROW

BY SAMARA AUMAN

Though I spent years trying to do so, I could not scrape away the memory of my lover dissipating into a nimbus of fireflies.

I refused to let my sadness soften into mourning; instead, I spent my evenings in my studio alone with my sorcery, trying to carve her back into being. Into living.

For three years after her disappearance, I refused to open my house to the breezes of spring. Nor did I let the bitter languor of summer sweep through my house—I feared that I would allow fireflies in. Though I dared not look, in my imagination they swarmed against the shojipanels, their evanescent light a reminder of my love and my failure to bring her back. I spent my daylight hours creating woodblock prints for my patrons; through the power of my skill, the portraits I carved, inked, and printed would almost seem to come to life, and in them the subject's essence was revealed in a way that everyday life could never display, only obscure. I would embroider silks with undulating patterns that swam with life so that my customers could hold the power of the sea in their own hands.

At night?

I would crush cherry blossoms between my thumb and forefinger and stir their essence into my inks, hoping to bring back the sunshine of an afternoon spent at a sakura-viewing festival.

I would carve the cherry wood I hoarded, the wood peeling away like petals softly opening into bloom. Each curl of cherry wood brought me closer to her. I would watch her form unfurl. In these portraits, she always stood gracefully, her back to me, but in the moment of the carving, she turned slightly, looking back. Her smile presaged a joke, and her hands were caught in mid-motion as though to hide her merriment.

I would stop myself before I stroked her face. I knew I would only feel the hardness of the wood, no matter how delicately I trailed my fingers along the whorls of grain that were her face. Reflections are powerful—the stuff that spells are made of—but they do not hold all the powers of the gods.

Though my magic could reflect the innermost secrets of any of Edo's folk, it could not bring that flicker of life to Chiyo.

As I carved each new iteration of her portrait, I wept. My memories of her would swirl about me, sweet with nostalgia, and just as difficult to capture as the fireflies I hunted in my youth. They were elusive, yes, but I knew I would spend the rest of my life chasing them.

The streets of Edo's red-light district always felt like they were rocking in the tumult of a festival. Laughter and night-proud proclamations of love echoed off the walls that separated it from the rest of Edo. It felt like a city unto itself—a city perpetually on fire and drunk on its own smoke.

My friends and I often met at a tea shop to while away the hours. On that spring-clad night my friends were laughing, arguing, and flirting with tea-girls. What a panoply of friends: kabuki actors, merchants, fellow magicians. Tanuki and fox-maidens. And a new woman.

My friend Ugiro saw me. When he approached, as graceful as ever, he said, "I cannot believe you two haven't met yet! How are you still strangers?" He dragged me to our friends' table.

"Hey, everyone! Suzuki, the lazy bastard, finally showed up!"

Half of my friends cried out in welcome. The rest were too caught up in the bubbles of their ebullience to notice.

Ugiro elbowed me. "Hey, introduce yourself. This is Chiyo!"

She half-turned from her conversation, and she caught me in a sidelong glance lit with life and hilarity.

In that moment, my words choked me; to speak would have been more difficult than coughing forth a river of pearls.

So went the years: my house a fortress, barricading me in and repelling any invading force of love, nature, or change. My nights spent closeted away with my magic, my pain, and my ink. Until one night, after perhaps a bit too much of our favorite sake, I left the shoji panel only slightly—slightly!—ajar.

At first, I thought it merely the effects of the alcohol that made my paper tremble. I steadied myself and moved the paddle again. Surely. Smoothly.

I felt the rhythm of her laughter in the movement of the paddle against the paper.

I lifted it quickly. The lines were clear and perfect. No mere drunken tumbling, this.

I touched her face, hoping that I would feel the smoothness of her skin against my hands.

I felt only paper.

Anger coursed through me, from my heart to my hands. I struggled not to shred the paper; even then I hoped to find her underneath.

"Why? Why can't I bring you back to me?"

Silence. No laughter now. No words of love.

I slammed the shoji shut, and then I tacked the new portrait to the walls of my studio with the hundred others—a collection of uneasy ghosts rustling without a breeze.

"You are as charming as a monkey begging for his raincoat," Chiyo said, handing me a piece of youkan. I bit into the sweet and laughed as it jiggled in my mouth. When you are in love, every sensation is a call to laughter.

"A monkey who appreciates the flavor of green tea candies on a summer's day." The taste opened up against my palate, and summer bloomed.

"Now, there's a poem for you. Three lines on a monkey eating summer candy in Edo."

"I don't know. It's a bit odd, don't you think?"

"Oh yes, city man. I, who come from the village, could not write a poem rarefied enough for city manners." She laughed, but with a note of bitterness. "We rustic folk know nothing of poetry."

"That came out badly. But, you do seem to know more of nature than I do." I dared to cup her face in my hand. "It almost seems as though every seasonal festival is a celebration of you."

This time, a real laugh—a laugh with the turbulence of water passing through clattering stones. I held my breath.

But then she smiled. "I'm not alone in my affinity for nature, city-dweller. Don't forget. I've seen your prints." A blush. "I love how you give nature another sort of life."

We let the matter settle there. As practitioners, we danced around our respective magics. It was a flirtatious dance, filled with secret smiles and deliberate missteps. However, as lovers, we danced only with our doubts, our fears of being discovered for who we were haunting our steps.

Though I kept my shojipanels shut, my prints still wavered in an unnatural breeze. Everywhere I turned, I caught glimpses of white. The prints fluttered, tugging at my attention as I attempted other projects. I hoped to hear her speak my name, but I only heard the sound of the indrawn breath of someone who is pondering before they speak. Over and over again.

At times, I paused my work and walked along the walls, watching her face. Multiplied, reflected. Mirrors properly aligned suggest eternity, but I found nothing of eternity in these prints of her—only an intensified longing.

I contemplated destroying them, of course. I thought of setting them on fire, drowning them in the Arakawa River, or shredding them to pieces and consigning them to the breeze like so many cherry blossom petals.

But in the face of loss, humans must be content with the most unsatisfying hauntings.

After minutes or hours, I would finally tire of my anger, and I would take my seat at my worktable. I wished that the light of fireflies would illuminate my work.

The door to my shop rattled open. No ghosts. No loves torn loose. Merely another customer, one with a generous smile and a generous girth.

"Hello! Every district in Edo tells rumor of this shop. Those rumors tell me that you have beautiful, mysterious items for sale here."

I assumed my shopkeeper persona. "Oh, those rumors are too kind! I do hope that you enjoy the wares that I have here today."

I set about introducing him to my shop. I showed him bolts of cotton patterned with fish that seemed to leap and splash as the fabric moved. His eyes lit up when he saw the mirrors, and his hand reached quickly for his money when he discovered the enchanted drums I had traded for.

As I wrapped his purchase, he noticed that I had not slid the wall to my studio back into place.

"Oh, what do you have back here? Something more marvelous?"

"Oh no, that's merely—"

He excitedly shouldered the panel along the track and entered my studio. No magic occurred—the prints did not suddenly disappear. They fluttered in place still, and they stared at the two of us with identical expressions.

He stood with his feet slightly apart, bracing himself. Still as a startled deer, I waited for his reaction.

He put his hands on his ample belly and laughed.

"Ah, how beautiful! It looks like your artist has been chasing perfection, my friend!"

"Perfection?"

"Some artists believe that the path to perfection is through the performing of the art, yes? It isn't the art itself but the process that brings one closest to perfection."

"I've heard similar."

"And your artist here. He keeps chasing that one moment. Over and over again. There's a beauty in replication, I'll grant you that, but I wonder what this beauty would look like if he tried some variation. Seasonal, perhaps?"

As I shook, as I trembled, the prints on the walls settled into stillness.

"I can't imagine that your artist is ready to sell those quite yet, eh? That sort never quits until they've gotten it right."

He pulled a leaf from the waistband of his yukata. "Maybe I will come back another day. I would love to examine your wares again."

Before I could thank him, he stepped out the door. I looked out the door after him.

I saw a tanuki in the street, prancing through the dust, trailing a small set of drums. Watching him and his joy, I thought that perhaps after three years, I should open wide my shojipanels that night as I worked. I looked forward to the taste of the breeze.

Night cloaked us for love's sake. Morning awakened us with a sparrow's song that sought to chase the sun away.

I wished that we could lie there through the birdsongs of every season. But that morning, it was only the sparrow.

I had not been chasing perfection—I had been chasing the reflection of my love. Trying to capture her reflection was like attempting to capture the stillness of an image in roaring river water—she was always moving. Happily, but with purpose and force.

I took the tanuki's observations to heart. I removed each print from the wall and added another layer to it—a robe of a different season. In one print, Chiyo wore a spring kimono bedecked in cherry blossom petals. In another, water lilies trailed along her hem (and oh the memories of our summer by the edges of the water—the river, the sea, the ponds). For each season, a kimono. For each kimono, a memory.

As I brought color to my prints, my studio seemed to come alive, curling its tendrils toward the sun. One morning after a long night of carving and printing, the bright fragrance of summer unexpectedly filled the air.

Rumor spreads like mercury down the streets of Edo. My reputation suddenly shone silver. My shop was seldom quiet, and the riot of the seasons inspired me to push my craft deeper than I had ever taken it before.

Years passed, and with it my proficiency with my arts grew. Once a secret held close by those who lived in the red-light district, I was now a legend unearthed. I was beloved of the cultural elite, for I seemingly had sprung from the cracks of Edo like morning glories at their feet. A sharp surprise, a beauty long hidden.

My name echoed across every alleyway, but I could not hear it from the one mouth I yearned to hear it from. Chiyo.

As I walked through my studio, I basked in the warmth of my memories of her. I could close my eyes and be transported to a summer festival: the taiko beat, the portable shrine on my shoulders, the savory yakitori, and the sweetness of her mouth.

When I opened my eyes, I was alone again. Festival fervor and the taste of love—both evaporated like mists in the daylight.

"Ugiro told me all about you before we even met, you know."

"Ugiro?" I asked. Ugiro was certainly a change of pace from what we had been discussing.

"Yes, Ugiro. Our friend? The one who introduced us."

"Oh, that Ugiro." I rolled over, and then realized what she had said. I sat up and turned to her. "Wait, what did he say?"

Her mirth waned. "Maybe it's time we were more honest with each other."

I rubbed my eyes, trying to disrupt any dreaming that may have settled there. "I thought we were talking about Ugiro?"

"We are. Were. What I am trying to say is that he told me about your real trade."

"Do you mean …?"

Chiyo looked me in the eye and put her hand over my heart. "Yes, he told me that you are a magician."

I was sure that she could feel my heart pound with her hand pressed against my chest as it was.

"Don't be scared. I know what it means to keep magic secret."

I sat there in the near-dark, shaken into silence. Our relationship was built on a solid foundation of witty banter and laughter, but I could not summon words to my lips.

"It really is disconcerting," she said, "how thoroughly you can disappear into your silences like this."

She looked at me, worry in the lines of her face.

"That's why he introduced us. He knew of both our magics." She frowned. "Do you hate me?"

In that moment, I knew I had to change her fear into something tenderer, less painful. "No, I love you. Thoroughly. I'm just surprised, that's all."

She smiled in relief. "He said that your magic was like the spring, always blooming. And mine? Well, mine is obviously summer: green, glowing, and growing." She removed her hand from my chest and took my hand instead. "Let me show you. Let's walk to the park."

The streets were buoyed by the townspeople's spirits as we walked to the empty park. She directed us to one of the small bridges there and gestured for me to kneel in the earth. She placed her hands over mine in the dirt.

In the quiet and the warmth of our seclusion, I felt like I had truly met her. I tilted my head to try and kiss her, but she stilled me.

"Wait," she said.

And as I watched, vines sprouted from the earth beneath our feet, grew and stretched and entwined themselves among the lattice work of the bridge. Flowers bloomed along their length, and suddenly I smelled wisteria in the night.

"Now you may kiss me," she said.

I found it easier to age than I had thought; every time I passed one of my portraits of Chiyo, my memories of youth rushed at me and overwhelmed my senses. My joints didn't ache as I scraped away at my stack of commissions, and I could drink several nights' worth of sake in one evening without feeling ill the next day (much to the nausea-wracked dismay of my friends).

But I couldn't force my magic to bring her back to me. She remained only a memory. I couldn't reach out to grasp *that* in the middle of the night.

Despite it all, I refused to love another.

My fame had extended so far that I was forced to take on students of my own. When I was young, I had thought merely to shape my life in an aesthetically pleasing way, like a bonsai master might. But age and fame had brought me pupils to continue my lineage of magic. With their training in my magic, a smear of red bean paste in their crimson ink would give them the exact hue of an amorous blush. Swiping a brush through the void between the stars on a moonless night would bring them a black as pure as a lover's hair. Their art would breathe.

They took care of most of the day-to-day business for me. On the days when I could summon the courage, I used the extra time to refine my prints of Chiyo. None of my students ever gathered *their* courage enough to ask me about them, however.

In the autumn of my fiftieth year (the season curled around itself with the sweetness of incense smoke), a woman walked into the store. A beautiful one. I was no stranger to the swiftness of beauty's thrusts; nor was I a stranger to the arts that people used to make themselves so. Fabrics and colors and safflower pigment for the lips. This woman, though, was different. I looked for her shadow and found a fox's instead.

My students ... I had not trained them well. There was stuttering, blushing, hiding behind bolts of fabric. I smiled at their youth and said, "How may I help, my lady?"

"I come in search of some art for my home. You know that you are praised as one of the most talented artists of Edo, so you should not be surprised that I would come to you. I seek a print on the theme of love, in that transition between spring and summer."

"That is very specific. I do take on commissions, but I am curious: why this commission?"

"Because I know you have the beginnings of it in your studio."

She slid past me and opened up my studio. The breeze that accompanied her set the prints of Chiyo fluttering on the wall. She frowned and moved among them, her posture now rigid and unforgiving. "This is all?"

"I am afraid I don't know quite what to say."

"I have felt you playing with powerful magics here for years! A decade! Two! And this is as far as you have come?"

She gestured, still graceful in her frustration. "How can you expect anything to come of this when you have drawn her alone? No nature, no seasons"—she glanced at me—"no lover."

She recentered herself. "I can feel that your heart is broken. But, if you want to accomplish what you have set out to do, look at the whole of her. All lovers want to be seen as the whole of who they are."

She paused. "If you ever finish this, I will buy it from you and treasure it. You know there is magic in my promise."

She walked out the door and faded into the sunlight. I sent my students home for the day and told them they would have the next three days free. Off they ran, hoping to inhale some of that last hint of magic that the fox had left in her wake.

No magician would ignore the advice of a fox when it came to ways of magic. We might tug at its hems, yes, but foxes live and breathe it. I knew what I must do.

I opened the shojipanels to allow the autumn air in. Leaves, brazen and golden, blew into the room and landed on my worktable. They scattered the prints, except for one with Chiyo dressed in her lotus kimono. The other prints, caught in the breeze, swirled out through the open panel.

I grabbed a block of cherry and began to carve. I set aside my eagerness and carefully began to carve the landscape that would frame her. Cherry trees in the foreground, yes, but her trees of summer in the background.

My magic swept through me. Every line was smooth. Perfect. Evoked a thousand memories from the ten thousand moments that made up our year of love.

I then began to carve the clouds, drifting away from spring to evaporate in the heat of summer. I knew that I had to connect the two of us in our magics. As I cut the curve of a wisp of cloud, I thought I heard Chiyo calling my name.

I sifted through my memories, trying to retrieve any moment that I could condense into a more potent image. I remembered how Chiyo always needed to feel the earth move beneath her feet.

A pathway, then, and a river. Both constant, both in motion.

And carrying the pathway over the river? A bridge. I could almost feel Chiyo's hands on mine as I replicated the bridge she had shown me that night.

With the last stroke, the scent of wisteria awakened. When I looked down beneath me, I saw that vines had sprouted from the floor and entwined themselves around my worktable's legs.

Snow cleaned the streets of Edo, sweeping loose the dustiness of workaday life. We sat inside my studio, legs warmed by the kotatsu, and looked through my woodblock prints. With the outdoors closed to us by the white weight of the snow, we strolled through my printed landscapes instead. Chiyo tipped more sake into her glass, and as a seeming afterthought, swished some into mine as well. She made sure to place the bottle far from the prints. Though she was reckless with her heart, she was careful with mine.

I brought over a draft I had been working on. Chiyo murmured appreciatively. I discussed the ebbs and flows of the lines that ran through the landscape. I gestured more wildly than I should have with my sake in hand.

"But there's still something missing!"

"The answer is obvious to me: we are."

"Oh, you would like me to draw you, eh? Well, let me find the shape of you, then." I lifted my hands to caress her, forgetting the sake.

She kindly helped me sop up the aftermath.

As she patted the last bit dry, she said, "I am serious. You should make a portrait of the two of us."

I laughed nervously. "Well, a portrait of you, I understand. Me, though? I would have to spend more time looking in my mirrors than I would prefer."

"Fine, then!" She laughed with faked indignation. "Maybe symbols of us?"

"Symbols?"

"Well, you're always talking about the power of reflections in your magic. And your prints are nothing if not powerful reflections. Perhaps symbols of us would work just as well."

"Ah, so, in your mind, the symbol is the reflection of reality? I like your way of putting it. What would be my symbol, then?"

"You're obviously a bird!"

"A bird? Not a phoenix or a dragon?"

"A sparrow," she said resolutely.

I guffawed and was grateful that I had already emptied by sake cup. I looked up and felt the heat of her glare.

"I apologize. May I ask, my dear, why a sparrow?"

"I can't forget what Ugiro told me the night I met you. A spring magician. For me, you will always be a harbinger of spring, of things beautifully beginning."

I blushed, I am not ashamed to admit.

"And sparrows are the birds of home. They greet you when you look out the window. They return happily in the spring. They are loyal to a particular place, and you to a particular person."

The headiness of love combined dangerously with the potency of drink. "Well, my love," I began, pompously trying to think carefully to live up to the power of her words. "You would obviously be, then ..."

"Fireflies."

She paused briefly, and she shone with a faint glow.

"The women of my village have a ... spiritual connection to fireflies. We hold festivals in the summer for them. Some of the women strongest in our magic are able to read our fates in the ways that they scatter."

"Sparrows and fireflies it will be, then."

Her skin had already grown taut and pale, though the fever was yet to come. Enrobed in the warmth of her regard, I didn't notice. I was content to gaze upon her, enraptured by the intimacy of her beauty. Sitting before me, she seemed lit from the inside by the fireflies she so adored.

Symbols are powerful magic, indeed.

Ah. That was the final step to complete it.

I had spent so much of my life trying to drag Chiyo to me—to change her, to change life and death.

I had not changed myself.

My chisel slid with ease into the cherry. With feather-lightness, a sparrow appeared, its wings spread as if preparing to land on a narrow perch. I knew that when I printed it, that small sparrow would land atop a beautiful woman's hand, and his love of her would be reflected in his homespun song.

I began to cry. If I completed this, I would fly away from this place forever. There was sadness there, even if I left it for the land Chiyo and I had imagined to pass a winter's night.

When I looked down at the cherry block, I saw that my fallen tears had formed into fireflies.

I touched them carefully. As my fingers moved over them, they came to life, flying around the room in a soft nimbus. As I began to apply the ink to my carving, they clung to me, embracing me. They enveloped me in their light and love. I chuckled, even in the midst of my tears. I had dreamt of such a delightful haunting for many years.

I placed the paper on the block and carefully pressed it. I evenly applied pressure across the whole of the print, not willing to lose any detail of my love to carelessness. When I was satisfied, I lifted the print—and there was Chiyo beckoning me home.

I hung it on the wall and then sat to contemplate it. I closed my eyes until I felt the gentle pressure of a kiss on my forehead. Chiyo's lips.

Then: "Suzuki, come over to me."

I walked my last steps and flew my way home.

The next morning, the studio was open to the wind and empty of all its previous magic.

Elsewhere in Edo a fox-maiden hung a woodblock print in a shadowy alcove. The print depicted a sparrow, having floated on the breeze between spring and summer, alighting on a lover's hand.

In the background, fireflies bloomed into a poem.

THE CHAMBER

BY H. R. BOLDWOOD

From the Journal of Dr. Wallace Fitzhughes

7 April, 1870
Baltimore

Dearest Wife,

Time has not assuaged my hunger for your lips, nor dulled their crimson blush in my mind's eye. Would that I could join your sweet repose, but the beating heart within my chest denies me. The very blood that gives it life is my sworn enemy.

Thoughts muddle and reason fades as I flounder in the swells of grief. Life is without joy or meaning. Days occupied with drivel give way to nights fueled by preternatural dreams wherein you cross the veil and lie with me. Here, yet not. Tangible smoke, a miasma as real as the mind allows.

Your moist, warm breath swirls in my ear, stirring a primal ache within. We kiss and join quickly—you and I, phantasm and man, writhing as one, tumbling across the silken sheets we once shared. Ours is a hunger that burns brightly—bright enough to bridge the planes of our existence. But in the morning, you are gone again, and the renewed pain of losing you is too great to bear.

Passion fettered by absence cannot be sated. Nocturnal trysts, fleeting hints of your perfume, and memories of your touch have left me with an unquenchable yearning that simply cannot stand. Therefore, I have devoted myself to the arduous task of finding a way to breach the void between us.

Sweet Margaret, after many hours of deliberation, I have struck upon a plan!

Part science, part madness, the concept I envision will allow me to join you in the nether. Know that I endeavor daily to this end and will stop at nothing to make it so. Wish me Godspeed.

Yours in life and death,

W

14 April, 1870

Dearest Love,

Exhaustion and melancholia distract me from my most precious project and have forced me to seek the services of the renowned apothecary, Winston Twitchell. The man comes highly recommended for the treatment of all manner of ills, including those of the heart and mind.

His Charles Street shoppe, regimented and pristine, was filled with row upon row of potions and powders the names of which were not in the least familiar to me. So busy was he, mortar and pestle in hand, grinding some concoction, that he failed to note my presence until I stopped mere feet away and cleared my throat. He turned with a start and stammered, asking how he might be of assistance. A bemused smile crossed his face when I introduced myself and advised that our housekeeper, Mrs. Lattimer, had recommended his services.

"A pleasure indeed, Dr. Fitzhughes." Twitchell scurried out from behind his counter and shuffled across the hardwood to shake my hand. "Lovely lady, Mrs. Lattimer—though something of a church bell. She announced the demise of your beloved wife some time back. Please accept my condolences."

I nodded in reply, somewhat rankled that my business had preceded me. When we chatted further and I admitted to being distracted by melancholia, Twitchell ushered me down an aisle past a collection of jars filled with bergamot, lavender, and pennyroyal—the largest collection of herbs I had seen in my life.

At the end of the aisle, he plucked from the top shelf a bottle labeled *Laudanum* and handed it to me. "Misery touches us all in time," he said, proffering a wistful smile. "But this opium and alcohol tincture should be of assistance. Take one spoonful each morning followed by two spoonsful at night to encourage restful slumber."

I paid the apothecary in full, and satisfied with my purchase, made to leave, but felt his gaze lingering on me.

"Dr. Fitzhughes," he called. "Forgive my impertinence, but our friend, Mrs. Lattimer, happened to share the most extraordinary tale when last we met. She claims that you are working on a means to open a ... a window of sorts into the void—to communicate with those who have gone before. Surely, she was mistaken ..."

That loose-tongued harpy, I thought, feeling heat rise in my cheeks. I met Twitchell's gaze with cool, silent indifference.

He persisted.

"I only ask because as a man of science myself, such an endeavor would be of incalculable interest to me. The opportunity of a lifetime, I might say. And it's entirely conceivable that my knowledge of chemistry might be of assistance to you, is it not? If Mrs. Lattimer happened to be correct in her ... assessment ... I would be prepared to offer you my services free of charge."

A preposterous idea, my sweet. I would never consider taking a partner. The danger would be far too clear and present. The mystical journey that lies ahead must be mine and mine alone.

"She was mistaken. Good day, sir," I said, pushing toward the door.

"Wait! *Please*," he called. "I beg you! At least let me see your creation. If for no other reason than I could attest to it, should you succeed in your mission someday. Record it for posterity, if you will."

Damn the man. He had me over a barrel. His very knowledge of my plans laid me bare and could at minimum lead to ridicule, if not my entire undoing. I had no choice but to appease him. Therefore, I agreed that he could visit my residence at eight o'clock the following evening, with the express understanding that he would be there only to observe my handiwork. Of course, I swore him to absolute secrecy.

Mark me, Love. The day's events are certain to change the course of my fate. I feel it in my bones. I simply do not know whether that change will be for better or for worse. Know that whatever the outcome, you are at the center of my every decision. You are the reason I carry on.

Until we meet again, my beloved,

W

15 April, 1870

Dearest Margaret,

True to his word, Twitchell arrived by private coach at the appointed hour of eight o'clock. Through the window, by lamplight, I discerned a man who looked markedly different than he had only the day before, when he had appeared giddy at the thought of laying eyes upon my creation.

The man I now bid enter averted my gaze and bore a nervous demeanor, as if he were uncomfortable in his own skin—skin shrouded by a pall only grief can paint. I sensed in that moment there was a far more intimate reason for Twitchell's visit than he had allowed. More's the pity that I had not perceived it when first we'd spoken.

"Where is it?" he whispered. "This invention of yours? And … *what* is it?"

I escorted him through the foyer, past the cozy lamp-lit rooms you and I shared, and then down the basement steps into the bowels of the house. Once Twitchell was at my heels, I removed a torch from the lime-plastered wall. A large bookcase swiveled open, revealing a darkened chamber before us.

"Behold," I said, sweeping my arm toward the unknown. "My psychomanteum."

Twitchell's eyes widened. "A preternatural portal!"

"An unrealized dream," said I.

Stepping across the threshold, I illuminated the room with my torch. "When in use, the chamber is devoid of all but the faintest candlelight. Note the walls, ceilings, and floors are draped in black, and the mirror hangs mid-wall before a single offset chair. This design is thought to draw spirits toward the candle's reflection. Their presence lifts the veil, and the mirror becomes permeable, allowing for a free displacement of energy. All is by design and as it should be. Many hours have I passed therein, seeking my beloved—to no avail. It pains me to say that my portal, as you call it, is not fully functional."

"But it shall be," Twitchell said, his eyes aglow in the torchlight. "Of that I am certain."

It was then he confessed the true nature of his visit, regaling me with a tale that mirrored the tragedy of my own. Mourning the loss of his daughter Elsbeth to consumption, he craved one last glimpse of her visage, and perchance a final embrace. He begged for his own opportunity to journey into the void.

His previous offer of partnership burned in my heart. The man had only wished to remedy his own loss. Much as that might have angered me, I bore him no ill will. I would have done the same had our roles been reversed. Still, the risk was too great—the dangers untold.

"I'm sorry, sir. No," I said, taking his arm and pulling him back toward the stairs. "You must understand. The chamber does not work! And I refuse to take responsibility for the outcome, should you for some unforeseen reason succeed."

Twitchell's sunken eyes sought mine. "Dr. Fitzhughes, grief has robbed me of many things, the least of which is pride. There is no peace for me. No sleep. No thought for the future. There is only an ache which swallows me whole. Have mercy, sir. Is it so much I ask? If I fail in my attempt, what cost to you?"

What indeed?

I reluctantly escorted him through the blackened void and tucked him into the oversized chair like a mother bird nesting its young, his eyes wide in terror or anticipation; I knew not which.

Profoundly moved, I grasped his hand. "Find your Elsbeth," I whispered, and then lit the candle and sealed him inside the abyss. Taking my place in a darkened antechamber, I watched through a hidden observation hole.

Imagine my dismay when he removed a small metal flask secreted within his jacket. I thought perhaps his frayed nerves required a strong libation. But when he removed the cap, a ghostly vapor bubbled o'er the top and down the sides of the flask. He took a goodly swallow of the unknown potion before replacing the cap, and shook the remains vigorously before lowering the flask to the floor.

Questions consumed me: what advantage would this tonic bring? How was it made? Be still, my racing mind, could it possibly work?

Twitchell relaxed and then gazed into the mirror, eyes heavy but unyielding to the shapes and shadows crafted by the candlelight. His breaths grew shallow and less frequent until his chest refused to rise, yet steam wafted from his mouth, as happens in winter's chill. Ice crystals etched the mirror's surface; indeed, the entire wall grew frigid—then a blissful glow transformed the apothecary's face.

"Elsbeth!" he cried.

Rising from his chair, arms outstretched, Twitchell embraced the unseen. "I shall never again let you go, child."

A tear slipped down his cheek and turned to ice. His joints popped and cracked like water contracting as it freezes. Before my unsuspecting eyes, his entire body froze en masse. Too astonished to look away, I watched his solidified body topple to the floor and sever at the articulations as if cleaved at the hands of a butcher!

Merciful God, what had we ... what had *I* done? Worse still, what lay ahead?

Despite the gruesome scene, I collected myself and devised a ruse for the returning coachman: Twitchell had elected to walk home on this warm spring night.

Following deliberate calculation, I disposed of Twitchell's remains, lest they be discovered and accusations fly.

Sweet Margaret, I fear the grip of madness, for the line between reality and fantasy is no more. The night is deep and I am spent. My eyes are weighted with all they have seen, my heart sickened by the unspeakable thing I have done. Pray, my love, that rest and the rising sun restore perspective.

Your Devoted Spouse,

W

17 April, 1870

My Darling,

I awoke to a visit from the town constable, prompt in his investigation of Twitchell's disappearance. I held true to my deception and offered nothing further. He tarried unnecessarily, observing me with a keen eye.

Despite my misdirection, suspicion is soon bound to fall on me like a swift sword. I can offer no explanation for the manner of his death, nor would my accounting of the evening's spectral events find favor.

This tragic, regrettable situation has left a number of loose ends. May they mire deeply in their hasty grave, lest my life forfeit.

How I envy Twitchell! That I could hold you without end as he now holds his dear Elsbeth. Fear not, my sweet, I shall find you. It is only a matter of when.

Yours,

W

19 April, 1870

My Beloved,

There comes an angry knock upon my door. The constable returns, sidearm drawn, accompanied by his men. Might some hungry hound have unearthed a grisly treat? Mayhap Twitchell's limbs scratched and clawed their way up through my garden soil to decry their contemptuous interment.

It matters not. I know my path of choice.

I'll not await the hangman's noose. The last of Twitchell's tonic passes my gullet even as I write. I return now to the chamber, that bleak and glacial tomb, to feel the frigid rush of death sweeping through my veins—to join you, my love, through the mirror's icy haze, and to share your embrace ever more.

Eternally Yours,

W

LAGNIAPPE

During a staff meeting one gloriously stormy night, the idea of having a section titled "Lagniappe" near the end of anthologies published by Brigids Gate Press was discussed. The staff unanimously voted in favor of the idea.

Lagniappe (pronounced LAN-yap) is an old New Orleans tradition where merchants give a little something extra along with every purchase. It's a way of expressing thanks and appreciation to customers.

The Lagniappe section might contain a short story, a poem, or a non-fiction piece. It might also feature a short novella. It may or may not be connected with the theme of the anthology.

The extra offering for this anthology is "The Keening," a darkly beautiful work of poetry by Cindy O'Quinn, a talented and powerful poet and writer of dark fiction.
Enjoy!

THE KEENING

BY CINDY O'QUINN

The world is closing all around me. Lid to a coffin, not mine, yours. I'm not next to you when I need to be. You are alone. No casket, only warmth from a velvet crematorium.

No wake or viewing. No sleep. No funeral, only death. Visitors not welcome. Onlookers will be prosecuted. Trespassers, wickedly eaten. Discarded bones, turn into chimes.

The tunes of hell, play on repeat, until I cut through. Breaking the spell. External wounds heal, not those inside. They haunt my mind as I search for you.

Stained glass glistens when you look back one last time. See the truth in light. The sound of thunder makes us wonder. Do first cuts burn like fire on the dead flesh you leave behind?

Silk to the touch, of my undying hand in yours. I open my mouth and inhale what's left of you. Cooling ash settles on my tongue. The new taste of you. Caramel and mesquite.

Lovers forever in the rising heat …

ABOUT THE AUTHORS

Valo Wing (they/them) is a recovering operatic soprano turned professional funeral singer. Their short fiction is published or forthcoming in Dread Stone Press, *Haven Speculative*, and *Cosmic Horror Monthly*. They are a Pitch Wars 2021 and Futurescapes Writers' Workshop 2022 alum. When not writing about unhinged lesbians or singing for dead people, they enjoy indulging an obnoxious velvet blazer obsession and drinking too much champagne. You can find them on Twitter @valo_wing.

Allison Wall is a queer neurodivergent writer. She has published short speculative fiction, personal essays, and book and film reviews. She founded and runs NEURODIVERSION, a newsletter that centers neurodiverse news, research, and current events. Connect with Allison on her website, allison-wall.com, or on Twitter and Instagram at @awritingwall.

Ariana Ferrante is an #actuallyautistic college student, speculative fiction author, screenwriter, and playwright. Her main interests include reading and writing fantasy and horror of all kinds, featuring heroes big and small getting into all sorts of trouble. She has been published by Eerie River Publishing and Brigid's Gate Press, among others. On the playwriting side, her works have been featured in the Kennedy Center American College Theater Festival, and nominated for national awards. She currently lives in Florida, but travels often, both for college and leisure. You may find her on Twitter at @ariana_ferrante, and on Instagram at @arianaferrantebooks.

Devan Barlow is the author of *An Uncommon Curse,* a novel of fairy tales and musical theatre. Her short fiction and poetry have appeared in several anthologies and magazines including *Solarpunk Magazine* and *Diabolical Plots.*When not writing she reads voraciously, drinks tea, and thinks about fairy tales and sea monsters. She can be found at her website: devanbarlow.com or on Twitter: @Devan_Barlow.

Ariadne Zhou is a programmer who enjoys reading and translating web novels in her spare time. She also has works published in *OFIC Magazine* and *Trembling With Fear.*

By night, **Desirée M. Niccoli** writes a blend of vicious romance and cozy horror, featuring monsters, villains, and the supernatural, and often served with (mostly) emotionally intelligent characters and heart. By day, she is a public relations professional living the nomadic military life with her husband and two cats Pawdry Hepburn and Puma Thurman. Although born and raised in Pittsburgh, Desirée has since lived in coastal Maine (where her spooky heart truly lies), Maryland, and Connecticut. She is the author of *Called to the Deep* and *Song of Lorelei,* the first two books in a paranormal romance series featuring vicious mermaids; and "Meat Cute," a short story in Brigid Gate Press's *Dangerous Waters: Deadly Women of the Sea* anthology. She can be found at www.dmniccoli.com.

Agatha Andrews is a writer that haunts old cemeteries and lurks in libraries and bookstores. Her stories are often a blend of the spooky and romantic, with enough of the spooky to be an active member of the Horror Writers Association. She lives in Texas with her family of humans and cats.

A. R. Frederiksen is a Danish writer of English speculative fiction, who is represented by Creative Artists Agency for her novels. Her short fiction has been published in literary magazines (e.g. *Factor Four Magazine*, *The Fantastic Other*, *Crow* and *Cross Keys*) and anthologies (e.g. Phantom House Press, Quill and Crow Publishing House). When she isn't at her desk writing stories, she works fulltime as a copyeditor and marketing assistant, while she freelances as a creative writing teacher on the side.

Rebecca E. Treasure grew up reading in the Rockies and has lived in many places, including Tokyo, Japan & Stuttgart, Germany. Rebecca's short fiction has been published by or is forthcoming from Flame Tree, *Zooscape Magazine*, *Galaxy's Edge*, Air & Nothingness Press, and others. She is an editor at *Apex Magazine* and a writing mentor. Rebecca reads, edits, and writes when she's not playing Stardew Valley or raising her children. She is fueled by cheese-covered starch and corgi fur.

Samantha Lokai is originally from the Caribbean and currently resides in England where she writes dark fiction, incorporating elements of neo-noir, gothic, folklore and horror. Her work has appeared in the award-winning *Strand Magazine* (Dec 2022 Special Holiday Issue) and *Dangerous Waters: Deadly Women of the Sea* anthology (Jan 2023 Brigids Gate Press). When not writing, Samantha can be found indulging in her love for books, nature, and her curiosity for the strange and unusual. You can connect with her on Twitter @samanthaslk1 for updates on future publications.

Geraldine Borella writes speculative fiction and has been published in anthologies, magazines, online and in podcasts. She's had over thirty works published by Deadset Press, IFWG Publishing, Rhiza Edge, AHWA/Midnight Echo, Antipodean SF, Black Ink Fiction, Horrorsmith Publishing, Brigids Gate Press, Shacklebound Books, Nordic Press and others. Geraldine lives in Far North Queensland, Australia, on Ngadjon-Jii land. You can find more about her at: geraldineborella.com/about, facebook.com/geraldineb4, and at mobile.twitter.com/geraldineborel2.

Fatmire Marke is an Albanian-American writer, educator and Historian. She lives on the east coast with her two children, husband and imaginary characters that keep her company. When she isn't writing literary or historical fiction, she enjoys diving into horror stories to quench the thirst for fright. Fatmire has written bilingual baby board books and a novella. This is her first gothic horror short story.

Theresa Tyree (she/they) grew up in the Oregon woods, dreaming of magic amongst the trees. She lives there still, with their platonic life partner and cat. As a nonbinary queer women, Theresa's favorite tales to tell are speculative queer stories that offer more representation and give her readers hope. You can read more of their work on their website, theresatyree.com. Follow her on Twitter at @theresatyree.

Dana Vickerson can be found in the concrete confines of Dallas, though she's most comfortable deep in the woods where she loves to sit and listen to the symphony of nature. When not crafting buildings, writing stories, or painting weird 3D-printed sculptures, Dana can be found analyzing horror movies with her husband or making elaborate paper dolls for her daughters. She's a slush reader for Apex Magazine and an active member of HWA and SFWA. Her short fiction appears in *Zooscape*, *Reckoning*, *Dark Matter Magazine*, and many other places. You can find her on Twitter @dmvickerson.

Marianne Halbert is an author from central Indiana. Her quiet horror stories have been described as "whimsical and terrifying" as well as "elegant and macabre". Her latest collection is *Cold Comforts* (Crossroad Press, 2019) and is full of slow-burn horror stories. Marianne's stories have been published by Brigids Gate Press, *PseudoPod* (Ep 776), (forthcoming) *Vastarien Magazine*, and more. Marianne is a member of the HWA. You can follow her on social media @HalbertFiction or learn more about her work at www.halbertfiction.com.

Ann Wuehler has four novels out, *Oregon Gothic* and *House on Clark Boulevard, Aftermath: Boise, Idaho and The Remarkable Women of Brokenheart Lane.* A short story, "Man and Mouse", appears in the April 2020 issue of *Sun* magazine. Her play, *Bluegrass of God*, is in Santa Ana River Review. Her short story, "Jimmy's Jar Collection", appeared in the *Ghastling's 13* and her "The Little Visitors" was in the *Ghastling's 10*. She has five stories placed with "Whistle Pig", "Maybelle", "Bunny Slipper", "Pearlie at the Gates of Dawn", "Greenhorn and Elbow and Bean". "City Full of Rain" debuted in *Litmag.* "Gladys", a short story, appeared in *Agony Opera.* The short story, the "Elephant Girl", was in the September 2021's the *Bosphorus Review.* "Pig Bait" has been included in *Gore*, an anthology by Poe Boy Publishing, back in October 2021. The "Witch of the Highway", a short story, appeared in the *World of Myth* in October 2021 as well. "Blood and Bread" will appear in Hellbound Books' *Toilet Zone 3, the Royal Flush*, due out in 2022.

The "Salty Monkey Mystery", a short story, appeared in the *Amazing Offer!* anthology from Brigids Gate Press."Lilith's Arm" just got an acceptance from Bag of Bones, to be included in their 2022 *Annus Horribilis* anthology.

Jessica Peter writes dark, haunted, and sometimes absurd short stories, novels, and poems. She's a social worker and health researcher who lives in Hamilton, Ontario, Canada with her partner and their two black cats. You can find her writing in venues such as *Haven Speculative, Howls from the Dark Ages*, and *Dangerous Waters: Deadly Women of the Sea*, among other places. You can find her on Twitter @jessicapeter1 or at www.jessicapeter.net.

Sasha Kielman is an attorney in Washington, DC. In addition to her story in this anthology, her short story "Between Heart and Home" was published by Tea With Coffee Media in *Living With Demons*, a dark fantasy anthology, in May 2023.

Celia Winter lives in Chicago and works in HR analytics. Her usually Jewish, frequently queer short fiction has been published in *Lemon & Lime* and *The Dark Magazine*, with a forthcoming publication in the *Days of Awe* anthology. You can find her on Twitter at crossing_winter, Instagram at crossing.winter, or Substack at celiawrites.

Vivian Kasley hails from the land of the strange and unusual, Florida! She's a writer of short stories and poetry. Some of her street cred includes Cemetery Gates Media, Brigids Gate Press, Vastarien, Ghost Orchid Press, Death's Head Press, and poetry in Black Spot Books inaugural women in horror poetry showcase: *Under Her Skin*. She definitely has more in the works, including her first collection. When not writing or subbing at the local middle school, she spends time reading in bubble baths, snuggling her rescue animals, going on adventures with her partner, and searching for seashells and treasure along the beach. She can be found at:
facebook.com/bizarrebabewhowrites
amazon.com/author/viviankasley
twitter.com/VKasley

Makeda K. Braithwaite's (she/her) current profession is a reader's dream, as an editor for the University of Guyana Press. She has been writing since she was a young child, scribbling on the back of receipts and filling notebooks as a teenager. Makeda is Guyanese and has been published once before in Hugo Award Winner, *Fiyah Literary Magazine*. When she isn't failing to learn new languages, she can be found on Twitter at @makedakb_.

Samara Auman is a speculative fiction writer who is always cultivating new intellectual curiosities: currently, that means how we define consciousness and the nature of the uncanny. She lives in the mossy Pacific Northwest with her husband and two appropriately mischievous cats. Her work has previously appeared in *Fireside Magazine* and *Clarkesworld*.

H. R. Boldwood, author of the Corpse Whisperer series, countless short stories, and Imadjinn Award finalist, is a writer of horror and speculative fiction. In another incarnation, Boldwood is a Pushcart Prize nominee and winner of the Thomas More College 2009 Bilbo Award for creative writing. Boldwood's characters are often disreputable and not to be trusted. They are kicked to the curb at every conceivable opportunity when some poor unsuspecting publisher welcomes them with open arms. No responsibility is taken by this author for the dastardly and sometimes criminal acts committed by this ragtag group of miscreants. H.R. can be found at:
www.hrboldwood.com
hrboldwood@gmail.com,
www.facebook.com/hrboldwood
twitter.com/BoldwoodH
www.amazon.com/H.-R.-Boldwood/e/B01LWY22MD

Cindy O'Quinn is a four-time HWA Bram Stoker nominated writer, and an Elgin, Rhysling, and Dwarf Star nominated poet. She is an Appalachian author, living and writing on an old New England homestead with her family.

ABOUT THE EDITORS

Heather Vassallo, co-founder of Brigids Gate Press, believes there are few things that can't be solved with tea, cookies, and a good book. Like nature, she abhors a vacuum. She enjoys reading a wide range of genres, but can't resist fairytales and gothic novels. She currently resides with her husband, son, and two horribly mischievous black cats under the vast prairie skies of the Midwest. She continues to believe the world is a place full of magic and wonder (and lost shakers of salt).

www.brigidsgatepress.com
Twitter: @BrigidsGate
Instagram: @brigidsgatepress

S.D. Vassallo is a co-founder and editor for Brigids Gate Press, LLC. He's also a writer who loves horror, fantasy, science fiction and crime fiction. He was born and raised in New Orleans, but currently lives in the Midwest with his wife, son, and two black cats who refuse to admit that coyotes exist. When not reading, writing or editing, he can be found gazing at the endless skies of the wide-open prairie. He often spends the night outdoors when the full moon is in sway.

www.brigidsgatepress.com
Twitter: @diovassallo and @BrigidsGate
Instagram: @s.d.vassallo

ABOUT THE ILLUSTRATOR

Elizabeth Leggett is a Hugo award-winning illustrator whose work focuses on soulful, human moments-in-time that combine ambiguous interpretation and curiosity with realism.

Much to her mother's dismay, she viewed her mother's white washed walls as perfectly good canvasses so she believes it is safe to say that she has been an artist her whole life! Her first published work was in the Halifax County Arts Council poetry and illustration collection. If she remembers correctly, she was not yet in double digits yet, but she might be wrong about that. Her first paying gig was painting other students' tennis shoes in high school.

In 2012, she ended a long fallow period by creating a full seventy-eight card tarot in a single year. From there, she transitioned into freelance illustration. Her clients represent a broad range of outlets, from multiple Hugo award winning *Lightspeed Magazine* to multiple Lambda Literary winner, Lethe Press. She was honored to be chosen to art direct both *Women Destroy Fantasy* and *Queers Destroy Science Fiction*, both under the Lightspeed banner.

Elizabeth, her husband, and their typically atypical cats, live in New Mexico. She suggests if you ever visit the state, look up. The skies are absolutely spectacular!

CONTENT WARNINGS

Star-Crossed by Valo Wing: misgendering, death

Remnant by Allison Wall: violence, violent death

Bleeding Art by Ariana Ferrante: none

Wandering by Devan Barlow: murder, anti-Semitism

A Haunted Person by Ariadne Zhou: emotional abuse

The Feast of Dead Man's Hollow by Desirée M. Niccoli: blood, death, murder, distress/grief, life-threatening situation, near drowning

Ribbon of Blue Poison by Agatha Andrews: parent death

As Twilight Falls on Sandthorn Hall by A. R. Frederiksen: death, hinted suicide, hinted mental illness

Silver-Plated Promises by Rebecca E. Treasure: death or dying, mental illness

Jacaranda House by Samantha Lokai: none

Desire So Fulminant by Geraldine Borella: animal cruelty or death, death or dying

The Cottage by Fatmire Marke: implied death, torture, abuse

Dracula in East End by Theresa Tyree: war, guns, sexism, blood, death, violence

The Moss-Covered Mirage by Dana Vickerson: none

The Phantoms of Wildridge Hall by Marianne Halbert: death or dying, suicide/self-inflicted harm

The Blackburne Lighthouse by Ann Wuehler: death or dying

Stainless by Jessica Peter: physical assault, murder, PTSD, self-harm

You Transfix Me Quite by Sasha Kielman: depictions of depression and PTSD, references to child abuse, implied self-harm, physical abuse, attempted arson

I am My Beloved's, and My Beloved is Mine by Celia Winter: death, violence, anti-Semitism

Forever Home by Vivian Kasley: death or dying, suicide or self-inflicted harm

The Die Has Been Cast by Makeda K. Braithwaite: death or dying, miscarriages/abortion, graphic sexual content, suicide or self-inflicted harm, abuse (verbal)

Firefly and Sparrow by Samara Auman: grief

The Chamber by H. R. Boldwood: sex, death, suicide

The Keening by Cindy O'Quinn: death and dying

MORE FROM BRIGIDS GATE PRESS

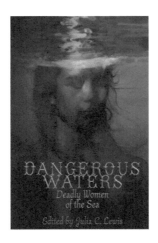

Malevolent mermaids.
Sinister sirens.
Scary selkies.

And other dangerous women of the deep blue sea.

Dangerous waters takes us deep beneath the ocean waves and shows us once more why we need to be cautious about venturing out into the water.

Featuring stories, drabbles and poems by Sandra Ljubjanović, John Higgins, Patrick Rutigliano, Candace Robinson, Emmanuel Williams, Desirée M. Niccoli, L. Marie Wood, Samantha Lokai, Christina Henneman, Gully Novaro, Christine Lukas, Alice Austin, Dawn Vogel, Victoria Nations, Mark Towse, Kristin Cleaveland, Ben Monroe, Kurt Newton, E.M. Linden, Eva Papasoulioti, Ann

Wuehler, Rachel Dib, A.R. Fredericksen, Daniel Pyle, Megan Hart, Ef Deal, Katherine Traylor, Juliegh Howard-Hobson, Simon Kewin, Elana Gomel, Lauren E. Reynolds, Grace R. Reynolds, René Galván, Marshall J. Moore, Ngo Binh Anh Khoa, Roxie Vorhees, April Yates, Kaitlin Tremblay, T.K. Howell, Kayla Whittle, Emily Y. Teng, Briana McGuckin, Tom Farr, Cassandra Taylor, Steven-Elliot Altman, Paul M. Feeney, Lucy Collins, Marianne Halbert, Rosie Arcane, Antonia Rachel Ward, Steven Lord, and Jessica Peter.

Medusa.
Cursed by the gods.
Slain by Perseus.
A monster.

So the poets sang.

The poets got it wrong.

Daughter of Sarpedon: A Tempered Tales Collection is an anthology of short stories, poems, and drabbles, ranging from retellings to completely new stories, from ancient to modern day

Featuring the talents of Eva Papasoulioti, Laura G. Kaschak, Linda D. Addison, SJ Townend, Christina Sng, Ann Wuehler, Amanda Steel, Ellie Detzler, Elizabeth Davis, Katherine Silva, Megan Baffoe, Rachel Horak Dempsey, Romy Tara Wenzel, Stephanie M. Wytovich, Die Booth, Rachel Rixen, Federica Santini, Thomas Joyce, L. Minton, Catherine McCarthy, Ai Jiang, Katie Young, Lyndsey Croal, Elyse Russell, Deborah Markus, April Yates, Theresa Derwin, Jason P. Burnham, Claire McNerney, Marisca

Pichette, Gordon Linzner, Patricia Gomes, Stephen Frame, Sharmon Gazaway, Kayla Whittle, Alexis DuBon, Sam Muller, Avra Margariti, Christina Bagni, Kristin Cleaveland, Eric J. Guignard, Marshall J. Moore, Owl Goingback, Renée Meloche, Cindy O'Quinn, Eugene Johnson, Alyson Faye, Jeanne Bush, and Agatha Andrews.

Sing O Muse, of the rage of Medusa, cursed by gods and feared by men ...

From the mists of time, and ages past, the muses have gathered; hear now their songs.

A web of revenge spun 'neath the moon;
A poet's wife who breaks her bonds;
A warrior woman on a quest of honor;
A painful lesson for a treacherous heart;
A goddess and a mortal, bound together by the travails of motherhood.And more.

Listen to the muses, as they sing aloud ... HER story.

Musings of the Muses, 65 stories and poems based on Greek myths, is an anthology of monsters, heroines, and goddesses, ranging from ancient Greece to modern day America. They, like the myths themselves, cast long shadows of horror, fantasy, love, betrayal, vengeance, and redemption. This anthology revisits those old tales and presents them anew, from her point of view.

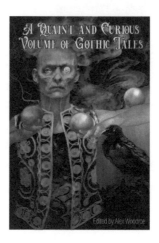

A Quaint and Curious Volume of Gothic Tales; 23 stories of madness, pain, ghosts, curses, unspoken secrets, greed, murder, and one of the creepiest collections of dolls ever. Ranging from traditional gothic themes to more modern tropes, this anthology is sure to please the reader ... and send a cold shiver or two down their spine.

So, come on in; enter the parlor, find a place by the fire, and experience the beautiful, dark, and occasionally heartbreaking stories told by the authors. The editor, Alex Woodroe, has passionately and carefully curated a powerful volume of stories, written by an amazing and diverse group of contemporary women writers.

Visit our website at: www.brigidsgate.com

Made in United States
Troutdale, OR
07/13/2023

11197023R10246